Fountain Garden

PAMELA BARON

FriesenPress

One Printers Way
Altona, MB R0G 0B0
Canada

www.friesenpress.com

First Edition — 2022

This is a work of fiction. Unless otherwise indicated, all the names, characters, businesses, places, events and incidents in this book are either the product of the author's imagination or used in a fictitious manner. Any resemblance to actual persons, living or dead, or actual events is purely coincidental.

ISBN
978-1-03-915322-6 (Hardcover)
978-1-03-915321-9 (Paperback)
978-1-03-915323-3 (eBook)

1. FICTION, SMALL TOWN & RURAL

Distributed to the trade by The Ingram Book Company

FOR
M. H.,
V. B. & L. B.

1

LEXI DAVIES KIRK

A gentle morning breeze blew in through the open crack of Lexi's bedroom window. The fresh air caressed her skin, soothing her as she lay in deep slumber, unbothered by the singing and dancing of the small birds on her windowsill. The tip of her nose was cool, but her body was warm, snuggled in her silky, lustrous sheets. She woke to that dreadful annoying sound—the first rude reminder of the day—that she had slept alone, once again. With eyes closed, her hands searched for her phone to stop the dream saboteur. The warrior in her was not ready to conquer any dreadful issues just yet, so with the power of her fingertips, she pushed off the reality of the day. The warmth and comfort of her beautiful bed compelled her to pull the blanket up to her chin and stretch her legs out to secure the perfect snooze position. She would enjoy falling back into a blissful sleep until the alarm went off again, and if it took a few minutes because her mind wandered leisurely to *that sultry place* ... then that would be okay. She loved that place, where she could conjure up the smallest of scenes and play with different endings, all of which ended with both of them naked. She had *him* on the brain. *He* was a stranger. Letting go into the fantasy, Lexi drifted off again, just as his rough hands grazed her thigh. He craved her as much as she craved him. The phone vibrated from under her pillow, disturbing her out of her dream. Lexi threw back her covers. *Oh, GAWD! Not already!* The second reminder that she had slept alone, reared its ugly head—the lack of aroma from a freshly brewed cup of coffee on her nightstand, lovingly made by her life partner. She willed herself up and fumbled to the bathroom disheartened that this was her new normal.

She felt sleep deprived as she glanced back at her reflection in the en suite bathroom mirror, taking notice of the new crow's feet under her eyes. At times Lexi did not even recognize herself anymore. Somehow the young, spirited girl inside her did not match who she now saw looking back at her. A girlfriend at yoga class told her that mirror-gazing could be quite therapeutic by boosting self-compassion and self-confidence, so she took a slow, deep inhale and exhale and stared intensely into her own soul. *How did you get here, Lexi Davies Kirk?* After pondering some of her life's decisions, harbored feelings of doubt that she had been carrying surfaced. They were disconcerting. Lexi looked away. It was time to toughen up and focus on the issues of the day: getting to her parents on Cody Island.

When Lexi told her husband Brock how stressed she was about her parents' health concerns, he suggested that she take care of her anxiety and wrinkles by seeing his dermatologist, "It will make you feel better," he had said. Brock fought against aging harder than her. *Forty-eight Yuk*! She finished brushing her long brown hair and then flipped it up into a loose French twist, adding pins to hold it in place. *Oh no, no, no …* She leaned in and pulled a stubborn, rogue grey hair from the top of her head. She knew she was lucky to still have a thick head of hair like her daughter and usually kept it up in a tidy up-do, unlike Malia's mess of flowing locks. In the old days, when Lexi was seventeen like her daughter, she was allowed just twenty minutes to get up, eat her breakfast, and jump in the truck with her dad to go help at the hardware store. He said that beauty was all about mental strength, drive and attitude, not what you saw in the mirror.

Brock was attracted to Lexi's magnetic carefree spirit as well when they first met. It amused him that she did little to impress him; she brushed her teeth and ran out of the house makeup-free, without combing her wild hair. She could pack her hippie-looking, island-bought hobo travel bags in under ten minutes when her handsome young fiancé would say he was whisking her away on a trip. After jumping on the bed with excitement and spending valuable minutes making out with Brock anywhere and everywhere, she would open her closet and mindlessly grab at whatever was hanging in front of her. By mid-trip, her clothes were tossed, tangled, inside out, mixed with clean and dirty, stained from bar beer, and smelled of cigarettes. That was then, so long ago. Now they both seemed like different people. *Had they become boring?*

2

DAY 1

An early morning fog blanketed Cody Island. A collection of tiny water droplets were suspended in the air outside Oscar's window of Fountain Garden residential care home. Oscar woke up, thankful for another day, and picked the sleep from the corner of his eyes. He had tossed and turned throughout the night, uncomfortable on his pillow, as he struggled to reclaim stored experiences that he was certain he had concreted in his brain. What he feared most in his elderly years was losing that blessed ability. The constant stirring during the long night's rest made him question his own sanity. His muscles were fatigued with soreness from his antsy legs constantly kicking in and out of the covers. Now, an angry neck that was all tight and cramped confirmed that his morning mood would emerge as irritable. His body felt icky under the damp white sheet and just as he attempted to kick it completely off, he heard it. *That fucking annoying voice*! The personality of one particular care aide at Fountain Garden rubbed Oscar the wrong way. Some days, the shriek of her voice could send him into a spiralling negative mindset that would last for hours. His morning routine, once awoken, involved lingering in bed until he deciphered if one of the voices he heard from the hall would be hers. That is how he would decide if he would have a good day or a bad day. The pain in Oscar's legs seemed to worsen when he was in a bad mood, so on a morning such as this, he would typically choose to use his wheelchair. With his daughter coming to visit, however, he decided to push through the pain and use his walker. He let out a big sigh of annoyance as he rolled his weight out of bed. The odds of him getting through the day without snapping at anyone were not looking good.

Oscar set his coffee cup down on the table in front of him and looked to his fellow resident, Ronnie, who was about to sit across from him. "Morning, Crusty!" Oscar said, taking note of the dried-up saliva and cookies still resting on the corners of Ronnie's mouth from the evening before.

Oscar watched as Liz pushed Ronnie's chair in to the table. The relentlessly positive, upbeat nurse noticed the dark circles under Oscar's eyes.

"I hope everyone slept OK last night," she said. "Goodness, wasn't that wind something else? It teased me out of my dreams a few times," she giggled.

Oscar looked at her and twitched his lips into a mouth shrug. It amused him that the curves of Liz's sixty-year-old body interrupted Ronnie's already scattered thoughts when she would lean in to place a tiny medicine cup on the table in front of him. The size of her double-D's appeared to make Ronnie slightly uncomfortable— but in a good way. The perky, full, and attention-seeking boobs were always there, every time the boyish man turned his head. Everyone knew Liz had a favorite uniform because she wore it often, and Ronnie liked it as much as she did. This particular ensemble was soft and worn, and the purple contrasted nicely with her bobbed, dirty blonde and silver-streaked hair. The stretchy material nicely accommodated her naturally growing hips and midsection, and it had a deep V-neck so air could move in and out freely on hot-flash days. She had told Oscar one day that she wondered if her uniform would outlast her career, and it was beginning to look that way with the looming closure of Fountain Garden.

Liz knew that Ronnie loved the way the soft stretched material hugged the roundness of her curves. When she leaned in to help him cut his pancakes and sausage, he would lift a bushy eyebrow and make a child-like giggle while making eye contact with an already side-smirking Oscar sitting across the table. "Easy boy!" Oscar would say to his table buddy to keep Ronnie's excitement in check. Liz was proud of being voluptuous. Her breasts had held firm even after three kids, and she knew they were her best feature. Her pendant necklace would appear and then disappear all day long, swaying in and out of the deep V of her top, mesmerizing Ronnie's gaze. She had shown him inside the locket one day. The tiniest picture of her gram's face on the left side and her mom and dad on the right. They had all passed on now. The residents at Fountain Garden, whom Liz cared for, had become her new family. In the old photo, her mother and father had been standing by a creek bed while on a summer camping trip. They expressed, that same day, how proud they were of Liz, their only daughter, for graduating from university. Liz had spent a long time meticulously cutting away at the picture so that at least their heads and part of their bodies would fit into the heart-shaped locket. Family was important to her and carrying them with her every day gave her continual strength and support, especially now that she was a widow and her children lived so far from home.

Holly, another one of Fountain Garden's precious residents sitting at the next table searched for her barrette in her ashy blonde and silver hair. She scoured the room, counting residents in her head. "Where's Edward?" she asked. Her hands continued to survey her own head until she found the rogue hair clip and then struggled to pull it out. Her question gave everyone pause. It would not be the first time that a resident of Fountain Garden didn't show up to breakfast for that dreaded reason they all secretly feared.

"He's *still alive* if that's what you are wondering, Holls!" Oscar shouted over his newspaper to his silver-fox friend, ensuring her that there were still five residents with beating hearts.

"He *SLEPT* in," Liz said as she shot Oscar a look, "it could be this weird weather we're having. I did not want to get out of bed either," she said, feeling the need to defend Edward. "I thought we were done with that fickle weather of the Pacific. My goodness, that was quite the downpour last night. Once this early summer fog completely lifts it will be beautiful out. This west coast island weather has challenged me and my flower gardens for many years now."

Holly peered out the damp window. "Well, we are supposed to get a spurt again later this morning, but it should let up in the afternoon sometime. What time is Lexi and the family getting here, Oscar?" she asked.

"Not sure. Later this afternoon, I guess," he said, throwing his newspaper on his walker beside him. "It's sure taking the aide a while to get my beautiful wife Anna ready this morning. She better not be caking Anna's face in make-up or I'll have something to say about it!"

"You sound *cranky* this morning, Oscar. I agree though," Holly said, "Anna is beautiful the way she is. I hope she gets to breakfast soon. The room feels empty with only three of us eating in here." Holly watched the wind blow the remaining raindrops sideways across the window. "I hope it dries up by the time Lexi arrives. Oscar, did you tell Anna that she gets to see her daughter and granddaughter today?"

"Yes, I did, Holls, but maybe I shouldn't have just in case Lexi had a change of plans *again*," he said.

"Oh, pooh-pooh, Oscar." She took a slurpy sip of her hot coffee.

"It wouldn't be the first time now, would it?" he said.

"Well, these young folks now-a-days have extremely busy lives. It is not *her* fault if something comes up," Holly said, "Don't mope, Oscar!"

"I know it's not *her* fault, Holly. It's usually Brock, that jackass she calls a husband. You know she is only coming because Liz told her that Anna and I are getting the boot from this place. She may as well have stayed in the city and waited for us there. This whole situation is ridiculous! I hate that our living arrangements have become her problem again. I managed to avoid the big city my whole life and now, at *this age*, I am being forced to move there! Whatever! Who cares about what us old people want, right?"

Liz tried to reason with him. "I care, Oscar," she said, "and Lexi *wants* to be here to help with this move. This is a tough time for all of us, and the support is nice."

"Well, seeing that cocky SOB Brock is not going to help my mood any," Oscar said, distastefully.

"Oh, for heaven's sake, Oscar!" Holly directed him to be sensible. "You have some mending to do. If Anna could talk, she would tell you that you are being a stubborn mule. I am *not* going to let you upset anyone this weekend. I won't! Just be nice to everyone when they get here and have your daughter's back for a change!" Holly continued to quarrel. "And do not embarrass yourself around Malia. Your granddaughter is still an impressionable teen. You are so bull-headed. You never gave Brock and Lexi a chance," she said, turning away from him toward the window, shaking her head.

Oscar reached for his pain pills with his shaky hand, dropping one back onto the table. *Oh, I gave that asshole a chance many times to prove . . .*

Liz saw Oscar getting wound up and tried to lighten the conversation. "Holly, you must be extremely excited too? I know Lexi is like a daughter to you as well and it has been a while," she said, shooting Oscar a look to lightly imply that he may have played a role in that fact.

The care aide entered the room, pushing Anna in her medical chair. She zigzagged Anna into position against the wall using one hand and pushed the brakes on with her foot. Then, she walked over to the kitchen area and grabbed a small condiment plate that held single servings of butter and assorted jams. The phone in her pocket rang and she answered it. Liz glanced a disapproving look at her as she approached the other residents while still talking on her mobile phone.

The aide saw her glare. "It's an emergency!" The aide said flippantly, disregarding Liz.

"Mm, hmm . . ." Liz pursed her lips at the woman.

"Strawberry or blueberry jam for your toast?" the aide asked Oscar, still holding the phone to her ear.

"Blueberry," he said.

She put two strawberry jams on his plate and walked off, whisper-shouting into the phone, "You were supposed to have her there a half hour ago. Get the lead out of your behind," she scowled.

Oscar growled at the aide, "Were you just trying to make conversation, or do you *just not give a shit*?"

"What . . .?" she said, looking over her shoulder.

Oscar shook his head, "Bah! Never mind." *You space cadet! There is no hope for humanity anymore, not here anyway.*

At the exact same time, Holly and Liz each grabbed a blueberry jam from Holly's table. Both women hucked their jams over to Oscar; Holly's jam landed mid-way on the floor and Liz's jam landed on Oscar's table. Tilting his head, he grinned at the women. Liz gave him a wink.

3

PACKING

Lexi could feel the anxiety building as she flipped open the lid to her perfectly rigid, leather carry-on bag. After years of accompanying her to her executive assistant job, it was still scuff-free. She had received it as a gift from her husband the night before she was to begin her new position. Lexi was standing at the foot of her imported Alaskan king-size bed, trying to choose from different outfits that she had laid out on her bedspread. Brock walked in and threw the supreme office-travel spinner bag on her freshly pressed black pants and then walked to the antique full-length beveled floor mirror and stood with his biceps flexed. "I picked this up for you after my workout. I am happy you are finally going to put all that education I paid for to good use," he said, as he admired his popping muscles.

Lexi opened the zipper of the hard-shelled exterior to see multiple small pockets for files and papers, and a bigger pocket that would accommodate her laptop. Straps would hold everything securely in place. *I'll stuff my favorite, cozy wrap sweater and flip-flops in this larger compartment,* she thought, *so that I can ditch my heels when I have to walk a block to my car at the end of the day.* She liked all the bag's organizational features.

"Burrows is a huge developer," Brock said, spiking his sweaty hair into place in the mirror. "Even *I* have collaborated with them to close some deals. You're a big deal now Lexi; you need to dress the part. It will complete your new identity as a successful career person," Brock continued. "People will take you more seriously."

She could remember thinking to herself, as she ran her hand across the rigid, black leather accessory feeling nervous about her new role, *Why wouldn't people take me seriously*?

Lexi pulled out her laptop and set it off to the side. She pondered how many items of clothing she should bring on the quick trip; four days and no one to impress. It would be a lot of sitting around in a care home. *For sure, the seniors that live there will not care what I will be wearing. Dad might comment, but that is it*, she thought.

She scanned her wardrobe once over, finding nothing appealing. Over the years, her wardrobe changed from Cody Island casual to city of Adasa office attire. She pushed a couple of suit jackets aside to reveal a large wicker box that held sundresses and shorts from what seemed like a long time ago now— when she and Brock would jet-set out to Turks and Caicos or St. Barts on a quick getaway. Those days were long gone. She rifled through the box, tossing clothes around undecidedly. Miniskirts; sexy tank tops; a lacey, black camisole; and a slinky, yellow bikini evoked old memories of home on the island. *I could still wear this,* she thought. Excitement fluttered over her as she held items from her past. She was proud that her body had somehow maintained itself over the years. Cutting down on eating bags of chips while watching TV at night with Malia was all she had to do to keep her slim figure. *I still got curves*, she thought, pulling at her small love handles . . . *tighter would be nicer though*. Touching her own skin made her sad suddenly. She wondered if there would ever be a time again when someone's hands, other than her own, would be touching her body.

Lexi's appearance had changed drastically from being a somewhat messy, young girl in dirty, ripped jeans and a T-shirt to a middle-aged woman in a dark plain skirt or pants and white, crisp, button-up shirt that had become her go-to outfit for work. Brock, a rich and gregarious man, offered her money and suggested she dress a little chicer, comparing her to his younger secretary. Lexi did not appreciate the sentiment.

Brock eyed her up and down one day, "Seriously though, why don't you go buy yourself something nice?" He handed her his credit card. "It's on me."

She knew he meant *sexier*, and it devastated her with insult. Early in their marriage, Brock could not keep his hands off Lexi, even if she was wearing a big, baggy T-shirt. Now, it seemed he had completely forgotten the free, unconventional young girl that he married. Looking back at what had transpired over the years, Lexi hurt with the realization that Brock seemed to tweak and will that free-spirited girl that she once was into someone that better suited his higher expectations.

"The girls in the office shop at Bella's downtown," he said, pausing to take a sip of his protein shake. "It's cute stuff . . ." Brock's voice trailed off as he left the room.

Screw YOU, Brock! She hated how chauvinistic he could be at times. Plus, she didn't see the point of trying to look cute in a work environment.

Lexi could feel herself getting flustered while recalling the past conversation and settled on her basic, solid white collared shirt and a rustic-colored tapered skirt from the wicker box. She packed her pyjama set, undies, a pair of jeans, one pair of shorts, a casual short sleeve T-shirt, another button-down blouse, and a simple tank top that she was sure she would never wear. It had been some time since she had felt the warm winds off the Pacific and the cooler evening sea breezes of the tiny island. She lifted the box to put it back in the closet and saw a red floral print material calling to her from a hole in the side. Nostalgic and hopeful, she reached in and pulled out the red sundress from the bottom and threw it into her bag.

Rayna's phone dinged. "Mal! He answered!"

"No way! What did he say?" Malia asked enthusiastically.

"He had early morning football practice." Rayna texted the boy back, giggling. Her phone dinged again.

"Summer practices are gonna kill me. I am jumping in the shower," he texted.

"Prove it!" she flirted.

He texted back. The girls screamed and huddled together on the bed in a rare moment of silence, mouths open, staring at the photo.

"OH MY GOD, he is SO HOT! Okay . . .what do we do?" Rayna said jumping up excitedly to stand on the bed.

"We *have* to send one back," Malia said, grabbing Rayna's phone out of her hand and jumping out of bed into action.

She yanked the comforter from under Rayna's foot, whipping it onto the floor.

"Back or belly?" Rayna asked as she flopped to her knees in her panties and loose camisole tank top.

"Belly. It makes your boobs look even bigger," Malia said, going down on one knee beside the bed, holding the phone in position, ready to snap a shot.

Rayna lay prone, her body angled so Malia could get a good view of her best assets. With one knee bent, she looked like a wild cat ready to attack the phone. "How's my butt looking?" Rayna asked.

"You need to arch your back more, Malia critiqued. "Your butt looks too small." Both girls cracked up.

"I *am* arching!" Rayna said, defending her form.

Malia took the picture and showed her.

"Yuck! Do it again," Rayna said, pulling her top down a bit further and adjusting her bust.

"Here, use this!" Malia reached over to her backpack and grabbed the airplane pillow that was squished into the handle. "Put this under you; it will help your butt look bigger," she said.

"You are a genius, Boo!" Rayna stuffed the pillow down below, propping her bottom up higher to give herself a rounder, fuller-shaped booty.

"Way better," Malia encouraged her. "Just show more cheek."

Rayna's phone alerted her with a text from the persuasive boy.

"Waiting," he'd messaged back.

The phone camera clicked four, five, and then six times while Rayna flipped her hair around, adjusted her undies, and played with sexy facial expressions.

"Knock, knock." Lexi was on the other side of the bedroom door. "Girls? I hope you are up and getting ready. Be ready and have your bags by the door in twenty minutes so the driver can load them up. I don't want to be late. It's the first long weekend of summer so the lines might be long at the airport. Malia Kirk! Are you hearing me? Get up and don't be late!"

"Ya, Mom!" Malia shouted, tossing the phone back to Rayna as she lay back down on the bed.

"Backpacks or carry-ons only!" Lexi said, "I don't want to check any luggage!"

Rayna stood over Malia on the bed, mocking Malia's mom by pointing her finger and whisper-yelling sternly, "Get up *now* and don't be late!" She giggled quietly and then back-flopped onto the king-size bed beside Malia.

"Shut up, Ray! She'll hear you!" Malia whispered back, slapping Rayna's arm. "Mom why are we leaving so early?" she called toward the door.

"Because we have to go downtown before going to the airport," said Lexi, looking down at a text on her phone feeling annoyed.

"Why?" Malia shouted.

"*Because* Malia . . . I accidentally brought a file home that Bob Burrows needs, and he needs it today apparently," she said, frustrated. "Just never mind and hurry up, please. I have to deal with this before we leave."

Lexi stormed away to her bedroom in a panic. *I can't believe I did that. I would demote myself, I swear.* It was bad enough that she had gotten excluded from the Tuesday meeting with her boss saying, "Well, I knew you were dealing with mediator stuff this afternoon, Lexi. I didn't feel the need to bother you." It made Lexi cringe that her failed marriage was getting in the way of her doing her job. In the last month, she felt excluded from important conversations and Bob seemed to be micromanaging her tasks a lot more than usual. Granted, her work had become sub-par and she had messed up pretty bad, having misplaced an important document while running out of the office early one day to save Malia and her distressed friends.

Malia had phoned her mom, freaking out that her car had a flat tire and that she and her teammates were late to their volleyball game. She had called her dad, but Brock wasn't picking up his phone. Hearing the urgency in Malia's voice, Lexi dropped everything and ran out of the office. The next day, after locating the missing document, Lexi apologized profusely to her forgiving boss, promised that she would be more professional, and that something like that would never happen again. Two days later, she disappointed Bob again by leaving him ill-prepared for a kick-off meeting when she printed out the wrong plans and set them on the conference table. Lexi saw the group of stakeholders laughing through the large glass and metal room divider. Bob did not look impressed. She knew she had embarrassed him. He had every right to be mad; it was Bob Burrow's name on the building after all.

"Is your dad coming this weekend?" Rayna asked Malia.

"Nope," she said, wanting to avoid a deeper explanation.

"When was the last time your mom got laid?" Rayna asked, shocking Malia with her question.

"Gross. I have no idea, but my dad is *never* around anymore. I don't know *exactly* what the deal is between them, but it's obviously bad," she said.

"Are your parents like, *full-on* separated now?" Rayna continued to pry.

"Let's just say, if Mom *had* Facebook, she would probably be considering changing her status."

"No wonder she's so moody," Rayna said.

"Ya, I feel bad for her," Malia shrugged her shoulders, appreciating her friends support and commitment to being a good sounding board, even though her comments sometimes felt invasive. "We were supposed to have this big family talk this weekend, in between dealing with my grandparents' big move, but now my dad is away with work *again.* Either that, or he is not coming because he is just avoiding telling me what I already know. It's whatever." Her heart sank with anxiety. "I just wish Mom and Dad would hurry up and figure their shit out. It would be nice to know they are both okay before I graduate and ditch them both."

"Maybe we can find her a little somethin' somethin' on this trip . . . a little somethin' tall, dark and nasty," Rayna said, as she rolled around on the bed, rubbing herself provocatively from her belly up to her neck in an attempt to be sultry.

"You little tramp!" Malia said laughing. "Don't be a dork!" She grabbed a pillow and whipped it at her half-naked friend. "She wouldn't Ray, she's too bitchy and sensitive these days!" An unpleasant feeling washed over her. She hated the stress and turmoil that presently existed in her small family.

"Mom, why are you dressed like you are going to work?" Malia yelled down from the top of the staircase, seeing her mom standing in front of the entrance closet mirror fussing to roll up the sleeves of her shirt.

"What's wrong with this?" Lexi asked. "I thought I looked okay today …"

"It's kind of work-ish. It's just not . . . *fun.*" Malia said.

"Really?" Lexi said, turning herself from side to side in the mirror, pleased with the fun rustic color of her skirt.

"It's a little nunnery. Sorry, Mrs. Brock," Rayna added, "You *could* be hot. You should show off that bod more."

Lexi went from anxious to stressed and self-conscious. She had heard Rayna's comment come right out of Brock's mouth before. "Well, I don't know how much *fun* this trip is going to be anyway." Her anxiety was heating her body up fast. "I'm going to leave it," she said, giving her white shirt a little extra tuck.

"Borrow something of mine then Mom," Malia pleaded.

"No, it's fine," Lexi said, getting more unsatisfied with her outfit with each passing minute. "I should look proper walking into Fountain Garden," she said, knowing full well that the words sounded *exactly* like something Brock would say. "You girls need to help me out on this trip. It's a stressful time for grandma and grandpa," she said, changing the subject. "I am relying on you. Don't forget girls, it can get chilly on Cody Island at night so bring hoodies."

"So, we are flying now instead of taking the ferry, Mom?" Malia asked, confused about the plan.

"Malia, I told you . . . we are flying there, and then, we are bringing grandpa, grandma and Holly back here to the city with us on the ferry in a couple of days. Oh God, I hope that nurse Liz was able to book the transfer bus for all of us—and that we all fit! It's not going to be easy—it's a stressful time for everyone at Fountain

Garden— so don't *you two* make things even more difficult for me," Lexi said, second-guessing her shirt one last time in the mirror. "I don't have time to change now anyway. Let's go, girls. We're late!"

Lexi felt sick to her stomach, thinking about the conversations about to take place with her dad. Oscar had finally settled in the care home on the island only to be informed that he and his wife would have to move again because the property was being put up for sale. Lexi's parents would have to relocate to a large, traditional nursing home in Adasa, a city which Oscar despised, near her and Brock, who he admittedly loathed.

Lexi could feel the pit in her gut grow as she pivoted her bag out onto the front doorstep. Back and forth, her mind bounced unnervingly between the two complicated men in her life. Lexi begged Brock to stay engaged with Malia during this difficult period and she thought it was a good idea that they go to the island together, as a family unit, one last time. In doing so, they could have much-needed honest, heart-to-heart conversations with Malia, and it would show their commitment as parents to make the divorce process as civil as possible. Two days before the trip, however, Brock ditched Lexi's plan once again with no regard. It was clear her relationship was over. She had drawn out the inevitable long enough in hopes of sparing Malia any pain, but that time had run out. It was time to stop avoiding the fearful conversation she needed to have with her daughter. Even if that meant doing it herself, without Brock. Lexi had been avoiding having to see her parents' reaction to the news of her dismantled marriage as well. On this trip, she was determined to disengage her father's sarcasm and negativity and remember that her aging parents deserved to know the truth, regardless of how much the discomfort of the admission would riddle her with embarrassment and humiliation. She did not look forward to the impending look of, *I told you so*, on her dad's face.

Lexi left her bag out on the front deck and came back into the house to take one last look on the top shelf of her entrance closet.

She pondered if she should concede and wear some old Cody Island apparel, like a hat that her dad bought her years ago from the island's meadery. *Maybe seeing this old hat and reminding him about the good old days will lessen the blow that his sweet, carefree String-Bean, who'd turned into a wealthy, big-city, success-driven daughter (who, in his eyes, had abandoned him) still cares about him and the way she grew up. OH, GAWD, I feel like a basket case today. Ugh.*

Feeling herself having a tiny inner meltdown, Lexi picked up an old blue and mesh cap from the shelf that she wore every day to work at the hardware store. It was soft and worn in, the brim shredded on one side. The lingering smell of sawdust evoked powerful emotions inside her. Her brain was somewhere between feeling utter failure and trauma of having to see people from her past and excitement and relief of going home to where she had often longed to be surrounded by those who loved her most. She looked at her hair, which oddly turned out quite lovely in the French roll and contemplated. *No. I won't.* She attempted to stop her own rant but failed. *I will not because I am not freaking seventeen anymore, because it will ruin my good hair day, and because that wild, hippie girl is long gone—sadly. Dad will have to accept that.* She tossed the hat back onto the shelf, catching the brim on the edge, leaving it half dangling. Lexi took one last look at her face, licked her index finger, and wiped some of her eyeliner off. *There! That's better.*

She stormed out of the house, away from the mirror, away from her identity tug of wars. When her luggage caught on something on the driveway, she kicked the wheels, sending the lightweight accessory spinning and sending a shooting pain through her big toe. Every little thing seemed to feel hard this morning. The choice to wear stylish summer ankle boots as opposed to sandals had been another difficult decision of the day, one she would ultimately regret. A flush of agitation came over Lexi again. *Just walking in, wearing a nice dress-suit triggered dad the last time he saw me.* Oscar had looked her up and down and asked, "Are you going to a funeral?" *Ugh. Get over it, Dad! Stop being mad at me for moving on like everyone else. Your little String-Bean grew up. I left the tiny island and its lack of opportunity. I did what no one expected me to do, and I left to go experience the world!* She cringed with sadness at her current situation with Brock. *How was I to know I would blow it? Maybe you were right dad. Maybe I should have stayed on Cody Island, taken over running the hardware store, and spent my adulthood caring for you and Mom like you wanted . . .*

Lexi felt riled up and acutely aware that she had become numb, thanks to her loveless, lonely relationship with Brock and somehow that stress extended to her relationship with her father. Maybe forcing herself to come to terms with her reality, telling her parents the truth about the state of her marriage, and getting out of that big empty mansion would be just what she needed.

"Girls!" Lexi yelled back at the house.

Malia and Rayna were distracted, admiring themselves in the entrance mirror.

"How's my pony in the back?" Malia asked.

"Uhm, it is perfectly poofy and hot, girlfriend! Hey, check this out. This cap is super cute!" Rayna said as she stuffed Lexi's old work hat in her backpack.

The girls jumped in the back seat with Lexi while the taxi driver loaded their bags in the trunk.

"I can't believe we are going to sit with old people for four days and miss the party of the year," Malia moaned.

"That's okay, Boo, I will perform my magic and get us invited to the next one too," Rayna said. The seventeen-year-old was super confident and found it easy to make friends with strange boys. "Even though *this* party was supposed to be *epic*!" she added snidely.

I will not engage in this conversation. Lexi thought as she turned to the window and ignored the girls in the car. She felt herself getting heated up, sweaty, and annoyed, remembering Malia's last comment during a fight they'd had two nights before. In the heat of the moment, Malia screamed, "You are ruining my life, Mom!" It seemed very overly dramatic. It was not like Malia to behave in such a way and Lexi decided that she better settle things with Malia's dad sooner than later because it was obviously taking a toll on her daughter. That reality made Lexi feel sick. The argument ended with Lexi making up for Malia missing the party by letting her bring Rayna to Cody Island. A girls' trip would be more appealing than the idea of spending four days with a sad, bored, pouting teen. Plus, if Lexi finally got the courage to tell Malia about divorcing her dad, she would have a friend there to console her. Hopefully, Rayna would be a good distraction for her and that would give Lexi more time to convince her parents that relocating didn't have to be a painful and negative experience.

"You are going to hate wearing those boots if it is warm out, Mrs. K.," Rayna piped up, interrupting Lexi's thoughts.

"Ya, Mom. Hope you packed flops in case we find sand?" Malia lifted her bare foot out of her sandal and wiggled her toes in the air.

"I did, but I feel like I have so much on my plate this trip, girls," Lexi said, "I doubt I will have time to enjoy any sand."

4

THE STROKE MAY 2010

Lexi's parents lived a humble, coastal life in a small, two-bedroom bungalow that had a private shady woodland area behind their home and sweeping views of the ocean sunsets out front. A small hedge divided their home and the similar home next door, which belonged to Hank and Holly Hill. The two wives, having been close since childhood, kept busy tending to their shared garden on one side of the house, while Oscar and Hank spent most of their evenings smoking and tinkering in Oscar's shed on the other side of the house. A wrap-around deck was home to two rocking chairs and a small lounger sofa that provided a stunning view of the ocean out front. Annabella preferred the rocker, and Oscar would have his afternoon snooze on the couch where he had permanently indented the cushions over the years. To Anna's annoyance, he would place his cigar ashtray right beside himself, instead of on the wooden table in front of him, and eventually, the distinct aroma had made its way through the upholstery, giving it an undesirable, lingering smell.

Holly and Hank had never conceived, so when Anna gave birth to Lexi, the new baby was a beautiful distraction for Holly while

Hank kept busy running Hill's Hardware Store in town. The bond between Holly and baby Lexi bloomed over the years and their relationship deepened, even more, when Hank suddenly died from colon cancer. Oscar took over the store to help keep it afloat. He was a good businessperson, and Holly had him to thank for maintaining the store's success.

Holly worked from home, doing the books for the store at her kitchen table, so she was able to help Anna take care of Lexi, especially after Anna landed a teaching job at the school during the week. On the weekends the women spent their days cooking, tending to the garden, and chauffeuring Lexi around the island for sports and activities. In the afternoons, Holly would routinely join Anna on the front porch for tea. The two women were inseparable. Holly claimed the other rocking chair on Anna's porch as "hers," and Anna left her favorite lavender sweater on the old chair to help Holly profess her spot. The two women believed whole-heartedly that they would grow old together, rocking and drinking wine, feeling forever grateful for the sunsets in front of them.

Years later, Anna found herself at Adasa Medical Centre, off the island and far away from home, where she received care and attention after a tragic stroke. In the early morning of mid-May 2010, Holly watched as Anna, with a shaken, inconsolable Oscar, was air-lifted away to Adasa city on the mainland where Lexi and her sixteen-year-old daughter met them. Lexi had reassured Holly that Anna was in good care in the city and that she would keep her updated often. Lexi's daily routine was dramatically changed by her mom's new condition and the presence of her dad in the city. Each day, she woke up at the break of dawn, gave Malia a loving kiss goodbye to send her off to school, and grabbed her to-go cup of coffee and her dad's small bag of freshly cleaned laundry to head to the city's downtown core. The almost hour-long commute allowed her to take a break from her worldly worries and prepare her game face for working for part of the day and then going to sit with her mom and dad at the inpatient rehabilitation unit.

Weeks passed and Oscar never left Anna's side. He slept on a cot beside his wife in her room. The days were long, so he had ample time to worry about the state of Hill's Hardware back home. Oscar's coworkers reassured him that they could hold down the fort on Cody Island and that they would watch over his property now that the end of June was approaching, and the island was getting busier with vacationers that were known to cause havoc on the beachfront. Oscar struggled to find contentment, having never liked the city. He had no desire to try to get comfortable there. Lexi's husband was absent for the most part and did nothing to make Oscar feel more at ease in the big center either. Brock popped into the rehabilitation unit a couple of times, talked about himself for the duration of the visit, and then said he had to leave early to get his workout in before going home. Oscar was mostly quiet when Brock was around, biting his lip while he sat in the corner, tapping his cane in annoyance. He worried that if he voiced his true opinion of Brock, it would hurt Lexi.

One day, after some coaxing, Lexi convinced her dad to walk a short way down the block to have lunch together at a busy park. Lexi soon realized that the walk was too much for Oscar because he quickly became tired, grumbling on and on about the city sucking his wallet dry and complaining of pain in both his legs. When she asked if he wanted to see her doctor in the city, he insisted that he had just missed his pain medication that day and that he had his health under control. When Lexi and her dad returned to the unit, they found Brock standing in the hall, just outside of Anna's room, flirting with the nurse. Lexi hoped that her dad hadn't noticed what was happening—but Oscar did. She avoided any discussion with him about her tumultuous relationship with Brock and instead, used her mom's recovery, as a good distraction.

Oscar and Lexi watched Anna struggle through therapy. Eventually, Anna's condition remained stable enough that the medical team told them that it was possible that Anna would be able to transfer back to Cody Island within a couple of weeks or so. In the meantime, it was explained, that the doctors would keep evaluating Anna's progress and that her living arrangements would need to be discussed further. Most of Anna's days were kept busy with her routine therapy or resting, so Anna agreed that Oscar should return to Cody Island and wait for her there. He could not wait to get out of the hustle and bustle of the city, but he regretted leaving Anna the minute he returned to the island and walked back into his quiet home. Oscar and Anna had seldom been apart over the years and this new situation he found himself in was a shock to his well-being. Over the next month, while waiting for Anna, Oscar became increasingly depressed, withdrawn, and overwhelmed with his new reality. Unable to communicate his feelings, he isolated himself in anger instead. He was still shocked that his beautiful, healthy wife suffered such a fate. The pain in his legs, which he was trying to hide from all his friends, was not helping his coping skills either.

On the phone, Holly kept asking Lexi, "When do I get my Anna back? Oscar said she was coming back soon! She has been there three months already, or is it four?" she said, confused, and lonely.

Holly was reassured by Lexi that it wouldn't be much longer before Anna would be back on Cody Island. After talking to Lexi, Holly went over to check on Oscar. In their conversation, she tried to help him understand that his home could not accommodate Anna's new needs, like the doctor insisted, and lightly added that there might come a day that he might struggle to take care of himself as well. At first, Oscar refused to accept that fact and asserted that after Anna's therapy in the city, she would be able to come home, and they could manage together. The rehabilitation team helped him succumb to the reality of his situation. The medics returned Anna to the island mid-August and brought her directly to Fountain Garden

Care Home. Oscar had no choice but to accept his new life without Anna but was beside himself with sadness.

The staff and volunteers at Fountain Garden were looking forward to welcoming Anna when she arrived. They were ready to provide Anna with the support and therapy she needed. Oscar and Holly were waiting patiently at the large entrance doors when she arrived at her new home. Lexi and Oscar had warned Holly that Anna had suffered a brain injury and that there would be long-term effects with her physical movement and well as speech. Even having been told that information and being somewhat prepared, Holly felt jarred when she came face to face with her friend. Using her inner strength and love for Anna, Holly pushed those feelings of shock aside, replacing them with joy that her friend was now home, and she could visit her every single day if she wanted to.

Holly wanted to do everything she could to help Anna with the transition to the care home. She popped into Oscar's house to ask if he wanted to help her grab certain items that she believed Anna would want in her new room, but he dismissed her, having already placed many of Anna's valuables in boxes.

Oscar's anger overcame him. "Keeping our stuff doesn't even matter now; it's not like she is here to enjoy it with me. I hate that place! I can't believe this is happening," he said.

"Anna needs us now, Oscar, more than ever!" Holly said, "This is not about you! It is not *always* about you! You are going to have to find a way to deal with this. If you find Anna's favourite sweater that used to live on the rocking chair out front, you let me know, Oscar Davies. She would want it! I mean it!"

With the changing of the season from summer to fall, so too had Oscar changed; he'd lost his motivation to do basic day-to-day things. He refused to eat a proper meal, gave up working at the hardware store, and forgot to pay some bills. Holly could not bear to see him like that any longer, so she called on Oscar's closest friends, Gunther and Vic, to help him, but he refused their support. Instead, he sat inside for days, just staring blank and emotionless from his living room La-Z-Boy chair.

Holly could see him through his big picture window and was sad and frustrated by the changes that she noticed in her friend. One day, she saw Oscar make his way outside and act more normal than she had seen him in a long time. Holly had a spark of hope that he was turning into his old self again. She sat on her front porch and watched him across the yard, banging things around in his shed. When she walked over to offer him her dinner leftovers, he seemed less than appreciative and tossed the paper plate on his shed tool counter, claiming that he would eat it later. That evening, when Holly walked her household garbage out to their shared trash can that sat on the invisible boundary line between their properties, she found her healthy, tasty meal thrown out.

It saddened Holly that she could not console Oscar. At the same time, she thought it was selfish of him to act in this way. She tried to convince him to stop pouting and visit Fountain Garden with her. "Come with me today, Oscar. Let's go see Anna together. We can ask Gunther for a ride," she coaxed.

Holly noticed that he wasn't going to visit every single day because driving had become an issue with the increased pain in his legs. Walking was not an option either, because even though the path through the back trees of Oscar's yard led directly to the back deck entrance of Fountain Garden, the walking shortcut was too difficult for him to cross over roots, fallen branches, and rocks with a cane or a walker. Holly was becoming aware that everyday tasks were getting increasingly hard for Oscar *and* herself. She came to the conclusion that her friend, who was once a lively, funny, mischievous man, was just sad and depressed and did not care much about anything anymore.

Anna had been settled into Fountain Garden for a couple of months when in early October, Holly called Lexi to insist that she come back to Cody Island soon to see her mom and to check if it was time to look at living options for her dad as well. Lexi wasn't surprised that Oscar's mental and physical health were struggling somewhat since living on his own but did not realize the level of help he needed. Lexi organized the weekend trip as soon as she got off the call with Holly and made plans to send Malia to a friend's house because Brock was out of town with work again.

When she arrived at home on Cody Island, she was sad to see her tired, solemn-looking father. Lexi learned that Oscar's mobility had diminished rapidly, and he was now alternating between a walker and a wheelchair, depending on his level of pain. Oscar, looking weak and shaken, could barely even hobble with his new walker and almost took a spill right on the driveway when he let go of the handles for a moment to give Lexi a hug. She held her dad in her arms, devastated to see him that way. She was shocked to walk around to the beachfront of the house to see a giant ramp built where the deck steps once were. When Lexi asked her father who had built it and *why* he had never told her that he had purchased a wheelchair, Oscar's response was that he and Gunther "whipped it up one day," and that "she had never asked." Lexi was distraught at how flippant he was and concluded that he must be in a lot of pain.

During the visit, Lexi learned that her dad was dealing with numerous obstacles. The doorway to Oscar's bedroom was too narrow for his wheelchair, so he opted to sleep on the small couch in the living room at night. The wheelchair could not fit through the bathroom door either, so even on a day when he was feeling excruciating pain, he was forced to manage to get himself to the toilet using only his walker. Numerous pills that were scattered across his coffee table were evidence that he had been suffering. Mounds of dirty, urine-stained clothes from unfortunate mishaps were piled on the floor. During that weekend, Lexi suggested that her dad move out of their family home. Oscar was appalled with his daughter when he realized that this was no regular loving visit and stated that he thought it was an ambush to take his whole life away from him.

While visiting with Anna at the care home, Holly explained to Lexi and Anna that she'd tried to help Oscar, but he'd refused out of embarrassment. Holly was frustrated with his demeanour and wanted to help him as much as she could but had issues of her own that needed tending to. Holly's yard and home had become a huge undertaking now that she did not have Oscar to keep her motivated. For years, Oscar had helped her by mowing, picking weeds, raking leaves, and keeping her hedge nicely trimmed. There was a noticeable change in the appearance of her yard when Oscar became sad and immobile. By the time the weekend was over, Holly, Lexi, and Anna had encouraged Oscar to move into Fountain Garden, where he could be with his wife and be supported and provided care himself.

At the end of October, with the help of his friend Gunther, Oscar moved into Fountain Garden in the room right beside his wife. Lexi tried to make it a habit to call him at least two or three times a week. Babs, the clerk at the front desk of Fountain Garden, would intercept the calls, explaining that Oscar was occupied. Then, she would pass the phone off to Holly (who happened to be there visiting) so the two women could catch up. Holly told Lexi that her dad was working out in the gardens, eating in the dining room, or having his bath or shower, or that he was already tucked away in his room too tired to talk on the phone. Holly reassured Lexi that he wasn't making less of an effort to connect with her, but that he was keeping himself busy again. "Your dad is finding more and more things to do, Lexi," Holly said excitedly, "You should come see your parents again and check it out for yourself."

Over the winter, Holly (tapping into her inner desire to have been a nurse instead of a bookkeeper for the hardware store) relayed news to Lexi about her parents. "Your mom is as well as can be expected, Lexi," Holly said. "Communicating is still super frustrating for her. Your dad, however, is cheering up and starting to feel like Fountain Garden is his home now. It is a safe place for him here, because you know, he has health issues too and . . . he is building relationships and making friends, slowly."

Holly always told Lexi things straight and did not mince her words. "Don't waste your time feeling guilty for not visiting us as often as you should, sweety. You aren't responsible for the demise of our age and health. But don't wait too long, Lexi dear, or none of us will be here anymore when you get here," she chuckled. "See you at Christmas honey!"

Lexi enjoyed Holly's dark humor and hearing it on the phone made her lonely for Cody Island more.

Three weeks later, Lexi was sitting at her desk at Burrows Developments when her phone rang. Holly's quiet, raspy voice came through. "I don't mean to bother you Lexi, but I have news." She explained, "I have made a decision. Old age is creeping up on me and if I move to Fountain Garden, I would be able to be with Anna every day and watch over her. I have been told they have a bed open."

"Mom is lucky to have you, Holly," Lexi said.

"The doc says I have a little rheumatoid arthritis and a little bit of high blood pressure, but nothing to worry about, honey," she said.

Lexi could hear Holly trying to downplay all her ailments. "Holly, you might like having people around to help you whenever you need it," Lexi said.

"Yes. It sure is quiet here without Oscar next door now and it would be nice to have some help with my medications. I cannot seem to keep them all straight these days," Holly said, "It would also be nice to not have to worry about how I am going to get to the grocery store anymore."

Chatty and thrilled with her plan, Holly kept Lexi on the phone for a half hour that day. Lexi did not mind the interruption at work and was thrilled when she heard the news, believing that Holly's presence at Fountain Garden would provide more stability and a feeling of familiarity for both her parents.

5

THE GLUE

Babs' sat in her high-backed office chair in the reception area of Fountain Garden. Her glasses slid down from her beady brown eyes and rested at the end of her nose. The coarse grey hair on her head appeared to have a mind of its own and the patch of flatness at the back was evidence of her dozing throughout the day, in her comfy chair, where she pretended to look out the window at the driveway and center courtyard. Babs enjoyed her quiet time when the residents were busy or napping. Sometimes, she would get lost in thought gazing at the world beyond the concrete walls, wondering if there had been something different out there for her.

She sat, eyes closed, and did not see Gunther pull up in his truck to the entrance of Fountain Garden.

Gunther entered the care unit with a bounce in his step. "Morning, Babs!"

"Morning, Mr. Gwilliam," she said, pushing her glasses up on her face.

He handed her a cup of piping hot coffee.

She took a giant whiff. "Ahhh! Thank you *so* much, Gunther! This old maid is tired *again* this morning," she said, taking a careful slurp and feeling a little butterfly flutter in her belly. "My feet already hurt, and it is only 9:30 in the morning. I needed this . . . but you know you didn't *have to . . .*" She only said it to be polite and loved the recurring gesture.

"Well, I know it's a big day with Oscar's daughter coming to town this afternoon. I figured you could use a little caffeine jolt to keep you motoring today. Breakfast is over and everyone is just doing their own thing now?" he asked.

"Yes, they are," she said. "It is a quiet time of the day. It gives me time to think about everything that is going on. I don't know if that is a good thing or a bad thing."

Gunther reached into the inside pocket of his oversized rain jacket. "Look what else I brought you, Babs," he said, holding up a glass frame for a photo. "I found *this* one yesterday sitting in the dust at the back of the store. When I told Vic you needed it, he said to give it to you and say it's from him as well—as a big thank-you for putting up with our buddy, Oscar," he said laughing.

On the corner of Babs' desk was a four-by-six picture of her and her sister Sherri, standing at a produce table at the local market. Both women had sunglasses on. Sherri had a basket in her hand and a big smile on her face, and Babs was holding a head of fresh lettuce and bright red tomatoes, looking just as gleeful. A jagged crack in the glass went through Sherri's face and shoulder, making her body look torn apart.

"I think it's the same size," Gunther said.

Giddy, Babs grabbed the picture frame. "It's going to be perfect, Gunther."

"I have to get to the store and open up," he explained. "Vic isn't feeling well today, and we can't rely on those little *shitheads* to do it. Wanna walk me out to my truck?"

"What would this island do without you, Gunther?" Babs said.

He held the entrance door open for her. She took the old frame apart while they walked outside to his truck.

"It's a little damp out here this morning," he said.

Babs was preoccupied. "I am so glad I convinced Sherri to come back to the island and live with me. I really wanted to help her in case her condition got worse," Babs said, running her finger down the photo.

"You sure did help her. You two were inseparable," he said.

"It was nice having her work here part-time with me. I loved those days. I remember telling her that she could stay at my place for free for as long as she wanted, but she insisted on giving me some rent. For a whole year I listened to her tragic and beautiful stories of experiences she had working at the palliative residence in the big city before coming to the island," Babs said.

"I am sure you have stories of your own," Gunther said.

"Yes, some. I guess," she said.

"Of *course,* you do," he said, giving her a nudge with his elbow.

"Even in her last days, riddled with cancer, she stated she had no regrets working much of her life in a facility where people would ultimately go to die. She was so giving and passionate about her work." Babs pushed her glasses up on her face, feeling emotional. "She had such a bubbly personality that could change the mood of an entire room just by walking into it."

"Well, I light up when *you* enter a room that's for sure." He kicked the dirt around with his boots and kept looking at the ground. "It would be a huge loss for this place if you were not around Babs. You are the glue around here." *It would be a loss for me—I know that!* he thought. "Plus, this isn't *just* work, these are your friends. Don't you think you would miss it? I think a place like this is worth fighting for."

"Probably, but I have been here a long time now Gunther. Don't forget, I am sixty-three! I worked my butt off as a nurse when this place was a full-on nursing home and then when it changed into a smaller care home and they asked if I wanted to be the unit clerk I thought—why not. At the time, I thought that maybe a position like that would be a good change and a slower pace, but it is amazing how the work never slowed down, even though the number of residents dwindled. Being short-staffed all the time has given us ladies quite the workload, and I don't know how much longer I can keep that up. Even if we did figure out how to keep this place up and running, I don't know if I would stay on—"

"Well, everyone on the island knows what you bring to the table, Babs. I would hate for you to sit at home every day and be bored. That's when age really starts to kick in!" he winked at her. "I gotta run, but I will be dropping String-Bean off here later this afternoon so I will see you then . . . maybe."

She smiled back.

"Take care of that new picture frame now! Don't set it where Ronnie can get a hold of it again!" He said as he lit a smoke and then jumped into his half-ton truck. Babs walked back toward Fountain Garden entrance and sat on the bench under the lattice structure. She could feel her pants getting damp, but she didn't care. She didn't want to go back in just yet. She sat back, pulled out a cigarette, and reflected on her life on the island.

In the early days of Bab's career, the nursing home was at full capacity with two very busy, fully occupied wings. Over the years, with people moving away or dying, the community was unable to keep doctors busy enough on the island, so the left wing of Fountain Garden was converted to a once-a-week clinic and the remaining residents were moved over to the larger right wing where there were seven resident rooms, not all of which were occupied. Now only the name remained the same, with a new owner and the building functioning only as a residential care home with a few loving, dedicated staff who considered themselves family.

Babs was the main administrative contact between residents, their families, and the physician and because the doc only made his way to the unit once a week, he relied on her to keep him updated with critical news and changing statuses. She was reminded of the arthritis in her wrists every time she had to deal with binders of papers and documents that needed to be hole-punched, sorted, forwarded, or filed away. She also transcribed for the doctor during his visits, which had become increasingly hard, not only because of her wrists but because her hearing was somewhat failing, and he had such a strong accent. Being the proud woman she was, Babs hid her ailments in front of others.

In the unfortunate incident of one of the residents passing away, she or Liz would contact the physician, the family, and the funeral home. It was always with such sorrow that she would have to relay this type of information. Babs had witnessed the passing of friends old and new. After contacting the appropriate people, she would assign an aide to gather belongings, mark boxes appropriately, and clean the room. Each time, Babs held strong emotionally. Regardless of everyone's heavy hearts, no staff member had ever seen Babs shed a tear while guiding the struggling caregivers to perform their duties during these moments. Only when the passing of Babs' sister, Sherri, entered her mind did she allow sadness to overcome her.

During the previous year, rumours of a permanent closure of Fountain Garden set a wave of panic through the community. People approached Babs with their concerns. She reassured the public that no such thing had been discussed yet, even though deep down she believed the closure seemed inevitable. She tried to avoid the topic until now. It was a scary thought for those wanting to remain in the community through their senior years but had a lack of support.

The new owner did little, if not nothing, to repair and keep the place up. When Babs and Liz approached him with their concerns, he fluffed them off with piss-poor excuses, and his lack of action told them it wouldn't be long before it would all come to a halt.

News eventually came that Babs was not to accept any new residents and the remaining residents were being asked to find new accommodations. The land was being sold. In the notice (in small print at the bottom of the page) it read, "We will do our best to give the staff and volunteers ample time to prepare for the closure and appreciate all their efforts in assisting residents in their relocation." Babs felt sick for the residents. Things were about to change quickly for everyone, and not everyone was happy about having to adjust and embrace a different lifestyle.

6

YOU COW

Holly had a long-time love–hate relationship with Oscar. Most days, she enjoyed his company and he, hers. It was familiar.

"What?" Oscar asked Holly, who was sitting beside him in her wheelchair, "Do I have a booger? I can feel you staring at me."

"NO, you don't have *a booger!*" she said rolling her eyes.

"Then what are you looking at?" he asked.

"You are quiet today, Oscar," Holly said.

"You like me that way, don't you?" he said tartly.

"Ha, ha, yes!" Holly chuckled, "Then I don't have to be mad at you for all the stupid things that come out of your mouth."

"I was just daydreaming. I burrowed myself down the rabbit hole of the past for a minute there," he muttered.

"Yes, I do that too. A lot, actually." She felt weirdly protected when she sat by him, like the old days when they would hang out together with their spouses at the local cafe in town. Holly knew Oscar felt lost without his sweet wife Annabella able to communicate with him in their usual way, and in her deep despair, she felt exactly the same. The two couples sat across from each other countless times over the early years of their life. Oscar and Anna on one side of the cafe table and Hank and Holly on the other during weekend breakfasts or afternoon teas.

Holly took a trying breath. "Not that long ago Anna and I would be sitting in the sun just like this and we could yuck it up for hours."

"I know, Holly," Oscar said. "I never could figure out how you two could spend every day together and never run out of things to say."

Holly smiled big. "It got to the point where we were literally finishing each other's sentences, whether we were talking about our workday, venting about things that bothered us, laughing about the latest gossip, or trying to analyze Lexi's life," Holly said with a smile.

"You girls . . . " Oscar said in a patronizing voice.

"Now, now, Oscar Davies!" Holly said, "Don't you pull that chauvinistic attitude with me. Do *not* tell me that when you, Hank, and Vic Charlie sat around at the store you didn't circulate any rumors or tell some tales during all those conversations. Even our good ol' friend Gunther Gwilliam got in on the smack talk, I bet—and that man is a gem." Assumptions and gossip were a normal occurrence on the small island. Holly knew the blabbermouths in the community had an opinion of her and Anna's relationship as well, especially how much time they spent together, but she never let the stinging remarks bug her.

"It was all harmless. We were just bored some days," he grinned.

She watched Oscar drift back into his quiet thoughts and remembered how the men used to enjoy talking in their presumptuous, all-knowing way about the local businesses, farming, who in the community was probably struggling or in financial deep water, and who was buying the latest toys. The four men, all tight-knit friends, had a daily routine: they'd get up earlier than the birds, make their way down to the hardware store in their half tons, and perch themselves down on their vintage wooden and steel industrial chairs. They would then spend countless hours smoking cigarettes and drinking pots of coffee from their favorite old mugs—mugs that were simply swished with water in the store bathroom sink and set right back on the counter. In their worn-out boots, beaten-up plaid jackets, and hats high and crooked on their heads, they sat, arms crossed, slumped in their spots. They discussed who needed to make trips off the island, who could help with vehicle or household repairs, and what vital purchases needed to be made. They would brag and name-drop mechanics and plumbers that they were in contact with from the city, and it made them feel important that they knew people.

One thing everyone had in common was that each household always had a repair or renovation on the go. This was a huge topic, especially for Oscar and Hank because they ran the local Hill's Hardware Store, and all the ongoing renos provided good clientele. Whether the project was small or large, it was explained with dramatic description. Each man's undertaking was described with huge importance and was considered very time-consuming (according to them) even though they had all the time in the world to have coffee every single day or lean up against the cashier counter at the hardware store for hours talking about it. Now, many moons later, at Fountain Garden, Oscar and Holly found themselves alone, sitting together, trying to press through the humdrum day.

Two hands grabbed the push handles of Holly's wheelchair and interrupted the moment of perfect silence, "Okay, Holly, let's get you out of the sun, okay? We don't want you to burn!"

Oscar looked over at the ambitious care aide, who smelled of antiseptic floor cleaner and snarled. "It's only 10:00 am.," he said, looking down at his reliable old brown leather watch to confirm.

"Now Oscar," she said, "Holly has fair skin, so she shouldn't sit out here that long."

He looked up at her with furrowed brows.

The aide, whom Oscar butted heads with on a daily basis, remarked, "You two weren't really talking, anyway."

"Where are you going to take her?" he scowled.

The aide snapped back, "It's 10 am. It's craft time."

He took a deep, trying breath. "Oh, for Christ's sake! Why? It's a nice morning, and we aren't in preschool! We'll move into the shade! Besides, it's supposed to rain later this morning so let us enjoy the fresh air before you bring us back into that prison to make some stupid ornamental crap that's probably going to end up getting tossed in the garbage anyway."

Oscar took a giant inhale. *You COW!* He continued fuming internally. His pain at the moment made it difficult to hide his emotions. He hated how power-trippy she was. It was always her way. She never asked anything; she told. She always seemed to be rushing and late for something. Her personality was light years different from Liz, Babs, or anyone else. He wondered how the others couldn't get as annoyed as he did. *Maybe dementia has its upsides.* Besides that, he knew that if Holly were that hot, she would ask for someone to help, and if she were tired, she would just gently close her eyes in the warm sun sitting right there beside him in her wheelchair.

"Well, I *was* trying to get a bit of a tan," Holly quipped.

The aide started to roll Holly away. Liz looked up from her medication cart and just as the aide passed her by, she reached out her arm stopping the chair with her hand. "Why don't you leave Holly right over there under the gazebo and once I give her these pills, *I* can move her back inside if she so desires."

Oscar glared at the woman. *I told you so, bitch!*

The disgruntled aide swung the chair around and moved Holly ridiculously to the center of the gazebo in the shade just to make a point. She lifted her hands abruptly from the wheelchair, clicking the brakes harshly and loudly, and walked back toward the building.

Ginger, another coworker with fiery red hair and piercing blue eyes, bounced out onto the deck. "Ah this sun is *spectacular*! Bring on the freckles. Finally, it's summer." She reached out and grabbed the other aide by the shoulder as they walked passed each other.

"Where are *you* going, Miss Sunshine!" she said teasingly to the cranky-looking aide. "Stay out here and soak in this Vitamin D with us. I checked on everyone; you can *relax* for a bit." Ginger's energy consumed an entire room when she was present. "The residents are all happy, and I gave Anna an epic ten-minute hand massage to relieve her achiness." Ginger twirled in a circle; her red ponytail spun in the air, vibrant under the sun. She stopped to look directly at Oscar, "Your wife was practically purring by the time I was done!" She giggled and grabbed her head to stop the dizziness.

The other aide disappeared into the building.

"I am sure Anna loved that, Ginger," Oscar said, nodding his approval. "You are quite the red gem aren't you!" He struggled to stand and made his way to the gazebo, screeching a chair out from under the table. He slid it right beside Holly and sat down. "Better get out of the sun myself," he said to her, "Don't want to ruin this perfect complexion."

Holly grinned slightly out of the corner of her mouth and kept her gaze forward, enjoying the morning breeze. She whispered to him, "You *are* lovable, Oscar Davies. Sometimes I feel like I know you more now than I did way back then."

7

LESSONS

Babs woke from her five-minute office chair power nap when she heard voices in the break room across the hall.

Ginger's voice travelled across the corridor. "It's more than just about letting them help us fold clothes and towels; you should have learned that in school."

"What is *that* supposed to mean?" The other aide asked, taken aback by the slight insult.

Babs entered the nurses' conference room and saw Liz, Ginger, Teddy (the volunteer) and the other aide sitting around the table. She closed the door over halfway to block the sound from trailing into the hallway. Babs could feel tension in the air.

"I just mean . . . I don't mean to be bitchy here but, we all learned about ageism, right?" Ginger asked the group.

The aide stared at Ginger with a blank look and then quickly turned to anger. "Do you really think I would have taken a job dealing with old people ALL these years if I didn't like old people?"

Ginger burst out, "*Old* people? You mean the *elderly*, or *seniors*?"

Teddy was laughing on the inside but kept his composure. He enjoyed working with a strong-minded group of people.

The aide was embarrassed at her own words. "You know what I meant, Ginger. So, obviously I cannot say anything right here. Holy cow, you are sensitive today." The aide threw her coffee toward the wastepaper basket, and it accidentally rebound off the edge, splattering the remainder of her drink up onto the back wall.

Babs gave a stern frown. "Hey, let's just relax and communicate effectively." She felt like the rising tension might be a result of the stress everyone was feeling about the closing of Fountain Garden. "Okay, everyone, let's not make this personal. I encourage you to express your feelings, but let's keep it productive and then let's go have a good day. Oscar and Anna's daughter is coming this afternoon and I want everybody happy and this place in tip-top condition."

Liz hated confrontation. "I agree with Babs. It's our last weekend working together, and I want to end this career on a high note. Everyone take a breath." She said as she turned directly to the aide. "I think what Ginger is *trying* to say is—"

Ginger held firm on her point. "I love you Liz, but you don't need to speak for me."

The aide raised her voice, "Do I need to remind you, Ginger, that I have been here a lot longer than you, I went to school *long* before you and, not that it's any of your business, but I graduated at the top of my class."

Oscar had rolled up in his wheelchair out in the hall and was being nosy. "How many people were in that class, one?" he said, laughing.

"Oscar! We do not need you chiming in. This is a private conversation!" Babs hurried over and shut the door.

"I feel like this is an ambush today," said the aide, looking fired up. "Like, what *in the hell*? You have never said anything before, Ginger, and now today you have a problem with me for some reason. I get enough of this shit at home. I don't need it here too."

"I'm just making a point, and for the record," Ginger explained, "I *have* brought it up before and things changed for a bit, and then after a while, *people* tend to fall back into old habits again . . ." *People, meaning YOU*, she thought. "So, I am bringing it up now, again. If I think someone is acting a certain way and it is not in the best interest of those that we are caring for then, I have every right to bring it to that person's attention. Right?" She looked at Liz for confirmation.

"Obviously!" The aide rolled her eyes.

"AND . . . if that person does not *want* to hear what the other person has to say then that's when YOU should join in, Liz," she said, motioning for Liz's approval, "to tell them that I AM RIGHT. Right?" Ginger busted out into laughter, knowing the level of tension she created.

Babs could tell that Ginger felt bad for starting an argument on Fountain Garden's last weekend.

Ginger tried to lighten the mood and exaggerated her smile to show all her pearly whites. The aide continued to have a sour look on her face.

"Why don't you get to the point so we can actually get some work done here today, Ginger." Babs urged them to finish.

Ginger continued. "I am just saying that what I took away from school is that, yes, all that other stuff matters—administering meds, assisting with personal care, consulting with other professionals about care plans, blah, blah, blah—*but,* in my mind, in a place like *this* especially, what matters even more is the personal stuff. I think creating a fun atmosphere and advocating for your resident to make sure they ALWAYS feel safe and comfortable should be the top priority."

Ginger looked directly at the aide. "Anna Davies is petrified of you. She changes her entire composure when you enter the room. I have seen you bathe her, and she literally tenses right up. Isn't the whole purpose of a bath to feel relaxed?" Ginger said.

"Is this true?" Liz asked, sitting up in her chair, looking at them both with utmost concern.

"That is a huge exaggeration, Ginger!" The aide said defensively, looking at Teddy and then at Liz, embarrassed.

"I am telling you that this is what I have observed," said Ginger. "I think you make her uncomfortable, not Ronnie, not Edward, not Holly, not Oscar . . . okay, well, Oscar can speak for himself on that," she said, chuckling, "but, with Anna, *yes*. I think we need to reassess our approach and reassess *constantly*. You are just a little *too* fast and maybe a little *too* rough for her." Ginger tried to tame her words knowing she'd have a better time getting her point across. "We could ask her daughter when she gets here if Anna has ever given her any indication that she is scared. I mean, I am sure Anna would have told us, but we should ask her daughter anyway. The thing about Anna is that we don't actually know what she is thinking; we can only speculate." Ginger saw the opportunity to throw out another issue that annoyed her. "And with Holly, I have seen you grab clothes for her to wear without even asking what she prefers. She can make up her own mind. This is a residential care home. We are just here if they need assistance, but they are free to make their own decisions."

Liz interjected, "I know the lines get blurry but that's *why* we are supposed to discuss each resident to make sure we are *all* on the same page." She cleared her throat to get Teddy to pay attention and look up from fiddling with his thumbs.

Ginger unzipped her backpack haphazardly to interrupt the mundane tone of Liz's professional voice. She felt herself getting bored and did not want Liz to go off on a lecture. "I just want to be on the same page for these last few days, so nobody has any stress. Let's make it fun. *Screw* routine!"

Teddy's head turned quickly to Ginger, surprised at her comment.

"Take your hard work to your next nursing home or hospital job and loosen up on this one for just this weekend, *please*," Ginger said, looking at the aide. She opened an Oh Henry! bar and stuffed her mouth, wanting to end the conversation. Speaking inaudibly, "I see the residents getting bored out of their tree some days so . . ." Ginger didn't miss a beat, grabbing the falling chocolate from her bottom lip. " . . . is it necessary to dust the whole floor today or water every single plant? Like really who cares about *that* anymore anyway."

"Ginger!" Babs interrupted. "Of course, we still have to care. I think you are getting off track here. Babs swung the door open wide. "I am going to do a quick round for you guys and make sure everyone is good and not needing anything. *Keep* talking and I will be right back."

Liz was disturbed thinking about Anna and what Ginger had implied about Anna feeling unsafe. "Okay, everyone, listen up now . . . ," ending the conversation and taking control of the room. She put on her reading glasses and reached behind her pulling a binder out of what they called the residents' cabinet because it held personal documents. She chose the one named Annabella Davies and set it on the table.

Silence blanketed the seriousness in the room. The aide and Ginger knew that Liz was about to school them and were acutely aware that they *both* probably needed it.

"Go ahead," Liz said, pushing the binder toward Ginger. "Open it up to 'History' and read the last handwritten entry page."

Ginger grabbed the book reluctantly and flipped it open, pulling an old, ripped paper out of a plastic sleeve. She choked up with emotions reading the first few words from the diary entry and set it back down on the table, unable to finish. Liz took the paper and read aloud.

The mood in the room was unsettling. When she finished reading the entry, Liz looked up at them, face reddened with empathy. "Imagine not having a voice. Imagine having a memory of this incident from your past . . . and that every time someone touched you unexpectedly, you are reminded . . . " She struggled to continue.

"The truth is, people don't always think of seniors as individuals that are still holding on to traumatic experiences but *sometimes*, that is not the case. We need to consider that in planning the resident's care so that they always feel safe. Whether it was a one-time incident or a lifetime of traumatic events, individuals are affected by their life experiences in unique ways. Memories are a powerful thing," Liz said, pausing to collect her thoughts. "Now," she continued, "we don't know if *this* is the reason she is responding this way to her care, but at this point, what matters is that she could have gone anywhere after her stroke and she chose this place as her new home. She is trusting us to give her the safest, most loving care possible. It's crucial to keep reminding ourselves of this. Just remember, not everyone comes in and divulges details of their past, so in the future, wherever you ladies end up working, don't EVER assume to know what goes on in people's lives, in the present, or in their past. Without Holly taking the time to write us this letter for her friend, we would not even know this happened to Mrs. Davies and while we figure out why she is feeling on edge about her baths or being touched in general, let's remember to be more delicate with her." She slid the paper back gently and closed the binder.

"Okay." The aide broke the silence, "I know sometimes I can be fast with the residents, Ginger. It is just my personality. I go home tired after work to three wired-up kids, a ton of chores to do, meals to fix, and an schmuck of a husband who is constantly nagging me to do more." The aide slumped back in her chair, defeated from trying to defend herself. Her face changed from defensive to sad and emotionally beaten.

"I understand that," Ginger said to the aide. "I do. But here, these people are our friends and with Anna especially, it is hard for her to communicate so I just want all of us to read the nonverbal cues better. That's all I am saying." She looked around the room at Liz and Teddy to make sure the aide didn't think she was being picked on.

Liz added, "And if we absolutely have to go into her room at night, let's just approach slowly and with tenderness." Everyone at the table shook their heads in agreement. "The residents' well-being always comes first. Their quality of life matters just as much as the workload. We need to find a balance. If you are struggling with your home life and it is making you stressed out, you should have come to me," she said, looking across the table at the aide, "especially if you felt you were bringing that stress into work with you."

Ginger looked at the aide and added, "I really don't mind picking up the slack if you want me to cover your remaining shifts so you can go get your life in order. I have nothing going on, the extra money would be nice, and I want to be around with Oscar and Anna's family coming." Ginger tossed her candy wrapper into the waste-paper basket.

Babs entered the room, having thought about the conversation. "Everybody good in here?"

They all stared at Teddy—a look you give a cute puppy.

"*I'm* good." He said, wondering why they were all looking at him.

Babs finished the conversation. "And *why* wouldn't the residents be helping with those chores if they want to? Involve them, guys. They love to help, and it might make the job go slower, but it makes the day go faster for everyone."

"I Agree," Ginger said, getting up from the table, she was done with this meeting.

The aide got up with a sour look on her face, not convinced that the conversation ended on a high note.

8

LUNCH

The residents moved in from outside around 11 am. when the rain hit. Oscar walked over to his wife with his walker and squeezed her arm as she lay reclined in her chair. Anna looked up at him, tense. *Is it still Friday? Did I miss Lexi's visit?* she thought.

Oscar gave her a smirk, "Are you getting as excited as I am, honey? We are going to have lunch and then it won't be long after that and we are gonna see our kid, finally." He lifted Anna's hand, gave it a kiss, and then sat down at his table.

Oscar grumbled all through lunch, making it blatantly obvious he was not a fan of catfish-salad sandwiches. It annoyed him that everyone else kept commenting how good they were.

"Mmm. Good." Ronnie shoved it in his mouth.

Edward agreed from the other table in his low voice, "Yup, very scrumptious."

"Yes!" Holly said licking her lips, "With the capers, shallots and celery . . . Mmm . . . and spicy mayo or is that mustard? Well, anyway, it *is quite* delicious."

Oscar took a few bites and threw the rest on his plate, making a big mess. "Blech! Have you ever seen what is inside of a catfish when you cut into it?" *This is mediocre at best.* "This is poor man's fish. I wouldn't feed this to my dog!"

"You have a *dog*?" Ronnie's eyes grew excited.

"Holy cow!" Holly blurted. "You are so hostile, Oscar! Don't have a hissy fit! How can you grow up on Cody Island and *not* like catfish?" Holly shook her head at his juvenile behavior. "People *pay* for this at the cafe."

"I wouldn't." Oscar got up from the table, grabbed two extra cookies off the dessert tray, and left the dining room in a huff, slamming his walker into the floor with each step.

A couple hours later, Oscar found himself in the hall, making his way towards the TV room, where the aide had parked Edward to watch his favorite exotic bird show, *Wing it with Elliot.* Oscar had changed from using his walker to his wheelchair to give his legs a break. The mid-morning confrontation with the care aide and the irritation of the distasteful food at lunch had gotten the better of him. His eyes swept the room with disgust, hating that this was the option for the moment. Choices were limited with the pouring rain. It was turning into a long, boring day. Even his stomach was cranky. He could feel the rumbling and bubbles building in his belly from the breakfast and the couple bites of lunch he had to stifle. Looking over his shoulder, he saw Teddy, the young volunteer, busy wiping the kitchen counters and tidying the lunch tables. The other aide rolled Anna down the hall towards her room announcing to everyone that she was going to change Anna's undergarments.

"We didn't need to know that!" Oscar yelled back at her. The aide was a hard worker, even Oscar could not deny that, but it didn't stop him from being annoyed with her constant rushing and fussing. The rest of the staff did their thing at their own leisure, and everything always seemed to get done. It was just her personality. Whether there were ten, five, or two residents to care for, she hustled and looked overworked just the same.

Oscar's belly rumbled again, and he could feel that it would be time for him to go to the washroom soon as well. Tightening and loosening his muscles down below, he played with his stomach to see how long he could last. Going to the toilet had become such an annoying task for all of them. It took energy and work. He had never had an accident, nor did he want one. He knew he was playing with fire when his stomach reacted to a meal this way, but he was in that kind of mood to take a chance. With an inner grin, and prankish intention, he used all his strength in his arms to quickly maneuver himself dead center of everyone in the TV room, stopping parallel to Edward, who was sitting in his wheelchair dazed and tired. Ronnie found an unused wheelchair at the end of the hall and decided to give his own legs a break. He entered the room from the far entrance and rolled toward the group. "Where should *I* park? I want to sit here too."

"Right here, Ronnie!" Oscar said. "We got room for *you*, right here." He motioned Ronnie to the other side of his wheelchair.

Ronnie beamed that he received a friendly response from Oscar and quickly rolled himself toward everyone spinning his chair abruptly, scaring Ed out of his trance. Oscar waited. He watched the aide come out of Anna's room and make her way toward the TV room. With the timing seemingly right, Oscar purposely and deliberately lifted his right leg to lift his buttock slightly off his wheelchair seat allowing all the bad air to be released. He tried to control the intentional fart thinking that if it was slow and easy, it wouldn't make a sound. *Success!* He lowered his weight, sat back down and waited for a moment until the smell reached his nostrils. *Awesome!* He was amused. He waited another moment to let it linger well into the air. Then he rolled himself out of the far entrance on the other side of the room. Looking over his shoulder to review the result of his success, he proudly watched Ronnie lift his chin like a puppy investigating the smell in the air. Oscar parked himself so he had a good view back into the TV room.

The aide walked in.

Oscar shouted at her, "Pretty sure someone shat themselves! You better deal with that!"

She looked around in disgust. "Okay, which one of you couldn't wait?" Finding herself standing between Ronnie and Edward, she shook her head. "Do you need to go to the bathroom Ronnie?"

"Nope," Ronnie said, shaking his head big from side to side.

She grabbed Edward's chair and released his brakes, bumping him awake, "All right Ed . . . "

"Where are you taking him?" Ronnie said.

In an obvious tone she answered, "I'm taking Edward to the washroom *again*, Ronnie!"

Ronnie reached under his leg where he had rolled up a piece of the newspaper and mumbled, "That's a bummer; I just got here."

Oscar smiled, proud that Ronnie had made a joke. *What a surprise she's going to have*, Oscar thought, watching her roll Edward out of the room, swaying him back and forth unnecessarily. She would be gone for at least ten minutes and that made it worth it in Oscar's eyes. *That's how I roll.* He left the area.

Holly, who had been watching by the far window at the end of the hall, commented over her shoulder, "You are an agent of chaos and mischief, Oscar Davies!"

"Just living my best life, Holls!" he said.

9

THE FLIGHT

Rayna managed to make them all late for the flight, having left her cell phone on the toilet tissue holder in the bathroom beside the check-in counter at the airport. The three of them arrived at the gate, scrambling for passports. Lexi was panting, annoyed, and regretted wearing her white button-up shirt, which was now damp with sweat.

Her phone rang. "Hello," Lexi said.

"Lexi!" Gunther said.

"Oh, hi Gunther!"

"You all set to jet?" he asked.

"I am. I was going to call you. It's so nice of you to take care of our accommodations for us. You are always so good to my parents and me."

"You sure you don't want to stay at *my* house? It's no trouble," he said.

"I know, but it is *a lot* to have three extra people, so I think it's best we stay at the motel. I am surprised there *is* a motel on Cody Island still!" Lexi said, laughing.

"Don't you worry your pretty little head about it, String-Bean. I got you covered," said Gunther.

"So, you *did* find us a place?" Lexi asked.

"Have a safe flight!" The older man hung up, shocking Lexi at the abruptness. She laughed at her old friend Gunther Gwilliam and how his age was starting to show through even on a telephone call.

Oh, for God's sake! Lexi struggled to reach the bottom of her large purse. Everyone in line was waiting for her to get out her ID and the lady with the mean Grade 4 eyes was not impressed that she was holding everyone up. She was in a full-blown sweat now and would have paid a million dollars to trade Rayna's inappropriate tank top just to get some material off her overheated body. *If this is what menopause is going to feel like, then kill me now,* she thought.

Malia had her brown hair in a high purposely messy ponytail. She wore a light pink tank top and a jean mini skirt with her new, light cream-colored sweater wrapped around her waist. Lexi approved (not that it mattered to the teen). Rayna was in a hot pink strappy, cropped tank that left little to the imagination. Her boobs spilled over her scooped neckline and her jean shorts with the frayed hem had a ripped hole, revealing even more of her one thigh. Lexi was mystified how the two girls had become friends and constantly reminded herself to keep careful watch on Malia to make sure she wasn't taking on too many of Rayna's traits. Lately, it felt like a full-time job watching the energetic teens. Brock's lack of parenting did not help; he practically flirted with Malia's friends, Rayna especially. It disgusted Lexi. This overly confident girl knew just how to get a reaction out of a man.

Rayna and Malia giggled continuously and were completely unfazed by Lexi's anxiety. Loving the attention of a couple boys in line, Rayna purposely allowed her backpack to slide off her shoulders, taking the strap of her tank with it.

"Ray! You are such a SLUT!" Malia whispered, giving her pony an exaggerated flip.

"Whaaat? Meee?" Rayna said, batting her eyes.

Lexi heard Malia's comment and shot her a disapproving look. *You two are a bit of a handful today,* she thought. Watching the girls reminded Lexi of herself at that age and how her mom would have handled the situation. Guilt entered her mind as she did the math on how many days had gone by since her last visit to the island. Time seemed to have gotten away from her, and between work, Malia's weekend sports tournaments, and her difficult marriage, visiting her parents had fallen on the priority list. *Oh, God, Mom, forgive me.* "Girls, I know it's your job as teens to stress me out, but could you rein it in a tad, please," she said.

The girls were loud and hyper in their seats on the plane, babbling about things that amused them on their phones. Lexi shushed them a few times, only to be ignored, and finally settled herself into the flight by resting her head against the window. The sounds of the loud engine on the smaller plane made it somewhat possible to ignore the constant chatter of the girls.

Lexi tried to doze, but her sporadic thoughts jumped from work to Brock to her father to how she was going to navigate the next few days without upsetting her father even more than he was. She recalled how bittersweet her high school graduation was. She had been so happy to be done with that phase of her life but sad that she had to say goodbye to most of her friends, who were moving off Cody Island to work elsewhere or further their studies in a big center. At the time, Lexi wasn't sure what she aspired to be, and her parents didn't want to spend money on college until she had a better idea of what she saw for her future. So, when Brock's family came to the island that summer, Lexi had her eye on him right away. He was young, very fit, and handsomely clean-cut. With a friend he had brought from the city, they ripped around on Sea-Dos in the ocean water. They were cocky, attention-seeking, and seemed way out of her league. She fantasized that this new stranger could be her way out of a boring future, working at a hardware store with a bunch of old men. Instantly, the two were wild about each other. Brock had the money to support her and maintain an unimaginable, anything-but-boring life, she thought.

"Cookies or pretzels?" the flight attendant offered, placing a napkin on Lexi's table.

"I am fine, thank you. I do not need to eat. It is only an hour flight," Lexi said as her mouth watered at the smell of Rayna's treats beside her. She turned her head to avoid the smell and wondered why she would care about calories on a day like this. Normally, her husband would make her feel guilty about eating sugar, but he was not there. She regretted not taking the snack.

"Mmm, yummy!" Rayna said, lifting the round chocolate treat up to her nose.

Eyes in a trance, fixed on the wing of the plane, Lexi recalled how her mom took pride in baking and preparing meals for her family. The aroma of the mouth-watering homemade butter and pecan tarts and cinnamon buns filled the entire space of her parent's tiny house. Lexi missed her mom's signature plate of pasta with mushrooms and creamy ricotta, topped with lemon and her delicious, prized asparagus sautéed in oil and garlic. Anna's meals were served at precisely 5:30 pm. It was just enough time for Oscar to get home from his work at Hill's Hardware, kick off his boots, and wash his hands. The three of them would enjoy a quiet meal at a perfectly set table. Oscar and Anna would have a glass of wine, and Lexi would have milk with her dinner. Only when all three were finished eating would they stand up together to clear the table. Lexi and her mom did the dishes, and Oscar—after sweeping the floor—would get garbage bags ready for their evening walks on the beach.

Lexi's husband was not a fan of eating with her parents. Brock said that he was just as hungry after the meal as he was before. One holiday evening, Lexi and her parents sat at the table staring at the beautifully plated food waiting for Brock. Lexi felt bad for her husband's rude behavior and Oscar was having difficulty hiding how ornery he was getting. Brock walked in the kitchen fifteen minutes late for supper (knowing full well the 5:30 pm. family routine) and said unapologetically, "Great run . . . got into the groove . . . you should have started without me." Oscar's hangry face filled with rage as Brock whipped his shirt off. "Wow it is hot out there," he said, reaching over the table and dripping sweat on the homemade bread to grab a pickle.

It was an evening ritual that, after a healthy meal, the family walked the waterfront with garbage bags in tow, clearing the sand of trash and debris. As a young child, Lexi learned from her parents that the simple routine was important for maintaining the coast that they called home, and the exercise was a bonus. Each day, even with all their efforts, it was surprising the amount of waste that washed up on shore with the tides. While Anna and Lexi filled their bags, Oscar picked all the large, sharp-edged rocks that he thought could be dangerous for Lexi or other children running on the sand. He made two significant piles, one down the beach a little north of his property, and another a bit south of his property.

When Lexi told Brock of the family routine, he laughed. "It's not exercise for me to pick rocks, Lexi." He shook his head, "I need to get my heart rate up." He had completely missed the point.

Lexi, feeling a trifle shaken from her memories, heard the pilot's voice on the intercom announcing jokingly that they were about to land in a completely different weather system. Through the foggy window, she watched a heavy rain plummet and bounce high off the tarmac.

Rayna's elbow struck Lexi's arm, sending a harsh pain up to her shoulder.

"Ouch!" Lexi yelled, grabbing her arm and shooting an irritated look at the fidgety girl beside her.

"Oops, sorry Mrs. Kirk!" Rayna said.

Her sugary apology was less than sincere and somehow the fake formality and tone of "Mrs. Kirk" didn't sit right with Lexi anymore. Maybe she *was* coming to terms with the idea that she would be a single woman soon.

"Rayna, just call me Lexi, please," she said.

The novelty of Malia and Rayna taking a trip together and their consistent giddiness had not worn off, even though they had stayed up late the night before watching movies and messaging boys. They continued to bounce off each other's energy.

The plane landed on the wet runway. A young man in a drenched yellow safety jacket taxied the pilot by waving his bright orange baton to motion him to stop on the ramp area. The girls made a high-pitched noise when they saw the young, handsome stranger standing out in the rain. *This is such a bad idea,* Lexi thought. *How did I think bringing you two on such a serious trip was a good idea?* Lexi pulled at her sweaty white button-up shirt. It was sticking to her back. *Holy hell! Could it be any hotter in here?* She hated her whole outfit now.

"Getting excited, Mom?" Malia asked.

"Yes," Lexi said, grabbing her purse from under her seat. "I am!"

"It's been so long since I have been here!" Malia explained to Rayna, "I couldn't come last time because I went with my *other* grandparents on a Christmas ski vacation to their Chalet. It was so awesome!"

"Duh! I know dumb-dumb, I begged you to take me, remember! I would rather have spent Christmas with your *rich* grandparents than stayed at home at my house of total boring!" Rayna said.

"Wow, it's like Brock is *in* this plane," Lexi thought. "If anyone heard this conversation, they would think you two sound like rich brats."

"I wish dad could have come this time," Malia said to her mom.

Lexi felt sick. *You are SO young still,* Lexi thought, smiling at her daughter, thinking about how she had begged Brock to join them. Once again, he abdicated himself of his fatherly duties and insisted he would rather discuss their "situation" with Malia alone after the weekend—after he got home from his "work thing" with his co-workers. Lexi wondered if one of those co-workers was his secretary. *It is only a matter of time that whatever Brock IS doing won't be my business anymore*, she thought.

10

OSCAR

Oscar had placed himself strategically in the hall to read his newspaper where he had a view of the entrance door and where he could see Lexi when she arrived. A window in the hall allowed him to keep an eye on the rain as well. He felt like he was going stir-crazy, so if the rain *did* stop, he had full intention of getting back outside to do something physical, like working in the garden.

Ginger, fiddling with the sleeves of her multicolored sweater (that by no accident complemented her blazing red hair) passed Oscar while he read his newspaper. "Oscar, have you seen Ronnie?" she asked.

"He's probably outside eating wood," he mocked, without even looking up from the paper.

Ginger gave Oscar a quick look of a disapproving parent and kept walking.

"I am just kidding, Red," Oscar said, as he pointed down the hall, "He's over there. I saw him eyeing up a plate of cookies near the entrance doors, but then he got sidetracked by the guppy fish. They were having a stare down."

"Yes. I see him now," Ginger said.

Oscar was amused at the length of time Ronnie could stay laser focused and mesmerized by the quick animal that suspended itself mid-bowl, seemingly staring back and communicating with Ronnie.

Ginger approached Ronnie in front of the fish tank. Oscar watched her put her hand gently on Ronnie's shoulder so she would not startle him from his gaze. "Ronnie," she said, noticing breakfast and lunch stains on his shirt, "I was wondering if you would like to come with me to wash up a little now that lunch is finished, and we could find you some fresh clothes to put on." He was usually pretty agreeable. "We want to look spiffy when visitors arrive."

Babs passed by Oscar in the hall. She had a grotesque look on her face from helping Edward with his unfortunate loose stool. In one hand, she had a bag of Edward's soiled garbage, and in the other, an aerosol can of Apples and Cinnamon Spray. She sprayed the vapor vigorously, up, down, and all around.

"For Christ sake's, Babs!" Oscar waved his newspaper around in the air to avoid the spray, "It smells like someone had a poonami in a bakery now!"

"I just want it to smell nice when your family gets here!" she said as she ran out of the building to chuck the garbage in the bin outside, her glasses falling off her face.

That's what they get for serving catfish, Oscar mocked in his head.

After some time, Ginger emerged from Ronnie's room, looking tired and overheated. Oscar looked up from his paper for a quick moment and noticed that she had taken off her second shirt and wrapped it around her waist. Ronnie paraded down the hall and stood in front of Oscar in his newly washed, long-sleeved, button-down, collared shirt with khaki pants. He had his hands by his side like a pleased child. "How do I look Oscar?" he asked, patting his chest and belly, taking a deep breath in to indicate he had a fresh-smelling wardrobe.

Oscar looked up again, annoyed. "You look exactly the same, Ronnie," he said, shrugging his shoulders and dismissing the man. He looked back down and continued to read.

"I'm getting company today," said Ronnie, repeating what he had heard earlier.

"No, *you're* not." Oscar rolled up his newspaper in his hand and repeatedly whacked it against his leg while he thought about having to see Lexi's husband again. Ronnie walked away, sensing Oscar's mood.

Oscar sat, recalling the early years when Brock took his daughter to exotic places in the first few years of their marriage. It was customary for the young couple to take three, even four vacations a year. Brock's family would foot the bill each time and ensured Lexi, only four months after the young couple had met, that a luxurious life was waiting for her in the big city. Oscar felt like this boy and his family had moved in on his daughter like a hurricane, and before he had even fully processed what had happened, he and Anna were given tickets to St. Barts to attend their daughter's extravagant wedding. Their baby was gone.

Oscar continued to sit idle, staring out the window, wishing the rain would stop—and then so too—could his stirring thoughts. He created a scenario in his brain. *I wonder if Brock has the gall to complain about Gunther's old, stinky truck when he's nice enough to pick them up at the airport. I hope that hoity-toity, smug son-in-law of mine gets oil and dirt all over his expensive clothes jumping in and out of Gunther's vehicle baby. That kid needs to learn to be humble and more appreciative of people.*

His memory flashed to six months earlier when, sitting around the Fountain Garden Christmas table, Brock sucked up all the air out of the room, telling of his successes, bragging about his accomplishments, and boasting about how easy his life was. Brock stated that he could not imagine being like an average person and dealing with everyday hardships. Then he went on to embarrass Oscar by announcing that "Oscar shouldn't have been *sad* to see his old house torn down. It was time!" Brock said. "The foundation was cracking, the windows were old, the hot water tank needed to be replaced, and you wouldn't let me buy you a new one," he said to Oscar, who sat fuming across the festive-looking table.

Oscar, red-faced and steaming in his ugly Christmas sweater, was mortified and utterly offended. He would rather freeze and give up showers than admit to taking anything from a son-in-law who was so arrogant. Gunther had kicked Oscar under the table in support of Oscar's rising blood pressure. All the older men at the hardware store knew how Oscar felt about Lexi's husband, and they all jumped on Oscar's pity train and agreed that the insolent kid had stolen their String-Bean, not only from Oscar but from the store and the community as well.

11

THE ARRIVAL

The plane sat still on the tarmac. *Open the damn door already.* Lexi's inner thighs were hot, damp, and sticking together in her skirt. *I NEED air and I want to go see this new development that everyone is ranting about. Standing on the same land where my childhood home once stood will be so weird!* She contemplated whether she would be super emotional or feel any attachment at all now that her house was gone. She could not imagine coming all this way and not going to see the property. *If the rumors are true, it will all look so different now, unrecognizable possibly,* she thought. Lexi took a deep sigh. *I just want to see Mom. Okay, get me off this plane, for goodness sake!*

Moments later, the door opened and the girls, with faces still glued to their phones, jumped up with anticipation, anxious to disembark. The rain slapped at Lexi's skin as she took her first step outside. *Home.* Her nostrils filled with jet fuel mixed with heavy humid air. A cool wet chill rose up her skirt as her boot heels clicked on the passenger stairs and exit ramp. *Oh MY GOD! FINALLY!* She felt her body temperature go down.

Rayna, still on the plane horsing around, was blocking Malia from exiting the aisle. The two girls, backpacks in hand, raced to the door and gasped as they departed the plane.

At the entrance to the old airplane hangar, an elderly man sat by the large door. The wet, wrinkly gentleman, in the oversized orange raincoat, managed to stand from the wet steel bench and approach Lexi as she stepped off the ramp, pivoting her roller bag. The man ignored the other five passengers, who quickly ran by him and entered the building, "Well, look who it is!" He said in his croaky voice. "It's been a long time *String-Bean*."

"Oh, that *is* you. Hello, Mr. Gwilliam!" Lexi gave him a big, warm smile.

"Stop that, Lexi! You know I hate it when you call me that! Bring it in, girl!" He grabbed her shoulders and wrapped her tight against his torn-up, dripping rain jacket.

All right, she thought, trying to avoid getting her white shirt more wet. *That's enough.*

His two-week-old beard scratched her when he let go. He had a familiar smell of plywood, coffee, and cigarette smoke.

"It's good to see you again, Gunther," Lexi said.

"Alotta folks are going to be happy to see you!" he said, stomping the excess rain off his feet.

Lexi chuckled at the inaccuracy of his comment. Gunther was exaggerating, she thought, considering the town's population had dramatically dwindled over the last ten years. In fact, she knew very few people in the area anymore. From talking with Holly, she learned that the popular local restaurant, Joe's Chowder, had been struggling and was now closed leaving the smaller Daphne's Cafe to tend to the community. The elementary school and high school had joined to become one small building, and anyone needing emergency care (like her mom had needed) was flown off to the mainland, where large surgical hospitals existed. Many of the locals that Lexi had known had either retired or moved on to supportive living facilities.

This left a few younger strangers to take over the businesses that managed to stay open, like the grocery store, the post office, the dockyard, and Hill's Hardware store with the adjoining cafe.

"You didn't think to dress for this weather, hey?" Gunther smirked, taking note of the girls' wardrobes. "You girls are going to get sick if we don't get you out of this chilly rain!"

"It's fine," Lexi uttered, shaking the rain off her shirt. Just then, a violent wind blew Malia sideways, pushing her into Rayna.

"It's just a quick downpour!" Gunther said, trying to reassure them.

Ya, right! Malia rolled her eyes at Rayna.

"It'll let up soon. Trust me," Gunther said, all knowingly.

Malia was blanketed under her light, cream sweater hiding her face. Rayna giggled as she whipped her wrinkled jean jacket out of her backpack and held it over her head.

Gunther pointed his shaky finger towards an old, blue ford half-ton truck. "That's our ride. Go ahead and hop in my truck, ladies."

Lexi and Malia ran to the truck, fighting the sideways rain while Rayna skipped leisurely around the puddles without a care in the world. Lexi jumped in the front, and Malia and Rayna hopped in the back seat.

Gunther hopped in the driver's seat. The rain jumped off his jeans and plastic orange jacket onto Lexi.

"I appreciate the ride, Gunther." Lexi forced a wet smile, taking in the gentleman's face. She thought he seemed a lot older now, even though she saw him just a few months ago.

"Well, I have some extra time today, so it's not a problem," he said, looking over his shoulder at the girls.

I bet your schedule is pretty much wide open every day! Rayna thought sarcastically. She rolled her eyes at Malia while she flipped her damp, flat ponytail hair up into a quick loose bun on the top of her head.

"I wouldn't pass up coming to pick you up, String-Bean. So, how's the big city?" he asked.

"Good, I guess," Lexi said.

Gunther adjusted his rear-view mirror, "So, you two cuties in the back finally had time to come see us on the island this long weekend?"

Malia and Rayna looked at each other simultaneously.

"Gross!" Rayna whispered to Malia.

Malia, putting on her waffle sweater, responded under her breath back to Rayna, "YUCK!"

Lexi wondered how many times she would have to hear the name "String-Bean" on this trip. Although she couldn't deny that the nickname did make her feel like home.

"It's been a few months, String-Bean," Gunther said, scolding. "I think the last time I saw you was the end of December." The girls were back on their phones, completely ignoring the conversation.

"I feel like I owe you so much, Gunther, after you helped dad pack up the house after he sold and then helped him move into Fountain Garden. Then, I heard you did the same for Holly just a month later. It was a lot of work for you, and I appreciate it," Lexi said, feeling guilty.

"Well, Holly, your mom and dad and I have been friends forever, so that was a no-brainer," he said, not paying her guilt any mind. "Most things sold in the garage sale, and the few things that were left I brought to Fountain Garden to help make it feel more like home."

"When you called that day to tell me that a guy had come to the island and was interested in purchasing not only mom and dad's property but Holly's as well, I was really caught off guard," Lexi admitted, "but then I thought about it and . . . everything happens for a reason, right?"

"You got that right, String-Bean. The timing was right, and the homes sold at a reasonable price. Those of us left here aren't getting any younger, so when these opportunities come up, and our health tells us it is time—you grab it. Your dad had trouble with the idea at first, too, but I think he was secretly a bit relieved he would have the money to pay for Fountain Garden for him and Anna. That place is old, but it isn't cheap. I am excited for you to see your pops. He is doing better, I'd say, finally found his place. Holly keeps him in check. Your mom too," he added, making direct eye contact with Lexi. "She's good, you know. The same, but good." His words were caring and gentle.

"After I talked to you during the holidays," Lexi said, "I did a little poking around myself and learned from the local island rumor ville—"

Gunther laughed out loud, "You mean the guys at the hardware store?" He did not include himself, even though he worked there as well.

"Yes exactly," Lexi laughed, "I was told that the man had intentions of demolishing our family home, along with Holly's next door, because he intended to build a mini camping resort!" She said, intrigued and surprised at the notion, "So, I guess you must know this guy now if he's a builder and doing all the work himself? He must use Hill's Hardware to provide much of his materials?"

"Oh yes, I know him *now*," Gunther said boastingly. "I only met him a few months ago. He kept his business to himself over the winter. He was more of a rumor for the longest time until he showed up at the store early this spring. He's ambitious, that Luke. It did not take him long. Apparently, he moved in giant machinery to excavate last fall before the ground froze. As soon as Holly moved into Fountain Garden and he had both properties in his name, he removed the two homes and levelled the waterfront lots to create one larger property. Then this spring, he built three tiny, seasonal waterfront cottages and added three RV parking pad areas. He is not finished everything yet, but it's sure coming along nice. You are going to get a big surprise."

"So, is it open yet?" Lexi asked.

"Yup. It's called Camper's Edge. It opened a month ago and has been surprisingly busy. News travels fast around here. He's gotten everything from hippie stragglers who show up with only a backpack on their arm looking for a place to crash for one night to city families with RVs full of belongings looking to get away. When I talked to him at the store, he said one day it can be crawling with children's screaming and the very next day it can be quiet and peaceful with a loner spending all day reading a book. He says it is very random and has already made for an interesting four weeks."

"Is it going to be opened all year round?" Lexi asked.

"I think so, but you should ask him *yourself*, String-Bean."

"So, what's this guy like?" Lexi said, digging for more information.

"He is a laid-back guy, that Luke. Most campers, he told me, are polite and tidy, but the odd ones leave behind evidence of a long night of drinking and early morning shenanigans. It does not seem to bother him much. I went to drop off supplies for his latest project about a week ago and the ground was covered in stale-smelling cans, cigarette butts, and mounds of seeds. Luke was sure happy his young helper, Teddy, showed up to work with him *that* morning."

"*That* sounds like a *fun* place," Rayna piped up from the back seat.

Gunther made a right turn and drove up the long private driveway. "This is it. This is the famous, *exciting* Fountain Garden. You girls are lucky. I think this rain is going to let up for you right away and we are going to have a beautiful evening." It was down to a light drizzle. "Look, that nasty cloud is passing over us now. The sun is going to win today! It can be really on and off around here. Those clouds leave as fast as they appear."

The girls looked up from their phones to see the vintage pedestal-style streetlights lining the road. An older-looking monument sign stood at the entrance to the property, identifying they had arrived at their destination. Parked on the edge of the lot was a white passenger transfer bus with a small, discrete graphic sign on the door representing the residential care home. There were no other vehicles. In front of the main door was a round cobblestone courtyard with a bench on each side for visitors to sit in the sun or lounge while having a smoke. Large planters of colourful, fragrant flowers added to the curb appeal. Just off to the side was a little nook made of wood and lattice. The structure was covered in vines, set among the trees, and offered seclusion from the weather for someone wanting to sit and relax without being out in the open.

"Cute," Rayna said with her face up to the window of the truck.

"It *is* cute, right?" Malia's excitement grew in her belly knowing she would be seeing her grandparents soon.

Like a perfect gentleman, Gunther jumped out and held the door open for Lexi.

So, chivalry is not dead? "Thanks—a million time over—for the ride, Gunther. We will be seeing you I guess." She gave him a big smile as she jumped out of the truck. "It was good to see you again, my friend."

"You sure *will* see me again. I'll drop your bags for you and you gals have a fantastic, long *overdue* visit."

Nice jab, Lexi thought. She was not insulted because he was right. It had been too long. Gunther had always pampered Oscar. They were best buds, and in any situation that Lexi could remember, they always had each other's back. She knew that comment was probably more from her dad, and she was happy that Gunther was still such a loyal friend to the family.

She noticed that Gunther was having a "moment" himself staring toward one of the windows of Fountain Garden. He just stood, waiting for something. *Weird,* she thought as she gathered herself. It was time to dig deep for some courage and calm her rising excitement. She couldn't wait to wrap her arms around her mom and dad.

"You gals still have time to visit with everyone today," said Gunther to Malia and Rayna, who had jumped out quickly, slamming the doors shut. "Right about now, all the residents are probably relaxing before their dinner. I have gotten to know their schedule pretty well. You should get some visiting in quick before everyone eats and then starts their evening routine. You will learn how things work around here fast. I will go drop your bags off at the cabins at Camper's Edge."

What? Seriously? Lexi shot a glance at Malia then looked back at Gunther. "So, there's *no* motel?" She was shocked to hear this news.

He ignored her question. "When you are done with your visit, just get Oscar to show you the path out back to get to the campground. It will be sunny and cleared up by then. You remember Lexi? It is not a far walk at all. It won't be raining anymore, so you girls will be fine."

Did he simply forget to tell me that we are not staying in a motel? Am I losing my mind right now or is HE losing HIS mind? I knew I should have insisted on taking care of accommodations myself. "Of course, I remember," Lexi said, biting the inside of her lip.

"There's already a large, hard-packed path from campers exploring in the trees out back of Fountain Garden. Remember the tiny trail that existed when *you* used to explore and play in the trees as a kid, String-Bean? I think those campers wander in the forest after a few brews until they find themselves at that rickety vine-covered fence overlooking the gardens of the care home, and then they probably get scared off, not knowing what the building is," he laughed.

"So *WHAT?*" the girls piped up, "*WHERE* will our bags be?" they asked, concerned.

"They will be in your cabins at the campground. Look for Luke when you get there. He is the new owner. He'll show you around," Gunther said.

"We're not talking like an outhouse-type of camping, right?" asked Malia.

"Nope, he made a real nice washroom facility out there. I was surprised. Pretty fancy crappers for camping, *I* thought. He is a handy guy, that Luke," he said as he jumped in his truck and then drove off.

12

FOUNTAIN GARDEN CARE HOME

Lexi held the entrance door open for Malia and Rayna as she read the sign on the glass. "Dr. Benjamin's office has now relocated to 17 Rocky Lane. Sorry for the inconvenience." The three women stomped the excess rain off their feet on the welcome mat and stepped forward onto the shiny floor that smelled of disinfectant. It was a large, bare, bland entrance where a visitor had to choose whether to turn left towards a set of two giant, plain closed doors or right towards another entrance with another set of basic closed doors. Lexi paused, questioning which way she had gone the last time she was here. The excitement of seeing her parents rushed through her body, making it hard for her to think.

The previous visit to Fountain Garden had been so stressful, with Brock less than pleased to spend the Christmas holidays visiting Lexi's parents in a nursing home. The interior of the building seemed so different now, without the visually stimulating holiday decor. Giant blue and silver cutout snowflakes had hung from the ceiling along with a starry Merry Christmas banner on the wall and multiple random crayon-coloured posters of Santa Clause. A plastic reindeer pulling a sleigh that held lighted gift box displays had filled the floor space. Lexi remembered chuckling that the area had felt a tad cluttered.

"This way, Mom!" Malia bounced to the right, "Look!" A small A-frame poster board sign rested on the floor. It read, "Welcome to FOUNTAIN GARDEN." On the wall to the right of the large doors entering Fountain Garden was a plastic, fluorescent yellow warning sign with black words, "CAUTION STAND CLEAR OF DOOR." Just below it was a large, flat silver button. Lexi could feel her nerves stirring at the bottom of her gut. She hoped this visit with her parents would be a success and that somehow, she would find the courage in the next couple of days, to be honest and real with them and her daughter about her divorce and her new life that was about to unfold. She motioned with her hand for Malia and Rayna to stand behind her, just as the two heavy doors opposite the room opened.

Ginger emerged through the doors. She was holding a tray with stacks of plastic cups. In an energetic voice, she called out, "Visitors! Go ahead; do not be shy around here! Just push the big silver button on the right wall and check in with Babs on the other side of the door." Rayna jumped forward with excitement and gave the button a good WACK, making an embarrassing echo throughout the entrance. The "wack" was followed by the sound of a faint buzzer that triggered the heavy doors to begin opening.

Really? Lexi thought that Rayna could be so childish. The large doors opened, and they all proceeded through. Three steps inside and the air had changed. It was heavier now. Lexi's nostrils filled with a heavy warm stench of chemical floor cleaner, antibacterial hand sanitizer, and a hint of *peanut butter cookies*?

Malia came out with a loud, "Oh, God!" She covered her mouth and nose with her hand to take a deep breath, her eyes watering.

Rayna threw her hands to her face covering her nose and mouth. "*Strong* smell!"

Ginger walked right by them, balancing her tray in one hand and holding her phone to her ear with the other. "Hey, Sweet T., I get to leave in about an hour," she said, "Liz has someone else coming in for the night shift, so I do not have to stay and work. I have a couple of errands to run, and then I am going to grab some take-out from the cafe, but then I can sneak over. Just leave the door open for me, lover."

Malia and Rayna looked at each other with raised eyebrows. *This girl was interesting.*

"Baby don't tease. I gotta keep my mind on work here! Mwah!" Ginger gave a giant smooch into her phone. Her fire-red ponytail bobbed with her bouncy steps when she took off down the hall.

Rayna was intrigued by the captivating girl. This place had already become more interesting than she had expected.

The large, heavy steel security doors shut, and the double latch clanged behind them. To the right was a hand-written sign taped to the front of the glass office door, "**All visitors must check in here.**" Lexi chuckled at the implied strictness of the bold letters and wondered how many visitors Fountain Garden received that it would require a unit clerk to sit there all day. She had learned from her last visit that signage such as this at Fountain Garden was more for due diligence than the seriousness it implied. Once inside the building the casual atmosphere, dress code and mannerisms were quite relaxed.

A large peg board hung on the wall. On it were sticker letters that said, "SAVE THE DATE" and a calendar that pointed out activities and special daily events. On Saturday, "Haircuts $10.00" and "Just kidding—they are free" written underneath it. Sunday had "Excursion Day—Mario's Market and Greenhouse" and "Ice Cream Palace" or "God, Gunther and Goodies (if the weather is bad)" written underneath it.

What the heck? Lexi thought as she burst out into a giggle.

Monday had "Music Madness" and "Plant your Plants" written underneath it. *Mom would love that, if only she could partake.* Tuesday was "Taco Tuesday" and "Tabbies and other Tails." *Interesting. Pet visits?* Wednesday was "ALL DECKED OUT" for bridge night. Thursday was "Paint with a Partner" and "Table Talk," as well as "Have You Heard?" and "What's in the News" written underneath it.

Lexi laughed again. *Like they need to set aside a specific day for gossip,* she thought, remembering full well how fast the tiniest piece of information could travel around the island, having experienced the consequences of tattletales as a teen.

Friday was "Movie and Popcorn". Lexi amused herself, thinking that her dad would *hate* everything about this. In the past, he always beat to his own drum and didn't like anyone telling him what to do. *Maybe Gunther was right about him settling in, and things were a lot different now that he was older.*

"Hello?" She called as she leaned over the admissions counter. The office was empty with the low sound of a radio playing over by the back wall.

"Hey there!" A short, stocky woman hailed the girls from down the hall. She waved at them, holding something white in her hand. "You can come down here. The rain stopped; everyone *just* went outside!" Then she disappeared out of sight around a corner.

"You know her, Mom?" Malia asked.

"Yes, she is one of the care aides here." Lexi started to walk down the corridor.

Rayna glanced over the admissions counter and immediately spotted a cigarette tucked behind a coffee cup. No one was looking, so she quickly swiped it.

The three of them sauntered down the hall, passing a fish tank that seemed excessively big for the small loner fish swimming inside.

"Even the fish die here," Rayna joked. "There were four in here yesterday, mwuahaha!"

"Ahhh. LOL. Good one, Ray!" Malia said, sliding her hand along the smooth, wooden hand railing.

When they reached the end of the hall, they turned right and met the aide at the entrance of the large dining area. The shorter, stocky woman knelt in front of an elderly gentleman sitting in a wheelchair. He struggled to stay perfectly steady while she pulled at his laces.

"Where are your Velcro shoes, Edward? These ones are such a pain in the butt." The young girls looked at each other, shocked at her brash comment. When she finished tying the man's lace, she stood up to acknowledge the three of them. They immediately noticed that she was holding an adult incontinence pad under her arm, "Lexi, right. I *heard* you were supposed to be coming."

Lexi remembered having met this aide before and that she was very forward in her words and noticeably hard working.

"I gotta pee right now or *I'm* the one that's going to need that diaper," Rayna blurted out.

"Ray!" Malia whacked her on the arm.

"Is this a washroom?" Rayna asked, pointing to a door beside the dining room entrance. "May I?"

"Sure. Go ahead." the aide said. Then she looked at Lexi and Malia and motioned them toward some garden doors. "If you guys go through the dining room and out through those doors, you will find everyone out on the deck. The sun is making its way out now, finally!"

Lexi and Malia walked through the eating area, through the garden doors, and out onto the wet deck. Lexi's heart skipped a beat when she spotted her mom sitting in her recliner chair.

"Welcome back, Lexi!" Babs shouted while wiping the rain off a white, plastic patio chair. "Watch your step; it is still slippery out here!" She pulled the chair closer to Anna's recliner and waved for Lexi and Malia to come over.

"Hi Lexi!" Liz said, closing the binder on her med cart. "Come ladies, Anna has been waiting for you. It's nice to see you again, Malia."

Liz put her hand on Anna's forearm, "Look who it is, Anna." Anna flinched when the nurse's hand alarmed her out of her rest. She turned her head slowly, squinting her eyes from the sun. She beamed bright when she realized that she was fully awake and looking at her daughter and granddaughter. The torture of the slowly passing time had halted in an instant, and the wait had all become worth it.

Lexi stood in front of her mom. Anna looked small, sunk into her medical recliner chair, surrounded by small pillows under her arms. She had on a light olive dress, and her hair was neatly combed. A light Afghan was draped over the bottom of her legs. "You look so good, Mom. It's so good to see you." Lexi said as she leaned down, kissed her mom on the cheek and then sat on the dry chair next to her. Anna's thin, sparse, little eyelashes blinked and cast a joyful look back at her.

"Hi, grams." Malia leaned over and put her youthful, smiling face in front of her grandma's.

Anna reached for Malia's arm. She stared back at her granddaughter, taking in her beauty. The frame of Malia's face and her smile reminded Anna so much of Lexi as a child. She could hardly contain herself in that moment. Her mind and muscles were so tired, but her pounding heart and overflowing spirit wanted to jump right out of her recliner and wrap her arms around her daughter and granddaughter in a giant group bear hug.

Ronnie walked up to Malia and startled her attention away from her grandma. "Hello!" he said, extending his arm abruptly. He was utterly unaware of her personal space, his stiff hand almost hitting her in the boob.

"Hello!" Malia said as she took a startled step back, avoiding the handshake.

Liz tried to redirect him. "Ronnie, maybe you should stay seated until the deck is completely dry?" she said, nudging him gently away from the family.

Seeing Rayna join everyone on the deck, Ronnie shuffled his feet swiftly toward her, "Hello!" he said, wanting to shake her hand.

Rayna hesitated to put her hand out, and when she did, he grabbed it with force.

"Hi!" she said, grimacing her face as he squeezed hard. "Whoa, cowboy! Easy up there, old fellow."

"I had a HORSE," Ronnie said.

"COOL!" She pulled her arm free, turned her back to him, and walked away.

Malia laughed as she watched Rayna try to avoid any further conversation with the man. "Grams, this is Rayna, my friend," Malia said to her grandma, waving Rayna to come over to the recliner.

Rayna approached and smiled awkwardly, "Hello . . . " Then, there was a weird silence. Rayna had forgotten that Anna could not speak. Uncomfortable in the moment, she stepped away from Anna's chair and wandered around the deck to find a place under the struggling sun to hang out by herself. She plunked down on a wet chair, rolled her shorts up to make them even shorter, and played on her phone while adjusting herself to stay in the remaining late afternoon warmth.

"We are here for a few days, Mom," Lexi said. "We are going to camp on our property and see what they've done to the place." Lexi dreaded that plan but tried to sound excited. "I will tell you all about it tomorrow." They continued to chat for a while. Lexi could see the thrill on her mom's face while Anna's eyes jumped back and forth between her and Malia. After anticipating the arrival to Fountain Garden all day, it filled Lexi's heart that her mom was just as excited to see her and Malia.

Malia tried hard to connect with her grandma. "I am going to go check out the ocean later, Grams; it has been so long since I've been here. I have been so busy with studying and sports. I wish you could watch me play volleyball. I am the setter, and I am good, actually." She wished she could come right out and say, "Sorry, my parents are assholes and *so* caught up in their own miserableness, that it has kept us apart." She just smiled instead, staring at her grandma's eyes, and felt that her grandma knew what she was thinking anyway.

Seeing that Malia could handle herself, Lexi got up to talk with Liz. "So, Liz? My dad? Where would he be?"

"Oscar is just down the path," Liz said, as she pointed Lexi away from the deck in the direction of the flower gardens.

"I guess you and I have a lot to chat about as well, with how the transfer is going to work back to Adasa," Lexi said.

"We do, but you just got here, so let's not worry about that now. Just enjoy your parents, and we can discuss the transfer later. Dr. Benjamin and I have the details for Tuesday pretty much taken care of anyway, Lexi. You and the girls are planning to take the ferry home to Adasa right? With your parents and Holly in the medical-transfer vehicle?"

"Yes. Thanks, Liz." She felt like a terrible daughter for not taking more control and getting more involved. Her and Brock's absence left Liz to handle a lot of her family's affairs. Lexi owed a great deal of thanks to the woman.

Oscar had squeezed his growing, old man bottom between the handlebars of his walker and was sitting in front of a shrub, holding a pair of gardening shears. He had a bucket garden hat on, and his face was flushed from bending over and working. His feet were planted among old dead twigs that he had already cut off but hadn't put in the waste bucket yet.

Lexi's heart raced when she saw her dad. She thought about how she used to run and jump into his arms when she was a little girl. Now, she approached slowly so she would not startle him.

"Hi, Dad," she said, squatting down at his side, minding her skirt.

"Well, ho-LY shit! Hi, Kid. Why are you here?" He put his hand around her shoulder and leaned to give her a kiss on the side of her forehead.

Lexi chuckled to herself. "Why do you think, Dad? To see you and Mom." He knew she was coming, so she wasn't sure why he was acting like he didn't. *Maybe he's as nervous as me,* she thought.

His eyes scanned her up and down, taking note of her wardrobe, "Did you come from work?"

"*No,* Dad, I didn't." In her mind, Lexi was shaking her head already, bracing for her dad's next critique.

"Well, I can't believe it. My *String-Bean . . .* You just get here?"

"No, I've been here for a bit," she said, and then felt bad about her answer. She worried he would be insulted that she didn't make it her first priority to find him. "This place looks nice. I peeked into a couple of rooms when I walked in. It looks cozy."

"About as cozy as living in a shipping container," he said.

"Oh, come on. It's nice. The last time I was here there was still snow on the ground, and I never got to see all this," she said, pointing to the lush gardens. "I love all the flowers."

Oscar was surprised that she brought up the last visit. He changed the conversation quickly. "You saw your mom when you walked in then?" he asked.

"I did. She looks good," she said.

"I'm sure she's happy to see you. It has been a while," he said, subtly lodging his complaint.

I get it, it's been a while . . . Her guilt kicked in again. "You are using your walker today?"

"Yes. It's a good day." He paused, and looked down, placing his hands on his legs. "I have good days and I have bad days. Today is a good day." He smiled, not remembering that he had used his wheelchair earlier when his legs were hurting.

"That's great, Dad. You look good," she said, trying to butter him up.

"Where are you staying?" he said, "I think they have a bed open *here*."

"Ha, ha, no. I have Malia and a friend here, so we are staying at that camping place on our old property," she said hesitantly, wondering if she had opened up an emotional wound that he was still carrying.

He looked down the path back toward the care home, "So . . . where's Alexander the Great?"

"You mean *Brock*, Dad? He couldn't come." She waited for a sly, insulting comment.

The corner of his mouth lifted into a condescending grin. He said nothing.

His reaction was tamer than she expected. *Maybe he's getting too old and tired to be contemptuous,* she wondered.

"Ya, Gunther told me where you are staying," he said, "It surprised me that you would want to do that."

"Do what?"

"Stay at that *campground*, although I guess your options are limited here. The motel in town is old, but it's still open, I think, if you don't want to rough it at a campground. Although, it is kind of roughing it by staying there too."

Really? Thanks a lot, Gunther, she thought, letting out a sigh. "No . . . It's fine. At least it's close. We want to be close to you and Mom, and we don't have a vehicle, so at least at the campground, the girls and I can walk back and forth to visit with you two . . . *and* Holly," she added. "We want to check out the new property anyway, and it's not like we are tenting. We are staying in cabins, I think . . . I hope."

His brain questioned why she said "girls." He hadn't heard her when she said that Malia had brought a friend. His brain felt overwhelmed now. His demeanor seemed to change from soft to hard, "Yeah, well, tell that new owner he's an asshole for me and that I know he dug up your mom's garden. He destroyed our properties.

Left nothing there—I heard—another city slicker out to make a buck. Actually, don't tell him. I will tell him *myself* if I ever see him."

She could see him getting riled up and wondered if his pain management was under control. "Do you want to come see your granddaughter?"

"I better in case it's *another* year before you bring her back here," he said.

It has not been a year! She rolled her eyes, got up, and started to head back without waiting for him. When she looked over her shoulder, she saw him trailing far behind. Watching him maneuver his walker shook her into sensitivity.

Malia watched her grandpa slowly make his way up the path to the deck with his walker. She had to look around Ronnie, who was standing practically over her, sweeping the remaining wet leaves—*and* the tops of her shoes.

"Grandpa!" Malia dodged Ronnie's broom, ran up to Oscar, hugged him tight, and tucked herself under his damp, sweaty arm.

"Look at *you*!" Oscar beamed when he saw his granddaughter. "I *don't know* you. You *look* like my String-Bean, but even prettier."

"I'll let that one go, Dad!" Lexi said, looking proud at Malia. Malia cuddled him tight, smiling ear to ear like an innocent little girl.

The clouds had completely blown over, and the sun was warming up the deck fast. Malia sat back down beside her grandma, Lexi pulled up a chair close to the other side of her mom, and Oscar stood nearby with his walker.

While Anna's family yammered on and complimented the staff about the hanging flowers that beautified the deck of Fountain Garden, Anna stared at her granddaughter. She was intrigued with the material of her sweater. It was not a material she had ever had the pleasure of wearing. She loved the light texture and the solid cream color. Two good-sized, walnut-looking buttons rested at the side of the neckline. *What a proper sweater for a girl your age,* she thought, wondering if the buttons were there simply for decoration. She had never seen such a pretty sweater like that before. Anna's wardrobe was years old and consisted of thicker, heavier material for when she was bone cold or very loose-fitting pastels. Most of her clothing items were buttoned all the way down the front in order to make changing as easy as possible. On Sunday, the aides would try to fancy her up like a dolly with a dress and a lightweight colorful scarf that would hang loosely around her neck. She would try to pull the scarf off with her good hand, but would fail, hurting the skin on the back of her neck in the process. *It was stupid,* she thought. She hated it. She detested the scarf, or anything tight around her neck, for reasons they could not possibly understand—and she could not tell them—what the stupid piece of material reminded her of and why it distressed her so much.

Anna heard Lexi telling someone that she wished she had more time to plant flowers or a garden at home, but then her voice faded away amid Anna's tired wandering mind. Moments later, her attention returned to the present again, combatting her weakness and medication. *The sweater looks so huggable, my beautiful granddaughter,* she thought in her exhausted brain. It looked like a kind of towel material that you would wrap a baby in after an evening bath. It was obvious to her that the cashmere and cotton waffle-looking sweater had been purchased in an expensive store. She wondered if Malia knew how blessed she was to have parents with money.

Her eyes closed in the warm sun to rest again for a moment. She was excited and tired at the same time. In her quick daydream, she saw glimpses of her young self in a flowy dress and snappy shoes that she had borrowed from Holly. Her body was free as she danced passionately, illuminating happiness in the room while a handful of friends mingled, smoked, and drank while listening to spirited music.

Anna's mind returned just as Malia extended her hand and laid it on the armrest of her recliner wheelchair. She stifled up her energy to reach up and lay her hand on Malia's young, healthy warm arm. Her sweater felt like butter.

"I am glad we came, Malia," Lexi said, leaning on the other side of the chair.

"I am too, Mom," Malia said.

"After this, we'll go to the property and see what's there. Maybe dad's wrong and the garden is still there, who knows," Lexi said, turning her attention to her mom, "I remember picking apples with you, Mom, when I was little, and then we made all those amazing pies. I used to stand on a stool right between you and Holly at the sink and help run the fruit under water . . . along with *all* the vegetables we picked from the garden. Remember? Nobody could make a pie like you and Holly, Mom."

"We used to make jars and jars of applesauce too." Holly rolled up in her wheelchair from freshening up after her afternoon nap.

"Holly!" Lexi and Malia jumped up. They both leaned in to give her hugs.

"Aww, my girls!" Holly said, "My angels are here!"

The breeze blew in Holly's direction, giving her that familiar whiff of urine mixed with baby powder. Saving her friend from embarrassment she quickly motioned to Liz standing at her med cart. "Liz, maybe Anna needs to . . . before dinner?" Liz came over right away and waved to Ginger, who responded quickly as well.

"We're just going to freshen up before dinner if you don't mind," said the vibrant woman, as she unlocked Anna's brakes and tilted the recliner up a bit more to roll her back into the building. "I am Ginger, by the way!"

"Of course; no problem," Malia smiled.

"Yes, definitely. That will give us a chance to chat." Lexi said, putting her hand on Holly's knee.

Oscar followed his wife back into the building, trying to keep up with his walker.

Anna knew that he would follow her inside. It saddened her that he appeared a bit uncomfortable, even with family. It had always been Anna that was the talkative one in groups and kept the energy alive in the room. As his wife, Anna witnessed Oscar and his daughter's relationship change after Lexi got married and she wished so much that they could find their way back to each other. Especially now that she was unable to communicate her feelings. *If I could talk*, she thought, *I would have a lot to say*.

Years back, Anna had been fearful as well of Lexi's quick decision to leave with Brock after dating long distance for only a few short months. However, she accepted her daughter's new relationship once she realized that Lexi was "all in" and there was no changing her mind. Anna tried her hardest to maintain a strong bond with Lexi, even after she moved off the island—by keeping the lines of communication open and always being a shoulder for the new bride to lean on.

Holly rolled her wheelchair a little closer to Malia. "Look at you," Holly said, "You are *so* tall now. You are gorgeous. I remember when you were this high." Holly extended her flimsy arm, her delicate palm down.

Malia gave her mom a quick side-eye and faked a little laugh to be warm with Holly.

"How are you, Malia? How old are you now?" Holly asked.

"I'm seventeen. My birthday is in four months. Holly, this is my friend Rayna," she said, waving at her friend to get off her butt and come over.

Rayna stayed sitting in the sun, "Hi. Uhm . . . Mal! Look. He answered back!" motioning to a reply she received on a text.

Malia left the adult conversation, craving some teen interaction.

"I have missed you, Lexi!" said Holly. "You know it was too long this time."

"I *know*. Life has been crazy, Holly," Lexi said.

Holly tilted her head, not interested in excuses.

"I know, I know!" Lexi said.

Holly did not waste any time getting into a serious conversation with her. "Oscar felt bad, after the *last* call. He knows he was wrong and he's ready to make it right, Lexi. He's been practicing you know . . . what he is going to say to you. I can tell. He gets really quiet, and I know he is thinking about you and Brock."

Lexi looked at the door, wishing her mom would come back out onto the deck.

Holly continued, "Your mom would tell you the same thing. He hasn't been happy . . . with himself, I mean. He feels like he overstepped when he fought with Brock last Christmas, and he knows it hurts you. Is that why you haven't been here in a while?"

"No, that's not why . . . I mean, maybe it has a little to do with it," Lexi said.

"You two need to patch things up, Lexi. None of us are getting any younger. Oscar knows he should have minded his own business when Brock said he had to cut the holiday two days short because of work. That was your decision as a family, and just because he was disappointed, he had no right to say anything, let alone cause a fight."

"I know that hurt Mom and Dad, having such a rushed holiday," Lexi said. "Pretty sure the tension at the Christmas table that day didn't help either. I also know that is no excuse—that I have let too much time pass since seeing you all. I realize that. I am thinking of maybe taking a step back from my job. Then I would have more time to visit, and it would be nice to spend more time with Malia before she heads off to university or to find a career. I have been kind of stressed out lately, so I think it's time for a change."

"Life is short Lexi. Try not to have stress in your life, honey," Holly said.

I agree, Lexi thought. "I feel like I can't even breathe anymore, Holly. I want to feel passionate about getting out of bed in the morning and I want the excitement of not knowing what tomorrow will bring."

"That's *me* every single day!" Holly giggled. "I would kill for excitement."

Lexi loved how funny and down-to-earth Holly was. She missed having her bright spirit in her life. Lexi looked at Holly's gentle, warm face and felt guilty for whining.

"Where is this *Brock* anyway? Is he here?"

"No, he didn't come," Lexi said, dropping her head and holding back tears.

No more questions were needed. Holly saw that Lexi was miserable.

Lexi pondered how much she should reveal to Holly, who was like a second mother to her. Anything she had to reveal was all YUCK and she had just arrived. She fought with her brain. Lexi didn't have a single memory of her mother that Holly wasn't in as well. Emotions began to well up uncontrollably and a constant repetitive banging in the background kept interrupting Lexi's increasingly anxious thoughts.

"What is going on, Lexi?" Holly persisted. "You are not yourself. It hurts me and your mom to see you any sort of unhappy. You will always be our baby."

Lexi knew, here in this strange place, that she was among family now. Face to face, there was no faking anything anymore.

The incessant banging continued to echo throughout the deck area. Rayna and Malia had moved their chairs a little further away to catch the moving sun and were leaning together, snickering at their phones. Ronnie was standing behind them, looking over their shoulder, swaying back and forth, just hanging out, in his mind, with his "new friends."

"I know you are keeping things from me when we talk on the phone. Sometimes you do not even sound like you, Lexi, and that *last* call . . . it sounded like you had been crying," Holly said.

Lexi took a long pause, looked around to make sure no one was listening and said, "I feel invisible. Brock doesn't love me anymore, Holly." She spoke low and paused to take deep breaths. "He talks to his secretary with more passion than me." *There is something so wrong with that.* She grabbed her head in her hands, startled at her own admission of a reality that belonged to her. She could not believe she was finally speaking these words out loud. Then, irritation ran through her again . . . "What is that *fucking* noise?"

"Shhh, Lexi! It's Edward. He has a leg thing . . . "

"Oh, *God.*" Lexi felt terrible for asking. Looking over into the gazebo, she saw the older stern-looking man sitting off in the corner with his foot banging persistently into the leg of the table. "That poor man."

The aide ran over to the gentleman to adjust his chair.

"Sometimes he bangs it so hard for so long it tears his skin, and he bleeds all over the place," Holly disclosed.

"Eew. That's awful," Lexi said sympathetically.

"Then his shoe flips off onto the floor, making someone have to dig it out from way underneath the table after each meal," Holly said, shaking her head.

"My gosh." Lexi stared at the quiet man.

Holly reached for Lexi's hand. "Lexi, you shouldn't have to beg for anyone's attention."

Oscar appeared through the garden doors with Ginger, pushing Anna in her recliner. "There we go. We are ready for dinner," Ginger said, looking down at Anna, who was looking fresh and beautiful in her dress that was now complimented by a lightweight, olive and cream summer scarf.

Lexi got up from her conversation with Holly and gathered herself. She felt mind-numbed. *That was enough truth for one day*, she thought. Walking over to her mom, she took control of her recliner chair from Ginger and parked it back over to where Holly was sitting.

Anna looked directly at Holly with agitation and a flushed face. Holly pushed the brakes down on her wheelchair and then stood up slowly to lean into Anna. She kissed her on the forehead and whispered, "You don't need to tell *me*, my love," sliding the scarf out gently from around Anna's shoulders. Holly flung the material on the nearby table.

"Oh, I thought it looked pretty on her," Lexi said. "It matched her dress."

"She doesn't need it. Anna doesn't like things around her neck. She never has. Plus, it makes her too warm," Holly said, winking at Anna. Holly always made Anna's needs a priority. The breeze blew the lightweight material off the table onto the deck. Holly left it there.

13
THE TOUR

Everyone was busy visiting out on the deck. The aide, still perturbed about the conversation in the break room, looked around, wondering if there was any point in tackling a new task before leaving for the day. Holly, Oscar and Anna were busy visiting with Lexi. Anna was changed and ready for dinner, so she did not need tending to, and Liz was busy doing nursing things. The two teen girls were off in the corner sunning their legs, Ed was safe and content under the tent gazebo, and Ronnie was wandering around somewhere with his broom and dustpan, happy as a clam. The aide stood still, having a unique, uncomfortably idle moment, looking around at everyone enjoying chitter-chatter under the sun.

Babs walked up behind her, "You look bored. How about giving the girls a tour?"

"I could do that. Good idea Babs," the aide said. She walked up to the teens. "Did you girls want a tour before I leave?" she said, looking at Malia and Rayna, "I'm on my way out. I could show you around the place quickly."

"Sure!" They both jumped up, having lost interest in the adult atmosphere. "Your shift is done?" Malia asked.

"Actually, my job here is done," the aide said. "I am sure you guys have heard, but this place is closing, so I am off to bigger and better things. The world awaits!" she said. They walked back into the dining area from the deck, "So, this is where we eat obviously," the aide said as she started her tour. "We do some of the cooking ourselves for breakfast and lunch and then for dinner . . . sometimes, stuff is dropped off by people in the community. Everyone is super nice here on the island. Maybe because they know they might be living here one day." She laughed as she adjusted some chairs to align with the tables perfectly. "Gunther comes in his truck and drops off a Meals on Wheels kind of deal from Daphne's Cafe in town as well. Teddy—he's probably about your age—does it too sometimes." Both girls perked up. "It works out well. Our friends over there are not crazy busy so they don't mind cooking us dinner . . . but if we *had* to cook dinner, we could." She talked super-fast and hardly took a breath. "We do have *some* food here, obviously. Sometimes a storm won't allow anyone to deliver, sometimes the power goes out, or on a couple of occasions, the cafe's ovens broke down. It's whatever," she said, waving her hand. "Liz and Babs figure all that out."

"So, *Teddy* . . .?" Malia was curious.

Rayna was doubly curious. "Is he a *man* or a boy? Is he Gunther's son or . . . ?"

"Oh, you girls will *like* him! He is not Gunther's son. Gunther never married or had kids. He's just a kid that lives here on Cody Island and works at Camper's Edge, the new campground through the trees out back."

Malia and Rayna cheered simultaneously, "That's where we are staying!"

Rayna whispered, "Dibs if he's cute!"

"Bitch," Malia whispered back, trying to keep up with the aide as she walked quickly out of the dining area.

"So, bathroom on the left and then the hall leading to the entrance which you came down," she said, pointing left to remind them where they came in. "When you entered you came from there, where Babs' office is. Coming down the hall, you walked by Mr. Ronnie G. Fitzgerald's room (Aka Mr. Fitz) which is number 101, which is right across from the old nursing conference room in the center . . . it's our staff room which we now call the 'Work with Wellness Room' so the volunteers are more comfortable going in there . . . then, continuing down to the 'Everything Room' which is where we do hair, crafts, sewing, and other stuff, and then you reach here, the dining area and deck. Straight ahead down this other hall," she pointed, "we have Mr. Oscar Davies, duh, your grandpa, here on the right in 102, then Mrs. Annabella Davies, your ever-so-sweet grandma, in the next room, 103, which is right across from the TV common area in the center, which they tried to call the 'Unity Room,' but that didn't stick." Her feet moved fast. The aide motioned for the young women to keep following her down the hall. "Then after Anna, we have Mrs. Holly Hill; she's 104. Ha, ha. Not her age, I mean her room number. She is best friends with Oscar and Anna from way back. I guess I don't need to tell *you* that Malia. Bit of a *weird* relationship *that* one . . . !"

Malia looked at Rayna questioningly.

"Then, turning left down the last hall . . . ," she continued to walk fast. "Keep up girls!"

The three of them ran into Ronnie who appeared lost, looking out a window. They startled him. He turned around holding a clear, plastic, juice glass in his unsteady hand.

"Whatcha got there Ronnie?" the aide said.

"Just the fish," he said in a matter-of-fact tone, holding the glass unsteady in his hand, making the water swish from side to side.

The aide looked at the poor, blue and silver guppy swimming around in the tiny space, bonking itself on the edges. "And *where* are you going with it?"

"I am taking it for a swim in the fountain outside," Ronnie said.

"Ronnie, you take *such* good care of our pants and . . . animal . . . I don't know what we would do without you," she said sweetly, "but not today, Ronnie, OK? Maurice, the fish, is *very* tired. I am going to bring it back to its home." She grabbed the glass abruptly and continued with her tour as she walked away. Malia and Rayna followed, leaving Ronnie standing alone.

"So down this hall there's another entrance to the TV room on the left," the aide rambled on. "Mr. Edward O. is in this room on the right in 105, then Perla May Lune's room, is 106. She died about a month ago. Her name was Perla May, but I only ever called her Perl because her skin was flawless and pretty as a pearl. Her room hasn't been cleaned out yet because her family didn't pick anything up. They live too far and said they don't care about any of it so . . . We are pretty sure her ghost is still walking around here . . . " Her fast pace seemed exaggerated, and the girls giggled amusingly while they kept up in stride. They wondered if the woman had this level of energy and breath all the time. "Then we have a spare room, 107, for whichever staff members are sleeping here at night to do rounds and make sure everyone is okay and then . . . Oh, don't mind all the mobile devices." She pulled up the red caution tape to let the girls walk underneath. "These are all extras from the other side of the building—that's falling apart by the way—so don't go over there." She pushed the walkers and wheelchairs with her free hand further toward the wall. "Some are extra donations from the community, some are from residents that have died here, and their families just never picked them up. Then," she continued, "we have the nursing room on the left and the main entrance. This is where you originally came in." She kept walking, flipped the fish back into the tank and then slipped into the Staff Room.

"So, about that *ghost*?" Rayna asked.

The aide gave a backhanded wave. "See you tomorrow, maybe!" she said, shutting the door.

14

BYE FOR NOW

"Alright, I am going to go grab the girls, go get settled in, and let you guys eat." Lexi stood up and kissed her mom on the cheek, sharing a quick eye gaze with her dad. "I will be back tomorrow, though."

"And the girls too?" Holly said in anticipation.

"For sure, they will come too," Lexi reassured her.

"I am so glad you are here, Lexi." Holly looked up at her, squinting in the sun. "Enjoy this time. Have a little fun. Find that sweet smile that I *miss* so much, honey."

The girls returned to the deck from their whirlwind tour of the care unit. Liz approached them on the deck with clear intention. "Malia, I was wondering if you and your friend, *if* you're interested, would like to help out a little while you are here. Just think about it . . . *no* pressure. I know everyone here would surely enjoy having you around."

"Uhm, okay," Malia said, surprised at the suggestion.

Rayna tugged Malia's arm, "Ya, we will *think* about it for sure." *NOT,* she thought.

Lexi overheard. "That is a nice idea, Liz. The girls will think about it for sure," she said, glancing at the two teens, wondering if they would be up for the task. "Alright, we will head out then. Goodbye everyone. It was nice to see you all again. Love you, Mom! Love you, Holly!" Lexi felt her dad's hand on her back.

"I'll show you out," Oscar said. "It's this way," he said, pointing to the path.

"Bye, Lexi! Bye Malia! Bye Rayna!" Ginger gave a big wave from the garden door, "Enjoy the camp, ladies! Don't be shy to ask that beautiful man for *anything*. He is fine as wine, that guy! I promise you will not regret it. He can make a girl's head spin I tell ya—and I don't even *like* boys!"

Everybody laughed at Ginger's comment. Lexi and her dad stepped off the deck onto the path. The girls pranced behind.

Oscar walked Lexi and the girls down the perfectly manicured garden walkway counter-clockwise around the lengthy circle path. The bright and colorful perennials were brilliant against the backdrop of tall deep, green foliage that lined the walkway. Gorgeous geraniums spread like a carpet amongst the green and silver shrubs.

"Thanks for walking us out, Dad, but I don't want you to be late for your dinner," Lexi said.

"It will taste like cardboard no matter what time I eat it," Oscar mumbled as he concentrated on maneuvering his walker down the path.

"Oh, that's *not* true." Lexi tried to encourage a positive mindset. "Fountain Garden looks like a wonderful place to live."

"Well, it wouldn't matter if it was—we're moving anyway," he said and then got quiet, not wanting to discuss matters in front of the teens.

The girls slowed their pace so Oscar would not feel rushed. They lagged behind him and Lexi, weaving playfully in and out of each other on the concrete path.

Lexi continued to chat, "This landscape is really gorgeous, Dad. Did you help plant all this?"

"Sure did. The butterflies love the asters and the daisies," he said, pointing to the lavender-blue and pink blossoms.

The girls jumped around on the path trying to catch the pretty creatures in their hands.

"Can you smell the catmint?" He pointed to a different, tall, spiky violet flower. "I can usually smell them, but this old nose is not working this afternoon. It malfunctioned the minute it got a whiff of my lunch today!" He made a disgusted look.

Lexi took a deep breath to smell the aroma of the catmint, lilies and russian sage. She walked slowly and enjoyed the gardens to stay with Oscar's pace.

The sounds of trickling water on stone became louder and louder as the four of them made their way closer to the farthest reach of the circle path. Coming around the turn the grand fountain appeared, surprising the girls with its mist and burble. It was tall and large in circumference. The brick and mortar piled on top of each other in layers and layers. Intertwining vines made their way into the crevices and tangled with spider webs. Thorns and wildflowers made their home in random spaces adding beauty to the old structure. The continuous stream of water rippled down over the wet, shimmering rock as the sun bounced off the water and pebbles below, revealing all the algae and debris skimming the surface. The graciousness of the structure seemed to demand a moment of contemplation or meditation, so they all paused to admire its impressiveness.

Rayna was unable to handle the seriousness. "Oh, so I guess *this* is why they call this place Fountain Garden," Rayna said, bursting out into laughter.

Malia reached for a dirty net that leaned against the structure. She swiped the slime floating on the surface of the water in a slow sweeping motion, unveiling the beauty of the rock below.

"Careful now, swipe the sludge, but leave the lily pads," Oscar said, showing ownership of the structure.

"Why?" she asked.

"Because the lilies block some of the sun, which helps keep the algae down," he explained.

"Cool!" Rayna and Malia said simultaneously.

"It's pretty," said Malia, feeling relaxed and happy.

"Pretty soupy!" Rayna said, unable to experience the beauty and depth of the moment.

"I try to keep it clean, but the wind is constantly blowing shi. . .t in there." Oscar tried to catch himself from swearing, but it was too late.

The teens laughed.

"I try to clean it out every day," he said.

"*You* do, Dad?" Lexi was impressed that he had taken an interest in keeping the fountain and gardens looking nice. It reminded her of how proud Oscar had been of his own yard on his old property.

"Ya, *me*. Sometimes I can get Holly to help too but lately, she just watches from the swing. My dear old friend is not as energetic as she used to be," he said.

Lexi was happy that her dad had a task or a job that kept him occupied. Rayna lost attention quickly and went and sat on the bench swing across from the fountain.

There was noticeable silence between Oscar and Lexi. "So much to say," she thought, "but not now."

Oscar looked a little shaky on his walker. He was ready for more pain pills, and it was getting hard for him to hide it.

"Well, Dad, we'll let you make your way back." Lexi looked at him, paused and then they both reached in for a hug. "We will be back in the morning. We are going to get settled in for the night. It has been a big day."

"Alright," he said, hating to see her go. "Sounds good. Hope you girls are comfortable over there. I sure do wish I still had a house that I could host you in."

Lexi put her arm around his shoulder and gave him a squeeze. "I know you do, Dad," she said.

Oscar was hoping for a better conversation with her, but the timing did not feel right and with Malia and Rayna around, he decided he would wait until tomorrow.

"Sleep tight, String-Bean," he said, trying to give his daughter one last side hug without letting go of his walker, feeling unsteady on his feet. He felt emotional about having his daughter in his arms again. "You too kiddo!" He reached for Malia's shoulder and gave her a heavy, loving shoulder shake. "And you . . . too," he said, turning to Rayna on the swing. He tried to remember her name but couldn't.

"Are you sure you are okay to get back, Dad?" Lexi asked.

"Don't be silly. I got lots of miles on me yet," he said. "After dinner, I am gonna hit the gym. It's leg day!" He hobbled off.

Lexi and Malia chuckled and watched him maneuver his walker around the fountain circle to make his way. They both felt guilty letting him walk alone.

"So, through here, I guess," Lexi said to the girls, pointing to a rickety gate between the tall hedges that led out into the dense cluster of thick, leafy trees. "I guess our adventure begins here." Shivers ran through her, walking through the glorious, climbable forest. It was just like she remembered. So familiar were the colors and damp, earthy smells.

"This is *so* cool in here!" Malia said as she walked along, brushing her hands along the lusty, sappy wood. "Ew, it's sticky!" she giggled.

Rayna asked, "How many times did you make out in these trees when *you* were a teen Mrs. Kirk?"

"Rayna! Call me Lexi or I am going to put you back on that plane."

"Okay, okay," she said.

"*Ya, Mom*! You must have done some partying in *here*. This is *awesome*!" The bright-eyed girls looked around at the mysterious green and brown natural surroundings.

"Girls! We are *out* of the city!" Lexi said, reaching into the bush to grab a walking stick.

Malia copied here. “Here's a good one!” She reached down onto the wet ground and grabbed a thick branch that had fallen to the earth. “The smell is strong in here. You can smell the bark!”

Lexi loved how enthusiastic Malia was. “I am glad you two are here. I wouldn’t want to be alone on this trip. I think this could be a good weekend.”

Malia whacked the brush as she walked through the shady path. “We should build a fort.”

“I built plenty of forts in my day,” Lexi said, “but the island storms wreaked havoc on them. Blustering winds off the ocean annihilated my flimsy structures!” she said laughing. The three of them scampered through the live woodland, getting sidetracked by any strange-looking rock or branch.

With her stick, Rayna scratched at the rich, green velvet carpet that blanketed the rocks. “This moss is so cool,” she said.

Malia copied her. “It is!” she said.

15

CAMPER'S EDGE CAMPGROUND

An opening appeared where the tree line ended, and the landscape changed abruptly. Luke looked up from measuring a board when he heard their muffled voices, and then he saw the bouncy, stick-holding, chattery bunch appear out of the lush greenery like a mirage. He and Teddy watched the three women as they stood in awe at the view.

Lexi and the girls stood at the edge of the over-sized lot, staring, absorbing, and letting the shock of the new view wash over them like an immense rolling tide. The ocean and sky ahead were the perfect aqua backdrop.

"Wow!" Rayna's mouth dropped open. "This is *incredible.* You used to *live* here?" she asked Lexi.

Lexi could hardly get the words out. "I did," she said, as her mind panicked, thinking about how her dad would react to the sight of his old property. *Oh God, Dad would trip UP if he saw this. His house is literally gone . . . This is so shocking.*

"Welcome!" Luke yelled, but the girls were so distracted that they didn't hear him. The tall, brawny stranger walked off the concrete foundation as he undid his tool belt from around his waist. He set the belt down on top of a shiny black and silver toolbox, making a noise when it hit the metal, and put his hands through his long, wavy, wind-blown hair.

"Oh, this *will* be fun," Rayna whispered, tugging on Malia's sleeve to notice the man standing on the grass and the younger helper climbing a ladder while staring back at them.

The scene flooded Lexi. A beautifully level concrete foundation pad was poured perfectly square among the fresh-cut grass where a large unfinished timber frame post and beam picnic shelter would soon provide shade for the campers. It was meticulous for a construction project: sawhorses lined up perfectly along the edge of the pad, corded tools were wrapped up neat and tight, big, looped extension cords lay on the plush ground and a brand-new level leaned against the shiny toolbox. The main columns that supported the structure were set on concrete, the Timber beams were installed, and the roof was over halfway completed with wooden rafters.

"So, what's left now, Luke?" the young helper called out to the man below.

"Tomorrow, I'll tackle the rest of the rafters and sheeting if you are around. You can keep working on the feature wall, Teddy. I might have to order a few more supplies," he said.

A sudden gust of wind blew, sending a pencil rolling down the sloped roof. Teddy caught it with his hand. "I think having one feature wall will be good," he yelled, "it will provide a good wind break." He turned around on the roof and took his first step down on the ladder with the pencil and a saw in his hand.

"Yup . . . be careful on that ladder, Teddy." Luke looked up to analyze the picnic shelter in progress. "We'll have it all finished tomorrow or the next day for sure." He turned toward the three guests. "As you can see, we have a few projects on the go around here. Sorry about the mess," he said, approaching Lexi, "I'm Luke, the new owner," he said extending his hand.

"Hi, I'm Lexi." She barely made eye contact while shaking his hand. Her mind was spinning. She looked around at the cabins, the RV area, the fire pits, and endless grass while Luke introduced himself to the girls. Wheelbarrows and shovels sat by freshly dug holes on the lot's perimeter. *Dad was right. The garden is gone; that's for sure,* she thought.

"I know who you are. Gunther told me you girls were on your way." He motioned over to his younger helper. "This is Teddy," Luke said, pointing to the young man as he stood on the grass wrapping up a long extension cord.

"Hi," Teddy said with a bright smile.

"Hey." Rayna and Malia answered in unison.

Rayna approached him, vying for his attention. "Is this important?" she asked Teddy as she picked the shiny item up off the lush grass and rolled it slowly between her two fingers coyly.

"Yes," he said, walking toward her to grab the item, "Thank you." He took it from her. "It's a wood bit to drill the holes for the main bolts." He motioned toward the developing structure and continued to over-explain, "The bolts hold the beams to the top of the columns. We wouldn't want to lose that," he said, throwing the bit on the concrete, realizing that Rayna wasn't listening anyway.

"I just set your bags that Gunther dropped off on the deck over there," Luke said, "I thought you girls could sort them out and pick whichever cabin you want. Two of the cabins have a double bed and one has two twin beds."

Lexi completely spaced, looking around the lot and out at the ocean. A flood of memories washed over her as she took in the view that she had forgotten she missed.

"You look like you need a sec," Luke said, "so I'm just going to keep working right over here, and you gals feel free to snoop around. You are the only ones here right now, so make yourself at home—I mean, comfortable." He regretted using the word "home" and didn't want it to sound like a stab to Lexi, who he thought looked a little troubled.

She walked to the front of the cabins and stood in the middle of the lot, looking around. It was hard to believe that both homes were gone. It was a bizarre reality. She tried to conjure up pictures in her head of her childhood, but they seemed blurry now.

"Come on, Mom. Let's check the place out." Malia grabbed her mom by the arm and dragged her around Camper's Edge.

They ran into the washroom facilities building. The bathroom had two entrances, one on each side. Each side contained two showers, two toilets, and a sink. Then they emerged and stood in front of the three small cabins looking at the wooden decks that were each home to two patio chairs. A few feet off each deck was a personal fire pit with two wooden lawn chairs and a log bench. On the side of each cabin was a small lean-to shelter for firewood.

Teddy watched as the guests explored. "You guys can use as much firewood as you want!" he yelled. "It's free and I will restock each morning," he said.

"Cool. Thank you!" Malia yelled back and shot him a big smile.

Malia and Rayna ran up to the entrance of one of the cabins and whipped the door open. It was small and rustic looking and boasted one tiny window that had already made home to a few dead bugs and spiders on the sill. Two twin beds almost took up the entirety of the room, and a small side table that boasted a simple lamp, a Kleenex box, and two water bottles filled the remaining space. A small square mirror hung on the wall.

"Small mirror," Rayna pointed out.

The teens ran back outside to see Lexi walking back from the three RV parking spots. She walked up to Malia and Rayna, shaking her head in disbelief. "He has created quite the spot here . . . those RV pads even have electrical, water hook-ups, individual fire pits . . . This place is no joke. It's no wonder it has been busy here already. I just can't believe . . . "

"Are you freaking out, Mom?"

"Uhm, I just need a sec to navigate these feelings," Lexi said as she took a long deep breath, blowing all the air out of her lungs to reduce her anxiety.

"*I* think it's kind of cool!" Malia was still riding her holiday high.

"Ya, this place rocks," Rayna said enthusiastically, still excited to be somewhere new.

"I *guess* . . . " Lexi said under her breath.

"Think of it this way, Mom," Malia said, trying to make her feel better, "it would be a lot harder to see someone else living in our *house*. Now the house is just a memory, and the bonus is, that we get to stay here! We couldn't stay here if someone was living here."

"Does it help a little too that the new owner is *HOLY HOT*," Rayna added. "He's kind of old but a *TOTAL SMOKE SHOW*!" Rayna moved Lexi and Malia's attention to Luke, who was lifting a heavy piece of lumber. Wearing shorts and work boots, his bronzed muscles popped out of his faded blue T-shirt while he exerted himself over by the work area. Teddy was standing nearby, flushed-faced, lifting and releasing the bottom of his T-shirt to let the breeze cool his body, "And his sidekick isn't too bad either!" Rayna said.

"Ya, it helps," Lexi and Malia said in unison. "JINX!" They laughed.

"That is a fine specimen of a man, for sure," Malia said as she zeroed in on Teddy.

Rayna grabbed Malia by her sweater yanking her, "Lose the sweater Mal! It's boiling out here! Let's go to the beach and taking selfies."

16

JOURNEY

After dinner, Liz was running between tasks that needed to get done for Edward and Ronnie. While passing Anna, sitting next to a window in the hall, she noticed a strained look in Anna's eyes. Without hesitation, she stopped and went down on bended knee in front of her wheelchair. "What is it, Anna?" she said, smiling. "That was incredible having your family here again, right?" Liz had a pen and a pad of pictures in her pocket if she needed it to communicate with Anna, but she chose, more often than not, to converse with her by reading her posture, expressions, and gestures instead. "It is going to be great having them here for two or three more days," she said.

Anna's eyes directed Liz towards her legs. Liz looked down and grabbed Anna's feet, still in her hard-soled shoes, "Are your feet hurting you? Let's take these off; you don't need shoes just to sit here," Liz said.

She undid Anna's lace, and with a struggle, slid her stiff shoe off her heel, flipping it onto the floor. Anna gave a heavy blissful sigh. Her eyes smiled at Liz, who mirrored a happy look back. It pleased Liz that she could give Anna some relief. She took off the other shoe, set both shoes off to the side on the floor beside the chair, and then stood up. "Do you want me to move your chair into the TV room, Anna?" she asked as she adjusted her Afghan and gave her shoulder a light squeeze. Anna nodded her head from side to side.

The sound of a plate falling and smashing on the floor from Ronnie's room made Liz look down the hall. "I have to go now," she said in a friendly whisper. She walked away from Anna to head down the hall, "I will be back, though."

Twenty minutes later, Liz knelt in front of Anna again, startling Anna out of her snooze. "Are you still doing okay, Anna? Would you like to go back to your room?" Liz figured that the day might have been too much for her.

Anna nodded, yes.

Liz assisted Anna to bed. The frail woman lay stretched out flat. Her muscles were relieved to be out of her chair but took their time to completely relax and get comfortable. She stared outside. The day was losing light. She wondered if Holly or Oscar were staring outside from their rooms as well. She pictured her daughter and granddaughter, snuggled in warm sweaters, sitting out by a campfire. Her heart felt full, but her brain felt gassed and overwhelmed from the short visit.

Her mind jumped to Holly and how the two of them, in the old days—after having soulful conversations on the beach— would sit and listen to the crackle of a toasty fire under a bright round moon that demanded attention.

Anna's mind fluttered back to her daughter, feeling weary in her exhaustion. She feared that the day's short visit with Lexi could have been her last and felt guilty that she couldn't have been more energetic for her daughter. Every single day was a gift now. Weakness swept over her. Looking out at the sky, something spoke to her. Would she be meeting it soon? Would this be a journey she could have better prepared for? Would she be leaving wishing she would have spoken more words to her daughter when she had the chance? Her mind scattered with thoughts. Who would be the last person she would see? *Hopefully, Oscar or Holly and not the busy-body, high-strung aide,* she thought. Her own sarcasm lightened her mood for the moment. What would be the last thing she would be doing? *Probably not much. What will I be wearing on the day of my final goodbye?* she thought girlishly. *Will I be warm and snug in my pyjamas or will it be on a bath day with my hair and nails freshly done? I better not have stupid shoes on.* Anna liked her feet and all her matching, fun-colored socks, and she preferred to be barefoot even more. She hated the hard non-slip clog shoes that everyone forced her to wear. They were the opposite of cozy, and she would want to feel comfortable in that last moment. The ugly shoes were a high grip, hard-shelled type of shoe that squished her right baby toe, forcing it to sleep and be numb most of the day. Thinking about it, it was ridiculous anyway; it's not like she was going to get up and walk away *so were the shoes necessary?* She knew deep down the workers put them on her so that they wouldn't accidentally crush her toes when transferring her, but it still made her grumpy. It was the most pleasurable moment when the workers slid the ungodly confining footwear off her feet at the end of each day. The thought relaxed her . . . *It would be so good to see my girls tomorrow,* she thought, *and I WILL be here to see them.*

Anna's sleep was often interrupted by the aide coming in to rotate her body and tuck a pillow under the lower of her back. She needed that now but knew from the sound of the laughter and chit-chat outside her door that, *whatever is happening outside the room is far more interesting than what is happening in here, I guess,* she thought. Her mind settled, and she drifted off. The voices finally stopped, and Liz came in to check on her. Anna was fast asleep, so Liz gave her a quick tuck, pulled the blinds a third of the way down the window, and walked out of the room.

17

END-OF-DAY ROUNDS

It was a part of Liz's routine to walk the halls one last time and pop into everyone's rooms at the end of her day. Making her way down the corridor, she heard knocking coming from Ed's room. When she entered, she saw him in a restless sleep, hammering his leg against the side of his bed. She snuck in and stuffed a pillow between his leg and the edge of his side rail. She had taken the time to duct tape a piece of foam to the inside of the bed while he lay snoring the night before, but it was on the floor the following day. Edward's constant movements had ripped it free, and eventually, it flopped over the rail. She was frustrated that his medications helped the muscle spasms but did not eliminate them. Finding just the right balance of medication was difficult; too high of a dose made Ed too drowsy and robbed him of his personality and too low of a dose didn't have any effect on his involuntary movements. Liz would have to go back to stuffing pillows every few hours all night long (on the bad nights) in order to save his leg from bruising even more. She worried about the day that his skin would finally give way on his ankle and his deep, dark bruises would turn into a gaping open wound. She couldn't imagine how Ed could ever sit through multiple dressing changes. With her hand on his side rail, she looked at her friend, cringing that he would detest a procedure like that if it were to become part of his regular care. If it were to happen, *she* would want to be the one to tend to him. The closing of Fountain Garden and having to see her residents move elsewhere, under someone else's care, gave her feelings of deep sadness in her belly.

She left Ed to sleep and continued her rounds. Entering the next room, Liz approached Holly, still sitting in her wheelchair, "Goodnight, Holly. Sweet dreams," she said in a low voice.

Holly reached her arm out to grab Liz's hand, "Thank you, Liz. It was a good day," she said. "You must think it's funny that we are all going to bed so early?"

"Not at all, Holly. Can I get you anything else before I shut down for the night as well?" she asked.

"No, I think I will sleep okay. I am tired, and I have my water, but thank you. I should sleep well, as long as Ronnie leaves me alone. His insomnia has been bad lately. I can hear him slogging around late at night with his slippers loud on the floor. It echoes through the halls."

"I know," Liz said, "he has quite the terrible sleep patterns. I told the aides to wake him if they find him snoring loudly in the TV room during the day. That's why he can't sleep at night."

"Sometimes I hear him shuffling papers or opening and closing drawers in the TV room late at night too!" Holly said.

"Well, actually, that might be me." Liz gave Holly an apologetic look. "I've had a lot on my mind and have had trouble sleeping myself."

"Don't get me wrong. I like the man," Holly added, "It would be boring around here without his energy. He can be quite funny," she said, smiling.

"You know, he loves to push the linen cart and sort all the colored socks, and he is surprisingly good at distributing them to everyone's rooms, so I will ask him to help out more during the day and see if that doesn't make him more settled at night."

"You are *so* kind and smart, Liz. We're so lucky to have you."

"I feel the same way about you, Holly. Do you need me to help you get ready for bed?"

"No, no, I am fine, Liz . . . but thank you."

Liz loved end-of-the-day conversations like this, no matter how repetitive. They left her feeling inspired even if she was dead tired or stressed. The residents reminded her of the reasons why she chose this career. Liz liked the validation she got from Holly. It felt good to be acknowledged for her years of work and it was surreal that it might be coming to an end at Fountain Garden.

She made her way to Anna's room. Her room always had a sense of calm and stillness, no matter how chaotic the day was. During her end-of-day routine, Liz would give Anna's blanket a little tuck under her feet to keep them warm and snug, and sometimes, if Anna looked like she would have a restless night, she would put her music box on low to help relax her. Then, she'd walk to the head of the bed, click on her tiny, low-lit red lamp, and lay her hand on Anna's to say good night. It was a beautiful closure to the day.

18

DASHED HOPES AND DREAMS

Holly squeezed between her bed and the window and reached up to grab the string to raise the blinds. After struggling to pull the old blinds up, she cracked open the window. She loved the feeling of a warm, damp, Pacific wind blowing through her window screen and the sounds that occurred in the middle of the night. Sitting back down in her wheelchair, she stared out at the bright moon, something that she and Anna had loved to do together. Since arriving at Fountain Garden, Holly had learned from Liz that there were sporadic nights when Anna would wake, unable to fall back asleep. It bothered Holly that she was not there to comfort Anna. She told Liz to make sure that Anna's blinds stayed open so she could stare out the window at thousands of stars instead of at something dull and dusty. "That would be way more appealing," she thought. "This could definitely be one of those wakeful nights with all the excitement and arrival of the girls. Especially knowing that the girls are just beyond the trees." Having them so close and anticipating the next day's visit excited Holly as well.

Holly's tired mind trailed to the countless nights she and Anna, as young teen girls, laid on the sand—hands locked—waves crashing in the background. They stared up at the magical lunar landscape, entertained by the bright round figure. "That moon belongs to us Anna," Holly would say. Holly had dreamed of how her life would plan out and said that Anna would always be in it. *I am glad I told her I loved her early on in our friendship,* she thought. From that moment, their bond had grown deep, genuine and unconditional. Holly never needed to name their relationship; she only knew that it felt right, and she could not imagine being without it.

She remembered feeling crushed when Anna met Oscar. Anna's parents had convinced her that her life would be secured by being married to such a well-known and respected man in the community. *I hate that you got swooped up, Anna,* Holly thought. The pain she suffered while watching the new couple from her neighboring porch was torture. In order to remain best friends with Anna, Holly had to find the strength to push down her feelings as best she could.

Holly got up from her wheelchair, feeling a little shaky in her fatigue, and slowly got ready for sleep. Climbing into bed, she clicked off her lamp and pulled the covers up to tuck herself in. She took a long sigh, ready to settle in with the ghosts of her mind. Her heart weighed heavy thinking about the past, about her own questionable marriage to Hank, and about the night her and Anna's relationship would forever be changed. Holly had never given her full heart to Hank, and he passed away, never knowing the truth. The past seemed so long ago now, and loneliness was a feeling that Holly had become accustomed to, but lately it weighed even more on her knowing that Anna's condition was not going to improve. She was losing her soul mate, and it killed Holly's spirit more and more every day. She settled in to the quiet; the nights could be excruciating at times.

19
THE CALL

"This is sick, Rayna!" Malia jumped from the floor to the bed, and then back to the floor, like a child.

"And it's *all* for us! Ha. Ha." Rayna spun around in a circle on top of one twin bed and then jumped over to the other. She whipped off her shorts and threw them on the floor. Dumping her backpack over the bed, she searched for her night shirt, which was just a thin, baggy white T-shirt. Malia followed suit and changed into her shorts PJ set. She folded her airplane clothes and set them in a pile on the little table in the corner.

A short time later, a rap came from the door.

"You girls good in here?" Lexi opened the door and peeked in.

They lay on the twin bed together. They had moved all the pillows in the room to the one bed and were leaning against them, heads practically touching while they snickered and texted on their phones. Rayna's leg intertwined with Malia's. Lexi shook her head, "Girls?" They looked up, "Are you good?" she asked again.

"Ya, Mom! Goodnight," Malia said.

"Goodnight? It's early! Don't you guys want to come and sit by a fire or something?" Lexi felt like a third wheel all of a sudden.

"Nope, we're good," Malia said, uninterested in mother-daughter time. Plus, the girls had seen Teddy take off in his little car earlier to go have dinner elsewhere, so there was nothing outside of the cabin that interested them at the moment. They were focused on their phones.

Rayna gasped, "Whoa! Chloe's dish'n the dirt!" she said, lifting her cell to Malia's face to show her a text, "*OH. MY. GOD*, Max is taking *Amy* to the party! *What* a dick! Chloe heard from Zack that Albert said that he wanted a break from dating Amy to reassess their relationship, so Albert went to the Blazers party alone and left Amy drowning her sorrows at Issy's house. Max was *at* Issy's house when all this went down and thought, 'Well . . . I guess that makes Amy single tonight, so . . .'" Rayna looked at Malia wide-eyed. "He better hope Zack is there to have his back tonight! Albert is going to *flip* his lid when he finds out!"

"No *freaking* way!" Malia yelled, fired up from hearing the juicy gossip of their friends back in Adasa city. "Tell her to keep us posted!"

Lexi shook her head, *GOOD GRIEF! I am so glad I am not a teen anymore!* She shut the door. The girls were fine and clearly amusing themselves. Seeing them reminded her that she had to go back to her cabin by herself. It was such a beautiful night. If she was that age, she would have been walking out in the dark, exploring and trying to meet people, but they were happy staying inside on their phones. Lexi was too stressed about Brock ignoring her phone calls to care.

Luke watched Lexi while he moved items around the yard and placed tools back into the shed. It was getting dark, but he could see her figure as she walked along the beach. Even with Lexi's head stirring in anxiety, the old habit of picking litter off the sand instinctively kicked in. She walked a few steps, stopped, looked at her phone, picked up garbage, tucked it under her arm, then looked at her phone again. She kicked the driftwood with her expensive footwear while waiting for Brock to call her back, wishing she had changed into flip-flops. *Wearing ankle boots was a stupid idea,* she thought. In an illogical way, she connected her bad wardrobe decision somehow to her loveless marriage. Blaming Brock for her inability to make good choices was easier than admitting that she should take control of her own life. The cans, plastic, and paper were piling up in her arms. She looked at her phone again.

Finally, it rang. "Hello," Lexi answered.

"You called," Brock said.

"*Yes*, I called! Are we *ever* going to talk? You should have come. You *could* have if you really *wanted* to."

"Lexi, I am at work surrounded by people right now," he said.

"That's *complete* bullshit. Look at the time Brock! You can't use that as an excuse anymore. You *never* have time to talk. I'm done trying to convince you to *want* to be with us. I thought we could handle this as a family."

He whispered into the phone, "First of all, I *am* still at work—even though it's late, and as for coming there, well, I am pretty sure Oscar wouldn't have wanted to see my face anyway . . . "

"This has absolutely nothing to do with *him*, Brock. I am talking about Malia. This would have been a good time to finally sit down with her, away from everything, and tell her what's going on," she said.

"I am meeting a new client tomorrow. There's no way I could have come this weekend. It wouldn't have worked anyway. It's a big client, Lexi," he said.

"Wow," she shook her head, "*WHAT DO YOU WANT ME TO DO*?" She walked on the beach, loose scraps of garbage and paper falling from under her arm.

"Just give me a sec . . ." he said.

Lexi could hear the faint sound of a door closing over the phone.

"I can't do this anymore, Lexi. We want different things. Just tell Malia if that's what you want. I can't live like this anymore."

"Well, I can't live like this anymore either," she sobbed. "You gave up on us a long time ago. It's so easy for you . . . " Lexi paced back and forth on the beach, getting even more worked up. "If you don't think you are hurting Malia are a *bloody idiot*." She threw down all the garbage in one spot.

"I promise I will talk to Malia when you get home," he said. "Honestly, it's better you talk to her first anyway. I don't know what to say and you are better at talking than I am."

"Wow!" *Wiping your hands of your responsibility to your daughter and manipulating me with a bullshit compliment just to take the easy way out,* she thought. "That's the first nice thing you have said to me in a year," she said sarcastically. "Well, I am glad you think I will be *so good* at telling our daughter that we are getting a DIVORCE! Ugh! You are the shittiest father! You are such a jerk!" she cried out. The despair and trauma of her failed marriage was on full display on the beach. "You know what? I don't care. If you don't want to talk to her, I will. I can't believe you are doing this, putting work before family once again, instead of handling this like a real man. You are teaching her that it's *okay* to be treated like this! I *fucking hate* this!" Tears poured down her face. She rubbed the snot from her nose onto her sleeve. There was silence on the other end of the phone.

"Brock! Brock!" she yelled.

He had hung up.

"*Fuck you*!" She screeched out in frustration.

Luke stood around the corner of the shed, out of sight, so Lexi could gracefully make her way back to her cabin in peace. Then he grabbed a black bag to go pick up the pile of garbage she had left on the sand.

20

TRESPASSING

The two girls hid in the dark, around the corner of the building, out of sight from anyone entering or leaving Fountain Garden.

"Hurry up, Babs," Rayna said, eyeing up the entrance door. "My ass is getting chilly out here."

Malia waited, snuggled close to Rayna while they watched for Babs to leave after her shift.

"I don't know if this is a good idea," Malia said.

"Yes. It is!" Rayna said, hearing the door. "Shhh. Here she comes."

They could hear Babs' heavy, hard-soled shoes crunching the gravel as she left the building. She looked relieved that her day was over, as she braced herself in the boisterous evening wind to light her smoke and take a long drag.

Rayna reached into her back pocket. "Good thinking, Babs. Look what I have," she said, lifting her cigarette up to Malia, "I scoffed it off the office counter when we walked in this afternoon." Rayna lit the smoke with the lighter, took a drag, and then handed it to Malia.

"COUGH, COUGH, COUGH."

Rayna quickly covered Malia's mouth, giggling, "SHHH!"

"How do you know the doors aren't locked now?" Malia asked.

"I don't! We'll try it and if it is, then . . . plan B. Maybe we can crawl through a window!" she said.

Babs' old car hadn't made it halfway down the driveway, and Rayna was lugging Malia by her wrist swiftly toward the door. She threw her cigarette butt casually to the side and grabbed the handle, looking at Malia. "Moment of truth . . . three, two, one," she said. The door swung open when she pulled. "Thank *you,* Babs!" she said with a mischievous smile. "We're going to see a ghost tonight, *and* it's a *FULL MOON*!" She said, trying to spook Malia.

"You're a lunatic!" Malia said, rolling her eyes.

They entered the dark-lit building and ran to the next set of doors that belonged to Fountain Garden.

Malia held her hand in place just over the large round entrance button, "What if someone sees the door open?" she said nervously.

"If they ask," Rayna said, "we lie and say Babs' let us in when she left."

"Why would she let us in this late?" Malia asked.

Rayna took a moment to think, "We'll say you forgot your sweater in your gramps' room."

"That's lame…" Malia said, whacking Rayna on the arm.

"You have a better idea?" Rayna laughed.

"Let's just NOT get caught! Okay, on the count of three. Okay, screw it! Bam!" She hit the button. The door opened, and the girls ran through quickly, veering to the dim, left hallway ducking and sliding under the caution tape. Malia's shirt got caught on the brake handle of one of the wheelchairs stacked against the wall. She tugged herself loose to catch up with Rayna, who had already squeezed through the parked chairs and was at the caution tape on the other side.

"Hurry up Malia!" Rayna whisper-shouted.

They stood, short of breath, heart beating out of her chests, at the door of 106. They looked straight into each other's eyes to gather up their nerves when suddenly, they heard a burst of laughter coming from Ronnie's room, down the other hall, "Oh, shit!" Rayna said, grabbing Malia's hand, pushing the door and yanking Malia hard to get inside the room. They were on the other side, both leaning against the door in the pitch black; only their breath sounds filled the stale air. "Your phone," Rayna muttered quietly, reaching for hers out her back pocket to put the flashlight on. Malia did the same.

The glow of their phone lights lit the room to reveal Perla May Lunes' last earthly home. Vanilla-scented candles hovered over the musty smell of confined air. Malia secretly hoped the information she received from the energetic care aide about the room being occupied with spirit was just a tale. Rayna moved around the room like a detective, flashing her phone light into every corner, scouring the simple room. Perla had her bed pushed right up against the window. The blind was closed. The head of the bed was raised, and her perfectly fluffed pillow rested on top. Malia approached and brushed her hand along the soft, pale, plum-colored Afghan material that was folded at the foot of the white bed. She felt her heartbeat calming after the dramatic entrance. A gentle Liz had left the room in meticulous order, just as Perla had kept it while being a long-time resident.

"I can't believe her family just left everything here. Look at all this stuff," Malia said.

Rayna opened the dresser drawer and pulled out a nude satin undershirt, "Sexy!" she whispered sarcastically, throwing it carelessly back into the drawer and pushing it shut.

Malia's curiosity drew her to the chest of drawers. She elbowed Rayna away from the cabinet. "Go check out the closet," she said to Rayna as she pushed her away. Swinging her light like a pendulum over the cabinet, Malia took a quick inventory to see if anything was interesting. She saw the usual bedroom novelties like a clock, a tiny box of Kleenex, a picture of a pretty woman in an old frame and other ornamental things. Her light caught the reflection of a gleaming gold and pearl necklace that rested on a wooden cross. She paused on it for a moment, wondering if it was real. Aiming her light down, she opened the second drawer and discovered a rustic leather album.

"Oh cool! I love pictures!" Malia said, grabbing the album and pushing the drawer closed. Plunking herself down on an old rocking chair, she opened the book that would unseal the history of Perla May Lune.

The sound of the sticky, plastic pages being separated echoed throughout the room. "What did you find?" Rayna questioned, rifling through old clothing.

"It's *her*! This must be her," Malia said.

"Obviously, it's her!" Rayna said, falling to her knees beside the rocking chair to help shine light onto the pictures.

"Wow, she was beautiful," Malia said.

"She was smokin hot!" Rayna agreed. "I bet she was a vixen, a hot commodity with the bad boys back in her day." She giggled while pointing to a picture of Perla May with some friends laying on a beach in bikinis.

Malia shook her head. "No way; she looked classy. She had a pretty smile. Look at this dress," she said, aiming Rayna's attention to another picture on the next page.

Rayna insisted, "Maybe she was actually a bitch, like a wolf in sheep's clothing, that stole everyone's boyfriends."

"You are so psychotic, Ray! Why do you have to be so dark all the time?" Malia was annoyed at her persistence in making the previous Fountain Garden resident out to be a villain or witch of sorts. *You can probably relate*, Malia chuckled to herself. "It looks like she had a lot of friends and did a lot of travelling," Malia said while inspecting the rest of the album.

Rayna quickly got bored of the photos and left Malia to study the images herself. She returned to the tall dresser and lifted a vintage clock laughing at its aesthetic. "Then I wonder how she ended up in this dump?" she said, scrunching her face as she pushed the clock to the back of the dresser, tipping the wooden stand-up cross that held the elegant pearl beaded necklace. "Maybe she was a Jesus freak," Rayna huffed with laughter. "Maybe she only loved God instead of men and was obsessed with touching herself in private!" she said in an exaggerated tone while moving her hand provocatively down between her legs.

Malia scowled back with a grin, "You're so gross, Ray!"

Rayna picked up the cross, tossed the necklace down on the counter, and twisted herself towards Malia aiming the cross directly in her face in a sacrilegious way, "Sweet JESUS! Pray for her, O Father God! Bless me and my skanky Boo here to see your almighty ways, O Lord! Forgive her for nasty thoughts and her constant desire to touch herself every day in such sinful ways O Lord. Please save her!"

"Eat shit, Ray!" Malia slapped the side of Rayna's wrist, projecting the cross through the air straight across the room. It landed on the bed. She went back to looking at the album, "It looks like she has a boyfriend here; it seems like it's the same guy in all these photos. I wonder why she never married. There are no wedding photos anywhere."

"Because she was smart and a beautiful dirty slut, I told you!" Rayna said.

Malia closed the album and stood to return it to the drawer. Rayna's humor made her feel like a bad person sometimes. Rayna blocked her phone's light for a quick second to make herself dark and slid the beautifully crafted necklace from the counter into her side jean jacket pocket. She grabbed a large square hairbrush from the top of the dresser and moved out of Malia's way. After returning the album to its place, Malia turned her phone light around toward Rayna, who tossed a wad of gray-white hair at her.

"Yuck, a dead lady's hair!" Rayna yelled.

"STOP Ray!" Malia said disgusted as she jumped back and wiped her hands down the front of her body to release any clinging hair. In that same moment a cold rush of air swept the room. It stopped both girls dead in their thoughts, stiffening them in fright. Frozen in terror, they stared at each other in the dark room, worried they were not alone. In the ghostly quiet, the girls heard a hanger moving across the rail from within the closet. Malia spooked instantly, squealed, and ran toward the door. Rayna flung the hairbrush onto the bed and was hard on her tail. Malia swung the door open and ran outside into the hall. With eyes large as saucers she gasped, "Did you fucking hear that, Ray?" her voice quavered.

"Sure did!" Rayna said, her eyelids drawn up high.

They bolted down the hall, fleeing the paranormal activity, back toward the front entrance. They flung themselves under the caution tape and ran through the scattered wheelchairs and walkers. Rayna's hip bumped a walker, launching a cane into the air that had been hanging on the side of it. It made a bang when it hit the shiny floor.

A pant-less Edward, in the room beside Perla May's, stepped out of his room—in his sundowning state—curious of the noise. Against his chest, he held a giant mess of hangers—from his full-moon—late evening tidy.

The girls were long gone.

21

EMBARRASSED

The fire felt hot on the front of Lexi's knees as she sat, mesmerized by the dancing, flickering flames of the campfire. The crackling, hissing wood was slowly calming her nerves. Luke walked up and stood beside her. "That conversation earlier was hard to miss."

She looked up at the tall, rugged man when he interrupted her hypnotic state, "Oh, God, that's embarrassing," she said, quickly using her finger to wipe her sad eyes of any runny mascara.

"I wasn't trying to listen," he said.

She was mortified that he had heard her talking on the phone with Brock. *How stupid we must have sounded arguing,* she thought. Her face paled with embarrassment.

"I don't assume to know any facts or your circumstance and I don't want to overstep my bounds here, but anybody that can bring a person to tears like *that* doesn't deserve to be a part of that person's world."

"I agree." She gave a big exhale, exhausted from her misery.

"May I?" he said.

"Of course," she said, moving over on the log bench.

He sat down beside her and gulped his beer.

Lexi moved her knee in slightly so it wouldn't accidently brush against his leg. When she stole a quick glance over at him she noticed his long, dark eyelashes.

"Turning into quite the local, hey? Buckwitt Ocean-Side brewery?" she asked, taking note of the label on his bottle and thinking it was a good conversation changer. "My family knows it well."

"Yup, made friends there right away," he said, gulping his beer. "Do you want one?"

A drink would be amazing right now, she thought. "Sure," she said, "Thank you."

He got up and walked away from the fire into the darkness towards his modern, thirty- foot-long pull travel trailer. For a moment, Lexi felt like she was in the start of one of her dreams. *Should she confide in this stranger? It would be safe because she would probably never see him again after this weekend. Maybe she should just enjoy the moment and resist the urge to dump her whole life story on him.*

She followed Luke, her curiosity taking control of her mind, to the top step of the door of his trailer.

"Permission to enter?" she asked.

"Come on in, check it out," he said. "Don't be shy. Feel free to snoop."

She was surprised to see how clean it was. The sleek-looking trailer was just as big on the inside as it looked on the outside. Lexi scanned the warm space. There was a living room with a fireplace, sofa and rocker recliner at the front of the trailer by the entry door. A spacious kitchen boasting beautiful cabinetry and a dinette area took up the middle of the trailer, and a door located at the back, was open, giving her a view into the primary bedroom. A dirty hat and jean jacket lay on the dining table with a couple of empty beer bottles, but somehow, it looked sexy, not messy. He turned around from closing the fridge and handed her a bottle of beer. She noticed his tanned hand was rough looking, unlike Brock's soft, perfectly manicured hands.

"Watching you and the girls today on the beach," he said, "I would say you gals look like you fit in rather good around here." He leaned against the fridge.

Oh, God, this is so awkward, she thought, leaning up against his counter not knowing if she should sit down on a chair or if they were going to go back to the fire. "I don't know about that," she remarked.

"Oh, now, don't be modest. Gunther told me that these were *your* stomping grounds a while back. He said you basically ran Hill's Hardware store in town and that you were the 'right-hand man' to your dad for years in that store. Sounds like a lot of people miss you working and living here," he said.

"A while back is right," she said starting to pace slowly around the trailer while sipping her beer. "It's a bit weird now. I feel out of place."

He watched her walk around the living room, looking up, down, and all around. Her hand grazed the top of the soft, micro-suede material of the recliner chair. She walked past Luke to check out the back of the trailer. "Truth is," she said, walking past a small bathroom, "I don't know where I fit in anymore."

She stopped herself from unloading her emotional baggage. Her curious eyes explored his room. A sizable bed layered in thick, plush comforters and pillows took up most of the space. A small lamp was on, making the room look dim and cozy. *Devil in a Blue Dress* and *The Buddha of Suburbia* laid on the nightstand. "Of course, he reads too," she thought.

"Well, it is nice having you here. You girls bring fun and pretty to this place," he said, flattering and flirty, sucking back his drink.

She walked back into the kitchen area as Luke reached to remove the dirty hat from off the table and toss it on the chair.

She couldn't help but think that those same words out of Brock's mouth would have sounded completely sexist, but somehow, he sounded charming.

Laughter came from outside at the fire pit in front of the girl's cabin. Lexi walked to the front screen door and looked out at the campsite. She saw the girls giggling in the lawn chairs in front of their cabin. Hearing her daughter's young voice made her feel nervous about being in Luke's trailer. She sipped her drink faster.

"So how long are you ladies here for?" Luke asked.

"Just the weekend. I have some things to figure out with my parents and then we are heading back to the city."

"Well, shoot. That's not a long enough time for me to figure you out," he teased.

Her stomach fluttered. She felt the chemistry in their interaction. She looked away nervously and then crossed her arms, still holding her beer, suddenly not knowing what to do with her hands or body.

"It looks different around here that's for sure," Lexi said.

"Yes, you probably have *some* sort of feeling about that I guess," he acknowledged.

"No . . . " she said, looking at him directly with a smile and dragging her answer. "My *Dad* probably does, but he's a grumpy old goat. We argue about pretty much everything lately. *I* think it's pretty cool what you've done here."

"Oh, *ya*? You think it's pretty cool?" he teased again. "Go easy on your dad. He has his reasons for feeling the way he does, I am sure. You are lucky to still *have* a dad. Some of us don't have that," he said.

"So, you're really going to live here? Like, all year round?" she asked.

"Sure, why not?" he said. "It gets a bit damp and cool in the winter but nothing a warm fire can't fix. It can be quite cozy."

She gulped her beer. *I bet*, she thought.

"I like the quiet, I like the trees," he said. "The ocean feels like it's protecting me from the chaotic world out there. I think I am done with the rush of life. I was spinning my wheels in the city, and it was time for a change."

"What did you do there, if you don't mind me asking?" Lexi said.

"I was a corporate fraud investigation officer during the day, and I side-gigged as a private investigator at night."

"Oh, wow!" she said. "That's . . . interesting . . . and now . . . this? That's quite the life change! So, this is your new home."

"Well," he said, standing up from the chair, "maybe not *here* exactly, but it's good for now. I'll probably build a house once this is all up and running and I get bored again. I'm not in any hurry, though. Just getting this place up and running is keeping me as busy as I want to be." He rubbed his couple day's-old scruff growth that was dark with a few random grey whiskers.

You are undeniably sexy. *Who IS this guy*? She pondered. "You are a man of many trades, I see. You make it all sound so easy. I could use a temporary hiatus from *my* life, but I have Malia to worry about," she said looking through the screen at Malia and Rayna still cracking up in their conversation.

"Oh, I think your daughter is just fine," Luke said, approaching to stand beside her at the door. His shoulder touched hers when he peeked through the screen to see what she was looking at.

Lexi's senses quickly heightened and so did the butterflies in her belly. She panicked and pushed the screen open a little too hard, sending it flinging.

"Well thanks for the beer," she said, walking down the steps.

"No problem, any time," he said.

Lexi's feet stepped onto the dirt, grounding her back in reality. She turned and gave Luke a quick memorizing glance as she walked away from the trailer.

"You let me know if you need anything, Lex," he said.

Lex? She smiled to herself; *I like it. So, we are definitely friends now,* she thought, giggling in her mind. She couldn't help herself, so she turned one more time to give him a final wave. He was leaning his buffed chest out of his doorway, hands up high holding the frame, so he wouldn't fall out.

Her knees swooned. *He was yummy.*

22

TINY ROOM

The tiny cabin felt like a fridge. Lexi grabbed her carry-on and flipped it onto the double bed, noticing a huge ugly scrape on one of the corners. *Figures!* She felt anxious being alone with her mind again. *Is this a sign I should quit my job? Quit my life as I have known it? Do what Luke did and make a massive change?* She kicked off her boots and removed her ankle socks to let her feet breathe. The wooden floorboards were cool under her bare feet.

She whipped her clothes off fast to race the chill that she anticipated on her body. Then she threw on her pyjama set and crawled into the crisp white sheets. Kicking the bed linen loose from being perfectly tucked, she adjusted and then readjusted until her cold feet were perfectly sausaged in the blankets. She lifted the bedding up over her cold nose and blew out a lungful of balmy air under the covers to warm herself up.

All the tense spots on her body released into a giant shiver and then relaxed, allowing the soft mattress to perfectly cradle her body. *Ah rest and rejuvenate*, she thought, motivating herself into a calm mindset. Her eyes panned the cabin from left to right, admiring the simple aesthetics of the room. The brown, beige, and green woodsy plaid drapes accented the comforter and décor pillows, giving it a complete cabin feel. *Simple and cute,* she thought. The small-scaled room triggered her brain back to fights she had experienced with Brock.

Were there signs in the beginning that she refused to see? She laid there with a sickened feeling of worry that she had disappointed her parents with choices that she had made, and she still held anger towards Brock for being so blatantly insensitive to her family's feelings over the years. Remembering his words that still burned in her brain, "You are crazy Lexi! Why should I find it more appealing to stay in your parents' 1950s, thousand-square-foot bungalow that smells of mildew from constant wet island weather than to be pampered at a Waikoloa Villa with my family in Hawaii?" The insolent tone of his voice still outraged her. Then he called the spare bedroom (where they slept in Oscar and Anna's house) "The Closet."

Self-reflecting on her own questionable actions, Lexi remembered that although it had upset her so much that Brock would insult her parents' home, she had taken on a few of his obnoxious traits herself. A couple of months after their fight, she stood in the lunchroom at her work. Looking down at her watch, she said to her co-worker, "It's two minutes to one. I better get back to my closet!" referring to her cubicle where she worked as a junior assistant. *Had she morphed into her husband?*

She contemplated how their marriage had changed over time. Lexi used to call Brock at the real estate brokerage firm where he worked and flirted as best she could over the phone, tempting him to come home early, but those days were over. She could not pinpoint when things began to change. They just did, and it devastated her. Brock blamed his competitive mindset and the expansion of the firm for his absence from home and refused to go to therapy. Before Malia got her driver's license, she would need someone to drive her to the odd activity after school. Brock would say that he could drive, but then at the last minute, something always came up at work, leaving Lexi scrambling. Recently, his secretary intercepted his calls and seemed pleased to turn Lexi away, saying, "Mr. Kirk is in a meeting, but I will be *sure* to pass on the message that you called." The young-sounding voice on the other end of the phone emphasized the word "sure" and the tone she used rubbed Lexi the wrong way. He never did call back.

A saddened, determined, and resilient Lexi did not want to give up on her relationship and had moments of hope when Brock would spend a whole weekend at home, but those moments were few and far between. He would lock himself away in his home office with a strong drink, basically ignoring the family and would come to bed late at night reeking of cigars and booze. His clumsy, drunken body would try to crawl on top of her only to pleasure himself, leaving Lexi feeling empty and depressed.

Brock also had a magnificent obsession for the gym, which was conveniently located in the same tower as his workspace, and his body showed it. Unfortunately, Lexi did not feel like *she* was benefiting from it anymore. It was more common for her to have intimate moments pleasuring herself to ward off the dreaded, self-pitied lonely days.

A few months back, she was picking up Brock's dry-cleaning in the downtown core. It was her day off and the warm sun put her in a positive mood. Brock's office tower was close by, so in a moment of courage and perseverance to bring a spark to their marriage, she decided to surprise him with his favorite gourmet Serrano ham, caramelized onion, and red wine panini. Unfortunately, her plan to connect with him as a loving wife backfired.

Looking at her reflection in the mirrored walls of the oversized elevator of the office tower that day, she fiddled with her hair and twisted from side to side in her favorite stretchy jeans, vintage T-shirt, and wrap sweater. She hoped her gesture to bring lunch would be well received by Brock. When the elevator doors opened to the twenty-fourth floor, the soft jazz music was instantly drowned out by a young woman's laughter and a group of sleekly dressed men talking over each other. She could hear Brock's voice dominating the conversation. Lexi was instantly irritated by the familiar tone of Brock's secretary and was taken aback at the conclusion that she was barely in her mid-twenties. The young woman in the tall heels and shapely black, fashionable dress exaggerated her laugh in response to his haughty mannerisms, and with her flirty touch, reached out to stroke Brock on the forearm. Lexi's heart dropped as she slowly approached the ambitious group of business people. Suddenly, she felt frumpy in her casual clothes. With a nervous stomach, she tucked the gourmet lunch bag under her casual wrap, while taking in the scene.

The professionally decorated space reeked of money and ambition. Floor-to-ceiling high-rise windows overlooked the downtown streets. Overpowering cologne lingered in the air. Fancy coffee drinks sat on the corner of large, glass desks that held sleek laptops and top-of-the-line computers. Behind each desk was a luxurious upholstered executive office chair. Tall palm tree plants sat beside filing cabinets that contained information about wealthy clients, and a mini office bar was situated in the corner by a large conference desk. Lexi's office at Burrows Developments was wildly dissimilar. It was a medium-size, basic office and did not have a spectacular view; it was certainly not as glamorous as this.

Brock spotted Lexi. With a look of annoyed surprise, he quickly revealed himself through the crowd to approach her, almost motioning her back to the elevator. "What are you doing here?" He said, looking at her casual attire up and down with disapproving eyes, making her feel minimal and insecure for being in such a posh atmosphere.

"Sorry to embarrass you." Her confidence and positive mindset were instantly beaten by his tone. She pulled her oversized wrap sweater across her chest to cover her T-shirt. "I thought I would surprise you with your favorite panini. I can see you are working hard!" she said, pushing the bag towards Brock's chest, crushed at his response to her presence.

"Don't do this, Lexi. Not here . . . and you know I am cutting carbs now!" he said.

Defeated, she got back on the elevator, left the building, and that was the last time she ever popped into his work again.

STOP, brain! Lexi yelled in her head as she lay in her cabin bed. *Relax and rejuvenate,* she repeated three times in her head like a mantra. Her racing thoughts finally settled. It only took a moment to take a few deep breaths and get to that quiet place in her mind.

His body . . . her hands . . . She was warming up fast. A large, pesky, incessant bug landed on her forehead, flew off, then landed again. "*Aww Seriously!!!*" She had just fully relaxed. Lexi pulled the blanket up over her head and tried to get back to that secret place in her mind. Moments later, the dream took over. *His bed felt soft under her naked body. She wasn't shy anymore. All her inhibitions let go. It was just the two of them . . .*

23

LIKE A DEER

"I have to wash this stank off me. Come Mal! Let's go to the showers now." Rayna said in a hyper tone, flinging her personal belongings out of her backpack and onto the floor. There was no organization to her misshapen mess. She tossed things to the side on the twin bed to figure out what she needed to bring with her to the washroom.

The sound of coins dropping in the machines triggered the showers to turn on. The girls yammered on and on over the loud running *shhshhshh* of the water, their giggly voices echoing throughout the camp. The water slapped the concrete floor as they lathered up their long hair in lavender-mint shampoo. The fragrant steam rose and billowed out of the opening in the wall to create a cloud of moving mist.

"I am so glad we didn't get caught tonight!" Malia said.

"That was fun!" Rayna said, "We should sneak in there again tomorrow night."

"No way! That was too freaky. We'll find something else to do. Ugh. So many tangles from the wind!" Malia complained. "I need a pound of conditioner! Throw me some over the top!"

"Don't you just hate it when wet hair falls and gets stuck in your butt?" Rayna said laughing.

Malia burst into laughter, "I KNOW! Then when you pull it out it's like the weirdest feeling . . ." She continued to crack up.

"Like pulling floss through your teeth but waaaay longer Ha! Ha! Ha!" Rayna howled, feeling loopy and over-tired from having little sleep the night before.

"Sucks about the party tonight," Malia said. "I bet it was epic."

"Well, it couldn't have been *that* fun because *we* weren't there!" Rayna remarked. "The summer has just started, so there's going to be parties every weekend now I bet. Besides, pretty sure we can amuse ourselves here. "Where did that hottie body—Teddy— go, I wonder?" Rayna said.

"Probably home if his work was done for the day," Malia said. "I assume he lives near here, or maybe he left to hang out with his friends. It *is* a long weekend."

"Well, we will have to find out. I don't know what they feed these island boys but d, d, d, damn, girlfriend, he was *fine* and usually where there's one, there's two or three, so we need to do some hunting tomorrow for some people to play with." Rayna turned off her water and jumped out of her stall. Seeing Malia's clothes laying on the wet floor under the half wall she reached her dripping arm underneath and swiped them up.

The water turned off on Malia's side.

"Where's the bag and my clothes?" Malia asked, stepping out of her shower.

"Right here," Rayna said from her shower stall.

"Throw my towel and PJs over the top of the wall," Malia said, shivering.

Rayna shuffled through the backpack. "They aren't in here," she said.

"Yes, they are!" Malia yelled. "They are in the blue backpack. The bag I *told* you to bring, Ray."

"Uh . . . well *I* don't have it. I only brought this one, the one with the shampoo and conditioner," she said from still inside her stall.

"Are you serious?" Malia asked. "I put my towel, underwear and PJs in the other bag that was on the bed."

"Well how was I supposed to know that?" Rayna said in a snarky tone. "You said let's just bring the ONE and share. When I threw the shampoo, and towel in *this* bag, I assumed your stuff was in it. I guess I wasn't paying that much attention. How did *you* not notice that you didn't have your clothes?"

"Because, bitch!" Malia shouted, "I was busy looking for coins, my toothbrush and toothpaste, and EVERYTHING ELSE!"

They both burst out laughing.

"Okay, I'll wait here," Malia said, "you go and grab my PJs, and a dry towel for me," Malia pleaded.

Rayna threw her towel around her body and gave it a boob tuck. "No way! Every man for herself. I am not coming back, so unless you want to sleep in here you are going streaking!"

"Rayna, don't be an ass; lend me your towel and go get my stuff!" Malia said panicky as she stood shaking like a wet dog.

"Nope," Rayna said, remaining stubborn as she jumped out of the stall. She loved to get a rise out of Malia, and the opportunity did not come up often.

"I HATE YOU!" Malia laughed, feeling frustrated at the same time.

Rayna gathered the backpack and both their belongings and walked backward out of the bathroom looking mischievous. "You know you don't *hate* me. You *love me!* Don't be a priss! You need to air out that cootchie of yours anyways! Bye, Boo!" Rayna sassed.

Malia peeked out of her stall and watched the wooden door slam shut.

Rayna yelled from outside the building, "Viewer Discretion is Advised!" She trotted off to her cabin pleased with herself and banged the door to scare Malia into thinking that she had locked her out.

Teddy walked up from the beach area holding two fold-up chairs that the previous guests had forgotten and that would have blown away in the night. He stopped dead in his tracks to watch the silhouette of Malia's naked body streak across the grass. She looked like a baby deer running in the night. With her long slender legs taking extra-long hurdles, she ran awkwardly, holding each hand over a boob. He squinted to see her nakedness through the fading campfire light. Malia reached for the door handle as fast as she could, "*I will KILL you Ray, if you lo . . .* " She swung the door open.

Rayna threw Malia's pyjamas at her. "I can see your goosebumps from here!" she said laughing. "There you go, Sweet Cheeks. Lesson learned."

24

DAY 2

The wind and rain blew steady through the night like a demanding white noise that failed in its attempt to drown out the incessant barking of an infuriating canine. Malia slept in, tired from flipping and flopping most of the night from listening to the windstorm and thinking about her parents and grandparents. She lay in an amazingly deep, early morning sleep when a text tone on her phone woke her. She opened her eyes, disoriented in her new rustic accommodation. She glanced around the cabin scouting for spiders and saw Rayna, with a bare leg, hanging half off the other twin bed. Picking sleep from the corner of her eyes, Malia read the time, "Ugh, it's only 7:15! Who the hell?"

"Is it someone from the party?" Rayna groaned.

"No, it's from Liz, the nurse," Malia moaned. "She says to 'feel free to come in around 8:30 am. if you and your friend still want to help out today. It would really be appreciated.'" Malia sighed, "Holy guilt factor," she said.

"*Screw that*, I gotta date with the beach and that hot little bod we met last night," Rayna said, rejected the idea from the other bed.

"I feel like I got no sleep at all with that wind last night. It was *so* annoying, and did you *hear that dog barking*?" Malia asked.

"Oh, ya! It sounded like he was right outside our door!" Rayna agreed.

"I wonder who's it is?" Malia said.

"I don't know," Rayna said, "but it is going to be hard to be polite if I come face to face with them this morning!"

A garden tractor with a harrow on the back drove by to head down to the beach area. Malia popped her head up to look out the window. "There *he is*!"

"Teddy?" Rayna found sudden energy to bolt to the door and whip it open. Standing in her baggy T-shirt and panties, she waved to Teddy until he finally looked over and waved back awkwardly.

Malia hustled to get herself ready for the day. "Could this mirror be any smaller?" she asked, jumping up on the bed to see if she could get a better view of her butt in her shorts.

Rayna popped in front of her to look in the mirror. "No doubt! Clearly, a man designed these rooms!" she said laughing.

Clothes were strewn all over the bed and floor. The table was covered in hair elastics, make-up, and hairsprays.

"Okay, I think I am ready. Let's go chill outside for a bit," Malia said, grabbing the water bottles off the side table.

"Just a sec!" Rayna dug her hands into her shirt to adjust her boobs higher in her bra and then inspected herself in the mirror. "We need to get this helping shit done fast and get into bikinis. I gotta get my tan on here."

Malia saw an old rag hanging over one of the lawn chairs out front and used it to wipe off the remaining rain and dirt from two of the chairs on the grass.

Rayna came out of the cabin, seeing all the lawn furniture in disarray, "What's going on here?" she said.

"It looks like Teddy's moving stuff around to clean around the fire pits," Malia said.

"Morning girls," Lexi emerged from her cabin and sat on her chair on her wooden deck. She grabbed a compact mirror out of her purse and used it to put on her mascara.

"Morning, Mom!"

"Morning!" Rayna said to Lexi.

"Did *anyone* sleep?" Lexi asked, staring in the mirror.

"Not really," Malia said, throwing the rag down on the grass and sitting down on the chair.

"Barely," Rayna agreed, grabbing one of the water bottles off the arm of the chair and then plopping herself down on the second chair near Malia.

"Did you guys hear that camper arrive in the middle of the night?" Lexi looked up from her mirror.

"Yup! I *think* they have a pet!" Malia answered sarcastically, looking over at the RV sight.

They all started laughing. A dog started to bark from inside.

Lexi got up and moved her chair off the deck to get a better view around the corner and to see the owner of the RV.

The barking suddenly stopped as if someone had given the dog a treat or picked it up. A moment later, the door to the RV opened and through the screen appeared a tall, voluptuous woman with high, matted hair, big framed sun-glasses, and an outfit that was something to be desired. She was jabbering to either the dog or someone else; the girls could not quite tell. She had the tiny canine in one hand and a piña colada in another.

"Mal! Check it out," Rayna said as she motioned Malia to look toward the camper.

"Good, God! That is quite the spectacle," Malia said, laughing.

Both girls looked over their shoulders to Lexi to see if she was watching as well. She was gazing at the new arrival with a smile on her face.

"Who wears heels camping?" Malia asked Rayna.

The oversized blouse fell loose over the busty woman. Bold, colourful abstract shapes plastered all over the material of her shirt. The woman's matching plastic hoop earrings swung when she turned her head and her hair was concreted in place, holding firm in the breeze.

Lexi was intrigued as she watched the woman who had her long, red spiked nails around the dog's fur with one hand and her tropical drink, complemented with a large piece of pineapple, dangled over the edge in her other hand. A small towel draped over her arm. She stepped cautiously as she descended the steps of the RV in her heels.

"Patsy, we don't have all day! If you want to see the ocean, we should get a move on."

"Hold your horses, Polly! I'm having a time finding the pineapple."

"I told you I cut a piece for your drink as well, but you were taking so long in the bathroom I put it back in the Tupperware container so it wouldn't get dried out."

"Well, my stomach isn't quite right this morning from that seafood you made me try on that monstrosity of a watercraft last night."

"Now, don't blame the food; you know how you get on ferries!" The first lady continued to yell up from the bottom of the stairs back into the RV. "You always get a little motion sickness with the waves. You get queasy on planes too; remember our trip to Hawaii last fall?"

"I think it's my inner ear problem . . . ever since . . . I don't see the Tupperware container anywhere, Polly!"

They nattered on. "I told you I left it on the counter by the toaster. Jeepers kreepers you don't listen, Patsy!"

"No, you did *not* tell me that, Polly! I assumed you put it in the fridge. *That's* where I was looking."

"Hurry up, Patsy! The sun is up, and Speckles needs her walk. You know we have to be mindful of her schedule. We don't need any hiccups in her routine, or she'll get distressed."

"Did you put her boots on? We don't want her getting sand in her toes while exploring this strange little resort you found; she would hate that! We need to protect her paws, or she'll spend the whole night scratching at them."

"Yes, I put them on. She is ready. We are just waiting on *you,*" the woman said.

"I'm coming . . . Just let her go, Speckles won't go far. You know she doesn't like unfamiliar places."

The woman set the mutt down and it pranced towards Malia and Rayna in its soft little rubber dog booties, looking to find the perfect grass.

"Finally!" The first woman said, looking back at the other woman who appeared at the door of the camper.

Rayna and Malia turned their heads rapidly towards each other, eyes large as saucers. They were shocked to see the look-a-like emerge from the RV. The other lady was the spitting image of the first. Their likeness was almost unsettling.

Lexi slowly zipped up her make-up bag while staring in shock at the twins. She had never seen anything like it.

"They're wombsies," Rayna said to Malia, giggling.

"Did you bring her float coat, Polly? She'll get tossed like a twig in those waves. Better get it on her before that nasty wind picks up again."

"I don't know if we want to be walking down there," the woman said. "It looks awful! It looks downright dirty with all that stuff the storm brought in. The sand is grotesquely littered this morning!" she said, looking toward the beach at all the seaweed and sticks. "That young man over there has a lot of work ahead of him," she said, pointing to Teddy working down on the sand. "Maybe there's a swimming pool we could just lounge beside."

Rayna heckled under her breath to Malia, "The dog has a *life jacket!*"

"It would have been nice to go exploring after we go to that amazing market we heard about on the internet, but we have to be careful not to miss the ferry later this afternoon!" the woman said.

Teddy drove up on the lawn tractor after clearing part of the beach of debris. He parked and walked toward the shed situated on the side of the lot. Malia and Rayna both perked up in their lawn chairs, attention diverted.

"Morning everybody." Teddy gave them all a wave and then disappeared into the building.

Damn, he is cute, Malia thought.

The little ball of fur had finally stopped turning in circles and left a perfect steamy poo just a couple feet from Rayna. "Just shit anywhere dog," she said, ridiculing the prissy mutt.

"Awesome," Malia said, grossed out.

"That's our good girl, Speckles!" The first lady called out proudly as she approached.

The second lady walked up, picking lint off her strikingly colorful, crisp striped blouse. She reached deep into in her giant purse. "I was sure I put that sunblock in here."

"Oh good, the helper boy is here!" The first lady said, seeing Teddy emerge from the shed wiping his hands with a rag. She removed her sunglasses, revealing the teal blue on her eyelids that gave her eyes a bright, wide-eyed appearance, "Hey there young man. If you wouldn't mind, could you wipe these chairs down so a lady can sit and relax and take in this view?" she said as she picked up a twig left on the lawn chair from the storm with her long, slender nails.

The second lady looked up from her purse, "Polly, just use the beach towel in your hand to wipe the wet off."

"I can't use *this*, Patsy!"

"Why not?"

"I don't want it to get wet."

"Well, that's just silly."

"Then what do you suggest I use on Speckles if she needs to be dried off, Patsy? She isn't going to like a wet towel."

"Well, she will be wet herself when you go to use it on her, Polly, so she isn't going to mind a little dampness on the towel!"

"*Ho-LY*! Malia sneered at Rayna under her breath, "These two are *batshit* crazy!"

"No, I am going to keep her out of the water," Polly said. "I brought it in case she wants to nap. She did not get much sleep last night with all that wind blowing. Scared the little wits right out of her!"

"You don't say . . ." Rayna said, in a sarcastic monotonous voice. *That annoying little canine kept the whole campground up!* she thought.

Teddy approached the girls at the fire pit area to clean the ladies' seats.

"Hey, Malia," he said.

"Hey," she replied with a wide smile.

"You guys survived the windstorm last night?" Teddy asked.

"Yup," Malia said.

Rayna chimed in, "It got scary there for a bit; it felt like trees were going to fall on us."

"Well," Teddy said, "Luke is camped here on the property if anything would have happened." He looked away from Rayna and over to Malia. "I popped by later in the evening to make sure everything was secure," he said looking right at Malia, "Actually, I saw you leave the bathrooms before I took off for home again—and you looked just fine." He winked and she flushed with mortification.

"Well, maybe you could bunk with us next time to keep us safe." Rayna said, trying to draw his attention.

Malia shot her a look. *Forward much?*

The new arrivals were still yakking back and forth. Patsy walked back to the trailer while Polly waited patiently for Teddy to clean her seat properly. "Don't forget the cracks, young man! The water sits in those cracks, and we don't need my pants to be soaking that up when I sit, do we?" She hinted to him to do a better job.

Patsy called back from her trailer, "I know we brought another one of those beach towels; now, where did we put it, Polly?"

The lady laid her towel on the sunny grass, picked up the dog and placed it on top. "There, Speckles, you take in this sun, baby girl and have yourself a little snooze before our walk." The dog looked up at her in a humanly way and then turned itself in a couple circles plopping itself down. "I think I know where that other towel is, Patsy!" The woman called as she walked back to the RV with her heels sinking in the grass. The moment she was gone the dog got up, pranced over closer to the girls and flopped itself down. It gave a big stretch, kicking off one of its boots and then flipped itself over, settling into a frog position with its belly flat on the grass.

The girls glanced at each other amused.

"If that dog could talk . . ." Rayna said.

"Right, Ray?" Malia laughed.

The girls watched Teddy work. After he cleaned the other two chairs, he unhitched the harrows and attached the wagon to his little tractor so he could deliver firewood. He hopped back on the machine. "Sorry about the noise of the tractor. I'm just going to fill your box," he said, pointing to the lean-to on the side of the cabin.

"Alright y then," Rayna snickered.

Teddy flushed. He drove over to the lean-to and neatly stacked the wood under the cabin shelter.

"You should have plenty of wood now for a good fire later. Let me know if you guys need anything else," he said to Malia, trying to open up a conversation.

"We will!" Rayna flirted hard. He jumped on the garden tractor and drove closer to the next cabin ignoring her.

"Ready, Ray?" Malia asked. "Let's do this before we change our mind."

"Fine! I just have to grab my phone off the charger," Rayna said, getting up and running back into the cabin.

Teddy saw an opportunity to chat with Malia alone. "So, you are going to help out at Fountain Garden today?" He said, while stacking the wood in a neat pile.

"I am," Malia said.

"If you guys are going to be around for lunch," he continued, "I can build up the fire so you can cook hot dogs or whatever. We have a barbecue too that we can haul over here from Luke's camper if you need that. Once we are done with this pavilion, the barbecue will be in there full time for everyone to use. So . . . ya, I'll be around. I *might* even see you at Fountain Garden, maybe."

"Okay, cool. Thanks, Teddy." Malia said. Her heart fluttered that he seemed to want to get to know her. *He's so cute. He seems nicer and more down to earth than the boys in Adasa.*

"I'm ready!" Ray said, emerging from her cabin holding her phone. She looked at Teddy, "You working here all day on this canopy—shade shelter—thing?"

"It's a gazebo, Ray," Malia said, laughing.

"No it's not, it's too big to be a gazebo. Isn't it?" Rayna asked Teddy.

"Well, Luke calls it a pavilion, I call it a picnic shelter . . ." he said, laughing.

Lexi walked up and interrupted the conversation, "I am going to come with you girls; wait a sec. I'll walk you." She wound her hair up in a loose scrunchy bun as she walked beside Malia and Rayna. "Whew, it's already *hot* out here today!" She looked around until she spotted Luke up on a ladder, leaning against the corner post of the wooden structure.

"Mom, what would you call this thing that Luke and Teddy are building?" Malia asked.

"I don't know—a pergola?" Lexi said.

Teddy, Rayna and Malia all burst out laughing.

"It's *not* a pergola, it has a closed roof!" Rayna said.

"My grandma in Adasa has a small pergola in her backyard by her pool and *it* has a closed roof," Malia said.

Luke chuckled, as he listened to the conversation from up on the ladder—amused with the debate, "Watch your step girls!" he said, looking down at them when they walked by. "I hope we didn't wake you this morning. Sorry about the mess again! Watch you don't trip on my cords or tools."

Lexi looked up at him, holding her hand flat at her eyes to block the blasting sun, "Looking good!" she said. *Oh, that sounded awkward,* she thought.

"Well, thank you!" Luke said with a seductive grin.

"I mean, the *pergola* . . . you are doing a lot of work around here." She tried to keep her focus off his shirtless body. His tool belt hung low on his jean shorts pulling them down just enough to show his stomach muscles and the top of his boxer briefs.

So, boxer briefs! Lexi thought. *That settles that.*

"Well, I thought it would be nice to have a place to gather and that provides some shade, but you still get this amazing view." He pointed out toward the ocean. "You guys can call it *whatever* you want," he said, grinning and loving the attention that his project created.

The girls walked away toward the back trees. "It's amazing Luke." Malia said. She liked the stranger and wanted to give her mom the okay to make a friend.

"You gals have a good day now," Luke said.

"So, I guess we'll see you later then." Malia yelled to Teddy.

"Yup. You will," he said.

Rayna put her arm around Malia's waist and leaned in to whisper, "You think he has a girlfriend?"

25

COFFEE, PLEASE

Once a month, all the residents would show up to the breakfast room still in their nightwear, with hair looking comically bedraggled and misplaced. It was acceptable to look rough in their robes because on *this particular* day, after breakfast, the residents would take turns going to the "Everything Room," which would be turned into a makeshift hair salon for the day. One by one, the residents would be taken from their place at the breakfast table and rolled down to the makeshift salon where Babs would be waiting with her clippers, and then after their haircut was complete, they would have the option to run through the showers or have a bath. Babs did not mind that she had been given the task of being a hairdresser when the previous stylist retired the year prior, but today would be a struggle for her because her breakfast was not sitting well, and she felt like she had been better off staying home in bed. She pushed through her nausea because it was the second day of Lexi's visit, and she knew the residents would want to look their best. Also, she would hate to put any extra workload on Liz since Liz was busy with the logistics of the closing of Fountain Garden. On "Hair Day," names were drawn out of her straw garden sun hat so that it was always random who would go first and who would have to wait.

How hard could it be, Babs had thought, when asked to fill in as the stylist. She found out the hard way, having taken a huge chunk out of the side of Ronnie's head the first time she had tried it. It had been a summer day, and she had decided to cut hair out on the patio, thinking that the wind would save her from having to sweep up the hair. She felt awful and embarrassed when everyone saw the bright red body fluid as it fell freely from Ronnie's head, staining the wood below his chair. To this day there was still evidence out on the deck of a haircut gone bad. Then after the incident, Babs felt bad and annoyed with herself for not being more aware that Ronnie was restless and did not fully understand the importance of the words, "Hold still!" He had managed to obey for the majority of the haircut but became restless and quickly turned his head just as the old clippers went in for a final cut. That very same day, Babs set out to buy a good set of new clippers that had the protective blade covers so that a mishap like that would never happen again.

"Are you girls going to be okay here?" Lexi stood at the garden doors of Fountain Garden with Malia and Rayna. She thought she should say hello quickly to her parents and Holly before venturing off to have some alone time. She needed time to think about how she would approach certain conversations. The "hello" would be fast, Lexi thought, so that no one would ask her if she wanted to help as well.

She peeked into the eating room. It looked like a spa for seniors the way everyone was sitting, seemingly waiting for breakfast in their robes—all except one lady. Lexi was a little surprised at how rough everyone looked and chuckled at the funny spectacle. Grabbing Malia's arm, Lexi said, "I don't see Mom in here yet, so just give her a big kiss for me and tell her I will be back later." She glanced around the room, feeling slightly anxious about how she should tackle the day. Once again, feeling like she didn't belong.

"Good morning, dad! Morning, everyone!" Lexi said, waving. "I will be back later; I just have a couple of things to do."

"Morning String-Bean!" Oscar said.

"Morning honey!" Holly said, and then she glanced over at Oscar while attempting to pat her hair down. *Say something to your daughter!* she thought. It was awkward for some reason, and Oscar wanted to say more, but he didn't.

Lexi whispered to Malia, "Good luck here and make sure you and Rayna find some food to eat. I will pick up stuff for later. I am going to go call your dad."

Malia knew what that meant. They would probably end up fighting. She didn't want to think about it. "Yes, Mom, *go.* We're good here. I'll see you later," Malia said, waving her off. "Go do *whatever*, Mom."

Lexi left. Oscar was annoyed with himself for being shy with his own daughter. *She'll be back,* he thought.

Ronnie fumbled to get his last button done on his collared shirt. The staff had reminded him numerous times the evening before that he should only wear his robe to breakfast in the morning, and he claimed to understand, but by daylight, his brain fell right back into his regular morning ritual. If he had looked in the mirror, he might have noticed that one side of his shirt didn't match the other because he grabbed one button from one side and then a random hole from the other side, paying no mind if they matched or not. Pleased with himself, he left his room and made a quick left toward the entrance to see if Babs had left a plate of peanut butter cookies on the office table, but to his disappointment, there were none.

Babs and Liz had strategically put Ronnie in the room directly across the hall so that on night shift, the nurses could sit in their meeting room and catch Ronnie if he wandered out of his room.

They would then attempt to intercept his mission to go pace the halls and wake everyone up.

Ronnie had woken up hungry, and all he could think about at that moment was food. After inspecting Babs' desk to find nothing, he turned back to make his way down the hall to the breakfast room. He noticed when passing the staff room that the door was slightly ajar. This door usually remained shut, so this bewildered him. Papers for scheduling, care plans, and an empty binder for the new arrival sat on the table along with a black carafe of still piping hot dark roast espresso coffee that Gunther had snuck in and dropped off for Babs a short time earlier. Today's early shift required something a little stronger to motivate Babs, and Gunther had taken the opportunity to come to her rescue.

The shiny container sparked Ronnie's interest, so he approached and peeked in to see if Liz was hiding behind the door. He knew Liz would *not* be pleased to see him enter the staff area because she constantly told him that this particular room was off limits. To Ronnie's delight, she was nowhere to be found. He entered, picked up five caramel candies that were laying on the empty binder and dropped them in his shirt chest pocket. Grabbing the still piping hot canteen of Babs' strong brew, he walked out.

The sun beamed through the large windows of the breakfast room. Liz had stopped dealing with her medicine blister packs for a moment and was trying to pull the blind down that was right next to Anna's medical recliner chair so that the blinding sun would be out of Anna's face. She noticed some dark, ominous clouds far off in the distance. “Something's brewing!” Liz said loudly.

Holly was preoccupied at another table, struggling to get a sugar packet out of the plastic, jam-packed sugar holder for her coffee that had not arrived yet. Mary H., the new resident, was across from

Holly, staring intently at a crossword puzzle. She wasn't filling in the answers with a pen because she didn't have one and didn't want to bother anyone by asking. She just read the questions and answered them in her head. Edward was alone at his table, staring intently at the newcomer. He stared at Mary as the constant bump, bump, bump of his hard slipper hit the floor. His right foot had made its way between the footrests of his wheelchair and was going rogue. Oscar was reading his newspaper and didn't even look up when Ronnie walked in holding the carafe of espresso coffee that he had stolen from the nurse's office.

"I like your robe, Oscar!" Ronnie said, looking at him with eyebrows held high.

Oscar pulled the robe over his chest and tugged on the belt, hating that Ronnie had brought attention to his attire. He had felt a little self-conscious this morning, having to sit at the table in his shower robe with his granddaughter and a newcomer in the room. Still, he was appreciative that Gunther had just bought him a brand-new navy-blue kimono robe to replace his old, thin, haggard, white one. At least this one felt a little dressy and was made with more expensive plush material.

Ginger and Babs were behind the counter, busy preparing breakfast, while Malia and Rayna watched. Liz looked up from her cart after writing something on a piece of paper. "Now that everyone is here, can everyone listen up for a second? I want to introduce all of you to Mary," Liz said. "She joined us late last evening and we are excited to have her here at Fountain Garden. Unfortunately, she is just passing through and will be leaving us tomorrow or the next day already, depending on when her family is ready to pick her up."

"Well, aren't we *all* going to be *kicked out* by then anyway . . ." Oscar was confused by her introduction.

Liz ignored him, "She is from the other side of the island, and her entire home is being repainted this weekend, so we get the pleasure of her visit until her place is ready for her again. We are delighted to provide a temporary home for you, Mary. So . . ." she said, looking at the quiet, pleasant lady, "welcome Mary!" She spoke in her professional voice with the kind heart that she was. "I would also like to say thank you to Oscar's granddaughter, Malia and her friend Rayna for giving us an extra hand this morning because we are short-staffed, and it is hair day." Liz directed her attention toward the newcomer again. "We hope you are comfortable here, Mary, and we will all do our best to entertain you for the couple of days you are here."

Oscar grumbled, "Well, if it's *entertainment* you are looking for, you came to the *wrong* place! Our standards are pretty low around here!" He knew the other side of the island had many large estates and found it amusing that she ended up in a place such as this.

"That's too bad you have to rough it *here* while your place gets reno'd," Oscar said to Mary.

"Actually, it worked out perfect," Mary said. "The motel is full for the long weekend and *here* I don't have to worry about meals," she said in a perky, positive tone. "Plus, the old motel doesn't really accommodate my wheelchair very well. I feel quite thankful and blessed you had a spare room."

Liz saw Oscar planning his next comment and cut him off before he said anything negative. "SO, let's *all* make Mary feel welcome today and," she said, leaning down toward the woman, "if you need *anything at all*, please ask any one of us."

Mary was looking at Oscar. *I will ask everyone but you!* she thought. She did not feel the need to familiarize herself with *this* stranger anytime soon. *He has a weird vibe about him.*

"Welcome, Mary!" Babs said from over the counter.

"Yes, we are happy to have you!" Ginger added.

Holly smiled at the little woman across the table. She had a blend of dark and light hair and warm eyes. *Too bad you couldn't have come earlier,* Holly thought. *I bet we could have been friends.*

"I'm Ronnie!" Ronnie yelled from sitting at his table with Oscar, "and this is Oscar!"

Oscar shook his head and shot Ronnie a rude look.

Mary smiled hesitantly and then looked back toward the strong-looking man with the chiseled jawline sitting at the table behind her. He sat tall and upright like a robot in his wheelchair with hands resting perfectly flat on the table.

"Weapons Sergeant Edward J. Oshanyk, Special Forces. Nice to meet you, ma'am," he said.

Everyone in the room perked up and then looked at each other for confirmation. Liz tapped Mary on the shoulder and very slowly nodded her head "no" to cue her to be leery of accepting everything as factual—and then everyone went about their business of breakfast. Liz continued to explain to Mary that the residents did not normally wear pyjamas and robes to the dining room. They both chucked, becoming fast friends. "I was wondering about that," Mary admitted, "I felt a little over-dressed here this morning."

Babs opened a conversation with Malia. "So, this is a big day, Malia! Have you ever volunteered at a residential care home before?" she asked. With her painted blue and mauve eyes peeking over her glasses, she filled a canteen with the resident's decaf coffee.

"No, it's my first time," Malia said, grabbing a box full of assorted little marmalades and peanut butter.

"And *you,* Rayna?" Babs said, handing her a plate of creamers to distribute to the tables, "Have you ever done work like *this* before?"

"Nope," Rayna muttered, walking away and placing the plate on one of the tables. She propped herself down by Edward on the seat of a walker she found against the wall and was rolling herself back and forth. *Probably the last time I ever will too,* she thought. "Mmm, coffee," she said, looking at the carafe in Bab's hand. "Could I have a cup of that?"

"You can," Babs said, "but it's decaf, just so you know." Our residents *do not* need any extra help in the bathroom department. This diet helps with that." Babs lifted the pureed prunes that Ginger had been scooping onto everyone's porridge.

"You still want some?" Babs asked Rayna, holding up the silver carafe.

"No thanks; no point in drinking that," Rayna said.

Rayna's voice caught Edward's attention from adjusting and re-adjusting his utensils, so the ends lined up precisely like soldiers on his placemat. He looked dead serious at Rayna, making her think that he was going to say something about her sitting right next to him. "I'll have a cheeseburger with *extra* ketchup, *and* fries, *and* a pop. Hurry up!"

Rayna looked back at Babs, laughing, "Do we have that?"

Babs peered over her glasses. "No, we do *not,* Edward," she said, fluffing him off.

"You girls probably don't realize that this place looked very different five years ago," Liz said, trying to spark a conversation.

Ginger walked around handing out porridge. "Ya, it used to be a full-fledged nursing home . . . until it wasn't!" she said.

"That's right! It's way *better* now," Liz said, smiling big, "thanks to Babs!"

Rayna and Malia were intrigued.

"Well, I made a few adjustments," Babs said bashfully, looking at Malia and Rayna.

"More than a few, Babs," Ginger said. "It went from being a typical, boring looking nursing home to a cozy looking care home thanks to the new decor, all the pictures on the doors and letting everyone bring in their own personal belongings from their homes like rockers, lamps, dressers, drapery, or whatever."

"Yes," Liz added, seeing that Malia and Rayna were staying interested in the conversation. "Babs is also the one that puts everyone's names on the resident's personal towels and robes. She is the one that suggested the music boxes in each room and the fresh flower vases and . . . we should give Ginger credit too . . . for replacing them when they die . . . the *FLOWERS* I mean! When the *FLOWERS* die!" Liz said panicky.

Everyone laughed.

"Yup," Babs said, as she lined up juice cups on a tray, "and then some big wig swooped in and thought he could buy it and make a quick buck by keeping it barely going. It's like he thought there would be no work in running a care home! He really let us down. The other side of the building is literally falling apart! I think he realized in a hurry that these places don't run by themselves."

"Yes, this place needs serious renovation on the north side of the building," Liz said. "Unfortunately, the owner has no interest in doing that and cannot see anyone else wanting to take over a care home that needs fixing either, so . . . the only option in his mind is to move us out and sell to get the most out of the land." Liz looked down at the documents on her med cart. "It's sad, but that has happened to many properties and businesses on this small island in the last few years."

The mood got quiet. Mary scanned the room, looking at all the sad, serious faces.

Ginger could not hold her emotions in, "So, what you are saying is that we are all *SCREWED,*" she mumbled.

"Ginger!" Liz looked up, shaking her head. Her heart sank seeing everyone's reaction. "It *is* unfortunate, *but* everyone is going to be fine! I will make sure of that."

"I wish *I* had a million dollars laying around," Ginger said.

"Don't we all, Ginger!" Liz agreed.

Ginger continued with her thoughts, "I would renovate the building, put a wheelchair-accessible, saltwater pool and cabana next to the gardens, and install an outdoor pizza oven!"

"Yup. That would be nice," Oscar blubbered. "Why not add a tennis or pickle-ball court and put a pool table under the gazebo while you are at it."

Malia pulled her chair up close to her grandma, who was in and out of napping.

Babs felt the urgency to divert the subject fast, "Well," she said, holding both hands over her stressed, grumbling belly, "that's enough of *that* talk." Looking out the dining window, she said, "if the weather does what it says it's going to do today, we will be glad we have an extra set of hands around here. All that patio furniture will have to be dealt with so it doesn't blow away, and the hanging flowers should be brought inside. We'll all have to keep an eye on that wind, and if it starts to pick up, we need to be ready to move fast."

Ginger, back in the kitchen area, nodded in agreement with Babs. "Malia, you can do a round of coffee, and we will finish up these toasts and bring them out," she said.

"Okay," Malia said. She scanned the room and saw Ronnie stand up at his table. He was struggling to hold a heavy black coffee carafe in his hand. She got up from sitting by her grandma and swiftly went over to him.

"Hi!" Ronnie blurted out loudly to Malia when she approached.

"Can I help you with that?" She asked, reaching for his cup. "Do you want to sit back down and let me pour this for you?"

"Sure. Uh, huh. You can do it," Ronnie said.

Oscar reached in front of his newspaper and pushed his cup further onto the table, motioning that he wanted some coffee too. "Thanks, kiddo. You have anything stronger than cream and sugar to put in here?" he winked.

"No, grandpa," she said, giggling.

Oscar watched while Malia poured and stirred in his cream and sugar. He couldn't believe she was finally right here in front of him. He was glad he chose to use his wheelchair today—he planned to keep up with the girl's young energy and had felt slow using his walker the day before.

Malia made her way around the room, pouring everyone a hot morning cup of coffee and stopped to help Holly's shaky little hands to add one packet of sugar.

Liz opened the lid to her large to-go cup, "I'll have some too; thanks, Malia."

"How long are you gals sticking around for?" Babs asked.

"Four days, Ray?" Malia looked over at Rayna, who had finally decided to help and was pouring juice into the plastic cups. "Or three maybe; you'd have to ask my mom."

"That's a nice holiday, but I meant today. How long will you be volunteering with us today?" Babs asked.

Ginger, with a pouty lip, said, "I can't remember the last time I was on a holiday." She walked by and picked up the napkins that Ronnie had dropped to the floor.

"Me either! No holiday for *me*!" Ronnie joined in.

"Ronnie, you have been on a mental holiday since I've met you," Oscar chirped while sipping his strong coffee.

Ginger commented, "I'm always working, and it's just too expensive to leave the island. T. and I find things to do that are free."

"You know what is *also* free?" Liz glared at Oscar and plopped his pain pills in front of him. "Kindness!"

Malia reached down to grab the cup from her grandma's feeding table. Before she could lift the cup, Anna reached over and grasped her arm. Happy that her grandma was alert enough to see her helping, Malia put the carafe down on the side table, leaned over her grandmother's chair, and embraced her in a tight hug. "Morning, Grams!" she said softly in her ear. "I am glad I am here with you today."

Babs and Ginger walked back and forth from the kitchen to the dining tables to deliver everyone's breakfast. Malia was assisting Anna with a tiny spoonful of her porridge while munching on a piece of toast herself. Holly was sitting with the quiet, elegant-looking newcomer, Mary, and was eating her toast turtle slow while looking out the window. Rayna joined Holly and Mary at their table to make it look like she was keeping them company but was ignoring everything and everyone while she played on her phone.

The familiar old, blue half-ton truck drove up the driveway and pulled right up to the entrance doors.

"Gunther's here for *recycling,*" Liz teased, knowing full well he would use any excuse to come to Fountain Garden to see Babs.

"Not just for the recycling," Ginger whispered to Liz as she stepped up to the window beside her.

Babs dropped one of the toast plates abruptly in front of Rayna, "Hand this out please, the rest are in the kitchen."

"Uhm, okay . . ." Rayna said, annoyed she was being asked to work.

Babs sprinted out of the room. They all looked at each other and laughed. When Babs was out of sight, Rayna and Malia joined Liz and Ginger at the window, smashing their faces up against the pane. Oscar tried to lean forward in his chair to see his old friend.

Holly's curiosity got the best of her, "What do you see, Oscar? I can't see that far."

"I see a wrinkly old-timer that's about to get eaten alive by one of the Golden Girls."

Liz shot him a dirty look.

Gunther jumped out of his truck and put on his dirty gloves. He walked to the entrance doors of Fountain Garden, where Babs was standing and holding the door open for him.

Malia gushed, "Aww, that's so sweet, hey Ray? Babs is crushing!"

"Is she into that old fart?" Rayna questioned Liz and Ginger.

Ginger said sarcastically, "Well, she didn't plaster her face in rainbow colors to impress *you two* today."

Babs' and Gunther disappeared into the building and then reappeared.

"Aww, she's holding the door for him *again*!" Malia said in a mushy tone.

Liz chuckled, "Oh, brother!"

Gunther came out of the building, carrying two blue recycling boxes stacked on top of each other. He and Babs walked side by side to the back of the truck, where he had purposely left the tailgate closed. Babs, like routine, struggled to open the rusty, old gate, but finally she managed, showing him that she was still a very capable woman. Gunther held the recycle box high and strong while waiting, to show her that he was still a brawny, strapping man. He pushed the boxes deep into the back of the truck and slammed it shut. Babs leaned against the side of the truck and pulled out her cigarettes from her uniform pocket. He leaned up beside her and reached out to take one.

"Aww," Malia said.

Holly and Mary were antsy in their seats, trying to see better out the window.

Ginger added, "OMG! Those two are totally adorable!"

Liz twisted her head toward Ginger, "*So sappy* you two!"

"Dude, she's got the *feels hard,* yo!" Rayna said to Malia.

They all stood staring quietly for a second. Liz reminisced about how long she had worked with Babs. She wanted her to be happy. "Yes, Babs *might* be a smitten kitten," she said.

"Or maybe it's purely *sexual*!" Rayna said.

Holly and Mary's eyes grew big. Oscar burst out in laughter.

"You think they actually *fool* around?" Ginger asked Liz.

"*Ahem*!" Liz cleared her throat, ready to defend her refined friend.

Ginger added, "He *does* still look viable."

Oscar joked, "I think Babs' clock stopped ticking a long time ago."

"OK *enough*!" Liz piped up when she turned and saw the expression on Mary's face. "So much for good first impressions here at Fountain Garden, hey Mary!"

"That's OK . . . who am *I* to judge?" Mary replied.

"Let's get everyone fed now, girls." Liz herded the young help back to work.

Edward approached Liz and reached up to grab a medicine cup from her hand. He asked if he and his pals could play bingo after breakfast. Liz told him she thought that was an excellent idea for an activity, especially having the help of Malia and Rayna there. It would be something fun for the residents to do, especially since it was Mary's first day at Fountain Garden. She sent Ginger to the TV room to grab the game.

Edward swiftly followed Ginger out of the room and passed her in the hall. "Hup! Need a *toilet!* He said in an urgent tone.

Ronnie was alternating his toast with his caramel candy and, with a full mouth, was trying to gulp his coffee. He left a trail of toast crumbs all over his table area. One piece of toast had fallen and was jam-side down by the leg of the table. It would, without a doubt, be stepped on later.

Oscar was irritated, "Ronnie, do you have to eat *so* loud? You know you're not going to shit for a week after all that candy."

"Hmm?" Ronnie kept chomping.

"You *are* a head-scratcher, I'll give you that, buddy," Oscar mocked.

The newspaper kept Oscar occupied so he wouldn't have to stare at the disgusting mess across his table. Liz had poured herself another giant to-go cup of coffee and creamer and sipped on it while she delivered medications to each resident. She was usually quiet and concentrated when giving out medications but was feeling more awake and gabbier this morning. Like happy, clucking hens in a pen, she conversed back and forth with all the women. The room was louder than usual.

Holly commented, "I heard on my radio this morning that the high winds will bring some rain as well."

After finishing his meal, Oscar threw back his pain pills into his mouth and tucked his newspaper under his arm. Bravely balancing his almost empty coffee on his lap, he rolled his wheelchair over to the women at the next table and parked beside Holly.

Mary, sitting concerned with the intrusion of the new stranger, stared at him questioningly. Rayna was feverishly texting on her phone, ignoring everyone. When Babs re-entered the room, there was a moment of awkward silence.

"*So*, how's Gunther today?" Liz asked.

Babs gave a shoulder shrug, dismissing Liz's question and walked into the kitchen without pause. "He's fine, I guess," she said, face blushing.

Oscar felt talkative. "It says that the storm might produce wind gusts of up to fifty miles per hour," he said to Holly. Looking over at Babs, he continued, "I know there's twine in the shed by the fountain if you want me to tie any of the vines or shrubs down. The girls could help me too."

Malia thought he must be feeling quite well today to want to get out of his wheelchair and help.

Even Liz was surprised at everyone's morning energy. She wondered if the arrival of Lexi and the girls had contributed to the liveliness in the air.

Babs, thinking about the flowers that she wanted to save from the pending storm and the ugly storm that was brewing in her stomach as well, walked over and grabbed the black canteen off the table while everyone was finishing breakfast. She shook it to see what was left. "Anyone want one last cup before we clean up?" She made her way around the room once more to fill everyone's cup, and Rayna got off her butt to help with the cream and sugars.

Oscar looked back at his table, where Ronnie sat alone. He watched as Babs approached Ronnie to top up his coffee. Ronnie grabbed the bottom of his shirt and lifted it up to his lips to use it as a napkin. He pressed the cotton material tight against his mouth and held it there as he turned and looked at Oscar with concern written all over his eyebrows.

"Uh-oh! I'd watch out Babs!" Oscar yelled across the room.

"What?" she said, standing by Ronnie's table, looking at Oscar and then back at Ronnie.

Ronnie's eyes grew large as saucers as the warm bile lurked its way up his esophagus and filled his mouth. His stomach churned again, sending him into a panic. In a moment of pure chaos, Ronnie screeched his chair back violently from his table, drawing everyone's attention. Watery, orangey vomit projectiled onto the floor and Babs, who was still standing close by, holding the almost empty canteen of espresso coffee.

"Aww *damn* it!" Babs yelled. She quickly grabbed her uniform shirt to get the puke droplets off. Feeling like the half-ingested food had sprayed onto her lip, she rubbed it off, smearing her red lip gloss over her cheek, making herself look like a half-made-up clown. Taking one step backward, her foot landed smack dab on the toast that was already lying there, and she slipped hard and fast to her bottom. With a bang, her wide butt hit the floor. The canteen flew out of her hands, smashed against the ground as her glasses flew off her face and landed under Oscar's wheelchair. Ronnie rushed to aid and tried to set his dirty, marmalade toast and candy puke-covered hand on the top of Bab's hair-sprayed mound, to indicate he was concerned that she was okay. Babs slapped his arm away angrily. Oscar convulsed into laughter and Holly spit her coffee all over her porridge bowl. Mary tried to politely hide her laughter behind her hand not wanting to offend anyone.

"*Oh, my GOD,* Babs! Are you *alright*?" Liz asked as she ran out from behind her med cart.

Babs growled back with a furrowed brow. Through her blurred, strained eyes, she could see Liz was clearly holding back a laugh as well.

"Ronnie are *you* alright?" Liz asked.

"Yup," Ronnie said, wiping his mouth with his shirt, "I feel better now." He sat back down in his chair.

Rayna was standing, not knowing what to do, "Mal!" She mouthed the words, "This shit is *funny*!"

"My *glasses*! I need my glasses!" Babs cried out.

Malia turned red, trying to hold her laugh in. She felt the urge to help in some way.

Ginger re-entered the room, not realizing the madness that she was walking into, "Hey guys! I have the Bingo for after—"

CRACK.

Malia had jumped up from her chair to help Babs and ran right smack into Ginger. The colored bingo balls leaped up and out of the plastic mesh basket upon impact and scattered as far as they could possibly roll on the dining room floor. Ginger dropped to her knees to try to retrieve them. Malia and Rayna scurried around on the floor in stitches and rallied with Ginger to collect the rogue, escaping balls.

Liz bent down to retrieve Babs' glasses from under the wheelchair, and when she came up, she knocked heads with Oscar, who had been bending over trying to find the glasses himself. The room got ridiculously loud. Anna's tired eyes swayed back and forth like a curious owl, distracted by the noisy commotion.

Teddy walked into the dining room holding a giant pile of freshly washed terry cloths. He stopped dead in his tracks, taking in the pandemonium.

From crouched down on her knees on the hard floor, Malia looked up at Teddy, surprised. "You work *here* too?" Malia asked.

Ten minutes later, the madness died down when Malia, Rayna, and Ginger finally finished gathering all the bingo balls.

"OMG, that was a lot!" Liz said, gathering herself and rubbing the top of her head to see if there was a bump. "I can still feel my heart pounding."

Holly felt fidgety from her coffee buzz. "So do I! My heart is racing, for heaven's sake!" she chuckled.

Ginger looked at Rayna (who stood feeling queasy and repulsed by the vomit on the floor) and laughed, "How happy are you that you decided to volunteer today?" she said, handing her gloves so she could help pick up the toast and remnants of breakfast that were stuck to the linoleum. Liz and Babs assisted the residents in leaving the dining area and then Babs disappeared, feeling like she had earned the right to get out of cleaning. Malia continued to clear and clean the tables and pile all the dirty dishes by the sink. She lifted the silver carafe of decaf coffee to throw it in the sink and was surprised to discover that it was full when it should have been empty. She suddenly realized that Ronnie's container may have been the wrong one to offer everyone and that she may have unknowingly treated the residents and staff with a strong dose of caffeine. She giggled to herself, thinking that it would be a good story to tell her mom later.

26

WHAT IS FAMILY, ANYWAY?

The aide, who had voluntarily joined the morning shift to assist with baths and showers, walked up to Anna in the hall after cleaning the tub and mopping the floor in the washroom. She bent down in front of Anna, who was lying in her recliner looking calm and refreshed. With her cell phone sandwiched between her ear and shoulder, she began tying Anna's hard-soled shoes. Anna woke from her medication-induced, post-bath snooze and caught part of the conversation.

The aide ranted, "Listen, I am not supposed to be talking on the phone at work, so what are we going to do? Go back and apologize for being late again. We have bills to pay! I'm only going to be here for a few hours. Stop complaining! You don't hear *me* complaining! You need to hang on to that job whether you like it or not!" The aide was quiet for a second while she tugged on Anna's lace. "I *had* to come to work today!" she shouted into her phone. "It's hair and bath day. I wasn't going to leave Liz empty-handed with everything that is going on. I will be home in three hours, and then

I can watch the kids, and you can go back to the shipping yard and beg for forgiveness!"

Anna knew in her mind that she should feel a certain type of appreciation about receiving help from this woman, but all she felt was annoyance. The aide, in Anna's opinion, was unable to see how lucky she was to be walking (or running rather) in these halls, chomping on her gum, and able to use her body as she wished. *Is THIS my family now?* Anna's body started to become tense and sore. *Are these people in these halls the people that I will have to spend the remainder of my life with? Family does change over time.*

The aide in front of her now was such a busybody and her communication style was drastically different than Liz's. *I bet you've always been a terrible listener,* Anna thought.

"Okay, mamma. These shoes are perfect for you for today," she said as she finished the last lace and slammed Anna's feet into place on her wheelchair recliner's footrests.

I am not your fucking mamma, and I don't want to wear shoes. I hate them! Anna screamed in her head. She wanted to kick the aide in the face. Since the stroke, she had found herself feeling more aggressive in her thoughts and towards people and appreciated the medication that was strong enough to break passage into the dark basement of her mind.

The aide walked away and left Anna alone to her thoughts. While waiting to catch a glimpse of her granddaughter again, Anna rested and felt appreciative that at least Liz could tell from the look on her face what she was thinking and feeling. Conversations and expressions were her biggest struggle now. She hated that everyone looked at her with pity when they saw that her body wasn't the same, but the fact that she couldn't speak like she used to—bothered her the most. Frustration led her to feel closed off from everyone, even Holly and Oscar. Visiting felt one-sided. Before her stroke, she and Holly would cut each other off in endless gab. Now, Anna found herself spacing at the clock on the wall or some other insignificant item when people talked to her. *Okay, it's been long enough, I gave this effort, now get out of my face*, she would think, more often than not. Her new condition depressed her.

Anna knew it was rude to just close her eyes in the middle of a conversation, but it was the *only* control she had now. When visitors carried on and on about the weather and other stuff that she did not care about, she would simply shut her eyes, hinting that they should stop yammering on and go away. She would rather sit in silence with someone than hear about the wind yet again or have to listen to their *hogwash* complaints about trivial things.

Everything became so difficult after her stroke. Anna remembered her heartbreak the first time Lexi had called after she had arrived at Fountain Garden. Liz helped Anna hold the phone in Anna's good hand up to her ear. The conversation left Anna sad and defeated. *Why did it have to be such a struggle? Lexi probably got off the phone and felt the same way*, she had thought. She knew Lexi was trying to connect with her, but it wasn't the same. As for Brock, the conversation would have felt too forced, so it was best he didn't even try.

After Liz hung up the phone, she looked at Anna and asked, "How was that?"

Anna saddened a half-smile and rolled her watery eyes. She felt blessed that Liz could recognize the fear and frustration. Liz had said to her softly, "You are safe. It is going to take some time, Anna . . . but I am here for you. We all are." Her words had calmed her in the moment.

Anna knew she was lucky to be back on the island, and it gave her enormous relief to live near Holly and Oscar, but it was different now. In the past, she felt safe with Oscar, and she could rely on Holly for anything. Now, Liz would be providing care and safety for her. This new relationship between Anna and her caregivers had grown fast and strong.

So, at this stage of the game, what makes a family, family? Anna felt guilty thinking that way. Instead, she said to herself, while accepting the soft touch of Liz's hand, *you are my people now. I appreciate you. I can't verbally tell you that, and it kills me, but I hope you know that you make every day a little bearable. You bring a little light into my dark, lonely life and for that I am forever grateful.* Anna knew Liz, being the kind soul she was, probably treated everyone the same way because she was that type of person, and that's what made her such an amazing nurse.

Anna's mind shifted drowsily back to thoughts of Lexi. *Where are you, my sweet daughter?* she thought, as her body relaxed and her heavy eyes closed again, falling into a deep sleep.

27

THE EVERYTHING ROOM

"Okay, here we go," Babs said, as she emerged from around the corner into the TV common area, having washed the mess of colorful gloss off her face. She pulled the first name from the hat. "Oscar, you're up first for haircuts."

"Whoop-de-doo," he said.

Babs was happy because he was the easiest with a quick buzz, and he could always stifle an interesting conversation with her. He agreed cautiously, noticing she appeared a little cranky.

Oscar rolled up to the door of the "Everything Room" where Babs had hung a stringed, plain homemade sign that said, "We are open!" He entered the room. Pattern quilts hung from the walls. Counters were cluttered with faux silk flowers, baby's breath, and greenery. Spools of thread were strewn across the ledge of the window, and small cans of colorful paint were stacked on a countertop. The floor was cluttered with cardboard boxes that held tubes of wrapping paper. Paint brushes that had been drying out for days lay out on paper towels beside the sink, and little vases (painted with creative attempts at artwork) were lined up on an old vintage table. A box high up on a shelf read, "Flea Market stuff."

He rolled into place in front of the long, arched, antique brass mirror. Babs tossed a cape over his body to protect him from the hair she would be razoring off and started dowsing him with the spray bottle. Water ran down the front of his face into his eyes. "Easy Babs," he said. "I know you enjoy this part!"

"I *do,* actually," she agreed in her monotonous voice.

"So . . . why you gotta be such an ass, Oscar?" she said, forcing a quick conversation as her stomach rolled over, giving her a wave of nausea.

He looked up at her in surprise, wondering if she was serious or being playful. "Jeez Louise! You okay, Babs?"

"Fine, I just have a weird stomach today," she explained. "You need to talk to that girl, Oscar. Lexi is only here a couple of days, and you are going to *regret* not making things right. I've heard you on the phone with her. You are *mean sometimes*. She can't help that she doesn't live here."

"Can't she?" he asked.

"You are being a *baby*," Babs continued. "Be happy for her. She's really made something out of her life going from a helper in a hardware store to an executive assistant with a huge development company." She placed one hand on her waving belly. "Get real with her and find out what's upsetting her. Maybe you should talk to her other half and fix what happened at Christmas."

"I don't hear any fat ladies singing," he joked.

"Yup," Babs shook her head. "You keep making jokes, Oscar Davies! You go ahead and stuff those feelings down, and don't be surprised if she visits you less and less—wherever you end up."

Wow! That was deep! he thought to himself, looking back at her in the mirror. Oscar liked Babs and appreciated her wisdom, "I'll tell you what Babs," he said, "you invite Gunther here for me tonight and I *will* talk to Lexi. I might even apologize for some of the things I said to Brock the last time they were here . . . maybe."

"I am *too old* for your baloney, Oscar. Don't mess with me!" she said, waving her clippers at him. "I will win. What's your play here?" she asked, looking at him questioningly.

"Just get Gunther here for me. I need a chatty chat with my buddy."

"Alright, but if I don't see some positive development between you and Lexi you are going to have to answer to *me*," Babs said, feeling the saliva in her mouth get warm and leaving a horrible taste in her mouth. She contemplated calling it quits and going home.

Ginger approached the door with Ronnie, who was rambling on about a puzzle and parked him in a wheelchair just outside the door in the hall.

"Are we going potty?" he asked, looking around.

She leaned down, slammed his brake into park and said in a manipulative voice, "Just stay here Ronnie and wait your turn. You are going to be *one sexy* dude when Babs is done with you!" He raised his eyebrows at her. She walked off in a hurry. "I have work to do now," she said over her shoulder.

"But, *why* am I in a wheelchair?" he yelled, looking down and around, super confused.

"Because I don't want you to walk around and miss your turn, Ronnie," she yelled. "Just stay put, you handsome little devil!"

Ginger's words did not make him feel any less confused.

Oscar took one final look in the mirror, "Good work Babs! Thank you, madame!"

"Don't forget Oscar," Babs said, pointing her finger at him.

He left the room, glanced over his shoulder, and saw Babs rubbing her belly with one hand as she reached in the closet for her broom and dustpan with the other. Passing through the door of the makeshift salon, Oscar reached to the left and flipped the sign that said, "We are Open!" to say, "Sorry we are closed." He motioned Ronnie to read it. Ronnie stared at the paper for a length of time.

Then, he unlocked his brake, and with a swift turn, bolted back to the TV room to solve the puzzle mystery.

Babs swept up the floor, filled her spray bottle to the top, and walked to the door to retrieve Ronnie, but he was gone. Everything was becoming incredibly irritating to her today. She particularly did *not* feel like herself. *"Oh, for Pete's sake!* Ginger!" she yelled down the hall. "Can you *please* bring Ronnie to the hair salon?"

Cutting everyone's hair was time-consuming and could take a better part of Babs' morning and at this point, she was not sure she would last. Oscar sat in the hall just out of sight from Babs with a big smile on his face. He knew that Ginger would probably be busy in the washroom assisting Edward. He smiled mischievously, knowing he had successfully screwed with everyone's day. He knew he should be nicer, with the closing of Fountain Garden nearing, but gave himself permission to be himself one more day and then maybe he would put in an effort to be good. *After all, no one else is going to amuse me,* he thought.

He looked down both halls to see which direction Ronnie would be coming from. In the distance, he saw Rayna walking past Mary in her wheelchair. The precocious teen wouldn't even have noticed the older woman because she was busy texting on her phone, but Mary extended her freckled little arm to stop her.

"You need something, Mary?" Rayna asked. *Please say no. Please say no. You are asking the WRONG girl!*

Mary grabbed Rayna's arm and pulled, forcing the teenager to lean in. Mary reached for the neckline of Rayna's deep V-neck T-shirt, and with the gentle tiny fingers of both her elderly hands, she pulled the shirt up higher to cover Rayna's young, perky boobs. "There! That's better, miss," Mary said.

Rayna, caught off guard, placed both her hands over her chest, suddenly feeling exposed and embarrassed by her wardrobe. Mary slid her hands out from under Rayna's and rolled away, almost running the teen over.

28

STRANGE ENCOUNTER

Mary grabbed a large-brimmed hat from a chair beside the garden door and went exploring outside. She didn't want anyone getting a hold of *her* hair. Wheeling down the path, she found the fountain, and parked beside the swing. She had been told that the structure's old, majestic beauty drew the residents to visit it every day. Now, seeing it for herself, she understood why everyone loved it. The impressive rock glistened, and the splashing droplets and clouding mist floated through the surrounding air making the sitting area feel like a spa when anywhere near it.

Those pennies deep at the bottom must be from years of wishes, I would imagine, she thought. *I bet this beauty has heard people's deepest thoughts and desires and, at times, excruciating prayers of hope.* Mary imagined family and friends sitting on the ledge and crying into the water in times of despair.

Lexi walked up to the rickety gate, having emerged through the trees. She opened it quietly so she wouldn't disturb Mary, sitting deep in thought. Mary looked up high at her to see from under her sun hat. "It's quite beautiful, isn't it?" she said to Lexi, pointing to the fountain.

"It's extraordinary; it really is." Lexi sat down on the wooden swing.

"So, tell me about this place. Lexi, right?" Mary asked.

"Yup, that's me." She inhaled deeply and then exhaled, exhausted. "I was raised here. My house was right through those trees actually," she said, staring into the loud, rushing water and getting swept away in her thoughts. "Where there is a *campground* now. I grew up playing in the sand by the ocean." She continued to get absorbed by the Zen sound of the bubbling water. "I watched my parents live an amazing life here," Lexi said and then paused, ". . . and I watched them struggle a little here too." She spaced into seriousness while Mary sat quietly. ". . . and then I met my husband here, and now I am here to admit to everyone that I am getting a divorce, sadly." Her mind came back to the present. She looked at Mary directly and smiled flatly.

Mary remained quiet and attentive.

Lexi teared up, thinking about the reality of her mom's health. "And my mom—she seems so tired. I worry that . . ." her voice trailed off. The two women stared at the water bouncing off the glimmering stone.

Mary broke the silence. "It seems that the universe is keeping you connected to this place," she said.

"I could not imagine why," Lexi said, disheartened. "I am *so sorry*! I just realized I do not even know your name and I don't know why I just dumped that information on you like that. You just seem to have this—I'm not sure—I just feel like I can talk to you for some reason. I haven't talked to anyone in a while. Not really, anyway." She shook her head embarrassed at unloading on the poor, elderly woman beside her.

"Do not apologize. *I* asked you," she said sweetly. "And my name is Mary, by the way. This place seems to hold special memories for you, and some complicated ones too. It might be just where you need to be. Give yourself time," Mary said, reaching her tiny, delicate hand to tap Lexi gently on top of her knee. "If you don't mind some advice from an old woman. Let yourself clear the clutter in your mind and feel what's in your heart instead. It won't guide you wrong. If you listen hard enough, it will tell you how to bridge the space between where you are now and where you want to be."

"I know. You are right, Mary. What I need to do, is talk to my dad."

"Your dad?" Mary asked.

"Oscar Davies," Lexi said.

"Oh!" Mary said, suddenly realizing who Lexi was and how she fit into the Fountain Garden scene. "Well, things have a way of working themselves out. Don't you fret about *him*, or anyone *else* for that matter. You do what *you* feel is right, don't ever intentionally hurt anyone in the process, and everything will work out. Don't fret, young lady."

Lexi stood from the swing.

"Are you going inside now?" Mary asked.

"I don't know what I should do," Lexi said, contemplating. "I am sure Malia and Rayna are fine. I should do some thinking before I talk to my parents."

"You should go embrace this beautiful island, Lexi," Mary said, "Let nature assist you in clearing your mind. Release all your cares and worries to these blessed natural surroundings. When you are alone, quiet, and free from distractions, it is easier to manifest strength—and then clarity will flow out of you—just like this masterpiece in front of us."

"I hope you are right," Lexi said, walking toward the gate. "It was so nice to meet you, Mary. I hope we can chat again sometime. This has been nice." Lexi disappeared into the trees feeling slightly uplifted by her chat with the riveting, magnetic woman.

29

TOWN CRUISE

Luke watched Lexi walk the perimeter of the property while talking on her phone. She looked serious and appeared to have long moments of silence. A couple of times, she paused dead in her tracks and reached her hand up to her head in a look of frustration. When she was finished on the phone, she walked up to where Luke was working.

"How goes the battle, beautiful?" he asked, as he climbed down the ladder.

"I fear I am the only one in the fight," she said.

He saw how disheartened and defeated she was from her toxic relationship, "You know what you need to clear that gorgeous head of yours? You need to go for a TC." He walked over to the toolbox, grabbed his truck keys that were laying on top, turned, and threw them at her.

She caught them in her hands, "A . . . TC?" She smiled big.

"Yes. A town cruise. Get out of here, girl!" Luke said.

"Alone?" she said.

"Yes, ma'am. Alone!" he chuckled. "Your soul thrives when you allow it to be alone and without distractions. The island is a great listener if you need to talk."

She was surprised at his deep perspective, "That's funny. I had an interesting interaction with a lady I met this morning who said the same thing, sort of—"

Luke smiled big. "Well, she sounds like a wise woman! Great minds think alike, I guess. If you happen to pop into the market, grab some grub for the fire. I'll stoke it up when I am done here."

"Are you sure, Luke?" She was already walking backward toward his pickup truck, excited to take off.

"Go on." He waved her off and walked away.

This guy had a way of making her feel safe, special, and unusual all at the same time; she thought as she opened the door to jump in. The truck smelled like Luke. Lexi took a deep breath in and tried to savour the manly aroma. Feeling hypersensitive and a little excited in the moment, she tried to hide her smile so she wouldn't look like a lunatic.

Brock would never drive a truck like this, she thought. His sparkling clean Cadillac SUV or his luxurious sports car didn't make her feel tingly down below like the pickup did.

The trip to town was an emotional roller coaster. Lexi's thoughts were split evenly between memories of the past and visions of what her future could look like if she were to move back to Cody Island somehow. She allowed herself to relish in the thought that Cody Island could, again, be *her* town, *her* dirt roads, *her* store, *her* people. She drifted into fantasizing that a man like Luke could be *her* man, and this could be *their* truck, and their life, just for a moment.

All her senses were alert and captured in the similar routine drive she had made as her dad's loyal sidekick on their short daily trek to the hardware store. Before getting her own license, Lexi would spend an hour working with her dad each morning, preparing to open the store. Then she would grab her backpack and walk the two blocks to her high school. After school, she would walk back to the store and help until closing or until her mom picked her up. She loved everything about working at the store. When she was little, customers would ask her where items were, knowing themselves, but they enjoyed her little hand taking them and showing them around. She loved the attention, and the customers loved watching her grow up right under their eyes. As the customers got older, so did she, and they relied on her expertise more and more.

She parked at Hill's Hardware and walked across the street to grab smokies, burgers, and buns from the grocery store, which was appropriately called "The Store." When she was finished, she threw her groceries in Luke's truck and walked up to the familiar glass door of Hill's Hardware and pulled the door open—something that she had done a million times before. She strolled down the aisles, looking at the merchandise. Her memory was playing tricks with her—there seemed to be fewer shelves now, and the pickings were slim. As Lexi walked through the store, she realized that *she* was a stranger now. She did not recognize the young man at the till.

The smell of dust, paints, cardboard, wood, and sawdust mixed in the air. *The shelves are definitely a lot barer now*, she thought. *Even the aisles seemed narrower.*

Lexi reminisced, up and down and around the aisles.

"Can I help you find something?" asked the young man behind the front counter.

"No thank-you, I am good! Just browsing," Lexi said.

A scruffy, haggard man in a plaid shirt came out of the coffee room, coughing, holding a cup and a pack of smokes in his wrinkly hand. "String-Bean? Is that you? I heard you were in town. Gunther told me you were back to see your mama and the old goat."

"Hello, Vic! Yes, I am back," Lexi said.

"I thought you might wander in here," Vic said. "I got something for you." He returned to the coffee room and reappeared holding an old, faded blue coffee mug that said Hill's Hardware on it. The blue cup was chipped on one side showing the white of the ceramic. He let out a cough. "You give this to that old fart when you see him and tell him I'll be around to bug him in the next day or two. I gotta see him before he leaves," he said, handing her the cup. "I can't believe Fountain Garden is closing soon. I am losing *all* my friends. With everyone being moved into Adasa city . . . I don't know if I'll ever see them again."

"Don't say that," Lexi said sympathetically. "You will see your friends again."

"I doubt it! That big crazy city is NOT for me. It's too busy and *loud*. I feel bad for Oscar. I know he struggles with the idea and feels the same way."

"Ya . . . I know." Lexi said.

"First the island had to say good-bye to you and now we all gotta say good-bye to your parents too. It doesn't seem fair." Lexi felt anxiety building in her gut. She was having enough issues processing her own emotions, let alone helping Vic work through his. She walked toward the storefront door and started to push it open, sensing that she could fall apart right there amongst the hardware if she were to continue to talk with her dad's friend.

"You come back now, Lexi. A lot sooner next time," he said.

She left quickly, jumped back into the truck, and threw the cup on the seat beside her, feeling drained after her short visit down memory lane. She drove slowly away from town, absorbing the view of the unique island homes and large immaculate acreages that were picturesque against the forested backdrop. She opened the window to take it all in. An intense gust of wind blew in and crossed over Lexi's cheeks and forehead. She took a giant inhale. The smell of the fresh air and the sensation on her skin from the open window seemed to open a part of her soul as well; a part that had been hidden for too long. A child-like yearning rushed through her—a wish and a need to have her mom sitting in the driver's seat and her in the passenger seat, having a loving and inspirational conversation like they used to. In that instant, a magnitude of uncontrollable sadness overwhelmed her. She pulled off to the side of the road and parked the truck by a cluster of trees on the corner of a plowed field. Lexi surrendered to the unresolved, trapped emotions of anxiety that were festering inside her, allowing them to pour out of her in streams of tears. Mentally exhausted, she leaned her head back on the seat and wailed to the swaying trees.

The wind calmed after a while, and so did she. She sat perfectly still, eyes closed, feeling her body and mind relax into a deep, restful state that led to a peaceful power nap.

An image of two women appeared. They sat close to each other on a beach blanket, watching a toddler frolicking in the sand in front of them. They were completely caught up in each other, laughing, smiling, and finishing each other's sentences. Only a few minutes passed before one touched the other in some sort of way. They were playful and thrilled to be in each other's company.

Time floated forward in her dreamscape.

The young mother sat on a pail in the garden, picking green beans. Another woman sat on the other side of the bountiful green row on another bucket. They were giggling, chatting nonstop, and eating what they picked. A handsome young man watched them while sitting on a deck, smoking. A little girl walked through the wet dirt. She laid her tiny hand on the woman's shoulder to keep balance while she tried to kick the mud off the bottom of her little rubber boot.

Her dreamer's eyes flickered while images shifted again to her younger self.

On the warm beach, the happy little girl with long legs sat on a blanket between her mom's straddled legs. The mom braided her daughter's long, brown, silky hair. Kneeling behind the smiling mother was another woman braiding the mother's hair at the same time. When the mom was finished weaving the girl's, she leaned down and kissed her daughter on the top of her head. When the friend finished braiding the mother's hair, she leaned down and kissed the top of her head. They all giggled playfully. The little girl felt safe.

The sound of a skylark trilling overhead through the open window woke Lexi from her power nap. She lifted her head from the seat, groggy and weighed down still from her dreams. She took a deep breath of fresh air to orientate herself. The wind over her dried-up tears made her skin feel tight. She gathered herself, put the truck into drive, and continued down the dirt road—just her and her memories.

30

MAKEOVER

Rayna had perched herself on a tall stool in the corner of the makeshift salon and was playing on an Etch A Sketch she had found in the TV room. She had never seen the toy before and was completely entertained as she attempted to draw. Ronnie walked passed her looking sharp, "Wow, Ronnie! Very handsome!" she said.

"I *know,* right?" he said, as he walked out of the salon, wound-free and proud as a peacock. He took his hand and flatly brushed his bang area over to the side of his head. She burst out laughing. He walked straight to his room and flopped onto his bed for a late morning nap.

Babs had lost all her energy. Her legs felt weak, and her queasy belly told her that she might need to spend some much-needed time on the throne. She would not last another haircut.

"Did you want me to go get the next person?" Rayna jumped down from her stool.

"Actually, I think I have to quit for the day," Babs admitted. "I am not feeling that great. I'll go lay in Perla's room and let my stomach settle for a bit."

"Aww, that's a bummer! Who was next? Maybe, *I* could do it! I have cut my own hair before. It's not hard." Rayna said confidently.

Babs thought about it and said, "It's Holly; she just needs her bangs trimmed a wee bit. She would have to agree to it, and you would have to be *so extremely* careful, Rayna. We don't need a blood bath on our hands!"

"Come on, Babs!" Rayna pleaded, "I can do it. I'm solid!"

Babs gave a questioning look. "Then, after you cut her bangs, she would like her hair dampened with the spray bottle and put in rollers. It's a big job, actually," she said, still wavering in her mind. "Are you sure you want to tackle this, Rayna? You would have to put that phone and game down for a whole forty-five minutes! Do you think you could handle that?"

"HA, HA, yes, I can. Let me do it, Babs! I'll go get her!"

"Okay, Rayna, if you need *anything,* I am just resting down the hall in the spare room," Babs said.

"I'll be good, don't even worry!" Rayna ran out the door and down the hall like an excited child, peeking into every room as she flew by.

"Rayna, stop running!" Babs yelled. *This is a huge mistake!*

Rayna found Holly in the breakfast room, chatting with Liz while Liz continued to vibrate from the morning caffeine and sugar jolt. "Madame! Are you ready for your appointment? I will be your stylist today. Won't you come with me?" Rayna said in a pretend professional voice.

Liz looked wide, "*You* are the stylist today? I don't think so Missy . . ."

"Babs said I could," Rayna said. "We are just putting rollers in." She omitted the bang-cutting part of the plan. "It's harmless!" she said, reassuring Liz.

"Where is Babs anyway?" Liz asked.

The sharp-tongued girl roared, "She's painting the bowl, I think!"

"Painting what bowl?" Liz asked.

Rayna let Liz continue to wonder and disappeared with Holly down the hall. "Come, my queen. We must beautify!"

Holly's pulse skipped in fearful thrill of being in Rayna's juvenile control.

An hour later, Rayna came back to the dining area with Holly, where everyone was gathering in anticipation of lunch.

Mary looked up, completely stoned-faced.

Oscar had to ask, "Is there something *different* about you today, Holly?"

"Very funny, Oscar!" Holly shot back. Her big bouffant hairdo was startling. Mounds of teased white hair sat high on her head, making her face look smaller than usual. Every hair had been carefully arranged and cemented in place with Babs' aerosol hairspray.

"She's runway-ready," Rayna said, "Who's next?"

Mary lifted her book up to cover her face.

31

THERE'S A STORM BREWING

Using the flat palms of their hands, Oscar, Ronnie and Ed simultaneously banged their dining tables, chanting "Hot dogs! Hot dogs! Hot dogs!"

Liz looked at Babs to see if she agreed that they had lost the battle over what to eat for lunch.

"I don't mind barbecuing for you. I can stay for a bit," Teddy offered, glancing over at Malia.

"I can help!" Malia added.

Rayna nudged her. "Me too!"

Oscar loved the idea of keeping the day outside for as long as possible. "Great idea! Let's get outside and get cooking. I am starving!" he shouted as he started to roll his wheelchair onto to the deck, knowing Ronnie would follow.

"Assemble!" Ed yelled, following the other men.

Liz liked the idea of a barbecue, "Okay, let's do it, Babs, but if those clouds start moving in, everybody *move* fast and *help* out."

"Do you guys need me to help with lunch?" Babs said, "I still don't feel quite right and think I should lay back down for a bit while you eat." The thought of smelling hot dogs made Babs sick. "Plus, you have Teddy and the girls to help."

"No, Babs. You go. We got this," Liz said.

While Teddy got the barbecue ready, Oscar took his granddaughter to investigate the shed to find some pails. He rolled his wheelchair into the dusty shack. "We'll use these to cover Babs' plants, and we'll find some big rocks to put on top," he said to Malia, handing her the old, dirty buckets.

"Uh-huh, those will make a good wind barrier," Mary agreed, approaching from the path, interested in what they were doing.

Ronnie walked up and stood at the shed door looking around, inspecting it curiously.

"What do you need, buddy?" Oscar asked Ronnie.

"Um . . ." Ronnie said, ". . . not . . .sure."

Oscar rolled his eyes, patiently waiting for him to answer. He looked on the counter and named the first random item he saw. "How about a measuring tape?" Oscar asked.

"*Yes*, a measuring tape," Ronnie said. "I have things that *need* measuring."

Oscar whipped the tape at him. It was tiny, lightweight, and belonged to Babs. "There you go!" he said. Off Ronnie went.

"Grab that burlap; we can wrap those new shrubs and use this," Oscar said, tossing his granddaughter the twine.

Mary watched Oscar and Malia work together to secure the plants along the path. Oscar was good with his granddaughter. He sat back in his wheelchair and gave her directions, forceful and deliberate in his words but praising her along the way.

"Good job, kiddo!" He said as he lifted his eyebrows cocky and proud, looking over at Mary.

With the help of Malia and Rayna, all the residents had taken their place under the gazebo outside. The smell of barbecue sauce lingered in the air. Rayna made a point to hang around the barbecue to be near Teddy. She prepared the plates, and he set the hot dogs in the buns with his thongs.

"You can hand the plates out," Rayna said in a bossy tone to send Malia away.

Teddy smiled at Malia and made eye contact with her whenever she came up to the table to grab another plate.

Ronnie walked up to Mary, startling her. He extended his tape long and started to measure the back and sides of her chair. "Forty-eight! Fifty-one!" he said in a loud voice. Then he moved down to her forearms, spilling her drink. She tried to shoo him away politely, but it didn't work. When his hand moved toward her chest, Mary slapped his arm away. He continued to yell out random numbers while he measured everything in his path, making it impossible for Liz to work. She had calculated and reviewed the same medication four times and still felt like she needed to recheck it. "Thirty-four! Eighteen and a half! Three and three-quarters!" he continued, staring at his tape with deep concentration. He moved on to Edward, sitting overly erect in his chair, waiting patiently for lunch. Ronnie measured every possible body part that belonged to Edward while the man sat stoically like a statue except for the rhythmic movement of his persistent leg. Quiet and expressionless, the large man looked around Ronnie to observe Holly's new appearance as she joined the group out on the deck.

"Wow, very coiffed, Holly," Liz said as she set Holly's pills beside her paper plate.

"Holly *farted*?" Edward piped up from his table.

Oscar saw an opportunity, "No, that's queefed, Ed, not coiffed . . . that's when—"

"Oscar!" Liz shouted, "Let's focus on lunch, shall we!" Liz always had one ear open when Oscar was around.

"Finish up that whole dog, Holly," Oscar said to her as she tried to pick it up without spilling. "You need to get some meat on those bones," he winked.

Liz settled Ronnie down with a giant plate of food, and everyone was suddenly quiet. Oscar looked down with the most pleasant appeal on his face. With eyes closed, he lifted his paper plate up with both hands to the tip of his nose and took a big whiff. "Ahhh." It was the most aesthetically pleasing masterpiece. The hot dog had basically tripled in size and was bursting with delicious hot juices that were seeping their way into the warmed barbecue bun. Without a doubt, this would be the most incredible meal he had had in days. The thought of taking a break from handfuls of walnuts, bland, tasteless vegetables, and cafe food excited him like a child. He would savor every moment. With each calculated bite, he would strive to have the perfect balance of bread, meat, cheese, lettuce, ketchup, mustard, and relish. He would take his time and allow his tongue to play, using the whole entirety of his mouth. He wouldn't even care if the bread or cheese got caught in his dentures because he wouldn't be having any major conversations during *this* meal. His mouth watered with every last bit of flavor until it was completely drained and void of every tiny morsel of dog.

The day could not get any better. Oscar's mood was completely heightened at that moment. His granddaughter was right in front of him, his daughter was close by, and the care aide was nowhere in sight.

Mary sat in the shade with a restful Anna, listening to the joyful conversations and laughing at the magical power of the simple lunch.

Liz set Oscar's pills down in front of him.

"My granddaughter being here is the only medicine *I* need, Liz," Oscar said, in a good mood.

"I will leave them here just in case, Oscar," Liz insisted.

"Well, screw it," he smiled and gulped them with his juice.

Malia felt someone standing extremely close to her back. She turned around to see Ronnie standing behind her, grinning with ketchup and mustard, smudged ear to ear. He had a disheveled appearance with his wrinkled shirt that had free-fallen drops of ketchup attached to the material that were about to roll further and further down. His measuring tape hung by the clip on his chest pocket, pulling his shirt crooked in a misshapen way. The flattened, tangled-up hair on the one side of his head indicated how he had slept during his nap.

"Napkin?" Malia said, handing Ronnie a handful of paper towels.

They had just finished lunch when the darkness began to roll in. Everyone hurried to get everything back inside. The wind became fierce, and leaves started to blow sideways across the ground. A couple of plastic chairs picked right up off the deck and tipped over. That's when panic set in.

"Take cover everyone!" Edward yelled.

A startled Mary was the first to leave the area. *"HOLY MOLY!"* Mary shrieked. She pulled her hat as far down over her head as it could possibly go and scooted fast off the deck to get inside the garden door.

Liz scrambled. She reached up and took the waving, hanging flower baskets down from the hooks. "Ronnie! Edward! Grab the buns and condiments and head on in!" she shouted in a frazzled manner.

Ronnie was chasing a plate on the deck that kept blowing just beyond his reach. Oscar grabbed each plant from Liz and rolled them two at a time into the building, balancing them on his lap. Every time he turned around, Liz was holding more plants. There seemed to be an excessive amount of hanging flowers. Malia and Rayna roared while they ran around with Teddy, trying to hold everything down, their hair slapping them in the face. The hilarity of the moment amused the teens. The three chased napkins and plates that had skipped down the garden path. They tucked themselves behind a bush, bursting into laughter. Holly sat in her wheelchair just inside the doors, eyes peeled to watch the commotion. Her hair hadn't moved. Babs came running down the hall having been woken by twigs hitting her window and alerting her of the wind. "My plants!" she yelled in a panic.

Edward, fighting the wind, clumsily rolled his way to the door in his wheelchair carrying the relish, ketchup, mustard, and some plastic glasses in a jumble on his lap. He stopped just inside wanting to keep watch on everything happening outside.

"Hurry, Ed!" Holly said, backing away from the door.

Fast on his tail, Oscar sprinted his chair with a giant spin of his wheels. "ED GET THE DOOR! HIT THE BUTTON!" Ed leaned to the side and slammed the automatic button with the ketchup bottle. Oscar barely made it in just as the door closed, and Ronnie ran smack right into the glass with a BANG; the juice he was carrying splashed straight up and out of the plastic container onto his face and shirt. The plates from under his arm all flew back into the windy atmosphere.

"Crisis avoided, Babs!" Oscar said, as he held up a plant with a childish grin on his face.

The haunting, dark grey scene moved in like a fast-moving wall. The atmosphere turned heavy with condensation. All the residents admired the strange-looking sky. It was awe-inspiring, and the quick thunderstorm had Holly's heart racing with anticipation. Sheets of persistent rain dropped the temperature quickly. It was beautiful to watch.

"Whew! So now what?" Mary said, shaking the excess rain and debris from her satin blouse, feeling quite invigorated from the excitement. "Shall we go to the sitting room?"

"What the hell is a *sitting* room?" Oscar asked.

"Yes, Mary," Liz interjected. "We have books and puzzles for you to enjoy in the TV room," she said, shooting Oscar a dirty look.

32

SHE'S A NATURAL

The storm kept all the residents busy inside for the remainder of the afternoon. Oscar opted to stay in the dining room with Ronnie to watch the storm taper off and read his paper. "Well, this pissing rain is a drag. Kind of shitty for you girls," Oscar said to his granddaughter. He was getting worried that Malia and her friend were getting bored.

Ronnie had a cross look on his face. "Excuse me," he said, "but my kid is in the room here," pointing his long, crooked pointer finger at Malia, "so you need to STOP using that kind of language Oscar *Daaavies*!"

Malia, sitting on the ledge of the window, looked up from browsing through a pile of old magazines and giggled. *Are they about to fight?* She wondered.

Oscar shook his head.

Ronnie gave Oscar a furrowed frown. "If you continue to talk like that, I'm going to have to put my hands around your neck and you'll be sorry! Then I'm going to get you thrown in jail you, Turkey Lurkey." He continued shoving napkins into the already full napkin holder. "Turkey Lurkey!" he said again.

Oscar noticed Ronnie's brain seemed to be on a continual loop now, and his body began to shake as he got increasingly frustrated. Napkins were falling onto the table and the floor.

"You couldn't fit those little hands around my neck Ronnie, but nice try," Oscar said.

Ronnie looked down at his hands to see if they were small.

Liz walked into the room wearing gloves. She pulled them off and threw them in the garbage. Sensing the tension in the air, she walked over and gently put her hand on Ronnie's shoulder, feeling the need to protect him from something Oscar possibly had said or done to wind him up, "What are you working on there, Ronnie?" she asked.

"Nothing. Just waiting for lunch. I could write you a letter while I wait," he said seeing Liz's pen clipped to her pocket, "Give me your phone number so I can send it to you."

Oscar smiled at Liz.

"We just ate Ronnie," Liz said, grabbing a bird-watching book from the next table and placing it in front of him on the table. She looked over at Oscar, "Are we all good here?"

"Yup," he said.

She walked into the kitchen area to grab a glass of water from the sink, laughing to herself about how she had become such a mother hen over the years.

Malia could see Ronnie's body tensing up and getting angrier at the table. The napkin holder flung out of Ronnie's sweaty, shaky hands and smashed on the floor. Oscar stopped reading and put his paper down, annoyed. Malia quickly picked up the holder, set it back on the table, and whispered in Ronnie's ear, "Do you want to come for a walk with me? Your job is done here, it looks like," she said in a kind voice to distract him.

Ronnie smiled, "Yes, that would be fun," he said, getting up from his chair. All the stray napkins that had fallen to his lap fell to the floor. He kicked them around with his feet and then followed Malia out of the kitchen area.

"She is a natural, isn't she?" Liz said to Oscar from over by the sink.

"Sure is. Quite fearless that one," Oscar said proudly.

33

QUICK AFTERNOON VISIT

Oscar approached Lexi, sitting on the couch in the Fountain Garden TV room.

"When did you sneak in?" he asked, pulling up and parking his wheelchair parallel to the couch.

"About twenty minutes ago. I just wanted to check on the girls. They have been here a long time."

"Are they going back to camp now?" he asked, "I haven't seen them in a few minutes."

"No. Malia and Rayna are curled up on Holly's bed, watching a movie. They said they will relax for a while and then they want to check out the Everything Room? Whatever that is . . ."

"I wanted to come back and give mom another big hug too," Lexi said, pointing to Anna's room across the hall. "She is sleeping now. She sure gets tired fast. It's fine, though, I know she needs her rest. After she fell asleep, I just moved out here," she said, patting the couch. "It feels good just to sit here and relax." There was a bit of awkward silence. *Please do not fill this nice quiet moment with sarcasm, Dad. I am too sad, too tired, and sometimes, you exhaust me in your old age.* Lexi braced herself. "Oh, I am supposed to give this to you," she said, reaching over and handing him the old mug. "Vic gave it to me to give to you. He said he will try to see you before you leave."

"Pff . . . leave. I don't want to talk about that," Oscar said.

Oscar sat looking serious. The two of them looked over into Anna's room where she lay sleeping soundly on the bed. "I wish your mom could talk to you. She would be better at this than me." The words stung her heart.

Lexi stared at her dad. *Was this the moment she would finally tell him?*

Oscar was focused on Anna's room. "Your mom was always better at everything than me," he said, taking a long uncomfortable pause. "And I know I am always saying the wrong stuff." His mind was struggling to find the right words, "How can I make you understand? I *do* think Brock is a patronizing dickhead. I always have, but I get he is your husband . . . "

Mary stopped dead in her tracks, having overheard Oscar's words from around the corner. *This father-daughter talk could use some work!* she thought. She chose to stay hidden and listen.

Lexi let out an annoyed grumble. "Nice, Dad."

Oscar piped up, "Now hold on! Let me try to explain," he paused. "Sometimes I feel like I could punch him in the face."

"DAD!" She shook her head. *This conversation is going to be a lost cause.*

Ronnie walked up with a mouth full of cookies and stood awkwardly in front of them, holding a plastic watering can for plants. "I'm watering the plants now," he said.

"Good for you, Ronnie; beat it! We're having a moment here," Oscar said.

Ronnie walked away to find a plant. "Beat it!" he repeated.

Mary, with her elbow on the arm bar of her wheelchair, put her head in her hand and shook it. *Ronnie, don't interrupt. Get out of there!*

Oscar focused his attention on Lexi, "Listen, it's not about him, it's about you. Your mother and I want the best for you *and* Malia and well . . . Does he really make you happy? You don't sound happy. You don't look happy, honey. I know you think I spend every day thinking about Brock and how much I loathe that guy, but I don't. I sit here thinking about the crap that *I* have to deal with," he said, slapping his legs with his hands feeling frustrated, " . . . and how I have let your mother down. I know where *I* went wrong in life, and in a lot of ways, I hate to admit it . . . but Brock reminds me, of me. Well, in some ways, except he has a shit-ton of money. He is a selfish man that only thinks of himself and, well . . . thinking back, I was somewhat the same."

Ronnie over-poured water into the planter by the television. The dirt overflowed and ran down the side and front of the counter, leaving wet muddy streaks.

"Ronnie, I think that's enough water, buddy, go feed the fish!" Oscar said, waving him out of the room.

Mary leaned forward to look around the corner to see what Ronnie had done. As she attempted to get a better view, he walked so swiftly by her, that he practically UN-waved her hair.

Oscar stared at Anna again, lying still in her bed. "I could have given your mom a better life," he said.

"No, Dad, that's not true," Lexi said, trying to comfort him.

"I just don't want to see you have to live like that honey—wanting more, wishing you had done things differently, wondering if there was something better for you. How can we repair this, Lexi?" He reached for her hand. "You deserve to be put first. You should be worshipped every single day. I know my charming personality hasn't made things easy for you and Brock either."

Mary nodded to herself, *Yes Oscar! Use your words!*

"You shouldn't have to beg for anyone's attention, ever! I hate that you don't think you deserve true happiness; and seem scared to be on your own. Jesus Christ, I hate that I have made you think you can't come to me."

She got teary-eyed and sunk into the couch, listening to his honest, fatherly words.

"I have been caught in my own miserable shit, and I have let you down," said Oscar. "I take full responsibility for what happened last time we were all together. I should have kept my mouth shut!" Her mouth almost dropped open at his admission.

"It wasn't just you, Dad." She felt angry that she had never heard Brock apologize. "I have to tell you that things between Brock and I—"

Oscar cut her off. "I am on a roll, here, kid. Let me say what I have needed so badly to say." He grabbed the arm of the couch. "Don't be afraid to be alone, you are *anyway,* String-Bean. You are married and you look so lonely. I can see it in your eyes. I know that look because I have watched our dear Holly look the same way for years. It's not too late for you. You deserve a ton of love, a great relationship, *or be by yourself,* whatever you choose, but do it for you, do it for Malia. Don't stay with Brock because he is rich, convincing you to, or because you think Malia wants you to, or because you are afraid. Don't do what, I worry at times, your mother did." He kept his hand on hers and she fought the urge to break down and cry.

Lexi's throat was completely choked-up and wouldn't allow her to speak and truthfully; she was melting into his words, words she had waited so long to hear. She didn't want him to stop—having missed talking and getting advice from him.

The sound of Liz's med cart rolling down the hall and stopping in front of Anna's room interrupted the raw moment. Liz glanced over at the two of them.

Lexi quickly pulled her hand out from under her father's grip and got up from the couch. "Let's talk more later, dad, okay?" She walked away, taking a deep breath and wiping her tears. Her brain felt numb.

"I am here for you, Lexi! I promise I will be better!" Oscar shouted.

"Okay, Dad!" she said, looking at Liz, feeling embarrassed. She walked down the hall, pulling her sleeves down to brace for the wind and rain on the walk back.

"Be careful out there, String-Bean! It's nasty! There could be falling branches!"

"I *know,* Dad!" Lexi didn't turn around; she just kept on walking. There was still so much unsaid.

34

FIVE O'CLOCK DINNER

Edward had placed himself on the end of Mary and Holly's table for dinner. His table was covered with numerous hanging planters that were to be hung outside after the wind calmed down. Ginger slowly motioned the spoon towards Edward's mouth, but he rejected it. His large stiff hand flung up, hitting the stew-filled spoon, launching the scoop high and clear across the table. Warm wet meat sauce splattered on Holly, "FOR GOODNESS SAKE!" Holly yelled disgustedly. "Why isn't he sitting at his *own* table? Why is he sitting with us ladies?"

Mary nodded in agreement, still shielding herself from behind her magazine.

"No! Rosy Carboni!" Edward pointed his rigid finger right in Ginger's face.

"Sorry, Holly," Ginger said, "I was just trying to motivate Ed to eat. I shouldn't have pushed." Ginger set the spoon down and got up to walk away giving him space.

Edward's leg thrashed against the leg of the table.

The constant noise of the thumping irritated Oscar, who was feeling the need for more pain meds. "Can we give him something *stronger* than food?" he said, "Seriously . . . is anyone listening?"

Malia ran up. "You're going to hurt yourself, Edward; let's just give you a scootch," she said with concern. She grabbed the back of his chair with all her strength and readjusted Edward to the center where his foot couldn't connect with the table leg. Oscar proudly looked at his granddaughter, even though he knew her efforts would probably be unsuccessful.

Ronnie came into the dining area ready to eat. When he sat down, Oscar noticed he had multiple strands of long thin rope hanging loosely around his neck. On his right hand, morsels of torn paper looked mysteriously stuck to his crooked, timeworn fingers that sparkled with glitter. Ronnie tried multiple times to detach the tiny scraps of paper, but the strange and annoying little bits held strong. Oscar watched, silently intrigued, as his friend continued to pick away at the pieces that moved back and forth between his sticky hands, attaching stubbornly to a different finger with each attempt. After some persistence, Ronnie finally abandoned the idea, leaning his face down into his bowl to take a messy slurp of his stew.

Oscar burst out laughing. It was clear that Malia and her friend must have had Ronnie helping with some sort of craft earlier— a craft that must have involved a good strong glue.

35

TO HELP OR NOT TO HELP

The residents all scattered after dinner—ready to unwind from the busy day. Rayna searched for Malia and found her in Holly's room. "What are you doing in here, Mal?" she asked as she watched Malia fold Holly's sweater and lay it on the back of the rocker.

"I'm just making the room nice for when Holly comes to bed tonight. *Helping*, remember? What we *agreed to* do . . . " she said.

Rayna walked over to the side table, lifted a photograph, snickered at the people in the image, and set it back down. In doing so, she shoved two ornaments to the side, shifting them on the table in a mishap way.

Malia was annoyed. "Holy, God, Ray! Do you have to make such a mess?" she said as she walked over to put the items back nicely.

"Dude. Chill!" Rayna said, oblivious to how she had irritated Malia. "So, what do *you* want to do when you are older, Miss Malia?" Rayna said in a super condescending voice. "Do you think you could handle a job like this?" She grabbed a caramel candy from a bowl that sat on Holly's side table, squeezed the candy from the wrapper into her mouth, and threw the wrapper down.

"Maybe," Malia answered.

"So, when you go off to college, what are going to study?" Rayna asked while looking out the window at the pillars of trees.

"I'm thinking of getting a science degree and then . . . ya. I guess I could transfer into nursing or something like that."

"Huh. Must be hard having to make all those decisions," Rayna said sarcastically. "Some of us don't have to worry about that, because we never had a shot of getting into uni to begin with." Rayna reached for another candy and grabbed Malia by the back of the neck and squeezed tight, "Open! You know you want one!"

"Ray!" Malia yelled and then felt the candy fly into her mouth.

"Holly loves you. She would *want* us to eat them!" She laughed and let go of Malia's neck.

"Holly loves my mom. I don't even know her, not really."

"Your mom—you—same thing," Rayna said.

Rayna admired herself in the mirror. "Getting old is going to suck. I'll rob a bank if I have to before I let myself get wrinkled and have saggy-ass boobs. I think they can even fix your vajayjay now, once it gets loose!"

"Oh my God, Ray, gross!" Malia tidied the hangers in the closet and shut the door.

Rayna continued to snoop and scan all the items in the room. Malia pulled the sheets back on the bed and fluffed the pillow while Rayna grabbed Holly's hairbrush from the counter and gave her hair a quick swipe to freshen it up.

Ginger walked in. "You shouldn't be using that, Rayna," she said.

"Whatever," Rayna said, shrugging her shoulders. She tossed the brush on the side of the sink.

"Do us all a favor, Rayna and do *not* work in the health field when you are older," Ginger said jokingly.

Malia looked at Rayna sympathetically, knowing that unless Rayna upgraded her marks, that wouldn't be an option anyway.

"Don't worry. No one would ever hire me anyway," Rayna said. "I'll have to work where people like your future rich husbands go to escape the mundaneness of your privileged 'missionary' life, and they need to rebel and pay for a little evil and spontaneity."

Ginger's eyes widened in shock, watching Ray dance loosely and offensively by herself. "You pretty little thing! You are so damaged!" Ginger said.

Malia cringed with embarrassment but remained fiercely loyal to her friend, "You whiny, self-deprecating whore!" She scolded Rayna playfully as she put her in a headlock and dragged her out of the room. "I am going to pretend I didn't hear that," said Malia. "Enough adulting and work, bestie; let's get out of here and see where everyone is."

36

PUZZLE

Malia walked around Fountain Garden, curious about the evening routine. Everyone appeared to be enjoying their quiet time. She saw Edward sitting and staring out the dining room window while Rayna talked with her mom on her phone at a nearby table. She continued to stroll down the halls while she pondered the excitement of graduation and checked her emails on her phone to see if she had heard back from the university admissions. Peeking her head into Ronnie's room, she saw that he was frantically rearranging his undergarment and sock drawer. When walking by the staff room, she overheard Liz, Babs, and Ginger discussing the resident's menu for the following day. Passing the door, Malia hastened her step so they wouldn't think she was eavesdropping. Sauntering around the building, she paused at her grandma's doorway to see Anna lying with her eyes closed in a peaceful, drowsy rest. It saddened Malia, thinking that her grandma, who she had known to have a gleaming, energetic personality, looked feeble and world-weary now. Her once rosy cheeks appeared pale with an underlying greyish tone, and her fragile frame looked almost childlike in the bed. Malia fought the urge to enter the room to hug her and moseyed across the hall where her grandpa was sitting in the TV common area reading the newspaper. Mary was in the room also, sitting at a small table for two off to the side doing a jigsaw puzzle.

She approached the quiet woman at the table, "May I?" Malia asked, pulling out the opposite chair.

"You certainly may," Mary said as she shifted the jumble of small pieces around on the table with her dainty pointer finger.

When Rayna finished talking on the phone with her mom, she popped into Oscar's room- having a quick moment of due diligence as a volunteer. She walked over to Oscar's nightstand and turned on the light. Then, pulling the sheets back just a bit—like she had seen Malia do, she made a nice little triangle. She slapped the pillow in an attempt to make it look better. Browsing Oscar's wardrobe, she pulled a suede, sandy-colored vest off the hanger. *Cool,* she thought, throwing it on the bed. Reaching up to a hook, Rayna pulled Oscar's suspenders down from behind hanging belts, went over to the mirror and attached them to her shorts. Tightening them and pulling her top down a little to exaggerate her bust, she admired her curvy figure in the mirror. After swaying from side to side for a minute or two, she grabbed the vest, kicked the door shut to the wardrobe, and left to find Malia.

Time passed, and Malia fell into a leisurely puzzle trance. She would often glance up from the table and get mesmerized by the luster of the beautiful colors of Mary's blouse. The lightweight satin fabric lay free over her delicate bony structure.

Malia's eyes wandered back and forth between Mary's blouse and the finger waves of her salt and pepper hair. The waves were placed with perfection, framing her tiny face. She was curious if the woman had accomplished this stylish, vintage look by herself.

Under Mary's strands of short dark hair, small diamond earrings sparkled from the lobes of her ears. When she moved her head to search the table for the perfect puzzle piece, the brilliant gems shimmered, elegant and simple.

Malia appreciated the comfortable silence and the easy company. Just being in Mary's presence somehow diminished her thoughts about her grandma's condition. She felt consoled—acutely aware at that moment— that she needed to be. Malia realized that she had probably benefited from Mary's company more than the reverse.

Liz entered the common area and approached the puzzle table, "Looks like you ladies are really making some headway here," she said seeing the outer border of the picture complete. Mary looked up at Liz when Liz rested her heavy hand on her shoulder, interrupting her focus. "It was nice of Malia to help today," Liz commented, placing a tiny cup of liquid medication on the table.

"The pleasure was all mine actually," Malia said.

Rayna entered the TV room with the sandy vest bunched tight under her arm and started to snoop around the area. Oscar looked up from his newspaper. He looked and then looked again at the teen. His brain was working hard to shuffle his thoughts. *Are those MY suspenders?* He thought, looking at Rayna as she walked over to an open cabinet in the corner of the room and shifted around the items. Stacks of old cassette tapes and a small boom box collected dust on the first shelf, and underneath, on the second shelf, she found puzzles, crossword books, scrap paper, decks of cards, and a couple of fiction novels. A bowl of random dice, a doggie bingo game, a variety of other games, and a Ziploc bag full of crayons and markers were also crammed onto the shelf. She grabbed the bag of markers and tucked it under her arm with the vest she had taken from Oscar's room. She found a pad of white paper and snagged it as well. "You ready?" Rayna said, looking at Malia. "Let's go back to camp now and build a fire or something. Come, come, Dorothy," she said in an exaggerated Disney-like voice.

Malia got up from the puzzle table. "What do you need those for, Ray?" she asked.

"I don't know," Rayna said. "Something to do on the beach or in bed if we're bored later."

They skipped down the hall, arms locked together, chanting, "Follow the yellow brick road, follow the yellow brick road, follow . . . follow . . . follow . . . follow . . . follow the yellow brick road . . . We're off to see the wizard, the Wonderful Wizard of Oz . . . "

37

BACK AT CAMP

"Oh, *thank God* they are gone!" The girls returned to Camper's Edge through the trees and noticed the RV had left.

Malia agreed. "YAAAS! *Peace* again!" she said, "and they took the bad weather with them too."

"I'm going to check out the ocean," Rayna said, whipping off her shoes. "Maybe I will jump in! I feel gross now."

Lexi, sitting on the lawn chair on the grass, heard Rayna's comment and was not impressed. She thought Rayna was implying that volunteering at Fountain Garden was a dirty job. She scowled.

Rayna ran passed Lexi on the grass, "I have hair down my shirt from cutting Holly's bangs."

"What?" Lexi asked Malia as she walked up, "She cut Holly's bangs?" looking questioningly at Malia. She felt bad for thinking the worst of Rayna.

"I'll explain later," Malia said, grabbing her mom's hand and yanking her up from her chair. "Rayna! I'm going to hang out with my mom for a few. I'll be right back and then let's change and do something."

Rayna yelled back, “Roger that, girlfriend! See you in ten.” She skipped toward the ocean, immersed herself up to her knees and swooshed around in the water, taking selfies.

Lexi grabbed Malia and hugged her tight. It felt nice, just the two of them, and she loved it when Malia hugged her back like her teenage daughter, not the young girl who yearned so badly to be an adult. *I wish we could stay in this moment,* she thought.

“That was a crazy day!” Malia said.

“Did you enjoy helping out?” Lexi asked.

“I did. Even more than I thought I would.”

“I am proud of you, Honey. I know it made your grandparents very happy.”

“I think I might help out tomorrow too, Mom. We’ll see. People are nice here.”

People? Lexi wondered. “Yes, that Teddy seems nice,” she said, smiling at Malia.

“Ya. Teddy’s cool,” Malia blushed. “I think it's awesome that he works at Fountain Garden *and* here at the camp,” she giggled. “The guys at *my* school never worked that hard!”

Lexi could see that her daughter had a crush. She gazed out at the ocean, quiet in thought.

“Are you okay, Mom?”

“I’m fine,” Lexi said, squeezing Malia’s arm. “I just got some things to figure out . . . and I will. I just need to know you are okay and that me and your dad love you more than anything.”

“Mom! I *do* know that! I want *you* to be happy, okay? So just figure it out and don’t worry about me. I swear, I am fine,” Malia said.

“I always worry about you. That’s my job!” Lexi said, feeling the weight of the tremendous responsibility of sending her daughter confidently out into the world.

“Well, my life is about to get crazy at the end of August. I know I am going to get accepted to university. I just know it—and when I do—I think it would be good for me to stay in the dorms right on campus, or at the very least, maybe in an apartment close to the university with friends. Then I can meet people and really focus on my studies so—"

Lexi interrupted her. "So, you are leaving me," she said with a smile, feeling jealous that Malia was excited about change and this next chapter of her life. Looking at the excitement in her young face was like looking in the mirror at herself years earlier.

"I am not leaving you; I just get a rush thinking about going and experiencing stuff, you know . . ."

"I do know, honey." Lexi gave her a kiss on the forehead.

A hundred feet over, Rayna was rolling around in the sand, looking provocative. She looked like a dog that had an itch or that was trying to mask it's scent. Luke set down a huge decorative wheelbarrow planter on the grass and took a moment to watch Lexi and Malia hugging on the beach. He could sense that things weighed heavy on the two beauties in front of him and was slightly curious to know more. He climbed back up the ladder to continue installing the rafters pondering how he could help alleviate the seriousness of Lexi's weekend. Lexi, Malia, and Rayna all made their way back to camp a few minutes later. Luke yelled down at Teddy from the roof, "Those girls look bored, Teddy. Why don't you show them the flower cups and potting soil in the shed? Let's transplant them into the hanging planters, so they're ready to be hung tomorrow. The day is going to be gone soon, that could be our last quick job, and then tomorrow there will be less to do."

Teddy, Malia, and Rayna went to gather everything from inside the shed.

"So, you work at both places," Malia said, handing Teddy the bag of potting soil to dump in the hanging baskets.

"I help out," he said, "They let us use their washer and dryer for our bedding and towels, so I do their laundry for them when I can.

"You look like you help with more than just laundry. I think it's cool you help. So, do you live nearby?" Malia asked.

"I live down the road at my grandma and grandpa's house," Teddy explained, "My parents travel a lot with work, so my grandparents became my guardians."

"Oh, wow," Malia said, intrigued.

"Ya, that's how I ended up helping at Fountain Garden. My grandpa—"

"Is *Ronnie* your grandpa?"

"Ha, ha, no—love that guy—but no. My grandpa passed away about a year ago, and I just kept helping out around there. Then I met Luke, and he gave me this gig as well."

"Oh. I am sorry about your grandpa," Malia said.

"That's okay," he said.

"So, school and *two* jobs; that's ambitious!" she said.

"Well, I have to save for university," he said. "My parents said they would pay for tuition, but I will have to come up with rent," he frowned. "What about you?"

"I have applied to three different places," Malia said, "and I am still waiting to hear back. I check my emails every ten minutes," she laughed. "I applied to the University of Adasa because it's close, and then two other colleges as back-up plans."

"That would be awesome!" he said. "I was so pumped when I got *my* acceptance letter to the University of Adasa!"

"Aww, you're so lucky. It sucks not knowing if I am accepted yet. Volunteering at Fountain Garden helped your application too, I bet," Malia said as she lightly packed the soil in the hanging planter with her fingertips.

"Maybe," he said.

"I enjoyed helping today. I get why you do it." Malia said, catching Teddy staring back at her.

Rayna was fiddling with the little plants in their individual cups. "I enjoyed it too!" she shouted.

They both looked at Rayna as if they were surprised that she was still in the shed.

Rayna felt like a third wheel. She put the tiny plant down. "Mal, I am going to go chill until we do that thing later for your grams."

"Sounds good, Ray," Malia said, happy to spend time alone with Teddy.

38

THE ESCAPE

Liz dimmed all the lights in the dining area as she chatted with Babs.

"So, are they gone now, Liz?" Babs asked.

"Yes, I think Malia and Rayna went back to camp a while ago. It was a long day. I think they were ready to go," she chuckled.

"They did good," Babs said. "I must admit I was impressed by both of them."

"Yes, that Malia is quite the girl. Did you see how proud Oscar and Anna looked? They couldn't keep their eyes off her," Liz smiled.

"Yes, that was cute," Babs said.

"Are you feeling better now?" Liz asked.

"I am," Babs said, "Having that rest earlier helped."

"Alright, Babs, you go for your "fresh air," and I am going to make this call to Ed's son and see if he will come in and visit tomorrow at four instead of after dinner. If he could come at *that* time, then that is one less person we have to deal with when we—"

Babs started to walk away, "That would work out great. I'll call Gunther too and make sure he is available for tomorrow as well."

"Perfect," Liz said. "Ginger is helping Ed shower and shave right now, and then she will take a break. I'll sit here alone in the dining room to make my call. That way, I can watch the weather and keep an eye on the deck in case something decides to blow away. It looks like Anna is having her evening nap, and everyone else is having some relaxation time. Good luck with that smoke in this wind, Babs. Go ahead and go home when you are ready. Rest up for tomorrow and feel better."

Oscar, having been eavesdropping on Liz and Babs' conversation, watched Babs walk down the hall to the front office to make her way outside.

"Now *that was* a day!" Oscar said, tugging on the armrest of Holly's wheelchair. They sat side by side at the entrance of the TV room.

"Right?" Holly agreed, "Can you believe today? It felt different, having them all around?"

"You know what, Holls? I think today calls for a celebration," Oscar said.

Holly lifted her eyebrow. "What do you mean? What are you plotting, Oscar Davies?" she asked.

He looked at his watch. "Come on, I'll show you," he said.

After some convincing, Holly found herself wheelchair-deep in Oscar's plan.

Outside of Ronnie's bedroom, Oscar pointed his shaky finger, "Quiet Ronnie," he shushed. "If you want to come with us, you have to do exactly what we say." He looked at Holly and winked.

"Yes," Holly added, looking up at Ronnie, "You are going to play an important part here, so pay attention, okay?"

Oscar motioned Ronnie to Babs' office door, "When I say go, you are going to sneak inside and grab the key with the *RED* tag in the top *LEFT* drawer," he said to Ronnie.

"Oh, that's easy," Ronnie said shaking his head.

Oscar and Holly both smirked.

"Holls, you keep watch for Babs out the side window," Oscar said.

"I see her!" Holly said, "She's sitting on the bench in the courtyard."

Babs had plunked her old butt down in the corner of the vine-covered nook to get out of the wind. She reached into her uniform pocket to grab her cigarette and cell phone. She looked forward to this moment each and every day. On a calm day, the warm sun, breezy air and large inhale of her smoke were the perfect remedy for stress. Sometimes she would even slip her feet out of her shoes and let the cold of the cobblestone rock make its way through her thin socks, giving her feet a cold spa-like treatment. Today, she pursed her lips tight around the cigarette hanging out of her mouth, so that the wind wouldn't blow it away. She called Gunther on her cell, but he didn't answer.

"Go! Go! GO!" Holly yelled.

Oscar gave Ronnie a push forward, accidentally slamming him into the glass office door. Oscar looked back down the hall to make sure Liz wasn't coming. Peeling his cheek off the window, Ronnie turned the knob and entered. He walked awkwardly, lifting his knees high off the ground to motion that he could step in a light, sneaky way. "Just hurry up, Ronnie!" Oscar said. Ronnie pushed the office chair back, practically throwing it to the back wall. "SHHH!" they shushed him.

"Okay! Okay!" Ronnie answered, putting his forefinger to his lips. He yanked the right drawer so fast, that it almost pulled right out of the sliders.

"Your *other* left, Ronnie!" Oscar whisper-shouted. "The other drawer!"

"Oh. Okay." Ronnie nodded his head and slammed the drawer shut making a loud noise. Holly and Oscar shook their heads at each other. He reached into the left drawer, picked up a large set of keys and raised his arm to show Oscar and Holly.

"Are there other keys in there?" Oscar asked hurriedly.

"Yup, RED ones!" Ronnie held up a key that had a red tag attached to it.

"Okay brainiac, grab those instead!" Oscar shouted. "Close the drawer! Put the chair back! Let's go!" Holly had already made her way to the double security doors, ready to assist in the escape. Her tiny hand, with fingers spread wide, hovered over the large circle button, ready to push to make the door open.

Oscar and Holly were aware that Babs had a stash of alcohol over in the other wing. She was smart enough to keep it there instead of on their side of the building. Babs knew that if Ronnie would find it one day and decide to consume it—it could lead to a heap of trouble. She only brought liquor out on special occasions, like a birthday, and even then, she limited everyone to one glass. Oscar had been thinking of grabbing it for a long time, but actually liked his friend, Babs, and didn't want to get her into trouble. Now, with the heavy news of Fountain Garden closing, he didn't really care anymore and thought it was likely that she wouldn't either.

"Ready!" Ronnie leaped forward practically falling onto Oscar's wheelchair as they both made a beeline to the door. Holly still had her hand up to push the silver button.

"Now?" she asked.

"Wait!" Oscar glanced at his watch.

"What do you mean wait?" she asked. "WHAT are we waiting for? My arm is getting so *tired,* Oscar!"

Oscar lifted his bum slightly off his chair to see Gunther just turning into the driveway. "K, now!" he said.

Holly slammed the button with giddy excitement, and the door opened. All three tried scurrying through at once, Oscar and Holly running their wheelchairs into each other. They halted fast at the entrance to the building, peeking their eyes out the front doors to ensure that Babs was still sitting, having her smoke in the nook.

"She's going to see us, Oscar!" Holly said nervously.

"Wait!" Oscar said with a grin, "Aw. There he is. *Mi Amigo!*"

Gunther pulled his truck right up to the front door of Fountain Garden. He jumped out into the wind and made his way to Babs with a gallop, holding a container in his hand.

"I thought you were coming to see Oscar later," Babs said.

"I heard you were feeling crappy!" he said, "We can't have that! I brought you some soup from Daphne's Cafe. Have you eaten dinner yet?" Sitting down beside her, he placed the covered recyclable bowl on the bench between them. He shook the debris from the wind off his cap and placed it haphazardly back on his head. He sat angled on the bench, eyeing up the entrance doors to see if he could see his best chum in full-swing monkey business.

Shyly, Babs picked up the container and raised it slowly to her nose.

"It's just soup, Babs, not a wedding ring," he joked.

"I know!" Babs said, embarrassed. "This was nice of you, Gunther."

"This is quite the cozy corner," he said.

Babs flushed, feeling old and awkward. Some days, she felt too stubborn to fully enjoy the company of a man.

"Clear!" Oscar yelled as the three rushed across the floor. Ronnie dropped the keys and made a loud noise. Oscar swiped them up fast and bolted to the doors of the other wing. Ronnie smacked the button to open the door, but it didn't work. "Hurry up!" Oscar yelled, looking over his shoulder toward the glass entrance doors. Ronnie hit it again and the door finally swung open. Oscar giggled and nudged Holly with his hands on her back, almost making her lose control of her wheelchair. "Come on, Holls!" he said, grabbing the back of her wheelchair and giving her an encouraging boost forward. The three of them paused just inside the entrance and scanned the unrecognizable room. Holly remembered the area, back when it was a functioning space when she had come to see Dr.

Benjamin for an appointment. Now, a large red and yellow plastic sign lay on the floor that read "Danger! Contaminated Area. Please Stay Out." Ronnie picked it up, attempted to read it, and then threw it aside.

The storage area was now a puddle from a water line break. Everything from that side of the building had to be moved or lifted off the ground and what remained was, for now, under large plastic tarps. Over the years, the rooms and halls of that side of the building accumulated furniture and boxes that enclosed personal items that belonged to the gentle souls who had left the living from within the walls of Fountain Garden. The belongings were stacked and strewn about the area, still waiting to be attended to. Unfortunately, many families chose to leave items behind rather than pick them up, and Babs never had the heart to throw anything out.

"Jesus!" Holly was shocked. Water stains had begun to seep through the ceiling, leaving streaks running down the walls. A stench of mildew heaved in the air.

"Gross!" Ronnie shouted, "I don't like it here."

Oscar agreed. "Well, if old age doesn't get us, continuing to live in this place will! Focus troops! Find the booze." Oscar said, drawing in their attention. He spun his wheelchair around to survey, "You look over there, Ronnie. It's probably in the old doctor's office," he said, pointing to a side room.

Holly made her way halfway down the hall and found a cane. She used it to poke and probe under the tarps and through some boxes that were lining the hall. In Gunther's chicken scratches, one of the boxes was marked, "Annabella Davies (deck stuff)." She threw the cane down excitedly and reached into one of the boxes. Tissue paper tossed up into the air as she threw handfuls of stuffing on the ground. Her pulse raced as she pulled out her hand-painted flower vase that she had made Anna years prior. She set off to the side. Underneath some crinkled-up newspaper was Oscar's stupid ashtray, which Anna hated so much and spent her whole life moving from the couch where Oscar would leave it—back to the coffee table where it belonged. Excited, she pushed the box to the side and grabbed the next one marked the same.

Oscar yelled, "Found the jungle juice!" holding up a bottle of whisky he had found in the hall cabinet. "Let's go, Holls! I grabbed a bottle of red wine too!" he said, with an old stale cigar hanging out of his mouth. "Ronnie, where *you* at?" Oscar looked towards the office and saw Ronnie trying to call someone on the office desk phone.

"Hello?" Ronnie yelled into the phone.

"Just a sec, Oscar!" Holly whipped the next box open and found multiple laundry Bounce sheets laying delicately and purposely over Anna's little quilt, the same one that had lived on Anna's rocking chair out on the deck for years. A moment of pure appreciation for Gunther washed over her. He had taken such care in packing her friends' belongings. Thrilled with her find, Holly whipped out the quilt and discovered that—carefully folded inside it—was her and Anna's soft knit button-up sweater. The unique lavender cardigan had belonged to Anna originally, but Holly wore it any chance she got when enjoying Anna's company during the many sunsets that they shared. She lifted it to her face lovingly and breathed her friend in deep.

"Alright, you two, we gotta blast before Buzz-kill Babs busts us for escaping!" Oscar yelled. "Ronnie, Let's GOOO! Babs will be pissed if we're in here."

All three rushed to the door, hearts racing like bad children about to get found out.

"Don't you feel bad, Oscar? Just a little?" Holly asked seeing the bottles piled on his lap. "What if Babs was keeping this for a special occasion?"

"We are alive *today*, Holly! It *is* a special occasion!" Oscar said, grinning big.

Out the doors, they hurried, rushing across the glass entrance doors, seeing Babs butting out her cigarette. With a quick smack of the button, they were back in Fountain Garden. Oscar wheeled his chair ferociously down the hall with two bottles of alcohol squeezed between his pant legs. "See you later, Holls," he called out, "I'll be by as soon as all the wardens go to sleep! We aren't washing our meds down with water tonight, my friend! I am ready to tie one on!"

A few moments later, Liz finished her call in the dining room and retreated to the nurse's office to relax and take a breath. "It will be a quiet night after such a crazy busy day," she thought.

39

MORE THAN A NIGHTCAP

Holly sat in her wheelchair, holding on to Anna's lavender cardigan, while waiting patiently for her company. Every few minutes, she would put the material up to her nose and breathe it in. She anticipated the door to her room opening. When it finally did, she could do nothing but grin.

"Are you sure nobody saw you, Oscar?" Holly asked.

"We're good, Holls!" he said. The whiskey and wine were in his lap with a bowl of ice that he stole from the kitchen. "And I brought a friend with me."

"Gunther!" Holly said, happy seeing him enter her room behind Oscar. "But where's Babs?"

"She's at her house eating my soup, hopefully," Gunther said.

"Alright, whatcha waiting for? Get a girl a drink!" Holly handed Oscar a plastic glass so he could pour her some wine."

Gunther made himself comfy on Holly's rocking chair.

TAP. TAP.

"Can I interrupt?" Liz asked from outside the door.

Inside the room, there was a pause and then quiet snickering.

"That depends, Liz" Oscar said coyly. "Are you here to be a Debbie Downer or a Debbie Doer?"

Liz peeked in. "Oscar, you guys didn't think you could get away with indulging without me, did you?" she said.

"Get your beautiful butt in here, Liz. We need to even this room out!" Oscar said as he poured two shots of whisky on the rocks. "We're drink'n old school tonight my friends!"

Liz entered the room holding the wooden chair from the puzzle table.

Gunther opened Holly's window to let the humid air of the evening blow through the room.

"Liz, I have a favor to ask of you," Holly asked as she handed Anna's sweater to her. "Do you think you or Teddy could throw this in the wash for me? It's Anna's, and I would like to freshen it up a bit."

"Of course, Holly," Liz said, taking it and draping it on the back of her chair.

The four of them sat for a good period of time, sipping and laughing while conjuring up memories of days gone past. The drinks went down easy.

Malia ran up to Rayna, who was standing with Ronnie in the dark hall of Fountain Garden, sliding her feet in her socks along the floor. "Okay, Ray, all the big lights are off except for the odd tiny night lights along the corridor floors, so we don't run into anything. It's perfect. All that is left to do is knock on everyone's doors and turn on the music in the TV room. We are ready to go."

"It's sure dark." Ronnie said.

"Shhh. Ronnie, hold still," Rayna said, guiding his long arm through the whole of the makeshift arm strap that was made of rope. Then she did the same to his other arm, like adorning a backpack, except it was no backpack he was wearing—they were cardboard angel wings. Little string battery lights were glued to the very edges of the wings to make them twinkle in the dark.

"Where are we going to put the battery packs?" Malia asked.

"We'll tuck them in the backs of our bras," Rayna said.

"He doesn't wear a bra!" Malia laughed.

"We'll just shove it down his pants," Rayna joked.

"Super inappropriate, Ray! No, we have to figure out a different way," Malia said, shaking her head.

"Let's put his suspenders on his PJ's and then loop them around that," Rayna said.

Malia looked wide at Rayna and then burst out, "Okay! Whatever works."

"Ronnie, just hang on to this for one sec until we are ready," Malia said, twisting his arm behind him to hold the little battery pack. He stood awkwardly. She ran into his room, grabbed his suspenders, and then came back to help him put them on. Malia and Rayna worked together to attach his angel wings securely.

The girls, giggling with excitement, quickly helped each other to put their own wings on. "This is going to be fun. I hope it works or we are going to look so stupid," Malia said to Rayna.

"Let's just agree—here and now—not to tell anyone back home that we did this," Rayna laughed.

"Agreed!" Malia said.

Their hearts raced, knowing they might get in trouble for being in the building at night without permission, but they didn't care. They had a vision of what they wanted to do, and nothing was going to stop them.

"Alright, this is where the rubber meets the road," Rayna said, "Let's see if this works."

The three stood in a circle, cracking up at how each other looked. The girls looked like pretty little butterflies. Ronnie, however, looked a little odd with the smaller wings against his broad back. They fell, crooked on his shoulder, the rope on the one side, struggling to hold strong. Malia adjusted his makeshift arm strap to make it good and tight and then grabbed Ronnie by the shoulders. "We need you, okay, Ronnie. It's going to take all three of us to make this look cool so follow our lead, okay? And *no* talking. Absolutely NO talking. We have to do this really, really quietly. Just keep following us and try your hardest to move to the music—*even* if you see Liz—just never mind her." Malia's heart was beating fast. "This is it . . ." She desperately wanted the plan to work. She stood, staring at Rayna, ready to turn on the lights.

"One, two, three," Malia and Rayna counted in unison. Malia clicked Ronnie's battery in one hand and her own battery in the other.

The wings lit up, and so did Ronnie's face. His big eyes glowed in the twinkly light, and his smile beamed ear to ear. They were all excited.

Ronnie turned in a circle, like a puppy trying to catch his own tail, mesmerized by the wings and excited about the adventure to come.

Liz heard a light tap, tap, tap from the other side of the door. She got up from her chair, tucked her glass behind a picture frame, and motioned to Oscar to hide the bottles of alcohol. She thought it was probably just Ronnie out for a midnight stroll. She opened the door to the dark corridor and heard the trumpet sheet music of Louis Armstrong's "La Vie En Rose" sweeping through the quiet building like an acoustic wave, finding its way to each resident. "What in the world?" she said.

Gunther and Oscar darted to the doorway, "What's happening, Liz?"

Holly set her wine down on her side table and tried to catch up in her wheelchair.

Shimmering wings of light danced by Holly's room and then faded down the dark hall, disappearing into the TV room. The tune of the trumpet filled everyone's ears. A moment later, down the other hall, another set of flickering angel wings danced eloquently in the shadows. Mary had wheeled herself out of her doorway, wearing her nightgown and robe. She sat in the musical moment with a warm smile.

While shuffling his bulky, slippered feet, a tall, awkward third angel followed suit, waving his arms like a child pretending to be a plane.

Oscar and Gunther burst out in laughter.

"SHHH!" The angel said as he looked back at them in the darkness with his finger up to his lips and then pranced away.

Oscar moved over, making more room for Holly to come and watch beside him. The four of them stood in the unusual, almost psychedelic moment, taking in the view of the wonderful spectacle. The beautiful energy of the moment, along with the pleasant effects of the alcoholic drinks, made the perfect recipe for happiness.

Ginger woke from resting and stuck her head out of the spare room just as Malia's sparkly wings rhythmically floated by. Rayna followed close to her, and Ronnie shuffled behind, illuminating the dark hall.

The three angels continued to dance and spin to the sweet musical sound that echoed through the halls, the twinkle of their wings flirting with the dark.

Edward loved the magical moment. He didn't feel the need to get out of bed. He laid with his milky eyes half-closed, listening to the melody and enjoying the merriment of what was happening outside his door.

Anna watched from her bed, staring out at the dark hall waiting for the majestic, winged angels to sway by. The glimmers of light would come and then go. She pulsed with anticipation.

The three angels twirled and spun in circles at her doorway. The heavenly figures were glorious and smooth in flight. Round and round, the wings whimsically floated through the dark night.

Mary approached her tipsy group of friends, "And you said there was no entertainment here, Oscar!"

Oscar smiled back at her, heart beating out of his chest for the pride he felt for his granddaughter.

The tune to "What a Wonderful World" came on, and the little angels slowed to hold each other's hands. They remained dancing in front of Anna's room while everyone else watched from the end of the hall. Swirling each other around in slow motion, the two girl angels continued to slide in their socked feet on the slippery floor to create a magical experience for everybody watching. The quirky third angel did his best.

The girls dazzled Anna as she lay watching. She wished she could spend an eternity in that blissful moment. The angel's movements were fluid to the soft music and made for such a magical sight, lifting Anna's body, mind, and spirit. She was inspired to be as free as what she was seeing in front of her.

Oscar was bursting with love and overwhelmed with what a fantastic daughter Lexi had raised and could not wait to tell her the next day.

Gunther leaned against the wall wishing Babs could be at his side. He wanted to share this experience with her. At that very moment, he decided that he would make sure that she understood that he felt that way.

40

LATE-NIGHT PARTY

It was late. A car pulled up from down the long driveway, shining its lights on Camper's Edge. Rayna woke from her bed and saw headlights shining through her cabin window. She popped up to ask Malia who she thought it was, but Malia was not there. She heard voices, and then the sound of doors slamming. Feeling her energy ignite again, she threw on her shorts under her loose V-neck T-shirt, wiggled her feet into her flip-flops and went out into the night to see for herself. She sat on a lawn chair in the dark and stared at the cold fire pit where she had a view of the loud campers, and a barely visible view of Teddy and Malia, who she saw walking down on the beach under the stars. Seeing the two of them enjoying each other's company annoyed her.

Malia looked up from the sandy beach toward the cabins and saw Rayna sitting on a lawn chair, the light of her phone screen illuminating her face as she scrolled. Malia continued her walk with Teddy.

Enough of this boring bullshit, Rayna said to herself, turning off her phone. She got up and walked toward the group of strangers setting up their tents.

"Hey there, pretty! Look, boys, a fellow camper," said the guy as he poured something onto the wood and lit a match. The flames went up high. WOOF.

"Hey," Rayna said.

"You alone?" the guy asked, as he reached into his pocket, pulled out a joint, and lit it.

"Yup," she said.

"Drag?" he said, extending his hand.

"Abso-fucking-lutely!" she said, giggling. *Finally, some fun.* She took a long toke.

"Here! Ready? Catch!" the other boy said emerging from the tent. He tossed her a beer over the blazing fire.

She giggled, twisted off the lid and chugged.

"Woaw, easy traveler!" the guy looked at Rayna and then looked at his friend.

Rayna sat down at their picnic table. The scratchy wood caught on the fringe of her shorts and was cool on her behind. Two others joined the fire after assembling their tent. The group rambled on, in drunk chatter, about nothing and everything. One of the strangers sat beside her and was clearly competing for her attention. Empty bottles and cans accumulated on the ground around the smoky fire. They offered her another beer and she took it.

Rayna watched as the guy walk away from the fire, towards the washroom building, swaying to keep straight on the uneven grass. Teddy and Malia were out of sight now and clearly didn't care where she was, so she got up and followed the stranger, looking for trouble. Pushing the washroom door open a crack, she could hear the boy stammering to get his words out on the phone with someone, *"Hola! Hola mi amor, ¿Cómo estás, mi chica?"* (Pause.) "I miss you!" (Pause.)

"I'm okay." "How are things in Cuba, baby?" (Long pause.) "No . . . it's all good, baby," he slurred, "I can't wait . . . "

Rayna, anticipating a simple challenge, smirked and shut the door quietly. She had never had a problem stealing someone's boyfriend, let alone from a girl who didn't even live in the country. In her drunk brain, she was bored and sick of hearing about everyone's fun, post-graduation plans, especially when she had none. She wanted to have fun *now.* She claimed the guy as her new toy of the moment, and was in the mood to play. The guy walked out the bathroom, zipping up his shorts. Rayna, in her loose V-neck T-shirt, leaned against the wall under the lamp right beside the washroom door. She had one knee bent and resting on the building, so he was sure to bump into her. He stopped abruptly and looked her up and down. She wanted his attention, and she got it.

"Hello, girl."

"Thanks for the beer back there," she flirted with slurred words.

"You going in here?" he asked, motioning into the bathroom.

"No . . . don't have to anymore," she said, sipping her beer slowly, letting the liquid sit on her lips afterwards.

"You sure?" He grabbed the V-neck part of her T-shirt and pulled it while he took a couple of stumbling steps backward into the bathroom door. She giggled drunkenly, pretending to lick the moisture from her lips—leaving her mouth open to seduce him. He moved his hands from her shirt up to her neck and aggressively slammed the door with his other hand, pushing her against it.

Teddy and Malia heard laughter blaring through the camp from the beach. The loud, new campers were partying strong by their fire.

"Maybe we should head back," Malia said with a worried tone. "So, *this* is what you guys deal with here, hey? Have you or Luke ever had any trouble with vacationers yet?"

"No, Luke is pretty laid back. Plus, he drinks whiskey before bed, so he can sleep through pretty much everything," Teddy said.

Every once in a while, the laughter and thumping party noise from the camp fluctuated from a low to a high volume. Malia noticed that Rayna wasn't sitting at the fire anymore.

"I am just going to check if she is in the cabin," she said, panicky.

"Okay, should I start the fire?" Teddy asked.

"Yes, do that." She said as she ran up to her and Rayna's cabin, opened the door, and peeked inside. "She's not in here, Teddy!"

"She wouldn't have gone over *there*, would she?" Teddy asked, looking over at the rowdy newcomers.

"I don't *know. Maybe.* Trouble attracts her," Malia said, shrugging her shoulders.

The guy's body was hard with anticipation. He grabbed Rayna by the back of her head and went for it. His mouth around hers. He was more experienced, and she could tell. Spreading his legs wider, he pushed up against her. Rayna could feel the strength of his leg muscles. He moved his body around, taking her with him and then forcefully pushed her legs apart against the sink counter. Rayna grasped his shoulder with her hand, pulling him closer to welcome the risky behavior as she held tight onto her beer in the other hand. His tongue went deeper. He held her butt cheeks in his grasp, fingers up her shorts, and pressed her in a waving motion against himself. He stopped kissing her mouth and moved his attention down to her chest. She managed to set her beer bottle on the counter, exploring her hands down the sides of his abs and lower stomach. Her fuzzy brain was willing to go further, and she wanted him to know. "YES!" she moaned. Their drunken movements were sloppy and uncoordinated—he kept motioning forward while she tried to undo his pants.

"Rayna, you in there?" Malia yelled, running up to the bathroom door.

Rayna's elbow hit her bottle and knocked it into the sink, making a loud noise.

"Ya, just . . . wait, don't come in," Rayna was full of his slobber.

Malia pushed open the door, "Ray! *What* are you doing?" she said, seeing the two of them in a heated mess. "Really? You're *drunk*?"

As Malia approached, the guy stepped backward, hitting Malia's arm in the process. Rayna mumbled something as she stood hanging onto the counter.

Teddy ran in and stood between the drunk guy and the girls. "I don't know who the fuck you are, but whatever you *thought* was going to happen here, *isn't* gonna happen, buddy. Get out of here and get back to your camp!" Teddy shouted.

"What the *hell* is going on in here?" Lexi stormed in, having heard the yelling from her open cabin window. She took one look at Rayna's face and fumed, "What do you think you are doing, Rayna?" She moved in the middle of everyone to get up close. Teddy backed up and stood in the doorway of the washroom watching. Luke ran up, sensing an altercation. He stopped and stood beside Teddy, seeing that Lexi had taken charge.

"And you!" Lexi scolded the grossly intoxicated young man, "You little PUNK! You think you are a big man, huh . . . Taking advantage of a drunk kid! You PIG! You LOW-life- SON-OF-A-BITCH!" she said, pushing him backward on his chest. The guy stumbled backward, hitting his back against the wall and then rebounded forward.

Teddy eyeballed Luke. "Aren't you going to do something?"

"Nope," Luke said, looking at Lexi, who was fired up and in the guy's face. "She's got this!" He leaned his arm up on the doorway.

The drunk guy slurred and spat, pointing to Rayna, "She *literally* said she *wanted* it!"

"You FUCKER!" Lexi yelled, grabbing him firmly by his muscle shirt. She yanked him out of the door and pushed him off the ledge of the washroom deck, making him stumble to one knee. "If I see your face again, I'm calling the cops!"

The guy's friend came over and helped him up. "We're sorry! So sorry, lady!" he shouted, holding one hand up to Lexi and pulling his friend away with the other.

"Take your loser friend and get the hell out of here!" Lexi seethed.

"I will!" the friend said, dragging him away toward the tents.

The music finally stopped and the noise at the camp teetered off to barely audible chatter.

"I am *so* over it!" Rayna slurred and stumbled while pulling her arm away from Malia, who was trying to hold her up. "Like *who* cares anyway?"

"*I* care, shithead!" Malia said, grabbing her arm again.

"You little *idiot*! Lexi said to Rayna, furious. "You are smashed out of your head, Rayna!" Lexi yelled, gasping for air to calm her pulse. "Get to bed!" she said, pointing toward the cabins. "I'll deal with you tomorrow!"

"We got this, Mom!" Malia motioned to Teddy to help her get Rayna back to the cabin. Walking past her mom with her heavy, sloppy friend, Malia said with a half-smile, "THANK YOU, Mom! I *love* you."

"It's not funny, Malia!" Lexi said, "and lock your door!"

"I know, mom. I will!"

Luke stood beside Lexi, watching Malia and Teddy try to balance their unbalanced friend. Camper's Edge was quiet.

Lexi was still steaming, "Scum," she said under her breath, looking toward the tent campsite on the far side of the lot.

"You are an amazing woman, Lexi!" Luke said walking beside her.

"I can't believe Rayna would pull that this weekend, with everything going on," she said, shaking her head in disbelief—still eyeing up the camp of drunk young men.

"You killed it—handled that like a pro. Those guys only reserved for the one night, I bet they are gone before you even open your eyes tomorrow," he reassured her. "I'll keep watch. I'll sleep outside in a lawn chair if I have to."

She looked over at him to see that he was staring right through her. "His sexy face is mood-altering," she thought as a shiver ran down her spine.

"I don't think sleep is in the cards for me tonight," Lexi said.

Luke laughed, "You'll sleep. I know a strong woman when I see one. I am beyond impressed." He touched her back lightly. Lexi thought he was about to lean in and kiss her, but he didn't. "I am going to go make sure that camp is shut down for the night," he winked and walked away toward the tents. "Have a good sleep, beautiful! I feel lucky that I get to see that face of yours again tomorrow."

"How old was that guy anyway?" Malia tried to pull the blankets from under the dead weight of Rayna's drunken body.

"I don't know," Teddy said, handing her a bottle of water to set near Rayna.

"Thanks, Teddy," Malia said smiling. "I'm glad you were here tonight."

"Ya, tanks, Teddy," Rayna repeated from her bed. "You guys are *the best*! *Just best!* You *reserve* each other." Her head dropped deeper into her pillow to pass out.

Malia looked at Teddy and rolled her eyes as she sat down beside Rayna on the bed.

Clothes, bags, make-up, hair accessories, and other stuff were strewn about the other bed. Teddy cleared a small area of the mess to sit opposite Malia.

Malia laid her arm on the side of Rayna's body, tucking her skunky, smoke-saturated hair behind her ear and off her face. "She *is* a good girl, you know," she said.

Teddy lifted his eyebrows.

"She *is* . . . she just . . . struggles . . . her life sucks, sometimes," Malia said, defending her friend.

"Well, she's going to feel *that* tomorrow," Teddy said.

They both chuckled. Malia pulled the covers up over Rayna's shoulder and gave her a tuck. Then she moved to the bed where Teddy was and sat beside him.

"I think I'm going to have a real mess out there to clean tomorrow after that crew leaves," Teddy said.

"I can help clean the campground up," Malia said, putting her hand on his knee.

"That would make it more fun for sure." He smiled, placing his hand on hers.

Rayna let out a snore.

"You think she'll remember any of this tomorrow?" Teddy asked.

"I don't know," Malia chuckled, "She didn't get the snuggles she wanted tonight, that's for sure," she laughed. "She's going to be surprised when she wakes up, and I am spooning her instead of that guy," Malia joked.

"You're a good friend, Malia."

"Not *that* good," she said batting, her eyes. *I'd rather be spooning YOU than HER,* she thought.

"I should go; it's late," Teddy said, giving her hand a squeeze. He stood up right in front of her, taking both her hands. Malia's heart raced. She got brave and leaned in for a long, soft kiss, excited about her courage and the blooming relationship. He pulled away and then placed his warm hands on her face, tugging her a bit closer to give a final, soft kiss. She felt comfortable in his arms and felt her heart falling hard and fast. To her disappointment, he pulled away again. "So . . . tomorrow then," he said, taking a step back, smiling sweetly.

"Ya, tomorrow, then," she swooned.

He left the cabin.

41

DAY 3

Everybody at Fountain Garden had a good night's sleep—even Ronnie—and woke up with smiles on their faces.

Anna woke with a sense of urgency to open her eyes and start the day. She saw Ronnie pass her room, wearing only his button-down shirt and holding his pants in his hands.

"Hi everybody!" Ronnie yelled as he scurried down the hall. "It's morning!"

Anna wanted someone to help her get up and get out of bed as soon as possible. *Had it all been a dream?* She thought. Had she really seen her daughter's beautiful face? Did she really witness Malia bouncing around the care home the whole day prior with her beautiful energy? She loved knowing that her husband had his twinkle back in his eyes also, something she hadn't seen in a long time. The hours, days, and months had become so boring and routine. The excitement of the last two days filled Anna's heart with such joy and made her want more. She missed it; she missed the exhilaration of anticipating a fun, unexpected day. She prayed today would be the same.

To Anna's delight, Ginger walked in to help her get up and get ready for the day.

A few minutes later, Holly pushed Anna's door open. "Anna, you up?" she asked, noticing a wrinkled-up gown, towel, and water basin on the roller side table. She waited until Ginger whipped open the curtain around Anna's bed. Anna tried to adjust her body to see her friend in the doorway. "Oh good; I was hoping you were getting ready," Holly said, seeing that Ginger had just finished giving Anna a quick bed bath and draped a fresh hospital gown on her. "It's going to be a beautiful Sunday, my love," Holly said, sitting in the doorway with a big smile on her face. "I told Liz to hurry up and come help you get ready this morning too, Anna. She'll be here in a second." The words pounded in her head. "She just went to get me some aspirin. My head hurts a little this morning for some reason. I need to fix that because we have lots to enjoy today, my sweet."

Liz walked by the TV room. She saw Mary, already up and dressed, sitting in the dim-lit room talking on the phone, "I can stay another day," Mary said, "I am honestly *completely* content here. It *is* only Sunday. One more day won't hurt, and I think I should avoid the paint fumes back at the house. You have a lot on your plate today, so—don't worry about me." Mary was silent for a second and then whispered, "I love you too!"

Liz entered Anna's room and shut the door for privacy. "Morning, my favorite ladies!" She went straight to Holly. "Your aspirin and a bottle of water my dear," she said, handing Holly a pill with a mischievous grin.

"Oh good, thank you; I must have slept on my neck wrong," Holly winked at Liz.

Liz chuckled knowing full well why she was hurting because Liz felt a little off herself this morning. She went over to Anna's sink and ran the warm water. "Is everyone excited for another visit with Lexi and the girls today?" She lathered up her hands by rubbing them together. The smell of lavender soap filled the air. "Ahh, I just love lavender, don't you guys?"

"It's Anna's favorite," Holly said, "She used to buy those soaps and candles by the case at the market—had them in every room of her house," she said, rolling herself over to Anna's closet and picking out one of her best dresses. She chose the ocean blue one that was bright and elegant.

Anna stared at Holly the entire time. There was so much she would have liked to discuss, especially about the sweet angels who had visited the night before.

Holly rolled close to Anna, who was sitting sluggishly on the side of the bed, her tiny frame propped up against Ginger. Ginger held Anna's scrawny shape tight in her arms. Holly noticed Anna's flimsy muscles were struggling to hold herself up. She studied her friend close, seeing her decline. *Maybe she's still just tired from yesterday,* she thought.

Ginger glanced over at Liz, wanting to make a note of Anna's weakness, but chose not to state the obvious and upset Anna or Holly, who had woken up in such a good mood.

"This button-up dress is one of Anna's favorites," Holly said cheerily. "Mine too."

Liz took the dress from Holly and held it in her arm. She and Ginger slowly and methodically undid Anna's hospital gown ties from the back of the neck and slipped it down from her shoulders. Without letting her body be shocked by the morning air, Ginger held the nightgown up at Anna's chest, keeping her mid-body covered and warm. Liz, sitting on the other side of Anna, lifted one of Anna's arms and slid it through the dress sleeve, wrapping the button-down dress around her back while Anna sat, weak, on the bed. Then Liz held the gown over Anna's chest, just as Ginger did, while Ginger grabbed the dress from the backside of Anna and brought it around to her front, maneuvering her arm into the other sleeve. As soon as both arms were in, Liz quickly buttoned from the top down, letting the nightgown fall from underneath the dress.

Holly watched in awe as Liz and Ginger moved slowly, carefully and methodically and wondered how long it would be before she would need that level of assistance. She cringed at the thought.

Anna struggled to hold her head up. She looked at her friend with a serious, *Do not pity me, Holly!* look in her eyes.

Holly sat up taller in her wheelchair and gave her friend a nod of positive energy to indicate she was sending her strength and resilience. In an attempt to comfort her, she started a light and fun conversation about their past together. "Anna, remember when we were teens, and we used to roll our skirts at the waist as soon as we left the house and were out of the parents' sight? Those were the days!" she said, handing Liz a pair of blue socks that matched Anna's dress. "I will never forget the look on your dad's face the night we came barreling in, late after the dance, and you had forgotten to tug your skirt back down!" She giggled. "Your parents always thought I was such a bad influence on you."

Anna smiled back at Holly, appreciating her friend and the distracting story.

Liz put the socks on Anna, and then she and Ginger transferred her into her medical recliner. Liz, in her diligent nursing mind, gave the routine instruction like she had countless times before. "Brakes on, Ginger?" she asked.

"Yup," Ginger said.

"Okay, on the count of three, stand and swivel, slowly and carefully, taking little baby steps, Okay?" Liz said, "I don't want to scare her. Don't let her legs twist and watch you don't accidently step on her little toes . . . "

They practically had to exaggerate how slowly they lifted Anna's body off the bedside, because she was so light that it felt like they could toss her up and out of their arms. Once in the chair, they tucked a light quilt around her frame and gave her matching, blue-socked feet a tuck.

"See, we don't need those hard shoes, do we Anna?" Liz gave her an understanding smile. "This was nice. Just the four of us here in the room together this morning. I am going to miss this." Liz looked at Ginger and then at Holly, who was at the sink grabbing a comb for Anna's hair.

"Stop! You are going to make me cry, I can't even think about it—" Holly said, lifting her hand up to Liz feeling overly sensitive with her hangover all of a sudden.

Liz realized that she had the ability to completely change Holly's mood, "You are *right*; let's go have an amazing day! I will see you at breakfast after you guys are done getting ready."

42

SUNDAY BREAKFAST

Anna napped soundly in her chair by the window. The morning routine took a toll on her worn-out, feeble body.

"This side of the island gets all those blustery winds, but I think today is supposed to be calm," Holly said to Mary, who sat across from her.

"Yes, you are right. It *is* much calmer on the other side. Have you spent much time on the other side of Cody Island, Holly?" Mary asked.

"Hell no," Oscar piped up, "That's where all the mucky-mucks live. Too rich for my blood over there."

"Oh, Oscar. You have such an attitude about people with money," Holly said as she looked at Mary and rolled her eyes.

"They stay on their side, and we stay on ours," Oscar said.

Liz joined the conversation. "Believe it or not, Oscar, some people with money are humble and kind," she said while getting medication ready for Edward, who was playing a slider number puzzle.

"Ya, *sure* they are," Oscar sneered.

Ronnie, distracting everyone from the conversation, walked into the breakfast room, arms full. He sat down, setting all the items on the surface in front of him; a plate with a cookie that slid right off onto the table, a set of keys, a Rubik's cube, and Babs' new photo frame that held the picture of her sister. Oscar put his paper down and looked at the odd man wearing giant black headphones. The cord hung down the front of Ronnie's shirt, attached to nothing.

Ginger bounced over in her blue jean, overall shorts. Her bright red hair was pulled completely off her face in her usual ponytail that sat high on her head. She lifted Ronnie's headphones. "Hey, buddy, want some morning mush?" she asked.

"Yes!" he yelled back at her face, making her jerk back.

Oscar questioned her work attire, "Nice outfit today, Red."

Ginger set down Ronnie's porridge and looked at Oscar's face inquisitively. She settled her persistent prying eyes on something unusual.

"What?" he said. Oscar liked the strange girl. She was spicy and usually up to something. She attached herself to him quite quickly once he arrived at Fountain Garden. She liked that his character was challenging at times and different from everyone else.

"You have layers, Mr. Davies," she would say, "and I am a patient girl. You can't scare me away." She didn't have a father, and oddly, she wanted Oscar's acceptance. Ginger bounced away toward the kitchen. When she came back, she stood three feet away from the table to keep her distance. She extended her arm out to Oscar— staying far away— holding his bowl in her hand.

"Your porridge, good sir," she said, "and will Mr. Professor Popeye be wanting porridge today too?"

"What?" Oscar asked.

"I see your prickly little friend popped in this morning. Will he be eating too?" Ginger teased.

Holly and Mary quickly looked over to Oscar's table, excited to see if there was someone else who had entered the room.

With an exaggerated lean, keeping her body far from the table, Ginger tossed the bowl in front of Oscar, making a bit of porridge spill out.

He shook his head at the entertaining girl, "Easy now Red," he said.

"I would come closer, but that thing popping out of your head is going to poke my eye out," she laughed.

"Jesus, Ginger!" Liz said. After all this time, Ginger could still surprise Liz with some of the weird stuff that could come out of her mouth.

"Get it then!" Oscar said as a joke. "Come on girl, permission to approach."

"Can I, Oscar?" Ginger got excited. She moved his bowl over and sat her overall-covered bottom on the end of the table to lean into the mysterious grey tentacle that protruded far out of Oscar's eyebrow. Her eyes probed closer at it.

"What are you waiting for?" he asked.

"I am worried it's going to peck at me if I come closer," she giggled

"Hurry up!" He shouted.

"C'mon you devilish, little tentacle, you." She positioned her fingers around the scary coarse hair and pulled, but it slid out between her fingers.

Ginger grasped it again.

YANK.

"OUCH! For Christ's sake, Ginger," Oscar yelled, popping his head far back. "Did you get it?"

"NOPE." She reached for his head to pull him back in. "Hold still!"

Anna opened her eyes from her nap to see all the commotion.

Mary's eyes were large as saucers.

Liz came over and leaned in to see better. "It's still there," she said, "I think you made it longer! Creepy!"

Oscar shot Liz a scrappy look out the corner of his eye.

"Sorry," Liz said, smiling.

Babs entered the room and approached, "Has anyone seen my photo of Sherri?" She walked up to Oscar and Ronnie's table, where people were gathered. "What's all the ruckus here?" Looking over her glasses at Oscar, she said, "Eww, it *is* an *unsightly* thing, isn't it?"

Ginger tried again.

YANK.

"Holy *shit,* that hurts!" Oscar yelled, pulling his head back again.

Mary put her hand up to her face to hide her giggles.

Holly snorted a laugh from her table.

"Come here. I still didn't get it," Ginger said, reaching to grab his head again.

Oscar leaned back and shook his head from side to side like a dog that was being forced to eat something it didn't like. "No, I have had *enough,*" he said frustrated but laughing at the same time.

"Don't be a baby!" Ginger shouted.

Liz howled. Tears were filling her eyes.

Holly continued to hoot with laughter and crossed her legs to stop herself from peeing.

Mary looked like she was vibrating as she tried to hold in her laugh.

"Ya, suck it up, Oscar," Babs said, bursting out in laughter as she grabbed her photo off the table.

"It's just dangling there now, taunting me," Ginger said. "One more time. I'll get it this time, I know it." Ginger stood up from leaning on the table and put Oscar's head in a headlock, holding her hand on his forehead.

"This is frickin ridiculous," Oscar said, red-faced from under her grip.

Holly saw Mary's ears perked up in shock. "Oscar! Stop swearing!" she said.

"Quite the funny business around here, I must say . . ." Mary grinned.

YANK.

The long, stiff hair shriveled in size. "Ahh! Ha-ha, you just curled it up now, Ginger!" Liz laughed as she walked past Mary, back to her medication cart. "There is really nothing to say, Mary. Everyone is crazy here!"

"Okay, I give up," Ginger said. She let him go and walked away. "Who wants toast?"

Liz could feel the change in the air. Everyone's spirits were high one moment and somber the next. She wondered if it was all because of the profound change everyone was anticipating. Feeling a little overwhelmed suddenly, with what was on her plate for the day, she saw an opportunity to bait the residents. If her plan worked, it would free up some time for herself to get some much-needed tasks done.

"They said we would see them at about four o'clock. Is that right?" Holly asked, inquiring about Lexi and the girls.

"Yup, four." Oscar said, as he popped his pain pills in his mouth with a swig of water. He could still feel the pulse in his forehead.

A loud grunt came out of Ronnie. He had finished his breakfast and had grabbed Ed's sliding square puzzle off the table. Frustration was building as he tried to break the individual tiny, numbered pieces out of the square with his large, clumsy fingers. He was having a difficult time placing them back in properly.

"What was Lexi's plan for this morning? Why do you we only get to see them at 4? Does anyone know?" Holly asked.

"I think Lexi was going to take the girls to the lake and then to the outdoor market to shop and show the girls around a bit," Oscar said all knowingly.

Liz interjected, "Yesterday was *quite* the day around here with all that young energy bouncing around. I am not going to lie. I had no problem sleeping last night!" she said, leaving out the part of the small nightcap in Holly's room.

"Me too," Holly said. "Slept like a baby."

Liz kept pushing the idea. "I think today will be *much* the same and the weather is beautiful *all* day with no storms in the forecast, so I sure hope I can make my energy last the whole day and be spry for the energetic girls later," she said, trying to use her power of suggestion.

Holly thought that if Liz, who was much younger than her, was concerned about maintaining energy, then maybe she should be too. "I think I might have a little siesta this afternoon, like Anna," Holly said, "I want to feel good later when the girls get here. My energy depletes fast lately," Holly admitted.

Mary agreed, adding that the previous day with her new friends was, *a lot*. "Probably a good idea," she said.

"I think that is wise." Liz said, happy she could dupe them to give her more alone time to juggle her responsibilities. "You will *all* be happy you did."

Ed, in his low manly soldier voice, wanted to join the conversation. "Hup! Yes, naps are essential; it's important to feel good."

They all looked over at the strong man who usually sat saying nothing, and snickered.

Oscar's competitive spirit kicked in, "Yup, I think some shut-eye might be called for today. I mean I don't really *take* naps, but it might be a big evening so I think I might take a little nappie-poo myself." He was too proud to admit that he snoozed in his chair or on the fountain swing almost every day. "You guys should probably entice Ronnie to rest too; he's looking a little squirrely over here," Oscar said, noticing his table buddy was talking in tongues under his frustrated breath and about to spiral into a frenzied attack.

At that moment, Ronnie threw the number puzzle clear across the room as hard as he could, shattering it against the wall. Tiny pieces flew in the air. One landed right on Anna's chest as she sat resting in her medical recliner chair. Everyone was stunned at Ronnie's behavior.

Oscar was amused, "Like I always say buddy! When things get tough—GIVE UP!"

43
MANY HATS

The girls trudged out of their stinky cabin, having slept in. The fresh morning air on Rayna's face offered momentary relief from her alcohol-induced headache.

"Here! Sit! Drink!" Malia handed Rayna a bottle of water and pointed to the patio chair.

"I will if you stop yelling," Rayna said. She sat in the therapeutic sun. From behind her big dark sunglasses, she watched Gunther drive his old half-ton truck into Camper's Edge and back up to the picnic shelter. Luke and Teddy walked over to the vehicle, opened the tailgate and started rifling through the lumber and boxes of hardware.

"It's all there. You boys should be good now," Gunther said.

"Thanks, Gunther!" Luke said.

"No problem; glad to do it for you. Helping you guys out with your project put a smile on Vic's face at the store today too," Gunther said, chuckling.

"Oh ya? Why's that?" Luke asked curiously.

"I wanted to brighten Vic's day, because he *sure* does miss Oscar's shenanigans around there, so when you called me at Hill's with your order, I made those two young punks have to go see Vic in the lumber yard for instructions on how to load it all up for me. Those two shitheads are always dawdling, goofing off, pretending to work, and talk'n shit about us old guys. Pisses me and Vic off—no respect! When they dragged themselves in to work this morning, I could tell those two young bucks had too many wobbly pops last night, that's for sure. Vic said the one kid looked pretty green when he was done loading all this material up! It didn't help his young, cocky pride either that I added to your list and sent him out back a second time to see ol' Vic to get the other heavy box of hardware, those galvanized nails and a slap for the feature wall you are building," Gunther added, "Vic says 'Hi' by the way."

"A slap?" Luke questioned. "You mean a slat?"

Gunther continued, "Nope! I told him—a slap! The kid didn't know any better, ha-ha. Boy, oh, boy! Did his punk ass get a surprise when he took it straight across the head from Vic— he found out the hard way what a 'slap' was." (His shoulders bounced when he laughed.) "It made Vic's day I tell ya! After the kid stomped away pouting, Vic called me on the radio to thank me—said it cheered him *right* up!"

"Ha, ha, ha!" Teddy and Luke howled.

"Ya," Luke said, "we had a bit of indulging going on around here last night too."

"Sure did," Teddy agreed and then kept quiet.

"Well, that's camping for you!" Gunther said as he lit a cigarette and looked up at the wooden structure with approval. "Look'n good so far! You boys better get busy. I'll leave my truck here for you to unload, and I'll borrow yours Luke. I have to go run those errands we talked about, so we are ready to rock and roll this afternoon!" Gunther jumped into Luke's truck and took off.

"Ready for *what,* this afternoon?" Teddy asked.

"Let's get after it, Ted," Luke said. "I'll explain later!"

Malia walked over to her mom's cabin just as Lexi came out. "Mom! You're a dish today!" she said.

"You think so?" Lexi said, looking down at her clothes, "You don't think it's too—" pulling her tank top up higher over her breasts and then tugging the bottom of her shorts down.

"Quit fussing, Mom. You look super cute. So, what's the plan for today? More visiting?"

"Um, I thought we could help out around here and enjoy the beach today. Let's not make a plan and just see how the day goes," Lexi said, reaching for her suntan lotion sitting on the lawn chair in front of her cabin.

"Wow!" Malia said sarcastically. "Okay—cool—let's not make a plan."

"And Rayna?" Lexi asked.

"Evil Ray came out last night; sorry about that, Mom," she said, pointing to her friend, kicking back and enjoy the morning sun."

"Uh-huh." Lexi shot a disapproving look toward Rayna, "How can that kid create such joy around herself one minute and then allow herself to be a part of something so toxic the next?"

"You know we're teenagers, right, mom?" Malia smiled big as she walked away, thinking it was too early for a serious conversation.

Luke appeared from behind the cabin, "Morning. Sleep well?" he asked Lexi.

"Hi," Lexi answered. "I slept not bad."

"I am giving out free mind, body, and spirit classes this morning. You interested?" Luke asked with a giant grin.

Am I interested? Tee-hee. "Um, sure," she said, "I don't know what that means but—"

He extended his arm to give her a pair of old dirty gloves.

NOT exactly what I was thinking, she thought to herself.

"Come on," he said, "We could use a hand around here to finish up. I have an idea for later today." Luke motioned Lexi to follow.

Lexi put on the gloves that smelled of dirt and wood, sending her brain into a spin of flashbacks of working in the lumber yard behind Hill's Hardware Store. *She did miss it.*

Teddy, muscles already poppin' in his T-shirt and with his cap on backwards, made his way from the truck to the building area. He carried a big, heavy box. Malia and Rayna had moved their lawn chairs up to the work area so they could chat with Teddy while he got the tools and hardware organized for the day.

"So, what are you guys working on now?" Rayna asked Teddy, having a split-second burst of energy. She jumped up and romped toward the construction area, snooping around playfully.

Lexi walked up to Rayna, ready to wring her neck.

Uh-oh. Rayna thought, seeing Lexi coming in hot. Her cellphone rang at that moment. She immediately lost interest in Teddy and wanted to avoid Lexi, "Oh, hey, wussup?" She said into her phone, trying to disappear quickly from the area.

"We're going to talk later, kid!" Lexi shouted to Rayna as she walked away.

"What's with the gloves, Mom?" Malia asked from her lawn chair, holding a bag of markers and a pad of paper.

Lexi looked at her daughter. "Malia, don't make fun. I am attempting to help," she said.

"There's more of those right there," Luke called to Malia, pointing to another set of gloves on his toolbox, "unless you are too busy this morning."

Malia flipped her pad upside down on the arm of her chair. "Nope! I can help!"

"Atta girl!" Luke gave her a big smile.

The morning sun got hot. Lexi and Malia were working up a sweat, hauling the remaining lumber from the truck. Luke and Teddy stood on the roof of the shelter, and the girls handed the remaining rafters up to them. Rayna moved from the lawn chair to the grass and laid her sluggish body on an extra blanket that she found in her cabin. Her shorts and T-shirt lay on the ground beside her, and her barely covered string-bikini bottom glowed in the sun. Crayons and markers were strewn all over the blanket, a highlighter rested behind her ear, and she was sucking on an orange lid while she colored on sheets of paper.

"Hey, lollygagger, you going to help out *at all* today?" Malia asked Rayna.

Bending and extending her knees back and forth like a toddler on the blanket, Rayna looked up over her large sunglasses. "Nope, I'm busy doing nothing!" she said.

"Your rear end is looking a little pink already. My Mom has lotion if you want it," Malia said.

"I'm good!" Rayna said, looking back down, continuing to color on her paper.

A few hours later, Luke stood on the completed roof, with a satisfied look on his face. "That's the last one. Heads up!" he yelled, "These sheets of plywood have a mind of their own in a breeze." He waited until the girls backed away and then threw down the last cut-off onto the grass. "Teddy, why don't you jump down and start cleaning up," he said.

"Here, Malia, catch!" Teddy yelled, throwing her the string line from on top of the rafters. He came down the ladder and took a piece of wood from her hand, "I can take that. I'll throw these cut-off pieces into the wheelbarrow, and I will take it over to the fire pit for later." he said to her.

Rayna, carrying a stack of papers, came over to check out the project. Her ponytail hung messy and crooked on the side of her head. Her big black glasses had slid down to the tip of her hot sweaty nose. The red on her arms and butt from being roasted to a crisp from the sun looked painful, but she did not seem to mind. "Wow, cool!" she said, holding all her pictures inward and close to her burned boobs so no one could see what they were.

"Props, girls! I am impressed," Luke said to Lexi and Malia as he jumped down the last two rungs of the ladder. "I really do appreciate all the help, everyone."

"We wear *many* hats, us gals!" Lexi said, putting her arm around Malia.

They all stood staring at the structure.

"That's enough for today, I'll get at the shingles tomorrow," Luke said, wiping the sweat off his forehead with his forearm. "I just need to do *one* more thing before I open a cold one . . ." He picked up his tool belt and a cordless drill from the grass and threw them into the back of the golf cart. "Why don't you girls go wash up and make yourself look even prettier—if that's even possible! Let's meet back here for a cocktail in an hour or so."

Rayna smiled at Malia.

"Not *you*!" Lexi scolded Rayna. "No cocktails for *you*!"

Malia laughed.

Luke drove away on the golf cart and disappeared into the trees without any explanation.

"That was weird!" Malia said to her mom.

Lexi laughed, "I think I know what he's doing. Come. I'll tell you."

"Yes. You guys have done more than enough. I got this!" Teddy said to the women, pointing to the wood and tools on the grass. "Thanks again for the help. That was fun." He said, looking solely at Malia.

"Come on girls, our work is done here!" Lexi said, grabbing Malia's head with her gloves still on, tugging her back toward the cabins.

"Aww, MOM!" Malia whined, wiping the dirt out of her hair. "Let's go peaches!" she said to Rayna, waving to her crispy friend. "Bring those markers and papers!"

44
SURPRISE

All the residents rushed out of the room after lunch, disappearing to go nap. Ginger walked around bored, "Where IS everybody?"

"They're all napping," Liz laughed.

"Do you need anything, Liz?" Ginger asked.

"Not at the moment," she said, "just make sure we are set for 4 o'clock, and call Babs to see if she needs any help with the food. I need some time to finalize the transfers that are happening tomorrow . . . and Ginger, I will be staying here again tonight so you can go home after dinner."

"Today is going to be such a fun surprise Liz," Ginger said excitedly. "You and Luke are geniuses. It is just what we all need."

Oscar walked up to Liz as she stood behind her medication cart by the entrance to the dining room. She looked up from writing something down on her paper, "Wow, look at you! Looking very handsome, Oscar," she said, feeling both excited and nervous about surprising Oscar and the other residents with a fun evening to finish her lifelong career at Fountain Garden. *Her and Luke's idea, if it planned out, would be bittersweet*, she thought.

Oscar stood by the door, leaning on his walker. His hand was a little shaky, but he worked hard to control it. He had on his best slacks and dress shirt. His hair was damp, combed neatly to the side, and he smelled of cologne. It felt, to Liz, like his family's presence had shaken things up in a good way.

"You must be very excited to see your girls. It is almost four o'clock," Liz said.

Oscar noticed the tables in the dining area were not made up "Are we eating out on the deck for dinner tonight?" he asked.

"I think so. It's a beautiful evening. I think we should," Liz winked at Mary, who was sitting on a chair close by, holding her sweater. Liz had revealed the secret plan to Mary so she could dress appropriately.

Ginger walked up, carrying a heap of blankets.

Oscar looked over his shoulder and down the hall, "Anna and Holls still in their rooms?" he asked.

"We are just finishing up," Ginger said, as she approached and set the pile of blankets on the other chair beside Mary.

"It's warm out, Ginger. I don't think we will need those," Oscar said.

"Well, it could be breezy off the—"

"Ginger, do we have everything?" Liz said.

"What do I know, right?" Oscar said. *Girls make such a hassle!* He rolled his eyes and made his way outside, following Mary.

Ginger bounced away. "Yes Liz. We're almost ready."

The phone rang, and Liz picked up. "Yes, that is perfect," she said. "Come now. We'll be out in two minutes."

Oscar and Mary made their way out to the warm deck to wait for everyone. They heard Gunther pull up on the other side of the fence gate and back the transfer vehicle up to the ramp. *What the hell is that old geezer doing now?* Oscar thought, trying to see him over the tall fence. The latch unlocked, and the double fence gates swung open. Gunther stood there looking spiffy and clean-shaven. Babs stood beside him in her Sunday best dress.

"Whoa, Babs!" Oscar said. "You are *looker* in that dress if I may say so. Holy shit! You two know something I don't know?" He looked over at Gunther, "What happened to your face, Gwilliam? I'm not used to seeing you look like that Mr. Fancy Pants!" Oscar smiled wide.

"Ha. Ha." Gunther said.

"I have fashionable attire," Babs said bashfully.

"Very pretty dress!" Mary said, nodding to Babs.

"Thank you, Mary! Not too bad for an old fuddy-duddy, hey?" Babs joked.

Ginger whizzed by Oscar with the handful of blankets, a Tupperware container full of old cassettes, and a dusty boom box. "Get the door for me, Gunther!" She looked at Babs and whistled, "Babs, you beauty. You are a *GODDESS*!"

Oscar questioned, "Is this ride for us?"

"For *me* maybe," Mary said, "but I think you have your *own* ride, Oscar."

Oscar was so caught up in his curiosity about what Gunther and Babs were doing he did not notice the golf cart approach quietly behind him from up the path off the deck.

"Dad!" Lexi called to him, "I have *your* ride *right* here!" He turned around to see Lexi getting out of the golf cart with a giant smile on her face. She looked beautiful. She tugged at her red sundress to make sure it was not showing anything inappropriate. The strappy sandals finished off her look in a young feminine way. Oscar hadn't seen this look on her in a long time. Her long brown locks hung down her back, and a few shorter ringlets waved freely against her rosy cheeks.

Oscar gleamed and walked toward her with his walker with a little pep in his step. "Don't you look pretty," he said.

"Thanks, Dad," Lexi said. "You are going to join us for dinner tonight at camp. What do you think about that?"

He was dying to see it, he had to admit to himself, and he was proud of his daughter for picking him up in style.

"Sounds good to me, String-Bean!"

"Hey, Oscar!" Babs called, waving him over to her, "Just a second. Come over here." She looked like she had another secret.

Oscar approached Babs and leaned in. She put her hand in her side dress pocket and pulled out a pair of tweezers. "Hold still," she said, reaching her hand up to his face.

Before he had a chance to move his walker back . . .

YANK.

"YOW!" he yelled, quickly putting his hand up to cover his eyebrow.

"*Now* you're ready," Babs laughed and squeezed his face with her warm hands.

"Thanks, Babs," Oscar said. He leaned in kissed her on the cheek.

"HEY, HEY, I saw that!" Gunther said jealously, flattering Babs with his comment.

Lexi helped her dad into the golf cart and strapped his walker to the back in the club storage area.

"And the others?" Oscar yelled to everyone standing on the deck.

"I got that covered, my friend!" Gunther confirmed. "This parade will be right behind you. We are taking the safe way!" he laughed.

"Hey, Liz," Oscar said, seeing her walk out onto the deck, "don't forget my *magic bullets*." Oscar looked over at Gunther, "and maybe my wheelchair, Gunther, just in case."

Gunther gave Oscar two thumbs up.

Liz ran up to the cart with Oscar's pills. "Just take them now, Oscar. A couple of minutes ahead of time won't hurt. Then you'll be good," she said, handing him his two pain pills and a bottle of water.

Lexi hopped on the cart, ready to chauffeur her dad.

"Anna is coming too, right?" Oscar asked Liz.

"*Yes,* of course, Anna's coming," Liz confirmed. "We'll have lots of help, and we are close if we need to come back. You two look so cute together," she said, giving Oscar her approval and encouraging him to relax and enjoy the moment.

"They *sure* do, Liz!" Babs said, loving how tickled Oscar appeared, sitting by his daughter in the cart.

"Pretty cool, I'd say," Gunther winked at Oscar. He stood by Babs waving "I guess we'll see you on the other side Ol' Buddy!"

"I hope *that's* not where we're going ha, ha. Not *yet* anyway!" Oscar joked.

Lexi and her dad drove off on the cart down the path until they reached the fountain and the opening in the forest trees where Luke had torn down the old gate so the cart could get through. "Whoa! What happened here?" Oscar leaned out of the cart to see the gate lying on the ground, having been removed from the fence and thrown off to the side.

"Oh, that's tomorrow's project!" Lexi laughed, "Ready for a strange trip down memory lane, dad?"

They disappeared into the trees.

Oscar did a double-take, and Lexi held her breath, bracing for her dad's reaction to the new view. The land where his livelihood once stood was changed dramatically. His heart tugged between shock and interest.

Luke approached the golf cart.

"Dad, I would like you to meet Luke, the owner of Camper's Edge," Lexi said.

Oscar hesitated, and then reached out to shake Luke's already extended hand. "So, you're the one," he said abruptly.

"Hello, Mr. Davies. Nice to meet you, finally," Luke said.

Lexi jumped off the cart to lift Oscar's walker off the back. Luke went to the back to assist her. "Let me get that for you, Lexi," he said, winking at her. "It's a great day for a gathering. Feel free to look around sir. Your beautiful daughter can show you everything."

"Uh-huh," Oscar mumbled under his breath. *Look around my OWN yard?* He thought. *Sheesh.*

Luke set the walker down on the side of the cart where Oscar was sitting, "There you go, Mr. Davies."

"All right now, just *hold on* there a minute, slick," Oscar said, wiggling his butt to the edge of the seat, "I have to tell my brain to tell my legs to get their ass in gear."

"Absolutely, sir," Luke said kind-heartedly. "Take your time. I will leave you to it," he said, stepping back from the area. "I will be over here if you two need anything."

Lexi looked at Luke apologetically, and he gave her an affectionate look back.

Oscar managed to maneuver himself off the cart and sturdy himself on the grass, "Okay, String-Bean, let's rip it off like a Band-Aid! Give me the tour."

Gunther drove up and parked the transfer bus. Ginger jumped out and open the back door, letting Holly come off the wheelchair ramp first. She looked fresh and happy; her thin little lips dolled-up with pink lip gloss. She dazzled in a light raspberry sweater and matching long wrap skirt.

Oscar surveyed her beauty from the grass, "Aww, Holls, I love it."

"Well, if you think I look snazzy, wait until you see our Anna!" Holly teased. "So, where is this picnic everyone was talking about?"

"Right over there," Oscar directed.

Babs helped Holly roll her wheelchair down the freshly compacted soil path toward the new picnic area. "Babs, S-stop!" Holly said loudly, gobsmacked at how different the property appeared. She stared at the new lot, trying to recall what her home had looked like, in that very spot, only a year before. She wondered if her brain had deliberately forgotten. "Please, I want to go over there, Babs," she said, pointing closer to the cabins and the ocean.

"Is this better?" Babs asked, moving her onto the grass to get a better view. "Holly, if this is too much for you—"

"No, I'm fine. Just leave me, Babs. I just need a second," Holly said, taking in the brand-new surroundings. *Why is it so hard to remember what my house looked like here,* she thought. *All my memories are of Anna—of Anna and Oscar's house—of Anna and Oscar's deck, yard, garden . . . It is like my life didn't exist.* Her hangover reared its ugly head again.

Oscar patiently waited for Anna to emerge off the ramp.

"Okay, Ronnie, you are next," said Teddy from on board.

Oscar rolled his eyes, growing more impatient.

Rayna emerged from around her cabin to join Oscar by the path. The spunky girl skipped toward him loudly in her light brown, high-top kick boots, her baby blue summer dress, and the old hat Lexi used to wear to work. Oscar's suede, sandy-colored vest hung loosely over her dress. Her hyper energy distracted his attention from staring at the transfer bus. He looked at her and then looked at her again. *I KNOW that hat, and that is definitely MY vest,* he thought. She jumped into position and stood right beside him to wait for Malia and Teddy to emerge from the bus. Fascinated with the irreverent-spirited girl, he stood in anticipation, waiting for her to say something about stealing his clothes, but she just smiled and said nothing. *These kids are so weird now . . .* He thought, continuing to stare at her. *I guess it looks better on her anyway.* The unusual girl left him quite speechless.

Malia watched as Teddy lifted Ronnie's armrest from his high back seat and unclicked his retractable seat belt. When Teddy reached over to help it revert back into the holster properly, he noticed Ronnie's eyes were glued to him, staring in an unusual way. Malia stood between the driver and passenger seat to stay clear. She was enjoying watching Teddy at work. *He looks super cute in his tight, short-sleeved polo shirt and shorts. I think we make a cute couple*, she thought.

"What's wrong with your muscles?" Ronnie asked Teddy, reaching for his bare arm. "I think your shirt is too small. How did you get them to look like that?"

"Well, I work out every day. You know me, Ronnie. I like work and exercise . . . and I eat really well," he said, trying to impress Malia.

"Oh, that's too bad." Ronnie made a repulsed face. "I exercise every day too," he said, proud as a peacock, "but I *never* want to look like *that*." His eyes surveyed Teddy's body up and down.

Oscar, heard the conversation coming from inside the bus, "Don't worry; you never will, Ronnie!" he said.

Outside the bus, Malia pointed Ronnie toward the large, covered pergola where he spotted Liz and Ginger's familiar faces. "Rayna, do you want to take Ronnie over to the others?" she said, seeing Rayna standing by her grandpa.

"Sure do!" Rayna bounced over to Ronnie, "Come with me Mr. Fitz, I will escort you to the partee!"

Mary rolled herself off the ramp. "Your stunning wife is coming, Oscar," she said, seeing the look of disappointment on his face.

Finally, Gunther and Teddy transferred Anna's recliner back wheelchair off the bus ramp. In an instant, the ocean smell flushed Anna's senses, and she realized she was somewhere familiar. She blinked, squinting under the bright summer sun until her eyes adjusted to take in the scene.

Teddy rolled Anna up to Oscar.

Oscar reached for the arm of her chair. "Aww, my sweetheart. Look where we are, my love. It's like déjà vu, right Anna?" He pointed toward the ocean. "This is for you, honey. This is *all* for you today." Her eyes settled on the light blue, tumbling water.

Still hanging on to the back of Anna's chair, Teddy said, "Shall we, Oscar? Let's find some shade for Anna, so you two can relax without the sun blasting on you."

Teddy pushed Anna's chair up the path, and Oscar followed slowly with his walker, his granddaughter by his side.

Ronnie sat in the warm sun, taking in the view. "*Glug. Glug. Glug,*" he gulped loudly, enjoying a sugary beverage that Babs had given him when she sat him down in the chair.

Luke was finishing mounting clips and strings of lights on the underside of the roof of the shelter. Lexi stood by the leg of the ladder, holding a hanging flowerpot to be raised up. He secured the last light in the clip and jumped down from the ladder, landing right in front of her. "You are looking *too* good right now, Lex," Luke said, looking at her flowery red dress. He took the flowerpot from her and made sure to grasp her hand in the process. She loved the compliment and had to stop herself from floating up into the clouds when he talked to her.

Babs was behind a small table by the barbecue filling plastic glasses with pink slush and where she could keep her eye on her sizzling crock pot. "It's quite simple, Mary, just a half cup of cranberry, half cup of orange, half cup of pineapple, and lemon-lime soda. My sister used to love this drink. Oh, and throw in some fresh limes if you have them too."

"Yummy!" Mary said as her taste buds came alive.

"Did we bring napkins?" Babs said, looking around and under the table.

Gunther jumped to her aid. "I'll go check if they were left in the vehicle, Babs. I am on it!"

Mary winked at Babs.

Ginger blew on the end of the boom box plug, "Okay, baby. Let's see if this still works," pressing the prongs into the extension cord. Hopeful, she pushed the "play" button and waited to hear the quality of the music.

"For crying out loud, it's not *that* old, Ginger," Babs laughed at her.

An upbeat tune filled the space. "HEY. I know this song!" Ginger yanked Rayna's arm, almost spilling her pink drink out of the teen's hand. "Dance with me!" she said, grabbing Rayna's drink and setting it down. They swung each other in and out of each other's arms, running into Teddy, who was trying to set up a large folding table. Luke and Lexi watched while Ronnie stood far back to stay out of the way of the dancing girls. Holly, having been sitting out on the grass in her wheelchair, heard the music and came back to relax under the shade of the roof. She needed a distraction from her nostalgic memories.

A car pulled up, and Teddy jumped into work mode. "A camper, Luke? Did someone book a spot for the night?"

"Nope, not that I remember," Luke said.

"I can take care of it," Teddy said eagerly.

"That won't be necessary, Teddy," Liz said as she walked away on the grass toward the vehicle. "I recognize who it is."

"Hi, Liz!" the care aide stood frumpy in her grubby gardening clothes, with hair a mess.

"Hi," Liz said, surprised to see her.

"Ginger called me," the aide explained.

"That's great," Liz said. "I am *glad* you are here! I just feel bad. It's your day off, and I know you are crazy busy."

"Are you okay, Liz?" the aide asked, "I know *I* sure woke up this morning wrestling with a ton of emotions."

Liz looked at her seriously. "I am sad one minute, then excited the next, and then absolutely terrified for my future," she said, trying to stifle a laugh.

"Well, I appreciate you, Liz, so I brought some stuff to help make your dinner party look pretty." She opened her trunk to show Liz a large box containing five beautiful white vases filled with freshly bloomed lilies and assorted flowers. In another box, she had three tall cream-colored candles.

"They are from my flower garden. I made my rotten kids help me put them together."

"Aww!" Liz laughed, "You are so thoughtful."

Oscar watched the women, admiring something in the trunk. He drove up to the back of her vehicle in the golf cart, "Whatcha got in there? Need a lift, stranger?" he asked the aide, wanting to make amends.

The aide was taken aback by Oscar's niceness.

Liz and the aide loaded the boxes in the back of the golf cart.

"You hop on," Liz said to the aide, "I'll walk."

Liz watched proudly as the odd pair drove off toward the pergola structure. She felt overly sentimental, having love for both of them. *I am probably just hungover,* she thought, laughing at herself.

Babs set a vase on the large, scratched-up folding table.

"I think it needs a wipe," the aide said, trying to remove a black smudge with her finger. She looked around at everyone hoping someone would take care of it. She walked away, inspecting the newly built structure and the view. "This is amazing here!"

"It is awesome, isn't it?" Malia agreed.

"Where did you go off to, Luke?" Lexi asked, noticing he had disappeared for a bit.

"Just to grab this," he said, holding badly folded white material, "and this." He turned to Rayna. "Here's the tape you asked for, sweetie." Rayna, still red as a tomato from her excessive sun exposure, grabbed the tape from Luke's hand and skipped away in her brown kick boots and cap backwards on her head. "Thank you, Luke!"

"I thought we could use this," Luke said to Lexi, handing her the white bed sheet—but she wasn't listening—she was distracted from recognizing the hat that Rayna was wearing.

"Is this for the table? Is this from *your bed*?" Lexi chuckled.

"No, it's from *your* bed," he teased.

There was an elevated mood among the group, and everyone was chipping in to help. The table was dressed immaculately. The white bed sheet, which created a makeshift tablecloth, was complemented by the white vases and lilies. With a final touch, the aide placed the cream candles perfectly on the table. Everyone gathered in silence talking in its elegance. "Well, it isn't Martha Stewart's dinner, but it's damn close," the aide said. "These gorgeous surroundings, all you crazy, beautiful people and this unbelievable backdrop helps too," she said, pointing to the rolling ocean.

"You are right! It is perfect!" Oscar said, feeling spirited himself. "I couldn't have said that better myself!" He sat off to the side, caressing Anna's arm while she lay in her recliner back wheelchair staring out at the beautiful canvas that—not that long ago—was her home. Her mind travelled back in time—the sound of the ocean waves drowned out everyone's voices in the picnic shelter. Her senses were alive one minute; then she'd drift off for a couple of minutes—then jerk awake with a gasp, like she was catching her breath. Oscar had seen her do this before in her sleep, years prior, during panic attacks, but it had become a seldom occurrence and wasn't until recently that they seemed to happen more and more. Oscar prayed to himself that if she *was* falling deep into memories, that they were the ones that would only bring her joy. He knew Anna's medication could sometimes push her into the shadowy recesses of the dark side of her mind. He hoped that bringing her to where her livelihood once stood wouldn't trigger any unwanted recall of an ugly experience that had taken place in the past—an experience that he too—spent years trying to forget.

Anna flinched out of restfulness again when Holly touched her other arm.

Gunther looked over at Oscar and Holly, who were looking at each other in concern. The four close-knit friends, stood together now in the shells of their elderly bodies, still concealing a painful, emotionally distressing event that their younger selves had shared. Being here on the property now, history was resurfacing in the memories of all of them—revealing that they were still bound together—in good ways and bad. They all secretly hoped that Anna, at this stage of her beautiful life, could finally and completely release her traumas and embrace the moment as cathartic, freeing, and liberating.

"Let's eat, shall we! Anna, are you hungry?" Gunther said over his shoulder while he began setting paper plates and utensils on the table. "We don't want it to get cold; Babs worked *very* hard on this amazing homemade meal." He wanted to make sure that accolades were given to everyone.

"Oh, Gunther. It is just sweet potato, chicken, and mustard dumplings," Babs said. "Go ahead and put these charcuterie plates on the table," she motioned to the aide. "Can someone help me with the cheesy garlic toast on the barbecue?"

"I can, Babs," Teddy offered

Gunther gave the remaining cutlery to Ginger to finish up and went and stood by Babs, ready to grab the crock pot to carry over to the table. He grabbed the steaming hot pot and Babs followed him with Anna's specially made puréed dish, feeling joyfully cognizant of how well she and Gunther worked together as a team.

"Is this seat taken?" Luke asked Lexi, pulling the chair out beside her.

"No, please, sit," Lexi said.

"This is cozy." Liz looked around from the head of the table.

Everyone took a spot.

"It's toasty under this roof." Oscar wiped a bead of sweat off his brow.

"It is," said Mary, rose-cheeked, tugging at her blouse to let the air flow in. "No need for a cardigan today."

Ronnie leaned into Ginger. "That lady talks funny," he said.

Liz raised her glass, "Well, I would just like to say a huge thank you to Luke for this wonderful afternoon. I can't think of a more beautiful place to spend the day. And to Babs and Gunther as well for putting this amazing meal together."

"Quite unexpected," Holly said, still struggling with the notion that she was eating at a campground right where her house once stood.

"Yes, this is amazing, Luke," Ginger agreed. "I feel so happy today . . . *and* sad—"

"Let's just enjoy the day, everyone," Babs' voice cracked. "What matters is that we are all here together right now." She stared straight across the table at Liz, who was welling up with emotion.

"Cheers, everyone," Luke said as he lifted his glass.

"Cheers!" Oscar said.

"Cheers," the rest joined in.

Lexi placed her hand on Luke's knee under the table and whispered, "Thank you for this."

They all sat quietly, enjoying the meal. Oscar helped assist Anna with her food and drink. Holly yearned to feel relaxed but struggled to reach deep inside herself to be happy.

45

MALIA

When dinner was over, everyone started to move about, feeling restless. Anna's face was grimacing, and her legs began moving from side to side. Liz rolled Anna's chair away from the table, concerned.

"Is there something wrong with my grandma, Liz?" Malia asked.

Lexi stopped talking to Luke to listen to what Liz was saying.

"She is probably trying to move herself to a slightly different position in her chair," Liz said, hiding her panic that her decision to bring Anna may have been the wrong one. Her shoulders dropped with guilt. She lowered her voice to talk privately with Malia, but everyone still eavesdropped. "When you sit in the same position for a long period of time the blood flow is reduced, making the area sore and painful. We don't want that because it can lead to issues like damaged skin and . . ." she paused, trying to rein in her nurse brain that tended to over-explain everything. "Anyway, the point is, it is super important to help her change positions or move her body, even a little, so the weight shifts to a different area. That helps." Liz scanned Malia's face to make sure she could handle the information. "I am so sorry; is this information bothering you, Malia?"

"No, *not* at all," Malia said, shaking her head. "I *want* to know. It makes sense to me and interests me. That *must* be uncomfortable sitting or lying all day long."

Oscar was proud of his granddaughter and was in awe of her maturity. *She's no little girl anymore*, he thought. Holly came closer to Oscar in her wheelchair, also concerned about Anna.

Liz leaned in to remove the little pillows that were tucked under Anna's arms to adjust her.

Luke wanted to help. "Teddy, give me a hand over here. Let's boost Mrs. Davies up a little in her chair to make her more comfortable," he said, approaching Anna's chair.

This man is amazing, Lexi thought to herself as her eyes jumped from him to her mom with concern.

Oscar couldn't help but be impressed with the stranger and noticed his daughter was a little dazzled as well.

Teddy came over from scraping the cheese off the barbecue. He and Luke stood on each side of Anna and everyone else backed out of the way. Oscar and Holly watched intently.

Malia interrupted, "Wait! I have an idea. Don't move her yet; I'll be right back."

They watched the teen run toward her cabin and disappear around the corner. They all waited in wonder. She smacked into Rayna, "Where have you been, Ray?"

"You know, *remember* . . ." Rayna said, indicating they had a secret.

"Oh, ya," Malia said. "Come on. We gotta give this to my grams." The two girls emerged; Malia held something baby blue with sleeping cows scattered all over it under her arm.

She ran up to the group. "It's my airplane pillow," she said, handing it to Liz. "Can I put it under her bum just like the butt pillow she has on that other chair I saw in her room?" she asked. "Look, see, it looks just like that other one and its memory foam so it's soft and it's round like the other one . . . and thick . . . " she said, trying to convince Liz that her idea was a good one.

Liz smiled wide at her. "Great idea, Malia!" she said, knowing it could not hurt and that she was planning to take Anna back to Fountain Garden soon anyway. "It will give some extra comfort for the short time she is here and for the ride back as well."

The two men lifted Anna gently and slowly enough for Liz to put the pillow under her bum in just the right place. "This will feel good on your tailbone Anna," Liz explained.

Anna blinked back at her communicating thankfulness.

Luke and Teddy boosted her a little bit higher in her chair. Both men were attentive to how light as a feather she was.

"I hope that's better, Mrs. Davies," Teddy said, smiling at the frail woman staring back at him.

Malia's heart mushed a little while watching Teddy. *You're so cool. I'm in LIKE, for sure!*

Lexi stood by Oscar, steadying himself on his walker, her eyes fixated on Luke.

"It's amazing Luke was able to lift her with those tinsel arms of his!" Oscar said quietly, winking at Lexi.

She appreciated her dad's discretion in his awareness of her attraction to Luke and thanked the skies that he wasn't calling her out on it directly. Oscar was right, too, she wanted to be close to Luke. She wanted to be associated with this man. He was so gracious, tender, and manly all at the same time, and he *did* have amazing arms.

"Thank you, Luke," Lexi said, stepping closer to him.

"You're welcome," he said. Lexi felt his hand touch her back in a friendly way, and it sent "feels" up her spine. It felt soon and a little wrong to have that reaction, but it had been so long since Brock had touched her.

Holly watched, with a melancholic smile, proud of everyone in front of her. Then she turned her wheelchair away from the scene and rolled herself back out onto the grass towards the ocean. She sat by herself, solemn.

Rayna sat back in her chair, watching and absorbing the scene. She was envious of these people and who they were as individuals. *I wish I didn't suck so much at life*, she thought in her seventeen-year-old brain.

"You are a force to be reckoned with, girl!" Liz said to Malia. "You are smart and a natural at being compassionate. You would be surprised at how many people struggle with that."

Like me, Rayna thought, overhearing the conversation.

"Not everyone finds it is easy to be a people person the way you are. Plus, you are a critical thinker. We use that term a lot in the medical field. You seem to be one—naturally."

Malia smiled proudly. The compliments from Liz boosted her ego, and she didn't mind that Teddy was right there listening.

"You should definitely contemplate the health field, but honestly, I think no matter what you choose to do in your future, you will be great at it. Maybe you and Teddy will both end up working in the medical field one day," she winked and walked away.

Malia leaned down and whispered to her grandmother, "I like her."

"That would be cool," Teddy said, shooting Malia a long flirty glance from back at the barbecue area.

Rayna's face looked defeated. It was hard for her to be the center of attention here. Her bratty ways were being ignored at this strange place and being herself was borderline uncomfortable.

46
A LITTLE CLEANUP

Luke took his drink and the black garbage bag that was sitting by the table and walked down to the beach. He moseyed along, sipping and enjoying the remains of the day. As he walked, he would reach down and pick up odd pieces of garbage and put them in the bag. Lexi joined her handsome new friend.

"I don't remember the last time I walked in nature and not on a treadmill. This is a nice change," Lexi said.

"That's sad," Luke said.

"I wish I could stay here forever and have more days like this," she said.

"Why can't you?" he asked her. ". . . if that's what you want."

"What I want?" Lexi repeated out loud.

"Yes, Lex. What *do* you want?"

To make out. She thought, laughing at herself. *Don't make this weird, Lexi.* She took command of her lonely brain.

"If you were at home right now, what would you be doing?" he asked.

"Nothing," she said. "I would probably be waiting for the phone to ring, but it wouldn't."

"You shouldn't wait for anyone," Luke said. "You should be out enjoying your life. You don't need anyone else to have a good time. What makes you smile? What do you enjoy doing?"

"Doing this," she said, picking up a granola bar wrapper and stuffing it into the bag he was holding. His presence had a strange and mysterious effect on her.

"Follow your heart Lex," he said. Her heart fluttered when the words came out of his mouth. "You deserve your own happy ending. There's a whole world out there waiting for you, and you are not going to find it sitting at home."

Ginger saw Luke and Lexi down by the water's edge. She grabbed a garbage bag from under the barbecue. "Can Rayna and I bring Ronnie down to the beach too," Ginger asked Liz.

"Liz looked out at the beach. "Of course, go. Just be careful, Ginger, right?" she said, her eyes motioning toward Ronnie.

Ginger grabbed the aide by the shirt, "You come too!"

"Are you sure you don't want help cleaning Liz?" the aide asked.

"Go, enjoy yourself!" Liz said.

Ginger and the aide each took Ronnie by the hand, "Let's go, Ronnie! We're going to explore the beach," she said, motioning for Rayna to follow them as well.

Babs looked at Gunther. "I guess we could go down to the beach too, just to make sure there's lots of help around. Care to join me?"

"I would love that, Miss Babs!" Gunther said, putting out his smoke.

Teddy and Malia followed behind shortly after.

Oscar sat with Anna under the shade of the roof. He watched Liz and Mary pull their chairs to the edge of the concrete pad to watch the young adults flipping off their shoes and running out onto the beach. Oscar squinted to see Teddy and Malia hand in hand, getting further and further away from everyone. Ronnie, getting brave, tempted the tide by walking closer to the water's edge. Oscar chuckled quietly, trying to avoid waking Anna from her after dinner snooze, when he saw Ginger and the aide yank Ronnie back from the tide and then scold him with their pointing fingers. Mary and Liz saw it too and burst out in laughter. Ronnie moved up higher on the sand and got distracted by some large shells after that.

"Want some company, Holls?" Oscar approached, moving his walker slowly on the freshly cut grass. He swung the apparatus to his backside and sat down on it like a chair beside Holly.

She shrugged her shoulders without looking at him.

"What's going on in that sweet head of yours?" he asked.

She welled up. "This is A LOT, Oscar. My house used to be *right* here . . . my life was right here . . . " She rested her hand over her mouth lightly, "And Anna . . . I don't think we have much time, Oscar . . . "

He put his head down, saying nothing.

"It wasn't enough time," Holly said sadly, her eyes downcast. "Why does it have to be like this?" she whimpered as her raw emotions surfaced. "I hate these fucking chairs!" she said, slapping her bony, brittle hands on her wheelchair. "I hate this. I hate *all* of it. It's like we're all just waiting to die! I'm *so* frustrated."

"Holls, don't," Oscar pleaded.

She persisted, "I feel like I'm dying inside Oscar and there's nothing I can do about it. I am going to leave this *useless* shell of a body one day, and I will never have had true love or figured out what my purpose was. Did my life have *any* purpose?"

"Holly, stop!" Oscar said. "That's *not* true. If Anna could talk, she would tell you that you *were* her perfect love and that the amazing life we all created here was partly because of you—because *you* were in it, Holly. There is so much I should have said over the years . . ." He tried to make it right—his heart filling fast with emotion.

Holly looked at him as a tear rolled down her face. She quickly wiped it away, trying to maintain herself in view of Liz, Mary, and Anna. "Oh, GAWD!" She buried her head into her hand. "I can't do this . . . please go . . . just leave me alone right now."

"I'm so, so sorry Holls," his voice cracked. Oscar had a surge of pain in his legs when he got up to go back to Anna. He knew Holly was in pain and getting more and more depressed watching Anna's health decline. He also knew her life did not plan out the way she wanted it to and listening to her express it was heart-wrenching for him. He felt the same. Ending up at Fountain Garden was *not* the plan. He and Anna planned to live out their days together in their house, and both secretly hoped they would just fall asleep on their porch one day—and not wake up.

47

1961

The plan for Saturday was to spend the day on the ocean and then bring the fishing party back to Oscar's living room, where the men secretly hoped the women would have an amazing dinner waiting for them.

"Gwilliam told me to tell you not to forget those new pliers, Oscar!" Hank yelled from off the deck where he stood waiting, "Hurry up. Gunther just pulled up and is waiting in the truck. You might as well bring that extra anchor and chain too, in case we have a mishap like last time."

"Ha, ha. I believe you *were* the mishap last time, Hank!" Oscar said, waiting for his wife to come out of the bathroom. Anna was struggling with a red wine-induced headache from the evening before.

Even as a married couple, Oscar and Anna enjoyed partying and gathering with friends as often as they could. The night before, however, was quiet, with only Anna and Holly sitting on the deck rocking in their rockers, wine in hand, until late into the night. Oscar laid on the deck couch with his eyes closed, drifting in and out of a beautiful, after-dinner, summer's evening sleep. When the women giggled, he would awaken for a few moments and lay eavesdropping, intrigued by their deep connection.

Oscar admired and sometimes envied Anna and Holly's comfortableness, respect, and loyalty that they had for each other. It was something that he had never seen between two women, having grown up as a single child to very conservative parents who mostly kept to themselves. Anna and Holly seemed to have their own language at times, and they shared many similar passions and goals. They never got bored of each other's company. Oscar felt lucky to be surrounded by such happy, beautiful energy.

It was getting late. Holly finally got up to leave. As Anna walked her down to the grass, their footsteps on the deck stairs woke Oscar out of his sleep. Through the crack of his sleepy eyes, he watched Holly grab Anna's hand, squeeze it, and then raise it up to her mouth and give it a slow, gentle, loving kiss. Her eyes were closed as she held Anna's hand to her mouth. Anna didn't try to pull away. Holly lowered Anna's hand from her mouth, and the two of them stood face to face, hands still clasped tight. The women stared at each other without speaking for the longest time, and then he heard the words come out of Anna's mouth, "I know, Holly. You make me feel some sort of way too. Goodnight, my treasure," Anna said. Their hands released, and Holly left.

What was happening? The grogginess in Oscar's mind lingered. *What was he seeing? What did THAT mean? Was his wife in love with her childhood friend?* His disoriented mind reeled as he lay there, heart pulsing in confusion, he pretended to sleep.

Pacing in his kitchen that next morning, Oscar waited impatiently for Anna to appear. He couldn't leave on his fishing trip without saying goodbye. Picking up Anna's wedding ring from a tea saucer beside the kitchen sink, he caressed it between his fingers, wondering if he would be able to find some sort of resolution for his scattered thoughts before setting out for the day. Finally, he heard the bathroom door open. When Anna appeared, her hair was in shambles, she didn't have any make-up on, and she wore his T-shirt. His wife, his chosen life partner, looked so beautiful to him.

Oscar had hardly slept. He didn't understand what he had witnessed between the two women. *Was it just a mere moment between two friends who love each other, or was it something deeper?*

It was Oscar's understanding that Anna's passion for him hadn't faded, so what he thought he had witnessed did not make any sense. *Had he been front row and centre to their friendship blossoming into something more? Could he be imagining it? . . . Probably. Everyone who knew Anna was in love with Anna . . .*

The anxiety and worry made him dread leaving her behind that day to go fishing with the men. His nerves were on edge, and there was a pit in his gut.

"Have fun, my love," Anna said. "Is Vic joining you, Hank, and Gunther on this fishing party too? Careful who you let drive our baby today. Don't let Hank sink that boat with all of you in it."

Funny. Was there a deeper meaning behind Anna's words? Would she care if something were to happen? he thought, looking at her intensely. He wanted to take her clothes off right there and make love to her, more romantically than they ever had before. Reaching down, he grabbed her left hand to slide her wedding ring on her finger. Anna smiled sweetly. The golf ball in his throat and his messed-up head stopped him from saying anything back. He felt less self-assured than he ever felt before and speaking without knowing the right words felt too risky.

"Come back to me, my love!" Anna said as she wrapped her long, slender arms around Oscar tight and leaned in for a kiss. Her lips were soft and much bigger than his, and she liked that. She loved to pucker them up to exaggerate her sensual smooch, turning her husband on every time. Oscar's hands embraced her tight. Belly to belly, breast to chest, it wasn't close enough for him today. He would rather relish in the moment than fall on his face in a fight that he wasn't prepared for.

Hank banged on the deck post from outside, "The fish are waiting, Davies! Let's go, you two!"

With resistance in his heart, Oscar gave Anna one last kiss goodbye and then drove away with Gunther and Hank to go meet Vic at the marina.

It was a small community with a handful of shops and services surrounded by pastures, hobby farms, and wineries. Entrepreneurs sold everything from fresh garden food, soaps and jewelry to jams, lotions, candles, and quilts. The hustle and bustle of the island market in the spring and summer kept tourists coming to visit from all over. The locals thrived on the money spent freely by the sun-kissed strangers. The coastline was full of every type of boat imaginable, from smaller fishing boats to large yachts. The warm season attracted family holiday shoppers, campers, and outdoor enthusiasts. Pompous rich men docked their yachts in the marina to relax and smoke cigars while they watched the raffish party-goers (rowdy with their offensive language) wreak havoc on the beautiful shoreline.

It was Saturday, and the market was bustling. Holly strolled among the tables, eyeing up all the delicious colors, shapes, and textures of the fresh produce. The bounce in her step was obvious. She was excited, anticipating a perfect evening. Four young women gathered around a table, shuffling through the mixed greens and vegetables to find the perfect item.

"You got some pep in your step today, girl!" said one woman.

"Well, it's a gorgeous day!" Holly said, exhilarated.

"Did your beau go out?" the woman asked.

"Sure did!" Holly said, "All four guys managed to get their butts out of bed this morning. They want to get it while the get-tin's good."

"Your guy too?" Holly asked the woman.

"Yes, mine left yesterday, I told him he's not fill'n any more of 'this' (her hands caressed the front of her dress) unless he can fill my freezer!" she laughed, "Although, I must admit, I hate it when he's gone. There was some mischief last night with three drunk troublemakers. When I peeked out my blinds, I saw three grotesquely intoxicated men abusing my perfect yard. They knocked over all my large potted plants on the path down to the beach, left beer cans strewn across my grass, and I saw one urinating all over my rhododendrons. I locked the door and just prayed they would go away. My hubby would have handled the situation a *whole* lot differently."

The tall lady laid her hand on the other woman's arm. "You should call when you feel scared like that, no matter what time of night. Do not be alone and frightened. Us neighbours need to look out for each other and each other's property during tourist season."

"I know, I love the excitement of spring and summer, but I could do without the lowlifes, the stinkers, and their blatant disrespect. It is appalling!" the woman said.

"Us gals should have tea later today on my porch," the other woman said, "We could chat about this more and discuss who is working what activity at the island Family Fun Fair coming up."

"I would love to join," Holly said, grabbing a bag of baby carrots, "but I gotta run, ladies! My basket is full, and the kitchen awaits."

As Holly bounced away gleefully, one woman looked at the other, "*The* kitchen or *Anna's* kitchen?"

The other woman snickered, "So I guess that means she's spending the day glued to the hip with Anna again. No surprise there."

Oscar, feeling physically present but with a mind miles away, sat on the boat as it rocked to the motion of the wind and waves. He couldn't get Anna off his mind. He tried to enjoy the blabber of the cockeyed men. Hank, Vic, and Gunther were well on their way to inebriation, their loud wisecracks competing with the noisy breaking waves. Oscar's mind, swaying side to side, tugged with thoughts that he should be at home giving his marriage needed attention. His grappling gut would not settle in the rolling waves. Anna hadn't even left him yet, he thought, and he was already lonely, feeling seasick and weak in his knees. He stared out into the expansive cold blue sea and imagined himself, being a weak swimmer, leaping in without a life jacket if his marriage was over. His brain urged him to get home to his wife. Maybe seeing her face again would confirm he was creating unwanted scenarios in his head for no reason and feeling overwhelmed about nothing.

The savory scent of dinner seeped through the window and front screen door.

"You were right, Oscar," Gunther said. "Glad we ditched that last line. Smell that deliciousness!" The shirtless, sun-kissed men ran up the steps with their sea legs, pushing each other like drunken children. Hank, with his two left feet, stumbled to keep pace with the others.

"Mmm! You got that right, Gunther," Hank slurred, "These women know the way to *my* heart."

Oscar anticipated a long night of having to entertain friends. He entered the kitchen, walked up to Anna as she stood chatting with Holly and wrapped his sweaty arms around her to kiss her on the neck. She spun around in her favorite summer dress and kissed him back— hard on the lips.

"You look beautiful tonight, Anna," Oscar said, looking at her pale-yellow dress and violet summer scarf around her neck.

"Thank you my love," Anna said, giving him a curtsy. She kissed him again on the cheek. "Grab a plate before it gets cold," she said, walking away to go change the music.

Her affection was exactly what he needed to relax his nerves and carry on with the evening.

The combination of all the ingredients made for the most pleasing aroma and delicious taste. The men filled their already alcohol-bursting red bellies and slurped their beer while sitting on the deck. The sun's last light disappeared over the horizon. The crashing surf sound echoed off the darkening ocean.

"We should light a fire tonight, Oscar," Gunther said.

"Ya, maybe in a bit," Oscar said, hoping Gunther would forget the idea with his next few sips. Oscar still had a lot weighing on his mind and wished everyone would end the evening early, including Holly, leaving him and his wife alone.

The women entertained themselves while cleaning up the dishes but soon abandoned that task for dancing and sipping wine while they absorbed the energy of the music. The screen door constantly slammed with people running in and out from the deck, smoking and visiting. Vic, Hank, and Gunther were steadfastly becoming blitzed, but Oscar, seeing Anna with Holly, wasn't enjoying the brew as he usually did. In an attempt to catch up to the men, the girls took a shot of whiskey and then bounced around on the living room carpet to the beat of the loud songs.

Night slowly passed. Hank struggled to stand and finally gave in heavily to the comfortable patio deck sofa. He lay satiated with a bellyful of goodness, fried from all the drinks on the boat, and beaten from the added blasting sun off the water. He was always the first to pass out, and knew he was lucky he had buddies that looked after him. Many a night, he would have woken up face down in the sand if Oscar, Gunther, and the boys had not made sure he got home safe.

"Looks like hurricane Holly came out to play tonight, hey buddy!" Gunther said to Oscar. "I think the girls are trying to compete with us."

Oscar looked at Gunther and gave him a side grin. Through the deck kitchen window, he could see Holly pouring a shot of alcohol down Anna's throat. Then they poured another, clinked their shot glasses together, and put another back. The girls maintained their fun for another couple of hours and had energy to burn. Their mood was intoxicating. They danced out on the sconce-lit deck, bumping into the furniture. Then, Anna grabbed the sweater she and Holly shared off the back of the rocker and ran out on the dark beach. Holly ran after her. They skipped in the sand and water, flinging their dress skirts high in the air while being chased by the dark, rumbling tides. Holly spun the brown-haired beauty around and around. Anna twirled with her arms in the air—the effects of the night's drinks peaking, giving her a warm rush through her body. She slipped her sweater off, whirling it around with her as she turned and then let go, letting it land somewhere on the soft, sandy earth. The women ran giggling inside to change the music when it stopped. Wearing out the carpet for another hour, swinging and twisting, they sang loud while spilling their wine. Both Oscar and Holly were infatuated with Anna, her body, and how freely and easily she moved. In their eyes, she was always the prettiest girl in the room.

"Boys!" Vic yelled through the screen door to Oscar and Gunther inside the house, "I'm headed out. Gonna walk my old ass home."

"Sounds good, Vic," Oscar said, relieved the day was coming to an end. "I'm calling it a night soon too."

Vic tripped loudly down the deck stairs, giggling like a small child.

"Hope Mr. Sauced is still breathing out there," Gunther shouted over the music, staggering back into Oscar's living room from grabbing another beer and the ashtray off the kitchen counter.

"Do you mean Hank? He's fine," Oscar replied. "That's what he looks like *every* day."

"Agreed!" Gunther said, "It was quite the task getting him into bed Thursday night after the 'meeting of the minds' at the store. It's no wonder he messed up on the orders Friday morning," Gunther said, slapping Oscar's leg to move over on the couch. "I felt bad for Holly when I walked into her house that night with Hank draped over my shoulder. From the look on her sad, pretty face and the table for two set up nicely in the dining area, it was obvious that Hank had stood up his wife again. He's been doing that a lot lately."

Oscar got a pang in his belly. *Does Anna feel that way about me?* He wondered if the men's actions didn't somehow push the women closer together.

The two men slumped back on the couch, watching Anna and Holly dance. Fast, then slow, embracing each other and then releasing each other's arms, still touching each other by the tips of their fingers. They flowed around the room in a drunken, sensual state.

Oscar noticed Anna's wedding ring lying on the coffee table by her sunglasses. His heart sank.

"Smoke?" Gunther asked, elbowing Oscar out of his restless thoughts.

"Ya, buddy, let's go outside," Oscar said. They wobbled to stand and made their way to the screen door finding things to hold on to on the way.

Each man leaned against a post on the deck and laughed at the loud wheezing and snorts coming from the couch where Hank lay passed out.

"It was a good day today, but it wasn't cool that Hank didn't show up for work yesterday morning," Oscar said. "The customers can get real pissy when they don't get their lumber. Can't say I blame them. This is going to catch up to Hank at some point, you know. Lately, he is sure to show up for the fun stuff, but he's letting responsibilities slide."

"Ya, I know," Gunther agreed. "I think it already is catching up with him. I think he knows it too," he said, exhaling a huge, long cloud of smoke.

"You could tell he was hurting today too. Was he over here last night?"

"No, he must have sucked back a few at home, alone," Oscar said. "Holly was here, with Anna." His belly felt nauseous.

"Well, I am glad he sucked it up and came out," Gunther said.

"I don't know if he dragged himself out of bed because he wanted to come fishing as much as he didn't want to stay home to fix that squeaky AC unit that Holly has been hounding him about for weeks," Oscar said, laughing.

"Well, regardless, when the fish are biting, and everyone's catching . . . " Gunther said, his fuzzy brain having trouble staying focused. "I heard even ol' Crusty—with his tin can of a boat—caught a few, and he's usually too blitzed to remember to throw his line in! He said his wife threatened to lock the door and withhold sex if he came home with an empty cooler, ha-ha. We should have gone out last week too; why didn't we?"

Oscar took a big puff of his smoke. "I couldn't because the store is too God damn busy, and with Hank shit'n the bed on some of the orders, I feel like I always gotta be around to pick up the pieces."

"You need to knock some sense into him, Oscar," Gunther said, punching his drunk arm in the air. "Hank is a lucky son-of-a-bitch to have Holly, I'll tell you that!" Gunther added as he coughed phlegm out of his lungs and spit it on the ground. "She's a good girl to stick around, and I bet she appreciates what you do for them and the business." He slid down the pillar as if his legs were giving out and sat on the step, leaning his head heavily on the post. He barely held his limp cigarette between his fingers.

"Hey buddy," Oscar said, "I think you should find somewhere to crash too."

"You are *right,* good sir," Gunther pushed himself up against the deck post. "My chariot awaits."

"You're not driving, Gwilliam!" Oscar said.

"Nope, I am *not,*" Gunther said, walking crooked and uncoordinated across the grass to make his way to his truck. "But I *am* going to lay my thick head down and pass out for a bit," he said, howling up at the sky. "Get inside before all the crazies come out Oscar!"

The music echoed out the screen door. Oscar leaned on the door frame to hold himself up. He looked inside but didn't see the girls. He mashed his face into the dusty screen and tried to focus his hazy, sun-burned eyes down the hall towards the washroom and bedrooms. He saw Anna come out of the bathroom and lean against the wall. Holly followed her and stood in front of her close. Oscar squinted to see better. Holly reached up and brushed a messy strand of hair from Anna's face. They stood for a time, face to face, the distance between them lessening more and more. Heart racing, he watched, breathing deep to regain form. Anna's hands reached up to caress Holly's arms, then softly moved up to her shoulders. *Why is she doing this?* Oscar was frozen as he watched his wife's delicate hands continue up, to hide under Holly's hair. His brain couldn't reconcile what he was seeing. *Had his fragile ego arrogantly dismissed Anna's needs? Had he not provided for her and loved her enough? Had their short marriage been a farce?*

48

BEAUTIFUL MISTAKES

Evening clouds were looming over the sunset. Everyone had made their way back from the beach and were hanging out under the picnic shelter.

"Hey, Wallflower!" Ginger plopped herself down on the edge of the warm concrete by Rayna, who had isolated herself from everyone. "This seems like a pretty cool family to holiday with." Ginger looked over her shoulder to see Teddy and Malia trying to jive on the concrete like they were at a high school dance. "I assume you guys are in the same class? Best buds, huh?"

Rayna looked at Ginger with a pouty look on her face and didn't reply.

"Well, you guys act the same," Ginger said, "you look the same, you kind of talk the same. To me, you *look* like besties."

"Ya, but she's the better one by far!" Rayna said.

"Oh, self-loathing!" Ginger teased. "I *am* familiar! Gimme the tea girl. What's up with you?" Ginger attempted to bond with the lonely girl. "Why are you wasting your time being jelly over your friend?" she asked.

"She has the looks without even trying, she can wear literally anything, and she kicks my ass in school *and* sports. Her mom is amazing. Even her *grandpa* is cool," Rayna said, motioning toward Oscar.

"Well, that might be pushing it! Ha, ha. Oh, you *are* in a funk!" Ginger joked.

"It's true. Everyone who ever comes into contact with Mal loves her and gravitates toward her. People only talk to me because I am her friend . . . and you do *not* want to know about *my* family. They are messed up, and super dysfunctional. Malia's family worships her, and I was basically a mistake," Rayna said.

"So, you were a beautiful mistake too, hey? Me too!" Ginger fixed her wind-blown ponytail, flipping her bright red hair directly on top of her head. Rayna was taken aback by her unique beauty and confidence.

"It used to bug me that everyone knew that," Ginger admitted, "but now I wear it like a badge. So, I was the result of a night of poor decisions . . . I was a surprise, so now I live my life *just* like that. My mom had issues. We had no money, she drank, and I have no idea who my father is. I gave up trying to figure that out. So, boo-hoo!" Her big blue eyes pierced into Rayna, keeping her attention. "I amuse myself by shocking others; nothing too crazy, but I am not afraid to try new things and experiment. I don't mean in a *bad* way either; don't misinterpret and distort my words, kid. If I walk in a room and everyone is sad, I try to go against the grain and be happy. When everyone else thinks something can't be done, I am the first person to try it, even if I fail. I wasn't stupid, I overheard some pretty hateful things when I was younger. This is NOT a big island. Everybody knows everybody's business around here, so it was hard coming from a family that struggled. It pissed me off and gave me the strength to try to be even larger in life, just to stuff it to everyone. This world is hard to navigate through, so you better find *your* inner thing that will push you, girl. It can be a crazy roller coaster ride, and no one is going to hold your hand or feel sorry for you, I can tell you that!" Ginger continued to assert her words, "You need to find *your people.* Find real friends who will stand by you and support you and have your back. Ditch the others! It looks like you *have* that in Malia."

"Well, she's going to go off to university and leave me in the dust, I am sure," Rayna said.

"You don't know that," Ginger said. "By the sounds of things, it's *you* pulling away from *her* because of your own insecurities." Rayna was shocked at her insight and forwardness. "You can sit back and feel sorry for yourself, compare yourself to others, and live in the shadow of everybody else or you can get off your cute little ass and rock this life out. *It's your choice, Rayna*! You guys can be best buds, but you still have to be yourself. You know what makes Malia so beautiful? Malia is busy just being Malia, and she's good at it. She seems genuinely herself. Stop trying to be her and *do you.* Just do you—and you will shine super bright."

Rayna continued to mope, "I could never be as successful as her know matter how hard I try."

Ginger had her arm around Rayna's neck, tugging her in. "What the hell are you talking about? You have some amazing money makers, *right* there!" she said, nodding her head toward Rayna's body.

"You mean my boobs?" Rayna asked in surprise.

"No dipshit! Your hands! Ha ha. I *do* like you! I think you would make a kick-ass hairstylist. I think you'd rock at *anything,* actually! Be creative! Stop self-loathing! Use that energy to hustle, girl! Go to school! Be amazing! Be unique! Start your own business! Get rich and stick it to everyone that doubted you!" Ginger gave Rayna's head a friendly push away from her when she stood up and then walked back over to Babs to help her clean up the food.

49

1961 PART II THE MONSTER

Holly had her hand on Anna's stomach, tugging at the material of Anna's pale-yellow dress. Anna giggled. Holly grabbed both ends of Anna's summer scarf that was hanging loose around her neck and pulled Anna back into the bathroom. Oscar opened the screen quietly, trying to restore his mental abilities. Chest pounding, he forged ahead into his music-filled house. His reluctant mind fought with his curiosity. Slowly, his hand guided him along his wall. When he reached the door to the washroom, he stopped, straining to hear over the melodies. He thought he heard movement, then silence, then breathing, then silence. The moment felt like the beginning of the end of his marriage. Forcing a peek around the corner, he saw them intertwined in each other's arms, holding each other in a loving, passionate kiss that he thought only belonged to him. Oscar's heart sank while he watched all their inhibitions let go.

Stopping to look at each other for an intense moment, Anna and Holly harmonized in thought that what they were doing was dangerous, risky, and complicated, but they were not in the right head space to think clearly. Instead, they allowed their emotions to spin and be free. Panting. Kissing. Almost giggling. They had gone there, to that place they had avoided for so long. Until then, they had an unsaid agreement that it was enough to hold hands, enough to run a hand through the other's hair, enough to rest their hands passionately on the small of each other's back.

Oscar stepped back in fear and hurried into the living room. His brain raced. He turned the music off quickly and ran to the screen door whipping it open aggressively. "Holly!" he yelled back, "Come with me to get Hank into bed. Everyone's gone. Let's call it a night."

His motive— to get her away from his wife.

Anna felt caught. Her woozy head whirled fast to come down from high, where she had been enjoying herself. *OH GOD! OSCAR,* she thought as she pushed Holly away.

Holly emerged out of the door of the bathroom, "What? Yeah? What?" she said to Oscar.

"*Let's go*!" He yelled from out on the deck in an angry tone. Holly came outside. Oscar yelled at her to grab Hank under his arm and lift his limp posture up off the couch.

"Okay! Alright, stop yelling, Oscar," she said. She didn't want to leave with her drunk husband, but she would. The moment with Anna was gone, and reality had kicked in.

"Go to bed, Anna!" Oscar yelled back into the house as he stepped off the deck.

Anna stood, looking disconnected on the other side of the screen door, making eye contact with only Oscar. Holly, annoyed under her husband's dead weight, pined for Anna to look at her, but Anna wouldn't make eye contact. Oscar and Holly dragged Hank next door, up the steps, and inside to toss him into bed.

Anna pushed the screen open and stepped out into the night. Hands over her mouth, she tried to replay the intimate moment she shared with Holly in her mushy brain. She sat on the first step, feeling numb, stomach-churning in an endless cycle of guilt. "Things would be different now," she thought, as she looked out into the twilight for answers but got nothing, her head spiraling. *How can I love two people the same but so different?* She stood and walked away from the house into the blackened space.

Anna walked barefoot in reverie and stayed in that elevated moment she had waited so long to have. She could still feel Holly's lips on her mouth. The stars above pulled her up into her dreamscape.

Swaying back and forth in the cool sand, she mimicked the joyful dance she'd had with Holly hours before and remembered that she had released her sweater, leaving it lying somewhere in the dark. *The sweater that belongs to Holly and me*, she thought. She searched to find it.

Anna was lost in thought as she sauntered the beach to clear her mind. Back and forth, her conscience swayed between her love for Oscar, her feelings for Holly and her uncertain future. She felt like she was floating outside herself as she tried to process the events of the evening when someone approached her from behind. Her sixth sense took over, quickly clearing her fuzzy brain. She remembered Holly telling her that the women at the market had been gossiping about some funny business on the beach the night prior. Instantly, Anna regretted leaving her house alone this late at night. Walking faster, her belly urged her to look over her shoulder. Her heart raced. *Turn the fuck around and look; do it!* She panicked. *Do it. Turn and look and see who the fuck it is,* she screamed in her head; her brain was surging in adrenaline. *Do it, NOW*! She did. OH GOD! A hooded man was right behind her. He ripped her summer scarf from around her neck, burning her skin. Every inch of her trembled in fear, sensing something horrible was about to happen. The hidden monster was like a tall shadow about to overtake her; his shoulder was well above hers. A large hand clasped her neck. She reached up to hit him off, but he grabbed her arm, twisting it hard to her side, then up her back, holding her vulnerable in his stern grip. Kicking sand up everywhere, her stumbling feet tried to run away. *Was this Hank? Had he seen her and Holly and was messing with her to get back at her?* She twisted in muddled thoughts. The evil man yanked her closer to him, shoving and waving her off balance in the sand. Slapping and punching with her free hand, she saw his dark eyes—he was a stranger. Scratching. Kicking. Screaming. She was desperate to get free, but he was too strong. Waves of terror washed over her, *PLEASE NO PLEASE NO PLEASE GOD PLEASE NO!* Tears flowed down her panting, bawling face.

The dark monster had a low, gravelly, drunken voice. "Where are you going so fast?" His fingers wrapped harder around her neck, maintaining his control.

She could hardly get the words out; her voice shook and rasped in flowing tears. "My friend is going to be here any second!" Her brain spiralled in panic.

There was a pause, like he was debating what to do next, while he breathed on her. "I'd like to meet your friend," he said with disgusting breath.

"Leave me alone! Please! I beg you!" She cried out again, fighting hard against his chest to put any distance between them.

He held her with terrifying force, keeping his mouth close to her face. She could taste his cigarette smoke. The friction of his gross beard rubbed and burned her sensitive skin. His smelly, greasy hair revealed itself from under his hood. It was happening so fast and yet it felt like time had stopped. He mumbled something, but she didn't hear it over her panicked breaths. His increasingly violent latch around her neck terrified her into silence. Her debilitating fear was no match for his strength as he shook her head back and forth like a rag doll. She pleaded to the heavens; *I don't want to DIE! PLEASE,*

PLEASE GOD STOP PLEASE I BEG YOU, I DON'T WANT TO DIE . . . OSCAR! HELP!

His thumb jammed into the soft of her throat, producing excruciating pain. As she gasped for air, a crushing blow to her upper cheekbone and eye knocked the screams in her head silent. The impact disabled Anna into shock, leaving her blinded and disoriented. His hand grabbed a fistful of her hair, holding her head tight and upright. A wet, revolting tongue entered and smothered her ear, leaving spit running down her neck.

"You KNOW you want it," he whispered in a crude tone.

He threw her down with overpowering force, and in a crushing assault, he kicked her in the ribs and then the stomach, hurling her damaged body around on the sand.

Her mind detached. Everything went dark. Time passed slowly as the vile monster overtook her.

"Come on!" someone yelled in the background, "Hurry up; let's GO!"

The violent criminal staggered up off his knees. He lifted her chin in his giant grasp, her hair smashed to her wet, snotty, sandy face, and with brutal force, punched her with pain that her body could not bear. She fell unconscious to the earth. In a final depraved act, he lifted her head like a rag doll and wrapped her scarf around her neck. Tying knot after knot, allowing her only a little breath, he pushed her back onto the sand.

The monster disappeared into the shadows, where hectic sounds of glass bottles clanged, and muffled voices echoed down the beach as a powerful boat engine pinned through the dark ocean water in the distance.

50

GUILT

The squealing fan elevated Oscar's nerves and interrupted his foreboding thoughts of the conversation he was ready to pounce on Holly. He broke the tension as they stood over Hank, who was conked out and oblivious to the world. "*What* are you doing, Holly?" Oscar asked.

Her voice shook. "I am *sorry*, Oscar. It wasn't to hurt you," she said, looking down at Hank, who lay drooling on the soft pillow of their marital bed, "or him."

"How did you think it wouldn't, Holly?" Oscar said. "How long?"

"I have felt like this for a long time," she said. "I can't speak for Anna."

"She married *me*! You have *no* right," he snarled.

"I know. We've never—" Holly's voice shook with tears at her admission.

"You are fucking everything up, Holly. Why are you messing with her brain? Why are you trying to ruin everything?" he asked.

"I know! I don't know!" She left the bedroom and made her way to the small kitchen of her and Hank's bungalow, face wet with tears and head still swimming from all the earlier shots.

Oscar chased after her. "You are being so fucking selfish!" he yelled as he slammed his fist on the table. He dropped himself hard on the chair, face red in his hands.

Holly ran to close the front door. "Don't yell, Oscar. That's not going to solve anything," she said.

"Don't *you* fucking tell *me* what to do, Holly," he screamed as he swung his hand straight across the table, launching a water glass clear across the kitchen. It shattered into countless tiny pieces that scattered all over the floor. He stood up, continuing to boil in anger, "I can't even look at you right now," he said, pacing around in the living room, shouting over the squeak of the window air conditioner fan. "The four of us have been best friends for as long as I can remember, and you have been lying this whole time? Does Hank know?"

"No, he doesn't," Holly cried.

"Well, he's not going to either," Oscar raged. "You are going to fix this. Whatever the fuck you thought—it's over. Anna is *my* wife! Tell her you were drunk and sick in the head, I don't give a shit, just fix this!"

"Oscar! I don't know if I—"

"I *mean* it Holly! I am not going to let *you* screw up the best thing that has ever happened to me. I swear, I will never trust you again. Live with it or move the fuck away!" Oscar stormed out of the house, slamming the door behind him.

With a trembling hand, Holly grabbed a broom tucked beside the fridge. Looking down at the shards of glass, feelings of guilt and humiliation swept over her. Wailing, she fell to her knees on the kitchen floor.

The island's late-night wind slapped Oscar in the face as he stood on the edge of Holly's porch. He walked back over to his house and stopped reluctantly at the bottom of his deck staircase, holding on to the railing as he struggled to get his mind right. Needing more time, he detoured and bolted to the side of the house, passed Gunther snoring head back and awkward against the window of his truck. Trying to calm the pressure in his erupting body, Oscar flounced around in his insanity in the waving maze of the immensely tall, shaded forest behind his home. His shaking hands feverishly brushing his messy hair off his red-raged face.

Up the deck stairs, Oscar's determined, heavy footsteps echoed out into the oceanfront yard. It wasn't odd, he thought, that Anna had left the door open for him, but it was strange she hadn't turned down at least some of the lights before going to bed. He was wound up, twisted in anxiety—ready to unleash his words on Anna— and hopeful that the house's appearance meant that she was waiting up to do the same. Dashing in and out of each room of the small bungalow, he discovered she wasn't there.

"ANNA!" He yelled for his wife in panic, his stomach wound into a giant knot. *Had she left?* "ANNABELLA! ANNA?!" *Was it all too much for her? Where could she have gone? She knew the beautiful beach could turn into evil dangers, especially alone at night.*

Oscar, trapped in worry, ran out of his house onto the grass to look around. The yard was dark and barely visible.

"Holly! Holly!" Oscar yelled from the bottom of her deck and then ran to Gunther's truck and banged on the window. "Gwilliam! Get up! ANNA'S GONE!" he screamed, scared. "Something's not right!"

The three of them looked out into the blackness toward the sand. Frantic screams boomed up to the twilight as they ran down the beach with urgency pounding in their chests. Holly spotted Anna's sweater among the driftwood. Picking it up, she heard Oscar's curdling cry for help. Anna lay in the sand like a frail carcass that washed ashore. Her perfect complexion was ravaged in bruises, blood, mucus, and tears. Holly fell to her knees beside Oscar as he cradled and wept over his wife. *What had happened to his beautiful wife?* Anna was dead quiet. Holly pulled Anna's skirt down to cover her mottled, shaking legs, and Oscar frantically struggled to untie the numerous knots that constrained her blue neck.

Gunther, struggling with his coordination, was stricken at the sight of his precious friend as she lay beaten, paralyzed in weakness, face against the bloodstained earth. His foggy protective brain filled with a clear, instinctive impulse of aggression. "I will kill them, Oscar!" He charged up to a rock pile and grabbed a large stone, sprinting off into the dark ready to inflict harm on his prey. Holly was crippled in her own distress and guilt.

Anna's dirty, battered body was limp in her husband's arms as he carried her home. Holly followed with Anna's sweater and scarf in her hand. In the desperate, dreaded night, Gunther scoured the coastline for his disgusting opponent, but found no one.

After seeking medical attention and returning home, Anna remained isolated inside the house. Oscar, Holly, Hank, and Gunther alternated taking gentle care of her, and tending to her battered body. Little conversation was had between the four friends. Anna avoided looking at herself in the mirror, disgusted with the sight of her bruises, swollen face, and cuts around her black eye and lip. Oscar gave Anna medicine to dull the pain and anxiety. Gunther dropped off homemade soups, and Hank covered a few of Oscar's shifts at the hardware store. Anna slept most of the day away, and when she was awake, she suffered in silence. Oscar couldn't muster the right words to comfort her. He longed for his wife, even though she was right there in front of him, but she was absent, trapped in the dark of her mind. Holly and Oscar sat in the rocking chairs on the deck while they tried to reconcile how the events of that fateful night unfolded the way they did. The unrelenting guilt of failing to protect Anna ate at them both. In her mind, Holly replayed scenes over and over, wracking herself in anxiety. Oscar did the same and decided he would never leave Anna alone and vulnerable again. Gunther sat quietly on the steps, feeling the misery of his friends, wishing helplessly that he could make it better.

"Do you want some tea, Holls?" Gunther asked kindly, "How about you, Oscar?"

Holly ignored the gesture and stood up to leave. On the last step, welled up in tears, she turned around to look directly at Oscar, "I am *so sorry*—for *all* of it," she said.

Oscar stared at Holly in silence for a moment. He stood up from his rocker. "I know. We will get through this, Holls," he whispered and then disappeared inside the house. The incident would never be discussed after that moment, but the catastrophic effect on all four of them would forever bind the four friends.

After many excruciatingly quiet days, Anna walked into the living room, dressed in the same worn-out T-shirt of Oscar's that she always wore. Oscar lay on the couch, depleted with emotional stress, watching his wife approach slowly. He lifted the blanket to invite her in. She moved cautiously, ribs and muscles still tender, leaving her short of breath with every movement. She lifted her feet under the blanket and tucked her bum and back into the warmth of his frame. His arm wrapped her. The tightness in his worried chest faded away when he saw her wedding ring back where it belonged. He cradled his hand around hers.

Annabella's free spirit was forever damaged to a degree, feeling unsafe walking alone at night and laden with a constant feeling of having to look over her shoulder. Her brain struggled with the perpetrator's description, and she blamed herself that the monster would probably never be held accountable for his actions. Time went on, and she and Holly fell back into their everyday routines, remained extremely close, but never allowing their relationship to go beyond friendship again. Anna had made her choice—Holly had to live with it.

51

PRESENT DAY

"Well, the music stopped playing, and the sun is going down, so I guess that's our cue," Liz said to Babs.

"Oh, I can fix that!" Teddy said, running over to put another tune on the music box.

Liz laughed at him, "Thanks, Teddy, but we really should pack up now." She turned to Luke, "Thank you so much for inviting us, Luke. It was such a great evening."

"Yes, Luke, I am glad we all got to enjoy it," Babs said while boxing up the last of the food items.

"What you built here is pretty damn cool, I agree," Gunther added, while folding up the table to get it out of the way.

"It was my pleasure," Luke said. "Everything is better if you can share it with someone else, right? I'm glad my simple wooden structure could create a place for you all to gather. Hopefully, we can do this again sometime. We are just missing one last thing." He walked to the corner, climbed halfway up the ladder, and reached to attach two extension cords. Loosely draped strings of tiny white patio bulbs lit up the square and surrounded the group from above. In the center, a multicolored disco ball of strobe lights spun magic through the air. The slow rotating colours bounced off the wood and hanging flower baskets, taking everyone's breath away. There was silence while everyone collectively embraced the moment.

In that instant, every individual under the wooden roof saw the genuine, giant smile on Luke's face and was either proud of him, wanted to be him, or be near him.

I want this person close to me forever, Lexi beamed. She thought, *this is the type of man that a woman could find both love and friendship with.*

Teddy changed the music to a soft melody and then turned to Luke, who winked at him with approval. The music seemed to move the flashes and twinkles of reds, blues, greens, and yellows that scattered and bounced off the roof. An electric feeling of unity, family, and connection washed over the group. Positivity and hope floated in the air like invisible, magical particles lifting everyone's spirit. Malia put her arms around Rayna and hugged her tight as they stared up at the ceiling.

Liz tugged the aide's shoulder into hers like a loving mom. "I am going to miss all of you," she said.

Gunther moved close to Babs. Their arms touched. His pinky found her hand, and with a graceful grin, she allowed him to take her hand in his. Her heart sparked at that moment, wanting to openly accept his love—love that she knew she rightly deserved. She stood, clasped in partnership with Gunther, tickled but perfectly poised.

Ronnie, with all his faculties in order, stepped forward into the center of the room with his face up, "It's like a moving rainbow. So beautiful!"

Oscar moved Anna's chair closer to Holly. Anna opened her eyes for a moment and delighted in the view of being surrounded by the people she loved and cherished the most on earth. Under the circling sphere of light, her spirit lay content. Oscar stood beside his wife, and Holly rested her hands on the other side of Anna's chair. Through the thin lids of her eyes, Anna could see the flashes of colour turning around and around. Images of her younger self and Holly dancing in her living room appeared and then disappeared. She was right back in 1961 in her happiest of daydreams. Holly closed her eyes and saw it too—her and Anna, dancing freely from any worries in the world. The memory was perfect. Anna looked the most peaceful that Oscar had ever seen. The spiraling colours reflected off her white hair and her pale, translucent skin. Holly realized right then and there that her friend had made peace with her life's memories. She envied her for being so serene.

52

WRAP IT UP

Off to the side, Mary had taken an Afghan and wrapped herself in it to ward off the end-of-day ocean chill. She sat snuggled, observing her new friends. The collection of everyone's beautiful energy and response to being together in that one blissful moment, thanks to Luke, filled her heart with blessings.

Luke pulled up a chair under the twinkling lights to join her. They leaned into each other just slightly.

Mary spoke softly to him. "What you have done here is a real gift to all these people. You *sure can* teach an old lady a few things."

"Thank you," he said softly, winking at her.

They sat for a while.

Lexi looked over at them and wondered what the two strangers had to talk about for so long. The fact that they were getting along so well did not come as a surprise to her. It only made her more interested in the charismatic man more. Besides, she also had experienced how Mary had "*something* about her" that drew people in.

Mary looked directly at Luke and finally released the words that she was dying to say, "If I haven't told you yet, I am very proud of you, my sweet, amazing *son*," Mary said, "and if you change your mind, there is plenty of room at the estate if you don't want to live in *that trailer*."

"I know, sunshine. That is sweet of you, Mom, but I am *good* here. I really am." He smiled at her with adoration. "I love you too . . . *Mom*," he whispered. "When are you going to let me introduce you as the most amazing woman I know?"

"Shhh," Mary said, tapping the armrest of her wheelchair. "Let's keep that our little secret for now."

He smiled, winked at her again, stood up, and walked away.

Everyone stood under the shelter, staring at the sky ablaze with color, enjoying the remaining last seconds of the majestic disappearing sun.

"This view is intoxicating," Lexi said, feeling positive.

"It sure is, Lex!" Luke said, resting his gaze on her face.

She blushed back at him.

Ronnie had picked up the remaining string lights and wrapped them around the golf cart, making it look like a float in a parade, but in doing so, made it virtually impossible to climb back into. He continued to tangle himself in a mess.

Liz giggled while sipping her pink drink. "He's just so . . . screwy in the cutest way," she said, tilting her head. "Aww!"

Oscar piped up. "It's like you can literally see his brain malfunctioning, like it's on repeat, saying ERROR! ERROR! ERROR!"

"Don't be mean, Oscar!" Liz said like a loving mother.

"I'm *not,* actually," said Oscar, surprised at his own admission. "I'm just *observing*." He looked over at Ronnie and hollered, "I'm gonna miss you, buddy!"

Mary rolled her wheelchair close to Liz.

"Are you ready, Mary? I think we're going to head back now," Liz said.

"That's perfect," Mary said, "I have an important phone call to make before bed, and it is getting a little late."

"Absolutely. The afternoon was wonderful, but it *is* time, isn't it?" Liz said as she snuggled a blanket around Anna, lying with her eyes closed, looking thoroughly bone tired. Liz called out to Ginger, "Mary is ready, and Edward's family just texted from back at Fountain Garden. They said they had a good visit with him at the home, but they are ready to head out. I should go back and help him wind down for the day."

"Sounds good," Ginger said.

"Can I come and help?" Malia asked Liz.

"That would be nice, Malia," Liz said. "You and Ginger could assist Anna while I go talk with Ed's family and make the plan for his pick-up tomorrow evening."

Malia looked at Teddy, "I'll see you later?" she asked, "We need to practice our dance."

"Absolutely," he said, grabbing her cream waffle sweater off the back of a chair and handing it to her.

Oscar kissed Lexi on the cheek. "I'm going to go back on the bus with Anna. I love you String-Bean. Thank you for this," he said.

"It was all Luke, dad," Lexi said.

He grinned at her and walked away, following Ginger and Anna.

Malia ran over to her mom and hugged her tight.

It caught Lexi by surprise. "Oh, okay," Lexi said, unable to lift her arms and reciprocate under Malia's tightly wrapped arms.

Malia whispered into her mom's ear. "He is *amazing,* Mom!" Lexi thought she meant Teddy, but Malia looked at Luke when she pulled away. "Enjoy yourself, Mom! He's a good guy, and you need a friend."

Everyone moved quickly to pack everything up and get back on the bus.

"Do you want these flowers and candles in your trunk?" Teddy asked the aide.

"I do, thanks," she said.

Teddy loaded up all the items, and the aide drove off.

"Whoopee!" Ronnie yelled from his seat. "Going on another trip!"

Teddy slammed the bus door shut.

Gunther and his lovely sidekick Babs gave a big wave to Luke and Lexi as the transfer bus drove off.

"Did you want to help me build a fire, Rayna?" Teddy asked.

"Teddy, I think I am going to go chill in my cabin and call my mom," Rayna said, "but I might come out by the fire after that."

"So, I guess that leaves us two," Luke said to Lexi as he turned the music up.

Lexi grabbed a dirty cup to throw into the plastic bag, but Luke grabbed her hand and set the glass back down on the BBQ table.

"May I?" he asked.

They walked to the center of the circling light and stood in front of each other. A moment of excitement rushed through her veins as she breathed in his cologne. He grasped her right hand and held it close to his chest. Her other hand lay comfortably on his broad shoulder, surrendering to the moment. They moved their feet slowly to the melody—bodies swaying together as one. She allowed herself to relax and melt into his arms.

53

GRANDMA ANNA

Malia entered the room just as Liz finished helping Ginger transfer Anna to bed.

"I put all the food back in the kitchen," Malia said to Liz.

"Thanks, Malia," Liz said as she walked out of the room.

Malia walked over and sat in the chair next to her grandmother as she lay with her arms across her stomach. Malia rested her arm on the bed and reached her hand up onto Anna, careful not to put her full weight on her grandma's belly. With eyes closed and body depleted of energy, Anna moved her fingers to search an inch or two ahead looking for her granddaughter. She found the familiar beautiful material that covered Malia's arm and gave a slow, soft pat. Then, giving in to fatigue, Anna rested her weary hands.

How precious time is, Malia thought.

"Now that she is in her hospital gown, you can help if you like," Ginger said quietly as she walked in holding a towel, washcloth and washbasin. " . . . to help wash her up for bed, I mean." She set everything down on the roller table. "Anna, would you be okay with Malia helping you get ready for bed?" she whispered.

Anna opened her eyes to nod "yes" to Ginger, and then closed her eyes again.

"*Only* if you would like, though," she said to Malia, giving her a reassuring smile, "Go ahead and raise her bed even more so that it is at a workable height for you and then pull the curtain to give yourselves privacy. You can undo her gown at the neck . . . *if* you are comfortable doing that. I'll go get us water. Use this to cover her," she said, setting a warm towel on the bed. "It's still warm from the dryer. She likes that. But *only* if you want to, Malia." Ginger walked out, holding the basin, closing the door completely behind her.

Malia reached down, feeling nervous, and took her grandmother's frail hand in hers. *Could she do this?* she wondered. Her heart skipped. She thought she could do it, and she wanted to, but would her grandma really want her to? She felt the light squeeze of her grandma's soft fingers around her youthful hand. She looked at her grandmother's partially shut eyes to see them looking back at her. Anna worked up a slow, simple smile.

"Okay," Malia whispered to her, "if you are sure," she confirmed again.

Anna let her hand go loose and fall to her side, closing her eyes again. Malia reached for the ties behind her neck. Finding the end of the string, she pulled it loose. She reached over her grandma with a cautious pace to pull down her gown, revealing Anna's delicate, bony structure. Her hands trembled. When she reached just above her grandma's breasts, she stopped and grabbed the warm towel to cover her. Anna's head relaxed deeper into her pillow as the warmth of the towel soothed her. She felt safe, drifting in and out of peaceful sleep.

A moment later, Ginger entered the room. Malia could hear her on the other side of the curtain, washing her hands in Anna's sink. Quietly, she made her way through the curtain to the other side of the bed, where she placed the basin. "Are you able to work over the side rail? If not, you can put it down," she whispered lightly.

"No, it's fine," Malia whispered back.

Ginger began to wash Anna's perfectly pale, worn-out body. The room was silent. Malia grabbed her own washcloth and copied every move that Ginger performed on the other side of Anna. The movements were slow, purposeful, and loving. Malia felt closer to her grandmother than she had ever felt possible and appreciated that Ginger was quiet and didn't feel the need to talk. Both stayed silent, remaining attentive to Anna's body, brushing her softly with the warm, damp cloth along her thin, fragile skin. When they were finished, Ginger smiled sweetly and handed Malia a clean gown. She took the cloth from Malia's hand, grabbed the basin and towels and left through the curtain.

"When you are done, lower the bed and give her the call bell," Ginger said from the other side of the curtain.

Malia gently laid the new gown over her grandmother, tucked the upper part just barely over her shoulders and left the gown loose. Anna opened her eyes and looked up at her granddaughter with pride. She covered Anna with her soft blanket and bent over to kiss her forehead. "I love you, grams." She lowered the bed as far as it could go, attached the call bell to the side of Anna's pillow and left the room. In the hall, Malia leaned against the wall and took the deepest breath she had ever taken, shocked at her own bravery and accomplishment. *Oh my god, did that just happen?*

"You did well, Malia!" Ginger said, approaching her with a pleased look on her face. "I really appreciate your help. Your grandma is so relaxed now, plus I have her night meds here," she said, showing her a small medicine cup, "so she is going to sleep like a baby."

"Okay, good. Thank you for letting me help, Ginger. That really was amazing. I felt like a nurse helping my grandma like that. Makes me feel like maybe—one day—I could be one."

"You should consider that for sure, Malia," Ginger said, walking into Anna's room.

Malia saw her mom sitting with Oscar in the TV room. "Oh, I didn't know you were here, Mom," she said, walking up to them.

"Yes, I just wanted to come say goodnight quickly," Lexi said, "and bring you this for your walk home." She handed Malia a flashlight. "Teddy gave it to me to bring to you. He's very thoughtful, that boy."

Malia lit up, "I'll see you back at camp then?" she said, looking excited to get back to camp to see her new crush.

"Yes honey," Lexi said. "You go; I won't be long."

"Did you walk here, mom? Maybe *you* should keep the flashlight." Malia said.

"Nope. I'm good. He gave me one too," Lexi chuckled, lifting up a small yellow light.

Malia ran up to Oscar, "Good night, grandpa!" she said, grabbing Oscar's head in her hands and giving him a playful kiss on the forehead.

"Good night, kid! Sleep tight!" Oscar said proudly.

Malia started to walk backwards toward the hall, shooting her mom one last look, *You can do this, Mom. Talk!* She said with her eyes. Lexi acknowledged her daughter with a smile before Malia turned and ran out.

54

TRUTH TIME

"She's a great kid, that granddaughter of mine!" Oscar beamed.

"Yes," Lexi agreed, "she makes me so happy. Do I make *you* happy, Dad?" Lexi asked, bracing herself to receive his answer.

"What I *am*, and always have been, is proud of you. There's a difference. I know what you have done. I know the courage it took for you to leave the island, Lexi. You were brave to put yourself out there, move to the big city, and create a whole new life. I couldn't be more proud of you for the amazing daughter you raised, for putting yourself through school, and for getting your career. You always held everything together, Lexi. I was always watching, don't kid yourself . . . and you did most of it *alone.*" He looked right into her eyes, and she burst into tears. "You did it alone, honey." He wiped his sad face. "I can't believe what *all* you have done. Your mother and I watched Brock put his work before you and Malia for years. It just made me so Goddamn mad, Lexi."

She wiped her tears, "Dad, we are over. Brock and I are done. My marriage didn't work."

Oscar sat quietly. His silence and lack of expression indicated he wasn't surprised. Lexi braced herself for the words that would emerge from his mouth.

"You are so special, String-Bean. It makes me sad to see you sad." He paused to clear his throat. "Find someone that appreciates you and fills your heart," he said, changing his tone, "or, if you want to be alone, then that is okay too." He gave her a pat on her leg. "That kid and his money came to the island and promised you the world, and now look at you, having to work so hard, stuck in an office all day, missing out on everything that is happening with Malia."

"Oh, Dad, lots of women work and raise kids. Let's face it; you and Mom were never really interested in my work." As the words came out of her mouth, she instantly regretted saying them. She knew they could ignite a fight—that was not her intention.

Oscar got defensive. "You know what, kid, I *don't* give a shit about the work you are doing right *now* because I don't think *you* do. When you say anything about it—you have no *heart*. You don't talk about your work with the passion and energy like you did when you talked about working at Hill's and out in the community here on the island. Besides that, I don't want to talk about your work, honey! You and I *barely* talk because, with Brock never around, you're always so busy doing everything. So, I'm not going to waste valuable time asking you about all that crap you're doing at your job. I care about what you are finally doing when you get home at night. I want to know what you and *Malia* are doing. I want to know if you guys went for a walk; you used to love spending all your time outside. Are you snuggling on the couch, watching a movie? Are you going to her sports games, shopping, or is she getting into trouble with that friend of hers? I don't hear you spending much family time together anymore, Lexi, and she is leaving for university soon. You might regret that one day, honey. No, Brock did *not* care for my little girl like he said he would! I know this sounds harsh, but you were eye candy for him. That's it! Look where that got you—"

"Dad, for the record, I chose to go to work. I wanted to work. I wanted something for myself."

"I don't know, honey; it sounds to me like you were reaching for something else because you were bored and lonely, and your husband was nowhere to be found. He wasn't at home, taking care of his family, that's for sure. Every time I called, that shithead was out with his bigwig friends, living it up with his fancy cars, fancy clothes, fancy trips and where was my baby? You were at home alone, not sharing in that big life with him. He has *not* protected my baby girl."

Lexi shook her head at how old school her dad could be in his way of thinking.

"He took you away, put you up in a fancy house, and left you to deal with everything on your own. That's not a *real* man. Money doesn't make a man, that's for sure, and that's no way to live, String-Bean."

"I didn't know this was going to happen, Dad. What was I to do, stay *here* forever? I thought I could make my life in the city work. I wanted to *be* somebody," she said, regretting her words again.

He sat up high in his chair, and his facial expression and composure completely changed. He was livid with her last comment.

"BE somebody? And Brock helped you do that? Is that what you are saying?"

"No," she said, sinking into the couch, tears rolling down her face.

"I know you girls nowadays can literally do everything on your own, better than us even, but . . . maybe if you would have stuck around here, maybe, just maybe, you could have found someone to fall in love with here, someone you could have built a life with. A man *or* a woman! Look at your mom and me. We were happy. And look at the life your mom could have built with Holly if *I* wasn't around. They didn't need me. Everybody knows they didn't need me . . . I don't even know why your mom stayed with me," he said, as his eyes trailed off, "But we all had a good life here."

He took a long pause to breathe. Lexi realized her dad was struggling with his own issues, more than she had been privy to.

"Jesus Christ! It makes me angry when you say you need to 'BE somebody!' What does that even mean anyway? You were *always* somebody. You are Lexi Davies!" Oscar said, completely dropping her married name, Kirk like it didn't exist. "You are smart and giving and loved by everyone that knows you. When you were here, you worked hard in your community, you helped your friends, you were there for your neighbors, and you were busier than anyone I knew. You practically ran that store by yourself, String-Bean," he said, taking a giant breath. "You were my right-hand man. We all missed you so much when you left. You don't even talk to your neighbors in the city!"

Her mind trailed to Luke, who had said something similar earlier.

Oscar continued to hammer his point. "You gardened with your mom and helped keep this island beautiful, and you literally walked the beach every day picking up garbage for fun. Who does that? You did all that stuff at your school. God, what didn't you do? When you left, you left a hole here; you were missed because you *were somebody*, String-Bean. You ARE somebody, honey! It breaks my heart that you don't think that. Who put it in your head that you had to live somewhere big, have a title, or a certain amount on a paycheck to be somebody?" Oscar couldn't resist. "Ya, I know who . . . "

"I know that this is a good place to live, Dad; don't get me wrong."

"Damn right it is, and everyone that lives here is 'somebody!'" he said, pulling a pill out of his shirt pocket and tossing into his mouth. He crunched it hard and swallowed it. She felt guilty that she was causing him pain.

"You think anybody looks at me now, here in Fountain Garden and gives a shit how I made a living? They don't give a shit. They see an old man in a wheelchair who they hopefully miss seeing at Hill's Hardware store because 'I' was there when they needed to find supplies and electrical wire and all that stuff after a windstorm flipped their greenhouses and sheds right out of their yards, and 'I' told them how to repair those things." Oscar had to catch his breath; his thick chest was trying to compensate. "And then after work 'I' drove to their house to help them *repair* those things . . . and then after *that,* they offered me dinner!" He was determined to get his point across, even breathlessly. "Then we all sat around at their old kitchen table together, as friends, and ate *together* because we were thankful to have each other in our lives. So ya, I *am* somebody, your mom is somebody, Holly is somebody. We all are."

"Dad—" she tried to apologize but he wouldn't let her.

"And you know what we talked about at that neighbour's kitchen table, honey? We talked about why I'm such a grumpy old asshole sometimes. It's because I miss my daughter that I feel I don't see anymore because she is off somewhere working for some big named company that doesn't know anything about the real genuine-hearted girl that she is, and to top it all off, she's living with a man who doesn't appreciate her and kiddo—that breaks my heart. You were always somebody String-Bean."

"*Dad*! Stop! You are going to have a heart attack! I shouldn't have said that. I honestly understand everything you are saying. Maybe I just needed to leave in order to really appreciate what I had here. I *know* I have to figure my life out. I am getting divorced. I'm not happy," she said, putting her hands on her forehead, exhausted. "I have so much to figure out. I want Malia to be proud of what I have accomplished, and I want to show her how I can stand on my own two feet."

"I agree," Oscar said, "so do it!" He reached for Lexi's phone that was lying beside her on the arm of the couch.

"DAD!" She tried to grab the phone.

Oscar leaned far back blocking her with his other arm pretending to talk, "Hey, Brock, my daughter doesn't want to be married to you anymore! She deserves better, she's better on her own actually! It's been a slice, pal." He smiled at her and tossed the phone on her lap.

She flopped herself back on the couch, smiling through her tears. She appreciated his attempt to be funny. Her mood lifted as she drew on her dad's strength in that moment, something she had not done in a long time.

"I love you, Dad," she said.

"I love you too, kid."

The light from her flashlight bounced off the tree trunks, cutting through the dark and illuminating the path that led her back to camp. Lexi felt surprisingly calm, confident and at peace, even walking alone through the dark forest. Why had she waited so long to talk to her dad? Every honest and raw word that rolled off his tongue—about his life on the island— inspired her to live her own truth as well. She felt stronger after their conversation. The heaviness of her worries seemed to weigh lighter now, and she felt hopeful, even with an uncertain future, because having her dad's support meant everything. She laid alone and happy, snuggled in her cabin bed and floated off into the fantasy.

She opened the trailer door and stepped inside, shutting it behind her. He lay reading beside the night lamp. He set his book down and got up from his bed. No words were spoken as he stood in front of her. His touch was slow as the tips of his fingers flirted with her thigh. His rough hands continued to explore and tease the sides of her legs, grazing her skin softly as if to ask permission. She felt a slight lift of her red sundress and the pressure of his full palms on her warm skin as his hands provoked her more. They were close in the darkness. Their breaths were heavy and inviting. He moved his mouth from the side of her neck to linger sensually over her mouth, then pulled away. All her little hairs were aroused in excitement while her body pulsed with heat. Her hands moved freely and willingly, surveying his muscular shoulders under his thin T-shirt; they grasped at his athletic build. His soft, seductive lips rested on her chin. She pulled back as if to say that she was still deciding. But she had already decided. She wanted the warmth of his body; she wanted to feel his skin against hers. Every part of her wanted.

55

MAKING ROUNDS

Night came. Everyone was nestled, quiet in their rooms. Ginger peeked her head into the staff room, where Liz sat at the table looking tired.

Ginger startled her. "Liz, I am going to go help Babs load some stuff into her car, and then I'll take off, okay?" she said.

"Okay, Ginger, thank you so much for today," Liz said, standing up to walk out of the room. Ginger grabbed her and gave her a quick hug before walking out of Fountain Garden.

Liz shut the staff room door. She walked slowly and quietly, knowing this would be one of the last evening rounds she would do. Walking in the dim hall, she noticed the aide had left a bouquet from dinner on Bab's office counter. She continued to walk past the guppy. *And who is going to take you?* she thought.

Liz checked in on Ronnie, who was absolutely gassed from the day. He was snoring loudly and sprawled crooked on his bed. She covered him up with a blanket and then left his room, continuing down the hall.

The Everything Room was dark, hiding all its disarray. Taped to the door was a bright new sign with large, colorful words on a single sheet of paper. Liz paused to admire it. It read, HAIR BY BABS, in bright orange, purple, and green marker and was outlined in sparkles. Underneath the words was an impressive drawing of a pair of scissors and a comb. Liz touched the paper. *Very, very, sweet that Rayna. Babs will be tickled,* she thought.

She walked around the corner into the empty TV room, making her way to the opposite entrance, tidying along the way. She turned the little lamp on to give a bit of light through the area in case someone woke up in the night. She stopped to look at Mary's finished puzzle and then moved on. *I'll take the plants home tomorrow,* she thought to herself, making a to-do list in her head.

Once she was back in the hall, she looked left to see Mary's door closed tight. *What an absolutely lovely woman. I won't disturb her again; she will call if she needs help.*

The door to Ed's dark room was open; his deep breaths echoed out into the quiet hall. *God, I hope your family discussing the move tomorrow didn't stress you out too badly,* she thought, closing his door.

She turned right and made her way back toward the hall that had Holly, Anna and Oscar's rooms.

A small night light lit up Holly's room. A soft tune played from her music box in the background. Liz peeked in and saw Holly sitting in her rocker with an Afghan over her legs. She was slowly turning the pages of her album and seemed content staring at pictures of her and Anna's life as best friends and neighbours. Liz left her to her memories. Anna's room was the last stop. Liz would not go to Oscar's room and disturb him—she was sure he would be content from the amazing day.

56

ALL THE LOVE

Liz took a deep breath and gently pressed the door to Anna's dark room open. She approached the bed with a gentle pace and set her hand on the side bed rail. Anna's frame was snuggled cozily in her sheets, her breath was slow, quiet and restful. *I am so glad today worked out,* Liz thought as she reflected on the success of the day. *I hope you enjoyed it somehow, Anna. I know I did. I am crushed that this will all be over soon.*

Through the darkness of the room, Liz reached onto the dresser to click the soothing, dim-lit, red-tinted light so Anna could locate the call bell if she woke. She looked at Anna through the red glow, taking in her features. *Mrs. Annabella Davies!* She said to herself, focused on Anna's tiny, frail face in the soft light. When she went to leave, she noticed that someone had closed the blinds. She walked over to the foot of Anna's bed and reached for the string to open them, knowing that was what she would want. She pulled slowly and quietly.

Liz's heart overflowed with emotion. A wave of tears pushed to the surface as her eyes scanned what was in front of her. Beautiful hand-crafted posters taped to the outside of the window read: "GRANDMA, YOUR EYES ARE SO BEAUTIFUL."

Liz squeezed the tears out of her eyes, smearing her makeup with her fingers.

"I FELT YOU SPEAKING TO ME WHEN YOU TOUCHED MY ARM, GRANDMA."

Her wet eyes jumped from poster to poster, her heart exploding inside her.

"OSCAR AND HOLLY REALLY, REALLY LOVE YOU."

"I WILL TAKE CARE OF MOM." The "I" had a line through it, and the word "WE" was written on top.

"WE WILL BE GOOD GIRLS." Two pony-tailed figures of the Malia and Rayna holding hands danced on the white paper.

"YOU ARE SAFE, GRANDMA!" A bright red heart balloon floated up into a starry night sky.

Liz had both her trembling hands on her mouth to smother her crying. She looked down at Anna and allowed all her emotions to fully surface before leaving the room. Her tears continued throughout the night, wetting the pillow of the staff room bed where she slept. Tomorrow she would be strong again.

57
LETTING HER GO

Oscar couldn't sleep, even though it was late, and he was tired. All his senses were being pulled to Anna. He sneaked quietly into his wife's room. His heart burst with emotion as he absorbed all the love from the posters on Anna's window. He pushed the release button to lower her side rail and moved his wheelchair as close to his Annabella as possible, wrapping his hand around her delicate bony arm. The curves of her figure caught his eye from the moment he saw her all those years ago. As a young woman, she had a healthy, muscular frame, and liked to wrestle and tussle with him. Her playful personality made it easy for them to want each other intimately. She was free with her body and danced like an angel, whether she was in the middle of the living room, barefoot on the beach, or naked in the bedroom. Under the weight of his hand, she felt so tiny and fragile now.

"I guess this is what our life has come to my precious, Annabella. Where did the time go, my sweetheart?" he said, rubbing his face. "I still need you, Anna." He pleaded in a whisper, wiping the tears wanting to flow free out of his eyes. "You are my person. You are my treasure. I have everything because of you. You are all I ever needed, even if you didn't always feel the same way. I always worried you would leave me Anna. I couldn't imagine a life without you in it, honey. You didn't have to stick with me, but you did, and I am so grateful, honey." He wept.

Anna tilted her head—in the tiniest way—toward him and used all her strength to keep her eyes slightly open. Oscar lifted her weightless hand, leaned over and kissed her light as a feather leaving tears to trail down her cool, translucent skin. He looked away from her and glanced out the window for some sort of relief from his anguish. "I will be better for Lexi. I won't let you down. The girls will be okay—I will make sure of it, my love."

58

DAY 4

It was a brand-new day. A vibrant and magnificent yellow, orange and red sun rose above the horizon. Holly entered Anna's room, having barely slept. It was 5:12 am. She put her brakes on and slowly and quietly flipped up the footrests on her wheelchair. Standing up, she balanced herself on the side arm rail of Anna's bed and then pressed the button to release it, so there was nothing between her and Anna. Lifting the bottom of her nightgown, she climbed up onto the bed and snuggled in on Anna's side.

Her head rested against her friend's bony shoulder and her hand laid gently on to Anna's blanket-covered chest to feel the slight rise and fall of her breath.

Inhale.

Exhale.

In.

Out.

They breathed together.

Her eyes scanned the posters unhurriedly and rested on the one that read, "YOU ARE SAFE, GRANDMA."

Holly prayed.

Anna rested in her lucid dream of dancing in a white dress, barefoot in the sand. Her body flowed easily, like a vibrant silhouette in the sun. She beamed with her girlish smile, radiating energy and love. She held a pale violet scarf in her hand. It blew freely in the wind.

The dream faded away and transitioned to another . . .

Oscar sat at the kitchen table, drinking his coffee. Holly was sipping tea from a cup, sitting on the counter in Oscar and Anna's kitchen as if it were hers. In her playful way, Anna twirled her body around the kitchen between her two favorite people—floating in love—teasing them with her attention.

Her mind went dark.

Oscar woke from his sleep hearing footsteps outside his door. He looked over to the clock on his dresser. It was only 6 am. The peacefulness and calm of the early morning turned into quiet commotion. Barely audible whispers and mutters turned to silence again. He lay there as his awareness heightened and his stomach filled with a sickening feeling. More footsteps walked passed his door, more sounds of rush and haste, and then no movement at all. Oscar knew. As his heart sank deeper, he maneuvered his old body to sit up and move to the edge of his bed. The quiet was deafening and scary. Fear in his belly turned to desperation to escape his room. He reached for his wheelchair and bound for the door. He looked right down the dim, quiet hall and saw Liz standing at the entrance to Anna's room motionless—staring inside. She turned her head, and in a low breath, she crushed Oscar's soul by barely managing the words, "I am SO sorry, Oscar. She's gone."

59
CHANGE

Lexi had received word from Liz in the early morning hours that her mom had passed on. Anna had let go of the present. She was free from time. Free from everything. Saying goodbye to her mom that morning was the hardest thing that Lexi would ever do. She and her dad had stood over Anna's bed sobbing and thanking her for the blessed life that she had so selflessly provided to them. Father and daughter, holding each other tight as they cried their hearts out—making promises to the universe that they would forever keep Anna's memory alive and live a life that would make her proud.

Lexi sat on the sandy beach in front of the glorious morning sun. Tears streamed down her cheek as she grieved in a quiet, intimate moment. She closed her eyes under the warm sky and let the light ocean breeze dry her salty tears. Now, as she sat alone, she could feel her mom's presence.

Malia approached her mom slowly, seeing that she was deep in thought while sitting alone. Walking up in her bare feet; and holding her flip-flops in her hand, she plopped herself down beside Lexi. "Mom. Are you okay?" she asked, wiping her runny nose.

Lexi sat with her arms wrapped around her tucked knees, rocking herself to find comfort in her sorrow. Malia copied her and leaned to the side to nudge her. "Hmmm? Are you?" she asked, looking at her mom with watery eyes and rosy cheeks.

"I am," Lexi said. "I am so sad, but I am okay too. How are you, honey?"

"I feel the same. I am going to miss grandma," she said, wiping her face, "but at least she is not in any discomfort anymore, right?"

They sat for a long time, hugging and staring out at everything and nothing. Lexi surrendered in that moment, in front of the expansive ocean, to accept that everything had changed. Just as she had to let go of her mom—she was ready to let go of herself. She looked at her daughter in awe of her strength and bravery and paused to take a breath and find her words. "I have been wanting to talk to you, Malia, and I am so sorry it has taken me this long," Lexi said. "Things are going to be different now when we get home."

"I know that," Malia said, tilting her head into her mom's shoulder. "Are you and Dad getting a divorce?"

"We are, honey, and you are entitled to feel any way you want about that," Lexi said, looking directly into her daughter's eyes.

"I just want you both to be happy again, Mom," Malia said, holding back tears.

"Me too," Lexi said. "I need you to know that we are going to be okay. I don't know exactly what the future holds, but we are all going to be okay. Your dad and I both want the best for you," Lexi reassured her. "We love you so much, honey. Our life is going to feel different, and look different, but we are going to make it work so that nobody gets hurt."

The two of them sat for a while, each absorbed in their thoughts.

"I don't know if this is the right time, but I have something to tell you, Mom," Malia said, holding up her phone.

"What's this?" Lexi asked, seeing that she had received an email.

"I got in, Mom! I got into university right in Adasa, and there are dorm rooms available too," Malia said, barely containing her excitement.

"Oh my God, honey!" Lexi felt a rush of joy for her daughter, "I knew you would get in! Your grandma is already looking after you."

"I think so, Mom!"

Lexi looked at her daughter—her sweet baby had grown up so quickly.

In her cabin, Malia was staring back at her reflection in the mirror. Looking at her favorite jean shorts and her casual loose tank top, she pondered what she would wear for the first day of university. The thought of possibly meeting up with Teddy on campus excited her. She could hear Rayna's flip-flops on the deck as she entered the cabin. Rayna sat on the bed, hair messy in her ponytail and eyes still tired from having been woke so early with the news of Malia's grandma. She sat quietly, watching intently as her friend got ready, prepared to be whatever Malia needed in a buddy that day.

"Up or down? I think up," Malia said, whipping her head down to make her hair fall toward the floor. Bunching her brown locks in her hands, she flipped her long hair back into a perfectly cute ponytail. "We're the pony posse again today." She stifled a sweet smile, trying to act fun and normal despite the sadness that lingered over the morning.

Something in Ginger's words from the day before, resonated with Rayna. In a rare confident moment, she reached up and pulled her elastic to release her hair from her messy ponytail.

"I think I'm going to try something different today, '' Rayna said, sitting on the bed.

"Good idea, Ray. Here let me help you. You have amazing hair!" Malia said, jumping behind her on the bed. She fluffed Rayna's hair, so it laid nicely down her back, grabbed two little sections from just over her ears, and twisted them to meet at the back of her head. She put the elastic back in to secure the two twists together and ran her fingers through the hanging hair strands to make everything neat. Malia pushed Rayna's back. "Go look in the mirror," she said. She stood behind her friend with her hands on Rayna's shoulders. "See! It's so pretty!"

"Ya. I love it," Rayna said, fiddling with a strand above her eye and pulling a tiny section to lay beside her face.

"I LOVE YOU! I am so glad you are here with me, Ray!" Malia said, bear-hugging her. "I want you in my life forever."

"I love you too, Mal!" Rayna reached up to embrace Malia's arms that wrapped around her.

60

BROKEN

Holly lay in bed, out of breath from crying. She couldn't fight her sadness and was depleted of energy. She dozed off and fell into a recurring ghostly nightmare that she could not escape; a scene of her and Anna holding hands and just as Holly asks Anna to 'please stay', Anna smiles, releases her clasp and vanishes into thin air. The sound of cardboard being dragged across the floor toward her closet woke her. Ginger was standing there, looking devastated as she worked to pack Holly's belongings.

Part of Holly thought she should get up and help Ginger, but depression overtook her, so she continued to lay in bed. She scanned the room with her eyes. Three small boxes were pushed off to the side on the floor and her dresser was bare. The picture of her and Anna embracing girlishly was gone. The ornamental angel was gone. She wondered if her three drawer dresser was empty now. Her whole life had fit into a few mere boxes.

Had her whole existence been boxed up quietly during one nap? *Anna was lucky she didn't have to stay and experience any of this,* she thought as she watched in silent torture while Ginger packed her things to be moved, yet again, somewhere new.

"Holly, I know you didn't eat breakfast. You must be getting hungry. It's almost noon, so if you decide to eat lunch, I have a plate for you. I can bring it here in your room if you don't want to be around anyone," Ginger said as she undid the top buttons of Holly's blouse and slid it off the hanger. She held it close to her chest, and with each meticulous fold, Ginger could feel emotions well up inside her. She bent over to tuck the blouse perfectly in the corner of the moving box, stood up, and reached for another item. Pushing the empty hangers aside, she reached to the top of the wardrobe and pulled down the soft, lightweight knit, sweater.

In her shaky voice Holly yelled, "No, don't pack that! It's Anna's."

Ginger scrunched the soft lavender material tight in her hands as her tears fell freely, "Oh, Holly. I'm sorry."

Holly felt paralyzed in fear and grief, her brain had become unbearably weak as she questioned her own existence.

Teddy walked in and saw both women in distress. He took the sweater from Ginger's hands, walked over to the bed, and placed it gently across Holly's side rail. "We don't need to pack this up. You might want it for the ride tomorrow morning. Let me get these boxes for you, Ginger," he said, bending over to lift the smaller box to stack them on top of the larger one.

"Careful, that box has photos in it," Ginger said.

"I will, Ginger. I got this," Teddy said. "You have been amazing to me the entire time I have worked here—let me do this for you."

Holly turned her head toward the window. Teddy and Ginger's compassion and young hearts made her feel as old as the trees beyond her window. The tall green forest was dead still. That's what she prayed for. Stillness and nothing. She didn't have the energy to tackle the days to come. She wanted her dark, foreboding thoughts to finally be over. Teddy and Ginger finished up and left Holly in the quiet. She closed her eyes toward the sky. Her body felt crippled and trapped in sorrow. She would have to be forced out of bed today because there was nothing to look forward to.

61

SORRY

There was a knock at the door.

"Come in." Ginger said from inside the staff room. She had just placed the binder labelled "Annabella Davies" in a box and wrote something on top of the lid.

"Hey," Rayna mumbled as she stood at the door looking abased.

"Hey you. You, okay?" Ginger asked, sensing that the young girl in front of her was just as sad as everyone else.

"Um, ya," Rayna said, "I guess." She reached into her pocket and pulled out Perla May's necklace. "I borrowed these. They are Perla's . . . *were* Perla's," she said, correcting herself.

"You borrowed them, huh?" Ginger took the gold chain and caressed the gritty, eggshell-colored gemstone. "That sounds a little hinky there, Chica!" She reached for Rayna's sheepish shoulders. "So, from self-loathing and self-deprecation to conscious-stricken—hmmm, that's *growth* girl, and you've only been here four days!" Ginger tried to shed light on the dark, sad day. She pulled open Rayna's pocket and dropped the round, delicate gem inside, patting the pocket with her flat hand. "You keep it," she said. "Go be *better*. Do what we talked about, okay, and come back here and visit me."

Rayna smiled and walked out of the room, knowing that she would forever be changed by her visit to Fountain Garden.

62

HEARTBROKEN

Oscar found an inconsolable Holly sitting on the swing by the fountain; someone had successfully urged her to get out of bed to sit in the comfort of the sun. She looked puny and emotionally drained as she stared blankly at the streaming water in front of her. Her legs snuggled in a tiny blanket, and Anna's cozy sweater draped her shoulders. Oscar felt sickened to his core as he rolled up in his wheelchair, feeling the heaviness that lingered in the air. When he approached, Holly didn't turn her head or acknowledge him. Her body tensed. His chest was panting, and his face blotched with sorrowful emotion. Holly's eyes looked beaten from crying, but her face held stern. They sat beside each other—their pain continued to surface from the deepest part of themselves, with only the bubbling sounds of the fountain in front of them.

Ronnie sat at the lunch table by himself, fiddling with his thumbs. He watched Babs over in the kitchen, putting cream cheese on two cinnamon-raisin bagels. Liz entered the dining area, looked over at Ronnie and gave a half smile, and then leaned on the kitchen counter to whisper to Babs. Ronnie's ears perked up to listen to what the serious women were saying.

"Have you seen Oscar and Holly?" Liz asked Babs.

"I think they're outside. They both refused to eat this morning," Babs whispered, shaking her head sadly.

Ronnie was upset having heard Babs' words.

"Don't worry about it, Babs. They will eat when they are ready," Liz said, "and if they don't—then that's okay too. Gunther is at the front door to help with the boxes; I just thought you should know."

"Oh," Babs said, "thanks for telling me." She picked up the plate and a glass of juice, walked over to Ronnie to place them both down in front of him, and then walked out of the room with Liz.

With clear intention, Ronnie grabbed the plate and walked the savory warm-smelling bread outside to the deck area to find his friends.

"Holly!" Oscar begged. "Please . . . " He reached out to touch her knee, stopping the swing from moving. "Please, Holls. I can't stand it when you are quiet."

A tear flowed down her pale, expressionless face. "I'm angry. I am so angry with you," her voice cracked. Her hands trembled as she wiped her hair away from her face. "You know that you always did *just* enough to make sure she would stay with you. It was selfish," she said in a low, stern tone as she stared straight ahead.

"I *know* you're angry," he said, validating her in hopes to ease her pain.

"It doesn't matter that you know; it's too late now. It was *our* fault that Anna got hurt that night. I would have been there for her if you wouldn't have dragged me out of the house," she said, turning her head to look at him dead on.

"That's not fair Holly," Oscar said. "As Hank's wife, you should have been helping with him too."

"I know, Oscar!" Holly shouted, "But . . . that's why she got hurt that night and then she changed . . . and you used her fear to somehow make it about *you.* You somehow made her believe that if she stayed with you, that you could protect her more." Holly started to bawl. Her shoulders dropped, and her posture became small. She needed a reason to understand why Anna didn't choose her all those years prior, and Oscar was willing to take the blame just to relieve her of her sorrow. In his sad mind, arguing with her now, about something that happened so many years prior, would be pointless. "That night ruined my life, Oscar!" Holly said, as she wept with her face in her hands.

Ronnie made long, decisive steps along the path, coming around the circle from the backside of the fountain. He stopped abruptly when he heard Holly crying. He peeked around the corner, shocked to see Oscar looking sad in his wheelchair and Holly grieving on the swing. Ronnie took a quick step back out of view and stood contemplating what he should do. He set the food down on the fountain ledge, pushed the small paper plate a little more around the corner in hopes that Oscar would see the bagels, and then quickly left the area.

Oscar slammed his brake down and hurled himself up clumsily to get out of his wheelchair. He reached over, grabbed the swing, and swung his body around to plunk himself down. He grabbed Holly around her shoulders and body to shield her from her sadness. His entire body pulsed with guilt. He rocked her, trying to console her while wrapped up in his misery.

Holly let her head drop against his chest. "She was *my* person! She is the *only one* who occupied my brain all these years."

"She was *mine* too," Oscar whispered with his head dropped.

"I don't want to do life with anyone else," she bawled uncontrollably.

"Stop, Holls!" Oscar pleaded, wrapping her tight.

"I don't want to be here, Oscar." She looked up into his swollen red eyes.

"Shhh," he whispered.

She crumbled like a tiny, scared kitten, burrowing herself under his arm.

"I loved her. I adored her." Oscar said, "You need to understand that Holly."

"But I think I loved her more," she wept.

"That's not true, Holly. It was just different," he said, trying to reason with her as he kissed her head.

Holly melted in despair. "I can't live like this. I have to be with her," she cried out. "We are supposed to be together." She sounded like a child begging and pleading; her desperation was raw, honest, and excruciating to watch.

Oscar's hands shook and his face quivered uncontrollably. He didn't know he could feel such deep pain. "You'll never be alone Holly," he said feeling gutted. "I am sorry for you. I'm so sorry for me." His heart broke into a million pieces.

The two of them sat for a long time, letting the rush of cascading water wash them of their anguish. "You are going to be fine Holly," Oscar said. "So am I. I'm going to take care of you. We are going to heal and find some sort of joy in this life together, Holls," he smiled at her. "Anna is still with us, I promise. She's just loving us from a different place now."

A violent gust of howling wind suddenly blew through the forest trees, muffling the sound of chirping birds and streaming water. Dirt and dry leaves resting on the fountain's stone ledge hurled into the air along with a swirl of dust and debris from the sidewalk. The plate Ronnie had set down flew off the ledge of the natural rock onto the ground. Oscar reacted to the whirlwind by quickly removing his arm from around Holly and using his hands to block the debris blowing toward their faces.

"Ugh!" Holly shouted, raising her hands as a layer of dirt gritted her wet face.

Oscar looked around at the settling wind. Blinking the dust and dirt from his eyes, he spotted the paper plate laying on the walkway and what appeared to be a piece of bread. "You, okay, Holls?" Oscar asked, sweeping the dirt off his shirt.

Holly brushed dirty leaves off her lap and off of Anna's favorite sweater. "Nooo!" she groaned annoyed, "Liz just cleaned this sweater. Damn it!"

"Uhhh, that's shitty! But I don't think its Anna's favorite any*more*!" he said sarcastically, leaning away from her."

Holly looked at him. "Don't be an asshole, Oscar," she whined, noticing the look of disgust on his face. "What?" she asked.

A bird screeched loudly above.

"You might want to clean it again!" he belted out, giggling through his dried-up tears, with his attention drawn to the sky above. Then he looked at Holly and pointed directly to the top of her arm.

She twisted her neck to look. "Oh, Christ!" she squealed, looking at the moist blob of white-brown poop sitting on her shoulder.

They both looked up in a panic to see a pair of pale, glaucous-winged gulls circling in the sky overhead. "Oh, shit!" Oscar yelled, throwing himself back into his wheelchair as a gull swooped down to sit on the ledge of the fountain to pick up a morsel of bread. "Hurry up, Holls!" Oscar burst out laughing, holding his hand above his head.

"OH God!" Holly shrieked, as she whipped the sweater off, and held it high to shield herself. Another bomb hit the seat of the swing just as she lifted herself up to retrieve her wheelchair. "Help me, Oscar!"

"What do you want *me* to do?" he yelled. "Come on, sunshine!" He spun his chair around to head down the path. "Follow me, my sweet Holly pooh-poo!"

63

THE LETTER

Liz entered the staff room. She needed to be alone. The melancholy environment had become too much for her to endure. She sat in her chair, blew her nose in a tissue and took a sad, long breath, wiping away her tears.

A beautiful handwritten letter was left on the table.

> *Greetings from Fountain Garden! I just resurrected a notepad I discovered in the bottom of your 'junk drawer' in the TV room. It has scores on it from four residents who appeared to play cards every single day for (it looks like) two full years and then they stop. It makes me wonder why they had to stop playing. I fear, maybe for reasons out of their control. I write this letter on the same notepad and hopefully, if these four sweet souls have already passed, they are enjoying being thought of at this moment. I am sure if I had more time here, I would be able to find many more treasures such as this. I am sorry for my hen scratching. I can't seem to be so steady anymore in my writing, but I have to keep trying because I am not for this*

computer era or texting on phones. As I now say, I am not of this world anymore. I am working on divine power for as long as that lasts. I feel old now, even as I write, that my left hand doesn't know what my right hand is doing, ha-ha.

This stay has turned out to be one of the nicest surprises. I feel like the universe had a plan when I was dropped into this special place called Fountain Garden. I have never met such colorful people who have so many dimensions to them. It was truly a gift to be able to spend time with you (even for a short time) and it weighs heavy, to the core of my soul, that underneath all that warmth, hospitality and energy, I imagine you are all struggling with the change that is upon you. This place is unique and questionable at times, but who really knows what normal or proper should be. It is distinctive and eccentric in the people who reside here, and it would be such a shame to close Fountain Garden's doors. It is a gift that should remain open for more people to experience the way I have felt.

I witnessed all of you feeling the effects of this change that is about to happen. I am in awe of your compassion and empathy for each other and your strength to stay positive. Even you, Oscar, in your own unique way.

It does not pass me by—the significance of the struggle and the symbolism that your beautiful fountain revealed to me, as a 'fountain' represents life, truth, and change. It would be an absolute crime to let that masterpiece of a structure be torn down. With that being said, I understand that you are slated to leave this coming week. So, I will do my best to have things in order as quickly as possible, with the help of others of course. What I am trying to say is, that 'it is payback time.' I have lived an extraordinary life, a life that had no real worries, I will admit. I believe in my heart that the time has arrived for me to give back all that I can.

I have contacted the owner of Fountain Garden and I will take care of all the required legal documentation and financial details this coming week. As the new owner, I hope I can persuade Liz, Babs, and the other staff to continue serving our remarkable community. That thoughtful, extraordinary man next door, Luke—who holds a very special place in my heart and who I am so proud to say is my SON—has agreed to take on the project. He has assured me that he knows big-hearted people in the community whom he can call upon to help him and I believe he is right after meeting all of you. I hope this news lifts your spirits.

I trust that Fountain Garden will use the funds wisely and if there is anything left over . . . maybe you could upgrade the Everything Room, because it appears to be in shambles.

Good health and well-being to you all,

Mary

Babs and Ginger stood at the door. They had called out for Liz a few times, but she didn't respond.

"Liz?" Ginger called.

"Liz?" Babs said, "We don't want to bother you, but don't you think we should start to pack up Ed and Ronnie's rooms? Or should we wait for their families to get here?"

"You know what, ladies, hold that thought." Liz stood up, smiling, eyes still glued to the letter. "I will be right back."

"Who's that letter from?" Babs asked curiously. "It's from Luke's mom, Mary!" Liz said, chuckling.

Babs and Ginger shot each other a look, "Mary?" They both said in unison.

"I gotta run! I have to go see someone for a few minutes," she yelled happily as she whacked the entrance door button, looking over her shoulder, "Don't do *anything* with Ed and Ronnie's stuff. Just go give support to all my angels. I won't be long." She ran off excitedly.

"Hey, Malia, do you think I could talk to your mom for just a second?" Luke asked, walking up to them as they sat looking out at the ocean.

"Ya, sure, Luke." Malia stood up, kissed her mom on the top of the head, and walked back up to the camp from the beach.

Luke handed Lexi the handwritten note from his mom. Lexi read it slowly through her puffy eyes and then looked at him. "I don't even know what to say. This is so wonderful—there are literally no words . . ." she said, her head spinning from what she had just learned.

"Don't say anything, Lex," he smiled at her warmly. "Just come back. Come back again and let's just see what happens, no planning, no expectations, no pressure . . . just come back."

Lexi was quiet while she continued to process what the letter meant for her family. "I don't want you to think that—"

"Stop," he whispered and shook his head. "Don't come back for *me;* come back for *this!"* He pointed out toward the calm, blue sea of glass.

The warmth of the morning sun and the perfectly calm ocean soothed Lexi's mind as she sat in comfortable silence with Luke at her side. She felt relief as she took a giant inhale of the salty sea air. The elements in front of her and feeling her mom's spirit close by filled Lexi's soul with peace, giving her hope for her future. *She would be back*, she thought, as she held the letter in her hand.

THE END

CPSIA information can be obtained
at www.ICGtesting.com
Printed in the USA
LVHW030620010423
743103LV00001B/10